COLLECTED GHOST STORIES

By LAFCADIO HEARN

Collected Ghost Stories
By Lafcadio Hearn

Print ISBN 13: 978-1-4209-7336-5
eBook ISBN 13: 978-1-4209-7399-0

This edition copyright © 2021. Digireads.com Publishing.

Cover Image: a detail of "Mitsukuni defying the skeleton spectre evoked by the witch Takiyasha." Ukiyo-e triptych by Utagawa Kuniyoshi (1798-1861) / Pictures from History / Bridgeman Images.

Please visit *www.digireads.com*

CONTENTS

From SOME CHINESE GHOSTS

The Soul of the Great Bell

She hath spoken, and her words still resound in his ears.

THE SOUL OF THE GREAT BELL

HAO-KHIEOU-TCHOUAN: c. ix.

The water-clock marks the hour in the *Ta-chung sz'*—in the Tower of the Great Bell: now the mallet is lifted to smite the lips of the metal monster—the vast lips inscribed with Buddhist texts from the sacred *Fa-hwa-King*, from the chapters of the holy *Ling-yen-King*! Hear the great bell responding!—how mighty her voice, though tongueless!— *KO-NGAI*! All the little dragons on the high-tilted eaves of the green roofs shiver to the tips of their gilded tails under that deep wave of sound; all the porcelain gargoyles tremble on their carven perches; all the hundred little bells of the pagodas quiver with desire to speak. *KO-NGAI*!—all the green-and-gold tiles of the temple are vibrating; the wooden goldfish above them are writhing against the sky; the uplifted finger of Fo shakes high over the heads of the worshippers through the blue fog of incense! *KO-NGAI*!—What a thunder tone was that! All the lacquered goblins on the palace cornices wriggle their fire-colored tongues! And after each huge shock, how wondrous the multiple echo and the great golden moan and, at last, the sudden sibilant sobbing in the ears when the immense tone faints away in broken whispers of silver—as though a woman should whisper, "*Hiai!*" Even so the great bell hath sounded every day for well-nigh five hundred years—*Ko-Ngai*: first with stupendous clang, then with immeasurable moan of gold, then with silver murmuring of "*Hiai!*" And there is not a child in all the many-colored ways of the old Chinese city who does not know the story of the great bell—who cannot tell you why the great bell says *Ko-Ngai* and *Hiai*!

Now, this is the story of the great bell in the Ta-chung sz', as the same is related in the *Pe-Hiao-Tou-Choue*, written by the learned Yu-Pao-Tchen, of the City of Kwang-tchau-fu.

Nearly five hundred years ago the Celestially August, the Son of Heaven, Yong-Lo, of the "Illustrious," or Ming, dynasty, commanded the worthy official Kouan-Yu that he should have a bell made of such size that the sound thereof might be heard for one hundred *li*. And he further ordained that the voice of the bell should be strengthened with brass, and deepened with gold, and sweetened with silver; and that the face and the great lips of it should be graven with blessed sayings from the sacred books, and that it should be suspended in the centre of the imperial capital, to sound through all the many-colored ways of the City of Pe-king.

Therefore the worthy mandarin Kouan-Yu assembled the master-molders and the renowned bellsmiths of the empire, and all men of great repute and cunning in foundry work; and they measured the materials for the alloy, and treated them skillfully, and prepared the moulds, the fires, the instruments, and the monstrous melting-pot for fusing the metal. And they labored exceedingly, like giants—neglecting only rest and sleep and the comforts of life; toiling both night and day in obedience to Kouan-Yu, and striving in all things to do the behest of the Son of Heaven.

But when the metal had been cast, and the earthen mould separated from the glowing casting, it was discovered that, despite their great labor and ceaseless care, the result was void of worth; for the metals had rebelled one against the other—the gold had scorned alliance with the brass, the silver would not mingle with the molten iron. Therefore the moulds had to be once more prepared, and the fires rekindled, and the metal remelted, and all the work tediously and toilsomely repeated. The Son of Heaven heard, and was angry, but spoke nothing.

A second time the bell was cast, and the result was even worse. Still the metals obstinately refused to blend one with the other; and there was no uniformity in the bell, and the sides of it were cracked and fissured, and the lips of it were slagged and split asunder; so that all the labor had to be repeated even a third time, to the great dismay of Kouan-Yu. And when the Son of Heaven heard these things, he was angrier than before; and sent his messenger to Kouan-Yu with a letter, written upon lemon-colored silk, and sealed with the seal of the Dragon, containing these words:

"From the Mighty Yong-Lo, the Sublime Tait-Sung, the Celestial and August—whose reign is called 'Ming,'—to Kouan-Yu the Fuh-yin: Twice thou hast betrayed the trust we have deigned graciously to place in thee; if thou fail a third time in fulfilling our command, thy head shall be severed from thy neck. Tremble, and obey!"

Now, Kouan-Yu had a daughter of dazzling loveliness, whose name—Ko-Ngai—was ever in the mouths of poets, and whose heart was even more beautiful than her face. Ko-Ngai loved her father with such love that she had refused a hundred worthy suitors rather than make his home desolate by her absence; and when she had seen the awful yellow missive, sealed with the Dragon-Seal, she fainted away with fear for her father's sake. And when her senses and her strength returned to her, she could not rest or sleep for thinking of her parent's danger, until she had secretly sold some of her jewels, and with the money so obtained had hastened to an astrologer, and paid him a great price to advise her by what means her father might be saved from the peril impending over him. So the astrologer made observations of the heavens, and marked the aspect of the Silver Stream (which we call the Milky Way), and examined the signs of the Zodiac—the *Hwang-tao*, or Yellow Road—and consulted the table of the Five *Hin*, or Principles of the Universe, and the mystical books of the alchemists. And after a long silence, he made answer to her, saying: "Gold and brass will never meet in wedlock, silver and iron never will embrace, until the flesh of a maiden be melted in the crucible; until the blood of a virgin be mixed with the metals in their fusion." So Ko-Ngai returned home sorrowful at heart; but she kept secret all that she had heard, and told no one what she had done.

At last came the awful day when the third and last effort to cast the great bell was to be made; and Ko-Ngai, together with her waiting-woman, accompanied her father to the foundry, and they took their places upon a platform overlooking the toiling of the molders and the lava of liquefied metal. All the workmen wrought their tasks in silence; there was no sound heard but the muttering of the fires. And the muttering deepened into a roar like the roar of typhoons approaching, and the blood-red lake of metal slowly brightened like the vermilion of a sunrise, and the vermilion was transmuted into a radiant glow of gold, and the gold whitened blindingly, like the silver face of a full moon. Then the workers ceased to feed the raving flame, and all fixed their eyes upon the eyes of Kouan-Yu; and Kouan-Yu prepared to give the signal to cast.

But ere ever he lifted his finger, a cry caused him to turn his head; and all heard the voice of Ko-Ngai sounding sharply sweet as a bird's song above the great thunder of the fires—"*For thy sake, O my Father!*" And even as she cried, she leaped into the white flood of metal; and the lava of the furnace roared to receive her, and spattered monstrous flakes of flame to the roof, and burst over the verge of the earthen crater, and cast up a whirling fountain of many-colored fires, and subsided quakingly, with lightnings and with thunders and with mutterings.

Then the father of Ko-Ngai, wild with his grief, would have leaped in after her, but that strong men held him back and kept firm grasp upon him until he had fainted away and they could bear him like one dead to his home. And the serving-woman of Ko-Ngai, dizzy and speechless for pain, stood before the furnace, still holding in her hands a shoe, a tiny, dainty shoe, with embroidery of pearls and flowers—the shoe of her beautiful mistress that was. For she had sought to grasp Ko-Ngai by the foot as she leaped, but had only been able to clutch the shoe, and the pretty shoe came off in her hand; and she continued to stare at it like one gone mad.

But in spite of all these things, the command of the Celestial and August had to be obeyed, and the work of the molders to be finished, hopeless as the result might be. Yet the glow of the metal seemed purer and whiter than before; and there was no sign of the beautiful body that had been entombed therein. So the ponderous casting was made; and lo! when the metal had become cool, it was found that the bell was beautiful to look upon, and perfect in form, and wonderful in color above all other bells. Nor was there any trace found of the body of Ko-Ngai; for it had been totally absorbed by the precious alloy, and blended with the well-blended brass and gold, with the intermingling of the silver and the iron. And when they sounded the bell, its tones were found to be deeper and mellower and mightier than the tones of any other bell—reaching even beyond the distance of one hundred *li*, like a pealing of summer thunder; and yet also like some vast voice uttering a name, a woman's name—the name of Ko-Ngai!

And still, between each mighty stroke there is a long low moaning heard; and ever the moaning ends with a sound of sobbing and of complaining, as though a weeping woman should murmur, "*Hiai!*" And still, when the people hear that great golden moan they keep silence; but when the sharp, sweet shuddering comes in the air, and the sobbing of "*Hiai!*" then, indeed, all the Chinese mothers in all the many-colored ways of Pe-king whisper to their little ones: "*Listen! that is Ko-Ngai crying for her shoe! That is Ko-Ngai calling for her shoe!*"

The Story of Ming-Y

THE ANCIENT WORDS OF KOUEI—MASTER OF MUSICIANS IN THE COURTS OF THE EMPEROR YAO:

When ye make to resound the stone melodious, the Ming-Khieou—
When ye touch the lyre that is called Kin, or the guitar that is called Ssé—
Accompanying their sound with song—
Then do the grandfather and the father return;
Then do the ghosts of the ancestors come to hear.

THE STORY OF MING-Y

Sang the Poet Tching-Kou: "*Surely the Peach-Flowers blossom over the tomb of Sië-Thao.*"

Do you ask me who she was—the beautiful Sië-Thao? For a thousand years and more the trees have been whispering above her bed of stone. And the syllables of her name come to the listener with the lisping of the leaves; with the quivering of many-fingered boughs; with the fluttering of lights and shadows; with the breath, sweet as a woman's presence, of numberless savage flowers—*Sië-Thao.* But, saving the whispering of her name, what the trees say cannot be understood; and they alone remember the years of Sië-Thao. Something about her you might, nevertheless, learn from any of those *Kiang-kou-jin*—those famous Chinese story-tellers, who nightly narrate to listening crowds, in consideration of a few *tsien*, the legends of the past. Something concerning her you may also find in the book entitled "Kin-Kou-Ki-Koan," which signifies in our tongue: "The Marvelous Happenings of Ancient and of Recent Times." And perhaps of all things therein written, the most marvelous is this memory of Sië-Thao:

Five hundred years ago, in the reign of the Emperor Houng-Wou, whose dynasty was *Ming,* there lived in the City of Genii, the city of Kwang-tchau-fu, a man celebrated for his learning and for his piety, named Tien-Pelou. This Tien-Pelou had one son, a beautiful boy, who for scholarship and for bodily grace and for polite accomplishments had no superior among the youths of his age. And his name was Ming-Y.

Now when the lad was in his eighteenth summer, it came to pass that Pelou, his father, was appointed Inspector of Public Instruction at the city of Tching-tou; and Ming-Y accompanied his parents thither. Near the city of Tching-tou lived a rich man of rank, a high commissioner of the government, whose name was Tchang, and who wanted to find a worthy teacher for his children. On hearing of the arrival of the new Inspector of Public Instruction, the noble Tchang visited him to obtain advice in this matter; and happening to meet and converse with Pelou's accomplished son, immediately engaged Ming-Y as a private tutor for his family.

Now as the house of this Lord Tchang was situated several miles from town, it was deemed best that Ming-Y should abide in the house of his employer. Accordingly the youth made ready all things necessary for his new sojourn; and his parents, bidding him farewell, counseled him wisely, and cited to him the words of Lao-tseu and of the ancient sages:

"*By a beautiful face the world is filled with love; but Heaven may*

*never be deceived thereby. Shouldst thou behold a woman coming from
the East, look thou to the West; shouldst thou perceive a maiden
approaching from the West, turn thine eyes to the East.*"

If Ming-Y did not heed this counsel in after days, it was only
because of his youth and the thoughtlessness of a naturally joyous
heart.

And he departed to abide in the house of Lord Tchang, while the
autumn passed, and the winter also.

When the time of the second moon of spring was drawing near,
and that happy day which the Chinese call *Hoa-tchao*, or, "The
Birthday of a Hundred Flowers," a longing came upon Ming-Y to see
his parents; and he opened his heart to the good Tchang, who not only
gave him the permission he desired, but also pressed into his hand a
silver gift of two ounces, thinking that the lad might wish to bring some
little memento to his father and mother. For it is the Chinese custom,
on the feast of Hoa-tchao, to make presents to friends and relations.

That day all the air was drowsy with blossom perfume, and vibrant
with the droning of bees. It seemed to Ming-Y that the path he followed
had not been trodden by any other for many long years; the grass was
tall upon it; vast trees on either side interlocked their mighty and moss-
grown arms above him, beshadowing the way; but the leafy obscurities
quivered with bird-song, and the deep vistas of the wood were glorified
by vapors of gold, and odorous with flower-breathings as a temple with
incense. The dreamy joy of the day entered into the heart of Ming-Y;
and he sat him down among the young blossoms, under the branches
swaying against the violet sky, to drink in the perfume and the light,
and to enjoy the great sweet silence. Even while thus reposing, a sound
caused him to turn his eyes toward a shady place where wild peach-
trees were in bloom; and he beheld a young woman, beautiful as the
pinkening blossoms themselves, trying to hide among them. Though he
looked for a moment only, Ming-Y could not avoid discerning the
loveliness of her face, the golden purity of her complexion, and the
brightness of her long eyes, that sparkled under a pair of brows as
daintily curved as the wings of the silkworm butterfly outspread. Ming-
Y at once turned his gaze away, and, rising quickly, proceeded on his
journey. But so much embarrassed did he feel at the idea of those
charming eyes peeping at him through the leaves, that he suffered the
money he had been carrying in his sleeve to fall, without being aware
of it. A few moments later he heard the patter of light feet running
behind him, and a woman's voice calling him by name. Turning his
face in great surprise, he saw a comely servant-maid, who said to him,
"Sir, my mistress bade me pick up and return you this silver which you
dropped upon the road." Ming-Y thanked the girl gracefully, and
requested her to convey his compliments to her mistress. Then he

proceeded on his way through the perfumed silence, athwart the shadows that dreamed along the forgotten path, dreaming himself also, and feeling his heart beating with strange quickness at the thought of the beautiful being that he had seen.

It was just such another day when Ming-Y, returning by the same path, paused once more at the spot where the gracious figure had momentarily appeared before him. But this time he was surprised to perceive, through a long vista of immense trees, a dwelling that had previously escaped his notice—a country residence, not large, yet elegant to an unusual degree. The bright blue tiles of its curved and serrated double roof, rising above the foliage, seemed to blend their color with the luminous azure of the day; the green-and-gold designs of its carven porticos were exquisite artistic mockeries of leaves and flowers bathed in sunshine. And at the summit of terrace-steps before it, guarded by great porcelain tortoises, Ming-Y saw standing the mistress of the mansion—the idol of his passionate fancy— accompanied by the same waiting-maid who had borne to her his message of gratitude. While Ming-Y looked, he perceived that their eyes were upon him; they smiled and conversed together as if speaking about him; and, shy though he was, the youth found courage to salute the fair one from a distance. To his astonishment, the young servant beckoned him to approach; and opening a rustic gate half veiled by trailing plants bearing crimson flowers, Ming-Y advanced along the verdant alley leading to the terrace, with mingled feelings of surprise and timid joy. As he drew near, the beautiful lady withdrew from sight; but the maid waited at the broad steps to receive him, and said as he ascended:

"Sir, my mistress understands you wish to thank her for the trifling service she recently bade me do you, and requests that you will enter the house, as she knows you already by repute, and desires to have the pleasure of bidding you good-day."

Ming-Y entered bashfully, his feet making no sound upon a matting elastically soft as forest moss, and found himself in a reception-chamber vast, cool, and fragrant with scent of blossoms freshly gathered. A delicious quiet pervaded the mansion; shadows of flying birds passed over the bands of light that fell through the half-blinds of bamboo; great butterflies, with pinions of fiery color, found their way in, to hover a moment about the painted vases, and pass out again into the mysterious woods. And noiselessly as they, the young mistress of the mansion entered by another door, and kindly greeted the boy, who lifted his hands to his breast and bowed low in salutation. She was taller than he had deemed her, and supplely-slender as a beauteous lily; her black hair was interwoven with the creamy blossoms of the *chu-sha-kih*; her robes of pale silk took shifting tints when she moved, as vapors change hue with the changing of the light.

"If I be not mistaken," she said, when both had seated themselves after having exchanged the customary formalities of politeness, "my honored visitor is none other than Tien-chou, surnamed Ming-Y, educator of the children of my respected relative, the High Commissioner Tchang. As the family of Lord Tchang is my family also, I cannot but consider the teacher of his children as one of my own kin."

"Lady," replied Ming-Y, not a little astonished, "may I dare to inquire the name of your honored family, and to ask the relation which you hold to my noble patron?"

"The name of my poor family," responded the comely lady, "is *Ping*—an ancient family of the city of Tching-tou. I am the daughter of a certain Sië of Moun-hao; Sië is my name, likewise; and I was married to a young man of the Ping family, whose name was Khang. By this marriage I became related to your excellent patron; but my husband died soon after our wedding, and I have chosen this solitary place to reside in during the period of my widowhood."

There was a drowsy music in her voice, as of the melody of brooks, the murmurings of spring; and such a strange grace in the manner of her speech as Ming-Y had never heard before. Yet, on learning that she was a widow, the youth would not have presumed to remain long in her presence without a formal invitation; and after having sipped the cup of rich tea presented to him, he arose to depart. Sië would not suffer him to go so quickly.

"Nay, friend," she said; "stay yet a little while in my house, I pray you; for, should your honored patron ever learn that you had been here, and that I had not treated you as a respected guest, and regaled you even as I would him, I know that he would be greatly angered. Remain at least to supper."

So Ming-Y remained, rejoicing secretly in his heart, for Sië seemed to him the fairest and sweetest being he had ever known, and he felt that he loved her even more than his father and his mother. And while they talked the long shadows of the evening slowly blended into one violet darkness; the great citron-light of the sunset faded out; and those starry beings that are called the Three Councilors, who preside over life and death and the destinies of men, opened their cold bright eyes in the northern sky. Within the mansion of Sië the painted lanterns were lighted; the table was laid for the evening repast; and Ming-Y took his place at it, feeling little inclination to eat, and thinking only of the charming face before him. Observing that he scarcely tasted the dainties laid upon his plate, Sië pressed her young guest to partake of wine; and they drank several cups together. It was a purple wine, so cool that the cup into which it was poured became covered with vapory dew; yet it seemed to warm the veins with strange fire. To Ming-Y, as he drank, all things became more luminous as by enchantment; the walls of the chamber appeared to recede, and the roof to heighten; the lamps glowed like stars in their chains, and the voice of Siĕ floated to the boy's ears like some far melody heard through the spaces of a drowsy night. His heart swelled; his tongue loosened; and words flitted from his lips that he had fancied he could never dare to utter. Yet Siĕ sought not to restrain him; her lips gave no smile; but her long bright eyes seemed to laugh with pleasure at his words of praise, and to return his gaze of passionate admiration with affectionate interest.

"I have heard," she said, "of your rare talent, and of your many elegant accomplishments. I know how to sing a little, although I cannot claim to possess any musical learning; and now that I have the honor of finding myself in the society of a musical professor, I will venture to lay modesty aside, and beg you to sing a few songs with me. I should deem it no small gratification if you would condescend to examine my musical compositions."

"The honor and the gratification, dear lady," replied Ming-Y, "will be mine; and I feel helpless to express the gratitude which the offer of so rare a favor deserves."

The serving-maid, obedient to the summons of a little silver gong, brought in the music and retired. Ming-Y took the manuscripts, and began to examine them with eager delight. The paper upon which they were written had a pale yellow tint, and was light as a fabric of gossamer; but the characters were antiquely beautiful, as though they had been traced by the brush of Heï-song Ché-Tchoo himself—that divine Genius of Ink, who is no bigger than a fly; and the signatures attached to the compositions were the signatures of Youen-tchin, Kao-pien, and Thou-mou—mighty poets and musicians of the dynasty of Thang! Ming-Y could not repress a scream of delight at the sight of treasures so inestimable and so unique; scarcely could he summon resolution enough to permit them to leave his hands even for a moment.

"O Lady!" he cried, "these are veritably priceless things, surpassing in worth the treasures of all kings. This indeed is the handwriting of those great masters who sang five hundred years before our birth. How marvelously it has been preserved! Is not this the wondrous ink of which it was written: *Po-nien-jou-chi, i-tien-jou-ki*— 'After centuries I remain firm as stone, and the letters that I make like lacquer'? And how divine the charm of this composition!—the song of Kao-pien, prince of poets, and Governor of Sze-tchouen five hundred years ago!"

"Kao-pien! darling Kao-pien!" murmured Siĕ, with a singular light in her eyes. "Kao-pien is also my favorite. Dear Ming-Y, let us chant his verses together, to the melody of old—the music of those grand years when men were nobler and wiser than tiday."

And their voices rose through the perfumed night like the voices of the wonder-birds—of the Fung-hoang—blending together in liquid sweetness. Yet a moment, and Ming-Y, overcome by the witchery of his companion's voice, could only listen in speechless ecstasy, while the lights of the chamber swam dim before his sight, and tears of pleasure trickled down his cheeks.

So the ninth hour passed; and they continued to converse, and to drink the cool purple wine, and to sing the songs of the years of Thang, until far into the night. More than once Ming-Y thought of departing; but each time Sië would begin, in that silver-sweet voice of hers, so wondrous a story of the great poets of the past, and of the women whom they loved, that he became as one entranced; or she would sing for him a song so strange that all his senses seemed to die except that of hearing. And at last, as she paused to pledge him in a cup of wine, Ming-Y could not restrain himself from putting his arm about her round neck and drawing her dainty head closer to him, and kissing the lips that were so much ruddier and sweeter than the wine. Then their lips separated no more; the night grew old, and they knew it not.

The birds awakened, the flowers opened their eyes to the rising sun, and Ming-Y found himself at last compelled to bid his lovely enchantress farewell. Sië, accompanying him to the terrace, kissed him fondly and said, "Dear boy, come hither as often as you are able—as often as your heart whispers you to come. I know that you are not of those without faith and truth, who betray secrets; yet, being so young, you might also be sometimes thoughtless; and I pray you never to forget that only the stars have been the witnesses of our love. Speak of it to no living person, dearest; and take with you this little souvenir of our happy night."

And she presented him with an exquisite and curious little thing—a paper-weight in likeness of a couchant lion, wrought from a jade-stone yellow as that created by a rainbow in honor of Kong-fu-tze. Tenderly the boy kissed the gift and the beautiful hand that gave it. "May the Spirits punish me," he vowed, "if ever I knowingly give you cause to reproach me, sweetheart!" And they separated with mutual vows.

That morning, on returning to the house of Lord Tchang, Ming-Y told the first falsehood which had ever passed his lips. He averred that his mother had requested him thenceforward to pass his nights at home, now that the weather had become so pleasant; for, though the way was somewhat long, he was strong and active, and needed both air and healthy exercise. Tchang believed all Ming-Y said, and offered no objection. Accordingly the lad found himself enabled to pass all his evenings at the house of the beautiful Sië. Each night they devoted to the same pleasures which had made their first acquaintance so charming: they sang and conversed by turns; they played at chess—the learned game invented by Wu-Wang, which is an imitation of war; they composed pieces of eighty rhymes upon the flowers, the trees, the clouds, the streams, the birds, the bees. But in all accomplishments Sië far excelled her young sweetheart. Whenever they played at chess, it was always Ming-Y's general, Ming-Y's *tsiang*, who was surrounded and vanquished; when they composed verses, Sië's poems were ever superior to his in harmony of word-coloring, in elegance of form, in classic loftiness of thought. And the themes they selected were always the most difficult—those of the poets of the Thang dynasty; the songs they sang were also the songs of five hundred years before—the songs of Youen-tchin, of Thou-mou, of Kao-pien above all, high poet and ruler of the province of Sze-tchouen.

So the summer waxed and waned upon their love, and the luminous autumn came, with its vapors of phantom gold, its shadows of magical purple.

Then it unexpectedly happened that the father of Ming-Y, meeting his son's employer at Tching-tou, was asked by him: "Why must your boy continue to travel every evening to the city, now that the winter is approaching? The way is long, and when he returns in the morning he looks fordone with weariness. Why not permit him to slumber in my house during the season of snow?" And the father of Ming-Y, greatly astonished, responded: "Sir, my son has not visited the city, nor has he been to our house all this summer. I fear that he must have acquired wicked habits, and that he passes his nights in evil company—perhaps in gaming, or in drinking with the women of the flower-boats." But the High Commissioner returned: "Nay! that is not to be thought of. I have never found any evil in the boy, and there are no taverns nor flower-boats nor any places of dissipation in our neighborhood. No doubt Ming-Y has found some amiable youth of his own age with whom to spend his evenings, and only told me an untruth for fear that I would not otherwise permit him to leave my residence. I beg that you will say nothing to him until I shall have sought to discover this mystery; and this very evening I shall send my servant to follow after him, and to watch whither he goes."

Pelou readily assented to this proposal, and promising to visit Tchang the following morning, returned to his home. In the evening, when Ming-Y left the house of Tchang, a servant followed him unobserved at a distance. But on reaching the most obscure portion of the road, the boy disappeared from sight as suddenly as though the earth had swallowed him. After having long sought after him in vain, the domestic returned in great bewilderment to the house, and related what had taken place. Tchang immediately sent a messenger to Pelou.

In the mean time Ming-Y, entering the chamber of his beloved, was surprised and deeply pained to find her in tears. "Sweetheart," she sobbed, wreathing her arms around his neck, "we are about to be separated forever, because of reasons which I cannot tell you. From the very first I knew this must come to pass; and nevertheless it seemed to me for the moment so cruelly sudden a loss, so unexpected a misfortune, that I could not prevent myself from weeping! After this night we shall never see each other again, beloved, and I know that you will not be able to forget me while you live; but I know also that you will become a great scholar, and that honors and riches will be showered upon you, and that some beautiful and loving woman will console you for my loss. And now let us speak no more of grief; but let us pass this last evening joyously, so that your recollection of me may not be a painful one, and that you may remember my laughter rather than my tears."

She brushed the bright drops away, and brought wine and music and the melodious *kin* of seven silken strings, and would not suffer Ming-Y to speak for one moment of the coming separation. And she sang him an ancient song about the calmness of summer lakes reflecting the blue of heaven only, and the calmness of the heart also, before the clouds of care and of grief and of weariness darken its little world. Soon they forgot their sorrow in the joy of song and wine; and those last hours seemed to Ming-Y more celestial than even the hours of their first bliss.

But when the yellow beauty of morning came their sadness returned, and they wept. Once more Sië accompanied her lover to the terrace-steps; and as she kissed him farewell, she pressed into his hand a parting gift—a little brush-case of agate, wonderfully chiseled, and worthy the table of a great poet. And they separated forever, shedding many tears.

Still Ming-Y could not believe it was an eternal parting. "No!" he thought, "I shall visit her tomorrow; for I cannot now live without her, and I feel assured that she cannot refuse to receive me." Such were the thoughts that filled his mind as he reached the house of Tchang, to find his father and his patron standing on the porch awaiting him. Ere he could speak a word, Pelou demanded: "Son, in what place have you been passing your nights?"

Seeing that his falsehood had been discovered, Ming-Y dared not make any reply, and remained abashed and silent, with bowed head, in the presence of his father. Then Pelou, striking the boy violently with his staff, commanded him to divulge the secret; and at last, partly through fear of his parent, and partly through fear of the law which ordains that "*the son refusing to obey his father shall be punished with one hundred blows of the bamboo*," Ming-Y faltered out the history of his love.

Tchang changed color at the boy's tale. "Child," exclaimed the High Commissioner, "I have no relative of the name of Ping; I have never heard of the woman you describe; I have never heard even of the house which you speak of. But I know also that you cannot dare to lie to Pelou, your honored father; there is some strange delusion in all this affair."

Then Ming-Y produced the gifts that Sië had given him—the lion of yellow jade, the brush-case of carven agate, also some original compositions made by the beautiful lady herself. The astonishment of Tchang was now shared by Pelou. Both observed that the brush-case of agate and the lion of jade bore the appearance of objects that had lain buried in the earth for centuries, and were of a workmanship beyond the power of living man to imitate; while the compositions proved to be veritable master-pieces of poetry, written in the style of the poets of the dynasty of Thang.

"Friend Pelou," cried the High Commissioner, "let us immediately accompany the boy to the place where he obtained these miraculous things, and apply the testimony of our senses to this mystery. The boy is no doubt telling the truth; yet his story passes my understanding." And all three proceeded toward the place of the habitation of Sië.

But when they had arrived at the shadiest part of the road, where the perfumes were most sweet and the mosses were greenest, and the fruits of the wild peach flushed most pinkly, Ming-Y, gazing through the groves, uttered a cry of dismay. Where the azure-tiled roof had risen against the sky, there was now only the blue emptiness of air; where the green-and-gold facade had been, there was visible only the flickering of leaves under the aureate autumn light; and where the broad terrace had extended, could be discerned only a ruin—a tomb so ancient, so deeply gnawed by moss, that the name graven upon it was no longer decipherable. The home of Sië had disappeared!

All suddenly the High Commissioner smote his forehead with his hand, and turning to Pelou, recited the well-known verse of the ancient poet Tching-Kou:

"*Surely the peach-flowers blossom over the tomb of SIË-THAO.*"

"Friend Pelou," continued Tchang, "the beauty who bewitched your son was no other than she whose tomb stands there in ruin before us! Did she not say she was wedded to Ping-Khang? There is no family of that name, but Ping-Khang is indeed the name of a broad alley in the city near. There was a dark riddle in all that she said. She called herself Sië of Moun-Hiao: there is no person of that name; there is no street of that name; but the Chinese characters *Moun* and *hiao*, placed together, form the character 'Kiao.' Listen! The alley Ping-Khang, situated in the street Kiao, was the place where dwelt the great courtesans of the dynasty of Thang! Did she not sing the songs of Kao-pien? And upon the brush-case and the paper-weight she gave your son, are there not characters which read, '*Pure object of art belonging to Kao, of the city of Pho-hai*'? That city no longer exists; but the memory of Kao-pien remains, for he was governor of the province of Sze-tchouen, and a mighty poet. And when he dwelt in the land of Chou, was not his favorite the beautiful wanton Sië—Sië-Thao, unmatched for grace among all the women of her day? It was he who made her a gift of those manuscripts of song; it was he who gave her those objects of rare art. Sië-Thao died not as other women die. Her limbs may have crumbled to dust; yet something of her still lives in this deep wood— her Shadow still haunts this shadowy place."

Tchang ceased to speak. A vague fear fell upon the three. The thin mists of the morning made dim the distances of green, and deepened the ghostly beauty of the woods. A faint breeze passed by, leaving a trail of blossom-scent—a last odor of dying flowers—thin as that which clings to the silk of a forgotten robe; and, as it passed, the trees seemed to whisper across the silence, "*Sië-Thao*."

Fearing greatly for his son, Pelou sent the lad away at once to the city of Kwang-tchau-fu. And there, in after years, Ming-Y obtained high dignities and honors by reason of his talents and his learning; and he married the daughter of an illustrious house, by whom he became the father of sons and daughters famous for their virtues and their accomplishments. Never could he forget Sië-Thao; and yet it is said that he never spoke of her—not even when his children begged him to tell them the story of two beautiful objects that always lay upon his writing-table: a lion of yellow jade, and a brush-case of carven agate.

The Legend of Tchi-Niu

A SOUND OF GONGS, A SOUND OF SONG—THE SONG OF THE BUILDERS BUILDING THE DWELLINGS OF THE DEAD:

> *Khiû tchî yîng-yîng.*
> *Toû tchî hoûng-hoûng.*
> *Tchŏ tchî tông-tông.*
> *Siŏ liû pîng-pîng.*

THE LEGEND OF TCHI-NIU

In the quaint commentary accompanying the text of that holy book of Lao-tseu called *Kan-ing-p'ien* may be found a little story so old that the name of the one who first told it has been forgotten for a thousand years, yet so beautiful that it lives still in the memory of four hundred millions of people, like a prayer that, once learned, is forever remembered. The Chinese writer makes no mention of any city nor of any province, although even in the relation of the most ancient traditions such an omission is rare; we are only told that the name of the hero of the legend was Tong-yong, and that he lived in the years of the great dynasty of Han, some twenty centuries ago.

Tong-Yong's mother had died while he was yet an infant; and when he became a youth of nineteen years his father also passed away, leaving him utterly alone in the world, and without resources of any sort; for, being a very poor man, Tong's father had put himself to great straits to educate the lad, and had not been able to lay by even one copper coin of his earnings. And Tong lamented greatly to find himself so destitute that he could not honor the memory of that good father by having the customary rites of burial performed, and a carven tomb erected upon a propitious site. The poor only are friends of the poor; and among all those whom Tong knew; there was no one able to assist him in defraying the expenses of the funeral. In one way only could the youth obtain money—by selling himself as a slave to some rich cultivator; and this he at last decided to do. In vain his friends did their utmost to dissuade him; and to no purpose did they attempt to delay the accomplishment of his sacrifice by beguiling promises of future aid. Tong only replied that he would sell his freedom a hundred times, if it were possible, rather than suffer his father's memory to remain unhonored even for a brief season. And furthermore, confiding in his youth and strength, he determined to put a high price upon his servitude—a price which would enable him to build a handsome tomb, but which it would be well-nigh impossible for him ever to repay.

Accordingly he repaired to the broad public place where slaves and debtors were exposed for sale, and seated himself upon a bench of stone, having affixed to his shoulders a placard inscribed with the terms of his servitude and the list of his qualifications as a laborer. Many who read the characters upon the placard smiled disdainfully at the price asked, and passed on without a word; others lingered only to question him out of simple curiosity; some commended him with hollow praise; some openly mocked his unselfishness, and laughed at his childish piety. Thus many hours wearily passed, and Tong had almost despaired of finding a master, when there rode up a high official of the province—a grave and handsome man, lord of a thousand slaves, and owner of vast estates. Reining in his Tartar horse, the official halted to read the placard and to consider the value of the slave. He did not smile, or advise, or ask any questions; but having observed the price asked, and the fine strong limbs of the youth, purchased him without further ado, merely ordering his attendant to pay the sum and to see that the necessary papers were made out.

Thus Tong found himself enabled to fulfill the wish of his heart, and to have a monument built which, although of small size, was destined to delight the eyes of all who beheld it, being designed by cunning artists and executed by skilful sculptors. And while it was yet designed only, the pious rites were performed, the silver coin was placed in the mouth of the dead, the white lanterns were hung at the door, the holy prayers were recited, and paper shapes of all things the departed might need in the land of the Genii were consumed in consecrated fire. And after the geomancers and the necromancers had chosen a burial-spot which no unlucky star could shine upon, a place of rest which no demon or dragon might ever disturb, the beautiful *chih* was built. Then was the phantom money strewn along the way; the funeral procession departed from the dwelling of the dead, and with prayers and lamentation the mortal remains of Tong's good father were borne to the tomb.

Then Tong entered as a slave into the service of his purchaser, who allotted him a little hut to dwell in; and thither Tong carried with him those wooden tablets, bearing the ancestral names, before which filial piety must daily burn the incense of prayer, and perform the tender duties of family worship.

Thrice had spring perfumed the breast of the land with flowers, and thrice had been celebrated that festival of the dead which is called *Siu-fan-ti*, and thrice had Tong swept and garnished his father's tomb and presented his fivefold offering of fruits and meats. The period of mourning had passed, yet he had not ceased to mourn for his parent. The years revolved with their moons, bringing him no hour of joy, no day of happy rest; yet he never lamented his servitude, or failed to perform the rites of ancestral worship—until at last the fever of the rice-fields laid strong hold upon him, and he could not arise from his couch; and his fellow-laborers thought him destined to die. There was no one to wait upon him, no one to care for his needs, inasmuch as slaves and servants were wholly busied with the duties of the household or the labor of the fields—all departing to toil at sunrise and returning weary only after the sundown.

Now, while the sick youth slumbered the fitful slumber of exhaustion one sultry noon, he dreamed that a strange and beautiful woman stood by him, and bent above him and touched his forehead with the long, fine fingers of her shapely hand. And at her cool touch a weird sweet shock passed through him, and all his veins tingled as if thrilled by new life. Opening his eyes in wonder, he saw verily bending over him the charming being of whom he had dreamed, and he knew that her lithe hand really caressed his throbbing forehead. But the flame of the fever was gone, a delicious coolness now penetrated every fiber of his body, and the thrill of which he had dreamed still tingled in his blood like a great joy. Even at the same moment the eyes of the gentle visitor met his own, and he saw they were singularly beautiful, and shone like splendid black jewels under brows curved like the wings of the swallow. Yet their calm gaze seemed to pass through him as light through crystal; and a vague awe came upon him, so that the question which had risen to his lips found no utterance. Then she, still caressing him, smiled and said: "I have come to restore thy strength and to be thy wife. Arise and worship with me."

Her clear voice had tones melodious as a bird's song; but in her gaze there was an imperious power which Tong felt he dare not resist. Rising from his couch, he was astounded to find his strength wholly restored; but the cool, slender hand which held his own led him away so swiftly that he had little time for amazement. He would have given years of existence for courage to speak of his misery, to declare his utter inability to maintain a wife; but something irresistible in the long dark eyes of his companion forbade him to speak; and as though his inmost thought had been discerned by that wondrous gaze, she said to him, in the same clear voice, "*I will provide.*" Then shame made him blush at the thought of his wretched aspect and tattered apparel; but he observed that she also was poorly attired, like a woman of the people— wearing no ornament of any sort, nor even shoes upon her feet. And before he had yet spoken to her, they came before the ancestral tablets; and there she knelt with him and prayed, and pledged him in a cup of wine—brought he knew not from whence—and together they worshipped Heaven and Earth. Thus she became his wife.

A mysterious marriage it seemed, for neither on that day nor at any future time could Tong venture to ask his wife the name of her family, or of the place whence she came, and he could not answer any of the curious questions which his fellow-laborers put to him concerning her; and she, moreover, never uttered a word about herself, except to say that her name was Tchi. But although Tong had such awe of her that while her eyes were upon him he was as one having no will of his own, he loved her unspeakably; and the thought of his serfdom ceased to weigh upon him from the hour of his marriage. As through magic the little dwelling had become transformed: its misery was masked with charming paper devices—with dainty decorations created out of nothing by that pretty jugglery of which woman only knows the secret.

Each morning at dawn the young husband found a well-prepared and ample repast awaiting him, and each evening also upon his return; but the wife all day sat at her loom, weaving silk after a fashion unlike anything which had ever been seen before in that province. For as she wove, the silk flowed from the loom like a slow current of glossy gold, bearing upon its undulations strange forms of violet and crimson and jewel-green: shapes of ghostly horsemen riding upon horses, and of phantom chariots dragon-drawn, and of standards of trailing cloud. In every dragon's beard glimmered the mystic pearl; in every rider's helmet sparkled the gem of rank. And each day Tchi would weave a great piece of such figured silk; and the fame of her weaving spread abroad. From far and near people thronged to see the marvelous work; and the silk-merchants of great cities heard of it, and they sent messengers to Tchi, asking her that she should weave for them and teach them her secret. Then she wove for them, as they desired, in return for the silver cubes which they brought her; but when they prayed her to teach them, she laughed and said, "Assuredly I could never teach you, for no one among you has fingers like mine." And indeed no man could discern her fingers when she wove, any more than he might behold the wings of a bee vibrating in swift flight.

The seasons passed, and Tong never knew want, so well did his beautiful wife fulfill her promise—"*I will provide*"; and the cubes of bright silver brought by the silk-merchants were piled up higher and higher in the great carven chest which Tchi had bought for the storage of the household goods.

One morning, at last, when Tong, having finished his repast, was about to depart to the fields, Tchi unexpectedly bade him remain; and opening the great chest, she took out of it and gave him a document written in the official characters called *li-shu*. And Tong, looking at it, cried out and leaped in his joy, for it was the certificate of his manumission. Tchi had secretly purchased her husband's freedom with the price of her wondrous silks!

"Thou shalt labor no more for any master," she said, "but for thine own sake only. And I have also bought this dwelling, with all which is therein, and the tea-fields to the south, and the mulberry groves hard by—all of which are thine."

Then Tong, beside himself for gratefulness, would have prostrated himself in worship before her, but that she would not suffer it.

Thus he was made free; and prosperity came to him with his freedom; and whatsoever he gave to the sacred earth was returned to him centupled; and his servants loved him and blessed the beautiful Tchi, so silent and yet so kindly to all about her. But the silk-loom soon remained untouched, for Tchi gave birth to a son—a boy so beautiful that Tong wept with delight when he looked upon him. And thereafter the wife devoted herself wholly to the care of the child.

Now it soon became manifest that the boy was not less wonderful than his wonderful mother. In the third month of his age he could speak; in the seventh month he could repeat by heart the proverbs of the sages, and recite the holy prayers; before the eleventh month he could use the writing-brush with skill, and copy in shapely characters the precepts of Lao-tseu. And the priests of the temples came to behold him and to converse with him, and they marveled at the charm of the child and the wisdom of what he said; and they blessed Tong, saying: "Surely this son of thine is a gift from the Master of Heaven, a sign that the immortals love thee. May thine eyes behold a hundred happy summers!"

It was in the Period of the Eleventh Moon: the flowers had passed away, the perfume of the summer had flown, the winds were growing chill, and in Tong's home the evening fires were lighted. Long the husband and wife sat in the mellow glow—he speaking much of his hopes and joys, and of his son that was to be so grand a man, and of many paternal projects; while she, speaking little, listened to his words, and often turned her wonderful eyes upon him with an answering smile. Never had she seemed so beautiful before; and Tong, watching her face, marked not how the night waned, nor how the fire sank low, nor how the wind sang in the leafless trees without.

All suddenly Tchi arose without speaking, and took his hand in hers and led him, gently as on that strange wedding-morning, to the cradle where their boy slumbered, faintly smiling in his dreams. And in that moment there came upon Tong the same strange fear that he knew when Tchi's eyes had first met his own—the vague fear that love and trust had calmed, but never wholly cast out, like unto the fear of the gods. And all unknowingly, like one yielding to the pressure of mighty invisible hands, he bowed himself low before her, kneeling as to a divinity. Now, when he lifted his eyes again to her face, he closed them forthwith in awe; for she towered before him taller than any mortal woman, and there was a glow about her as of sunbeams, and the light of her limbs shone through her garments. But her sweet voice came to him with all the tenderness of other hours, saying: "*Lo! my beloved, the moment has come in which I must forsake thee; for I was never of mortal born, and the Invisible may incarnate themselves for a time only. Yet I leave with thee the pledge of our love—this fair son, who shall ever be to thee as faithful and as fond as thou thyself hast been. Know, my beloved, that I was sent to thee even by the Master of Heaven, in reward of thy filial piety, and that I must now return to the glory of His house: I AM THE GODDESS TCHI-NIU.*"

Even as she ceased to speak, the great glow faded; and Tong, re-opening his eyes, knew that she had passed away forever—mysteriously as pass the winds of heaven, irrevocably as the light of a flame blown out. Yet all the doors were barred, all the windows unopened. Still the child slept, smiling in his sleep. Outside, the darkness was breaking; the sky was brightening swiftly; the night was past. With splendid majesty the East threw open high gates of gold for the coming of the sun; and, illuminated by the glory of his coming, the vapors of morning wrought themselves into marvelous shapes of shifting color—into forms weirdly beautiful as the silken dreams woven in the loom of Tchi-Niu.

The Return of Yen-Tchin-King

Before me ran, as a herald runneth, the Leader of the Moon;
And the Spirit of the Wind followed after me—quickening his flight.
LI-SAO.

THE RETURN OF YEN-TCHIN-KING

In the thirty-eighth chapter of the holy book, *Kan-ing-p'ien,* wherein the Recompense of Immortality is considered, may be found the legend of Yen-Tchin-King. A thousand years have passed since the passing of the good Tchin-King; for it was in the period of the greatness of Thang that he lived and died.

Now, in those days when Yen-Tchin-King was Supreme Judge of one of the Six August Tribunals, one Li-hi-lié, a soldier mighty for evil, lifted the black banner of revolt, and drew after him, as a tide of destruction, the millions of the northern provinces. And learning of these things, and knowing also that Hi-lié was the most ferocious of men, who respected nothing on earth save fearlessness, the Son of Heaven commanded Tchin-King that he should visit Hi-lié and strive to recall the rebel to duty, and read unto the people who followed after him in revolt the Emperor's letter of reproof and warning. For Tchin-King was famed throughout the provinces for his wisdom, his rectitude, and his fearlessness; and the Son of Heaven believed that if Hi-lié would listen to the words of any living man steadfast in loyalty and virtue, he would listen to the words of Tchin-King. So Tchin-King arrayed himself in his robes of office, and set his house in order; and, having embraced his wife and his children, mounted his horse and rode away alone to the roaring camp of the rebels, bearing the Emperor's letter in his bosom. "I shall return; fear not!" were his last words to the gray servant who watched him from the terrace as he rode.

And Tchin-King at last descended from his horse, and entered into the rebel camp, and, passing through that huge gathering of war, stood in the presence of Hi-lié. High sat the rebel among his chiefs, encircled by the wave-lightning of swords and the thunders of ten thousand gongs: above him undulated the silken folds of the Black Dragon, while a vast fire rose bickering before him. Also Tchin-King saw that the tongues of that fire were licking human bones, and that skulls of men lay blackening among the ashes. Yet he was not afraid to look upon the fire, nor into the eyes of Hi-lié; but drawing from his bosom the roll of perfumed yellow silk upon which the words of the Emperor were written, and kissing it, he made ready to read, while the multitude became silent. Then, in a strong, clear voice he began:

"*The words of the Celestial and August, the Son of Heaven, the Divine Ko-Tsu-Tchin-Yao-ti, unto the rebel Li-Hi-lié and those that follow him.*"

And a roar went up like the roar of the sea—a roar of rage, and the hideous battle-moan, like the moan of a forest in storm—"*Hoo! hoo-oo-oo-oo!*"—and the sword-lightnings brake loose, and the thunder of the gongs moved the ground beneath the messenger's feet. But Hi-lié waved his gilded wand, and again there was silence. "Nay!" spoke the rebel chief; "let the dog bark!" So Tchin-King spoke on:

"*Knowest thou not, O most rash and foolish of men, that thou leadest the people only into the mouth of the Dragon of Destruction? Knowest thou not, also, that the people of my kingdom are the first-born of the Master of Heaven? So it hath been written that he who doth needlessly subject the people to wounds and death shall not be suffered by Heaven to live! Thou who wouldst subvert those laws founded by the wise—those laws in obedience to which may happiness and prosperity alone be found—thou art committing the greatest of all crimes—the crime that is never forgiven!*

"*O my people, think not that I your Emperor, I your Father, seek your destruction. I desire only your happiness, your prosperity, your greatness; let not your folly provoke the severity of your Celestial Parent. Follow not after madness and blind rage; hearken rather to the wise words of my messenger.*"

"*Hoo! hoo-oo-oo-oo-oo!*" roared the people, gathering fury. "*Hoo! hoo-oo-oo-oo!*"—till the mountains rolled back the cry like the rolling of a typhoon; and once more the pealing of the gongs paralyzed voice and hearing. Then Tchin-King, looking at Hi-lié, saw that he laughed, and that the words of the letter would not again be listened to. Therefore he read on to the end without looking about him, resolved to perform his mission in so far as lay in his power. And having read all, he would have given the letter to Hi-lié; but Hi-lié would not extend his hand to take it. Therefore Tchin-King replaced it in his bosom, and folding his arms, looked Hi-lié calmly in the face, and waited. Again Hi-lié waved his gilded wand; and the roaring ceased, and the booming of the gongs, until nothing save the fluttering of the Dragon-banner could be heard. Then spoke Hi-lié, with an evil smile—

"Tchin-King, O son of a dog! if thou dost not now take the oath of fealty, and bow thyself before me, and salute me with the salutation of Emperors—even with the *luh-kao*, the triple prostration—into that fire thou shalt be thrown."

But Tchin-King, turning his back upon the usurper, bowed himself a moment in worship to Heaven and Earth; and then rising suddenly, ere any man could lay hand upon him, he leaped into the towering flame, and stood there, with folded arms, like a God.

Then Hi-lié leaped to his feet in amazement, and shouted to his men; and they snatched Tchin-King from the fire, and wrung the flames from his robes with their naked hands, and extolled him, and praised him to his face. And even Hi-lié himself descended from his seat, and spoke fair words to him, saying: "O Tchin-King, I see thou art indeed a brave man and true, and worthy of all honor; be seated among us, I pray thee, and partake of whatever it is in our power to bestow!"

But Tchin-King, looking upon him unswervingly, replied in a voice clear as the voice of a great bell—

"Never, O Hi-lié, shall I accept aught from thy hand, save death, so long as thou shalt continue in the path of wrath and folly. And never shall it be said that Tchin-King sat him down among rebels and traitors, among murderers and robbers."

Then Hi-lié in sudden fury, smote him with his sword; and Tchin-King fell to the earth and died, striving even in his death to bow his head toward the South—toward the place of the Emperor's palace— toward the presence of his beloved Master.

Even at the same hour the Son of Heaven, alone in the inner chamber of his palace, became aware of a Shape prostrate before his feet; and when he spoke, the Shape arose and stood before him, and he saw that it was Tchin-King. And the Emperor would have questioned him; yet ere he could question, the familiar voice spoke, saying: "Son of Heaven, the mission confided to me I have performed; and thy command hath been accomplished to the extent of thy humble servant's feeble power. But even now must I depart, that I may enter the service of another Master."

And looking, the Emperor perceived that the Golden Tigers upon the wall were visible through the form of Tchin-King; and a strange coldness, like a winter wind, passed through the chamber; and the figure faded out. Then the Emperor knew that the Master of whom his faithful servant had spoken was none other than the Master of Heaven.

Also at the same hour the gray servant of Tchin-King's house beheld him passing through the apartments, smiling as he was wont to smile when he saw that all things were as he desired. "Is it well with thee, my lord?" questioned the aged man. And a voice answered him: "It is well"; but the presence of Tchin-King had passed away before the answer came.

So the armies of the Son of Heaven strove with the rebels. But the land was soaked with blood and blackened with fire; and the corpses of whole populations were carried by the rivers to feed the fishes of the sea; and still the war prevailed through many a long red year. Then came to aid the Son of Heaven the hordes that dwell in the desolations of the West and North—horsemen born, a nation of wild archers, each mighty to bend a two-hundred-pound bow until the ears should meet. And as a whirlwind they came against rebellion, raining raven-feathered arrows in a storm of death; and they prevailed against Hi-lié and his people. Then those that survived destruction and defeat submitted, and promised allegiance; and once more was the law of righteousness restored. But Tchin-King had been dead for many summers.

And the Son of Heaven sent word to his victorious generals that they should bring back with them the bones of his faithful servant, to be laid with honor in a mausoleum erected by imperial decree. So the generals of the Celestial and August sought after the nameless grave and found it, and had the earth taken up, and made ready to remove the coffin.

But the coffin crumbled into dust before their eyes; for the worms had gnawed it, and the hungry earth had devoured its substance, leaving only a phantom shell that vanished at touch of the light. And lo! as it vanished, all beheld lying there the perfect form and features of the good Tchin-King. Corruption had not touched him, nor had the worms disturbed his rest, nor had the bloom of life departed from his face. And he seemed to dream only—comely to see as upon the morning of his bridal, and smiling as the holy images smile, with eyelids closed, in the twilight of the great pagodas.

Then spoke a priest, standing by the grave: "O my children, this is indeed a Sign from the Master of Heaven; in such wise do the Powers Celestial preserve them that are chosen to be numbered with the Immortals. Death may not prevail over them, neither may corruption come nigh them. Verily the blessed Tchin-King hath taken his place among the divinities of Heaven!"

Then they bore Tchin-King back to his native place, and laid him with highest honors in the mausoleum which the Emperor had commanded; and there he sleeps, incorruptible forever, arrayed in his robes of state. Upon his tomb are sculptured the emblems of his greatness and his wisdom and his virtue, and the signs of his office, and the Four Precious Things: and the monsters which are holy symbols mount giant guard in stone about it; and the weird Dogs of Fo keep watch before it, as before the temples of the gods.

The Tradition of the Tea-Plant

SANG A CHINESE HEART FOURTEEN HUNDRED YEARS AGO:

There is Somebody of whom I am thinking. Far away there is
Somebody of whom I am thinking.
A hundred leagues of mountains lie between us:
Yet the same Moon shines upon us, and the passing Wind breathes
upon us both.

THE TRADITION OF THE TEA-PLANT

"Good is the continence of the eye;
Good is the continence of the ear;
Good is the continence of the nostrils;
Good is the continence of the tongue;
Good is the continence of the body;
Good is the continence of speech;
Good is all. . . ."

Again the Vulture of Temptation soared to the highest heaven of
his contemplation, bringing his soul down, down, reeling and fluttering,
back to the World of Illusion. Again the memory made dizzy his
thought, like the perfume of some venomous flower. Yet he had seen
the bayadere for an instant only, when passing through Kasí upon his
way to China—to the vast empire of souls that thirsted after the
refreshment of Buddha's law, as sun-parched fields thirst for the life-
giving rain. When she called him, and dropped her little gift into his
mendicant's bowl, he had indeed lifted his fan before his face, yet not
quickly enough; and the penalty of that fault had followed him a
thousand leagues—pursued after him even into the strange land to
which he had come to hear the words of the Universal Teacher.
Accursed beauty! surely framed by the Tempter of tempters, by Mara
himself, for the perdition of the just! Wisely had Bhagavat warned his
disciples: "O ye Çramanas, women are not to be looked upon! And if
ye chance to meet women, ye must not suffer your eyes to dwell upon
them; but, maintaining holy reserve, speak not to them at all. Then fail
not to whisper unto your own hearts, 'Lo, we are Çramanas, whose
duty it is to remain uncontaminated by the corruptions of this world,
even as the Lotos, which suffereth no vileness to cling unto its leaves,
though it blossom amid the refuse of the wayside ditch.'" Then also
came to his memory, but with a new and terrible meaning, the words of
the Twentieth-and-Third of the Admonitions:
"Of all attachments unto objects of desire, the strongest indeed is

the attachment to form. Happily, this passion is unique; for were there any other like unto it, then to enter the Perfect Way were impossible."

How, indeed, thus haunted by the illusion of form, was he to fulfill the vow that he had made to pass a night and a day in perfect and unbroken meditation? Already the night was beginning! Assuredly, for sickness of the soul, for fever of the spirit, there was no physic save prayer. The sunset was swiftly fading out. He strove to pray:

"*O the Jewel in the Lotos!*

"Even as the tortoise withdraweth its extremities into its shell, let me, O Blessed One, withdraw my senses wholly into meditation!

"*O the Jewel in the Lotos!*

"For even as rain penetrateth the broken roof of a dwelling long uninhabited, so may passion enter the soul uninhabited by meditation.

"*O the Jewel in the Lotos!*

"Even as still water that hath deposited all its slime, so let my soul, O Tathâgata, be made pure! Give me strong power to rise above the world, O Master, even as the wild bird rises from its marsh to follow the pathway of the Sun!

"*O the Jewel in the Lotos!*

"By day shineth the sun, by night shineth the moon; shineth also the warrior in harness of war; shineth likewise in meditations the Çramana. But the Buddha at all times, by night or by day, shineth ever the same, illuminating the world.

"*O the Jewel in the Lotos!*

"Let me cease, O thou Perfectly Awakened, to remain as an Ape in the World-forest, forever ascending and descending in search of the fruits of folly. Swift as the twining of serpents, vast as the growth of lianas in a forest, are the all-encircling growths of the Plant of Desire.

"*O the Jewel in the Lotos!*"

Vain his prayer, alas! vain also his invocation! The mystic meaning of the holy text—the sense of the Lotos, the sense of the Jewel—had evaporated from the words, and their monotonous utterance now served only to lend more dangerous definition to the memory that tempted and tortured him. *O the jewel in her ear!* What lotos-bud more dainty than the folded flower of flesh, with its dripping of diamond-fire! Again he saw it, and the curve of the cheek beyond, luscious to look upon as beautiful brown fruit. How true the Two Hundred and Eighty-Fourth verse of the Admonitions!—"So long as a man shall not have torn from his heart even the smallest rootlet of that liana of desire which draweth his thought toward women, even so long shall his soul remain fettered." And there came to his mind also the Three Hundred and Forty-Fifth verse of the same blessed book, regarding fetters:

"In bonds of rope, wise teachers have said, there is no strength; nor in fetters of wood, nor yet in fetters of iron. Much stronger than any of these is the fetter of *concern for the jeweled earrings of women.*"

"Omniscient Gotama!" he cried—"all-seeing Tathâgata! How multiform the Consolation of Thy Word! how marvelous Thy understanding of the human heart! Was this also one of Thy temptations?—one of the myriad illusions marshaled before Thee by Mara in that night when the earth rocked as a chariot, and the sacred trembling passed from sun to sun, from system to system, from universe to universe, from eternity to eternity?"

O the jewel in her ear! The vision would not go! Nay, each time it hovered before his thought it seemed to take a warmer life, a fonder look, a fairer form; to develop with his weakness; to gain force from his enervation. He saw the eyes, large, limpid, soft, and black as a deer's; the pearls in the dark hair, and the pearls in the pink mouth; the lips curling to a kiss, a flower-kiss; and a fragrance seemed to float to his senses, sweet, strange, soporific—a perfume of youth, an odor of woman. Rising to his feet, with strong resolve he pronounced again the sacred invocation; and he recited the holy words of the *Chapter of Impermanency*:

"Gazing upon the heavens and upon the earth ye must say, *These are not permanent.* Gazing upon the mountains and the rivers, ye must say, *These are not permanent.* Gazing upon the forms and upon the faces of exterior beings, and beholding their growth and their development, ye must say, *These are not permanent.*"

And nevertheless! how sweet illusion! The illusion of the great sun; the illusion of the shadow-casting hills; the illusion of waters, formless and multiform; the illusion of—Nay, nay I what impious fancy! Accursed girl! yet, yet! why should he curse her? Had she ever done aught to merit the malediction of an ascetic? Never, never! Only her form, the memory of her, the beautiful phantom of her, the accursed phantom of her! What was she? An illusion creating illusions, a mockery, a dream, a shadow, a vanity, a vexation of spirit! The fault, the sin, was in himself, in his rebellious thought, in his untamed memory. Though mobile as water, intangible as vapor, Thought, nevertheless, may be tamed by the Will, may be harnessed to the chariot of Wisdom—must be!—that happiness be found. And he recited the blessed verses of the "Book of the Way of the Law":

"*All forms are only temporary.*" When this great truth is fully comprehended by any one, then is he delivered from all pain. This is the Way of Purification.

"*All forms are subject unto pain.*" When this great truth is fully comprehended by any one, then is he delivered from all pain. This is the Way of Purification.

"*All forms are without substantial reality.*" When this great truth is fully comprehended by any one, then is he delivered from all pain. This is the way of . . .

Her form, too, unsubstantial, unreal, an illusion only, though comeliest of illusions? She had given him alms! Was the merit of the giver illusive also—illusive like the grace of the supple fingers that gave? Assuredly there were mysteries in the Abhidharma impenetrable, incomprehensible! . . . It was a golden coin, stamped with the symbol of an elephant—not more of an illusion, indeed, than the gifts of Kings to the Buddha! Gold upon her bosom also, less fine than the gold of her skin. Naked between the silken sash and the narrow breast-corslet, her young waist curved glossy and pliant as a bow. Richer the silver in her voice than in the hollow *pagals* that made a moonlight about her ankles! But her smile!—the little teeth like flower-stamens in the perfumed blossom of her mouth!

O weakness! O shame! How had the strong Charioteer of Resolve thus lost his control over the wild team of fancy! Was this languor of the Will a signal of coming peril, the peril of slumber? So strangely vivid those fancies were, so brightly definite, as about to take visible form, to move with factitious life, to play some unholy drama upon the stage of dreams! "O Thou Fully Awakened!" he cried aloud, "help now thy humble disciple to obtain the blessed wakefulness of perfect contemplation! let him find force to fulfill his vow! suffer not Mara to prevail against him!" And he recited the eternal verses of the Chapter of Wakefulness:

"*Completely and eternally awake are the disciples of Gotama!* Unceasingly, by day and night, their thoughts are fixed upon the Law.

"*Completely and eternally awake are the disciples of Gotama!* Unceasingly, by day and night, their thoughts are fixed upon the Community.

"*Completely and eternally awake are the disciples of Gotama!* Unceasingly, by day and night, their thoughts are fixed upon the Body.

"*Completely and eternally awake are the disciples of Gotama!* Unceasingly, by day and night, their minds know the sweetness of perfect peace.

"*Completely and eternally awake are the disciples of Gotama!* Unceasingly, by day and night, their minds enjoy the deep peace of meditation."

There came a murmur to his ears; a murmuring of many voices, smothering the utterances of his own, like a tumult of waters. The stars went out before his sight; the heavens darkened their infinities: all things became viewless, became blackness; and the great murmur deepened, like the murmur of a rising tide; and the earth seemed to sink from beneath him. His feet no longer touched the ground; a sense of supernatural buoyancy pervaded every fiber of his body: he felt himself floating in obscurity; then sinking softly, slowly, like a feather dropped from the pinnacle of a temple. Was this death? Nay, for all suddenly, as transported by the Sixth Supernatural Power, he stood again in light—a perfumed, sleepy light, vapory, beautiful—that bathed the marvelous streets of some Indian city. Now the nature of the murmur became manifest to him; for he moved with a mighty throng, a people of pilgrims, a nation of worshippers. But these were not of his faith; they bore upon their foreheads the smeared symbols of obscene gods! Still, he could not escape from their midst; the mile-broad human torrent bore him irresistibly with it, as a leaf is swept by the waters of the Ganges. Rajahs were there with their trains, and princes riding upon elephants, and Brahmins robed in their vestments, and swarms of voluptuous dancing-girls, moving to chant of *kabit* and *damâri*. But whither, whither? Out of the city into the sun they passed, between avenues of banyan, down colonnades of palm. But whither, whither?

Blue-distant, a mountain of carven stone appeared before them— the Temple, lifting to heaven its wilderness of chiseled pinnacles, flinging to the sky the golden spray of its decoration. Higher it grew with approach, the blue tones changed to gray, the outlines sharpened in the light. Then each detail became visible: the elephants of the pedestals standing upon tortoises of rock; the great grim faces of the capitals; the serpents and monsters writhing among the friezes; the many-headed gods of basalt in their galleries of fretted niches, tier above tier; the pictured foulnesses, the painted lusts, the divinities of abomination. And, yawning in the sloping precipice of sculpture, beneath a frenzied swarming of gods and Gopia—a beetling pyramid of limbs and bodies interlocked—the Gate, cavernous and shadowy as the mouth of Siva, devoured the living multitude.

The eddy of the throng whirled him with it to the vastness of the interior. None seemed to note his yellow robe, none even to observe his presence. Giant aisles intercrossed their heights above him; myriads of mighty pillars, fantastically carven, filed away to invisibility behind the yellow illumination of torch-fires. Strange images, weirdly sensuous, loomed up through haze of incense. Colossal figures, that at a distance assumed the form of elephants or garuda-birds, changed aspect when approached, and revealed as the secret of their design an interplaiting of the bodies of women; while one divinity rode all the monstrous allegories—one divinity or demon, eternally the same in the repetition of the sculptor, universally visible as though self-multiplied. The huge pillars themselves were symbols, figures, carnalities; the orgiastic spirit of that worship lived and writhed in the contorted bronze of the lamps, the twisted gold of the cups, the chiseled marble of the tanks. . . .

How far had he proceeded? He knew not; the journey among those countless columns, past those armies of petrified gods, down lanes of flickering lights, seemed longer than the voyage of a caravan, longer than his pilgrimage to China! But suddenly, inexplicably, there came a silence as of cemeteries; the living ocean seemed to have ebbed away from about him, to have been engulfed within abysses of subterranean architecture! He found himself alone in some strange crypt before a basin, shell-shaped and shallow, bearing in its centre a rounded column of less than human height, whose smooth and spherical summit was wreathed with flowers. Lamps similarly formed, and fed with oil of palm, hung above it. There was no other graven image, no visible divinity. Flowers of countless varieties lay heaped upon the pavement; they covered its surface like a carpet, thick, soft; they exhaled their ghosts beneath his feet. The perfume seemed to penetrate his brain—a perfume sensuous, intoxicating, unholy; an unconquerable languor mastered his will, and he sank to rest upon the floral offerings.

The sound of a tread, light as a whisper, approached through the heavy stillness, with a drowsy tinkling of *pagals*, a tintinnabulation of anklets. All suddenly he felt glide about his neck the tepid smoothness of a woman's arm. *She, she*! his Illusion, his Temptation; but how transformed, transfigured!—preternatural in her loveliness, incomprehensible in her charm! Delicate as a jasmine-petal the cheek that touched his own; deep as night, sweet as summer, the eyes that watched him. *"Heart's-thief,"* her flower-lips whispered—*"heart's-thief, how have I sought for thee! How have I found thee! Sweets I bring thee, my beloved; lips and bosom; fruit and blossom. Hast thirst? Drink from the well of mine eyes! Wouldst sacrifice? I am thine altar! Wouldst pray? I am thy God!"*

Their lips touched; her kiss seemed to change the cells of his blood to flame. For a moment Illusion triumphed; Mara prevailed! . . . With a shock of resolve the dreamer awoke in the night—under the stars of the Chinese sky.

Only a mockery of sleep! But the vow had been violated, the sacred purpose unfulfilled! Humiliated, penitent, but resolved, the ascetic drew from his girdle a keen knife, and with unfaltering hands severed his eyelids from his eyes, and flung them from him. "O Thou Perfectly Awakened!" he prayed, "thy disciple hath not been overcome save through the feebleness of the body; and his vow hath been renewed. Here shall he linger, without food or drink, until the moment of its fulfillment." And having assumed the hieratic posture—seated himself with his lower limbs folded beneath him, and the palms of his hands upward, the right upon the left, the left resting upon the sole of his upturned foot—he resumed his meditation.

Dawn blushed; day brightened. The sun shortened all the shadows of the land, and lengthened them again, and sank at last upon his funeral pyre of crimson-burning cloud. Night came and glittered and passed. But Mara had tempted in vain. This time the vow had been fulfilled, the holy purpose accomplished.

And again the sun arose to fill the World with laughter of light; flowers opened their hearts to him; birds sang their morning hymn of fire worship; the deep forest trembled with delight; and far upon the plain, the eaves of many-storied temples and the peaked caps of the city-towers caught aureate glory. Strong in the holiness of his accomplished vow, the Indian pilgrim arose in the morning glow. He started for amazement as he lifted his hands to his eyes. What! was everything a dream? Impossible! Yet now his eyes felt no pain; neither were they lidless; not even so much as one of their lashes was lacking. What marvel had been wrought? In vain he looked for the severed lids that he had flung upon the ground; they had mysteriously vanished. But lo! there where he had cast them two wondrous shrubs were growing, with dainty leaflets eyelid-shaped, and snowy buds just opening to the East.

Then, by virtue of the supernatural power acquired in that mighty meditation, it was given the holy missionary to know the secret of that newly created plant—the subtle virtue of its leaves. And he named it, in the language of the nation to whom he brought the Lotos of the Good Law, "*TE*"; and he spoke to it, saying:

"Blessed be thou, sweet plant, beneficent, life-giving, formed by the spirit of virtuous resolve! Lo! the fame of thee shall yet spread unto the ends of the earth; and the perfume of thy life be borne unto the uttermost parts by all the winds of heaven! Verily, for all time to come men who drink of thy sap shall find such refreshment that weariness may not overcome them nor languor seize upon them; neither shall they know the confusion of drowsiness, nor any desire for slumber in the hour of duty or of prayer. Blessed be thou!"

And still, as a mist of incense, as a smoke of universal sacrifice, perpetually ascends to heaven from all the lands of earth the pleasant vapor of TE, created for the refreshment of mankind by the power of a holy vow, the virtue of a pious atonement.

The Tale of the Porcelain-God

It is written in the FONG-HO-CHIN-TCH'OUEN, *that whenever the artist Thsang-Kong was in doubt, he would look into the fire of the great oven in which his vases were baking, and question the Guardian-Spirit dwelling in the flame. And the Spirit of the Oven-fires so aided him with his counsels, that the porcelains made by Thsang-Kong were indeed finer and lovelier to look upon than all other porcelains. And they were baked in the years of Khang-hi—sacredly called Jin Houang-ti.*

THE TALE OF THE PORCELAIN-GOD

Who first of men discovered the secret of the *Kao-ling*, of the *Pe-tun-tse*—the bones and the flesh, the skeleton and the skin, of the beauteous Vase? Who first discovered the virtue of the curd-white clay? Who first prepared the ice-pure bricks of *tun*: the gathered-hoariness of mountains that have died for age; blanched dust of the rocky bones and the stony flesh of sun-seeking Giants that have ceased to be? Unto whom was it first given to discover the divine art of porcelain?

Unto Pu, once a man, now a god, before whose snowy statues bow the myriad populations enrolled in the guilds of the potteries. But the place of his birth we know not; perhaps the tradition of it may have been effaced from remembrance by that awful war which in our own day consumed the lives of twenty millions of the Black-haired Race, and obliterated from the face of the world even the wonderful City of Porcelain itself—the City of King-te-chin, that of old shone like a jewel of fire in the blue mountain-girdle of Feou-liang.

Before his time indeed the Spirit of the Furnace had being; had issued from the Infinite Vitality; had become manifest as an emanation of the Supreme Tao. For Hoang-ti, nearly five thousand years ago, taught men to make good vessels of baked clay; and in his time all potters had learned to know the God of Oven-fires, and turned their wheels to the murmuring of prayer. But Hoang-ti had been gathered unto his fathers for thrice ten hundred years before that man was born destined by the Master of Heaven to become the Porcelain-God.

And his divine ghost, ever hovering above the smoking and the toiling of the potteries, still gives power to the thought of the shaper, grace to the genius of the designer, luminosity to the touch of the enamellist. For by his heaven-taught wisdom was the art of porcelain created; by his inspiration were accomplished all the miracles of Thao-yu, maker of the *Kia-yu-ki*, and all the marvels made by those who followed after him;

All the azure porcelains called *You-kouo-thien-tsing*; brilliant as a mirror, thin as paper of rice, sonorous as the melodious stone *Khing*, and colored, in obedience to the mandate of the Emperor Chi-tsong, "blue as the sky is after rain, when viewed through the rifts of the clouds." These were, indeed, the first of all porcelains, likewise called *Tchai-yao*, which no man, howsoever wicked, could find courage to break, for they charmed the eye like jewels of price;

And the *Jou-yao*, second in rank among all porcelains, sometimes mocking the aspect and the sonority of bronze, sometimes blue as summer waters, and deluding the sight with mucid appearance of thickly floating spawn of fish;

And the *Kouan-yao*, which are the Porcelains of Magistrates, and third in rank of merit among all wondrous porcelains, colored with colors of the morning—skyey blueness, with the rose of a great dawn blushing and bursting through it, and long-limbed marsh-birds flying against the glow;

Also the *Ko-yao*—fourth in rank among perfect porcelains—of fair, faint, changing colors, like the body of a living fish, or made in the likeness of opal substance, milk mixed with fire; the work of Sing-I, elder of the immortal brothers Tchang;

Also the *Ting-yao*—fifth in rank among all perfect porcelains— white as the mourning garments of a spouse bereaved, and beautiful with a trickling as of tears—the porcelains sung of by the poet Son-tong-po;

Also the porcelains called *Pi-se-yao*, whose colors are called "hidden," being alternately invisible and visible, like the tints of ice beneath the sun—the porcelains celebrated by the far-famed singer Sin-in;

Also the wondrous *Chu-yao*—the pallid porcelains that utter a mournful cry when smitten—the porcelains chanted of by the mighty chanter, Thou-chao-ling;

Also the porcelains called *Thsin-yao*, white or blue, surface-wrinkled as the face of water by the fluttering of many fins. . . . And ye can see the fish!

Also the vases called *Tsi-hong-khi*, red as sunset after a rain; and the *T'o-t'ai-khi*, fragile as the wings of the silkworm-moth, lighter than the shell of an egg;

Also the *Kia-tsing*—fair cups pearl-white when empty, yet, by some incomprehensible witchcraft of construction, seeming to swarm with purple fish the moment they are filled with water;

Also the porcelains called *Yao-pien*, whose tints are transmuted by the alchemy of fire; for they enter blood-crimson into the heat, and change there to lizard-green, and at last come forth azure as the cheek of the sky;

Also the *Ki-tcheou-yao*, which are all violet as a summer's night; and the *Hing-yao* that sparkle with the sparklings of mingled silver and snow;

Also the *Sieouen-yao*—some ruddy as iron in the furnace, some diaphanous and ruby-red, some granulated and yellow as the rind of an orange, some softly flushed as the skin of a peach;

Also the *Tsoui-khi-yao*, crackled and green as ancient ice is; and the *Tchou-fou-yao*, which are the Porcelains of Emperors, with dragons wriggling and snarling in gold; and those *yao* that are pink-ribbed and have their angles serrated as the claws of crabs are;

Also the *Ou-ni-yao*, black as the pupil of the eye, and as lustrous; and the *Hou-tien-yao*, darkly yellow as the faces of men of India; and the *Ou-kong-yao*, whose color is the dead-gold of autumn-leaves;

Also the *Long-kang-yao*, green as the seedling of a pea, but bearing also paintings of sun-silvered cloud, and of the Dragons of Heaven;

Also the *Tching-hoa-yao*—pictured with the amber bloom of grapes and the verdure of vine-leaves and the blossoming of poppies, or decorated in relief with figures of fighting crickets;

Also the *Khang-hi-nien-ts'ang-yao*, celestial azure sown with star-dust of gold; and the *Khien-long-nien-thang-yao*, splendid in sable and silver as a fervid night that is flashed with lightnings.

Not indeed the *Long-Ouang-yao*—painted with the lascivious *Pi-hi*, with the obscene *Nan-niu-ssé-sie*, with the shameful *Tchun-hoa*, or "Pictures of Spring"; abominations created by command of the wicked Emperor Moutsong, though the Spirit of the Furnace hid his face and fled away;

But all other vases of startling form and substance, magically articulated, and ornamented with figures in relief, in cameo, in transparency—the vases with orifices belled like the cups of flowers, or cleft like the bills of birds, or fanged like the jaws of serpents, or pink-lipped as the mouth of a girl; the vases flesh-colored and purple-veined and dimpled, with ears and with earrings; the vases in likeness of mushrooms, of lotos-flowers, of lizards, of horse-footed dragons woman-faced; the vases strangely translucid, that simulate the white glimmering of grains of prepared rice, that counterfeit the vapory lace-work of frost, that imitate the efflorescences of coral;

Also the statues in porcelain of divinities: the Genius of the Hearth; the Long-pinn who are the Twelve Deities of Ink; the blessed Lao-tseu, born with silver hair; Kong-fu-tse, grasping the scroll of written wisdom; Kouan-in, sweetest Goddess of Mercy, standing snowy-footed upon the heart of her golden lily; Chi-nong, the god who taught men how to cook; Fo, with long eyes closed in meditation, and lips smiling the mysterious smile of Supreme Beatitude; Cheou-lao, god of Longevity, bestriding his aerial steed, the white-winged stork; Pou-t'ai, Lord of Contentment and of Wealth, obese and dreamy; and that fairest Goddess of Talent, from whose beneficent hands eternally streams the iridescent rain of pearls.

And though many a secret of that matchless art that Pu bequeathed unto men may indeed have been forgotten and lost forever, the story of the Porcelain-God is remembered; and I doubt not that any of the aged *Jeou-yen-liao-kong*, any one of the old blind men of the great potteries, who sit all day grinding colors in the sun, could tell you Pu was once a humble Chinese workman, who grew to be a great artist by dint of tireless study and patience and by the inspiration of Heaven. So famed he became that some deemed him an alchemist, who possessed the secret called *White-and-Yellow*, by which stones might be turned into gold; and others thought him a magician, having the ghastly power of murdering men with horror of nightmare, by hiding charmed effigies of them under the tiles of their own roofs; and others, again, averred that he was an astrologer who had discovered the mystery of those Five Hing which influence all things—those Powers that move even in the currents of the star-drift, in the milky *Tien-ho*, or River of the Sky. Thus, at least, the ignorant spoke of him; but even those who stood about the Son of Heaven, those whose hearts had been strengthened by the acquisition of wisdom, wildly praised the marvels of his handicraft, and asked each other if there might be any imaginable form of beauty which Pu could not evoke from that beauteous substance so docile to the touch of his cunning hand.

And one day it came to pass that Pu sent a priceless gift to the Celestial and August: a vase imitating the substance of ore-rock, all aflame with pyritic scintillation—a shape of glittering splendor with chameleons sprawling over it; chameleons of porcelain that shifted color as often as the beholder changed his position. And the Emperor, wondering exceedingly at the splendor of the work, questioned the princes and the mandarins concerning him that made it. And the princes and the mandarins answered that he was a workman named Pu, and that he was without equal among potters, knowing secrets that seemed to have been inspired either by gods or by demons. Whereupon the Son of Heaven sent his officers to Pu with a noble gift, and summoned him unto his presence.

So the humble artisan entered before the Emperor, and having performed the supreme prostration—thrice kneeling, and thrice nine times touching the ground with his forehead—awaited the command of the August.

And the Emperor spoke to him, saying: "Son, thy gracious gift hath found high favor in our sight; and for the charm of that offering we have bestowed upon thee a reward of five thousand silver *liang*. But thrice that sum shall be awarded thee so soon as thou shalt have fulfilled our behest. Hearken, therefore, O matchless artificer! it is now our will that thou make for us a vase having the tint and the aspect of living flesh, but—mark well our desire!—*of flesh made to creep by the utterance of such words as poets utter—flesh moved by an Idea, flesh horripilated by a Thought*! Obey, and answer not! We have spoken."

Now Pu was the most cunning of all the *P'ei-se-kong*—the men who marry colors together; of all the *Hoa-yang-kong*, who draw the shapes of vase-decoration; of all the *Hoei-sse-kong*, who paint in enamel; of all the *T'ien-thsai-kong*, who brighten color; of all the *Chao-lou-kong*, who watch the furnace-fires and the porcelain-ovens. But he went away sorrowing from the Palace of the Son of Heaven, notwithstanding the gift of five thousand silver *liang* which had been given to him. For he thought to himself: "Surely the mystery of the comeliness of flesh, and the mystery of that by which it is moved, are the secrets of the Supreme Tao. How shall man lend the aspect of sentient life to dead clay? Who save the Infinite can give soul?"

Now Pu had discovered those witchcrafts of color, those surprises of grace, that make the art of the ceramist. He had found the secret of the *feng-hong*, the wizard flush of the Rose; of the *hoa-hong*, the delicious incarnadine; of the mountain-green called *chan-lou*; of the pale soft yellow termed *hiao-hoang-yeou*; and of the *hoang-kin*, which is the blazing beauty of gold. He had found those eel-tints, those serpent-greens, those pansy-violets, those furnace-crimsons, those carminates and lilacs, subtle as spirit-flame, which our enamellists of the Occident long sought without success to reproduce. But he trembled at the task assigned him, as he returned to the toil of his studio, saying: "How shall any miserable man render in clay the quivering of flesh to an Idea—the inexplicable horripilation of a Thought? Shall a man venture to mock the magic of that Eternal Molder by whose infinite power a million suns are shapen more readily than one small jar might be rounded upon my wheel?"

Yet the command of the Celestial and August might never be disobeyed; and the patient workman strove with all his power to fulfill the Son of Heaven's desire. But vainly for days, for weeks, for months, for season after season, did he strive; vainly also he prayed unto the gods to aid him; vainly he besought the Spirit of the Furnace, crying: "O thou Spirit of Fire, hear me, heed me, help me! how shall I—a miserable man, unable to breathe into clay a living soul—how shall I render in this inanimate substance the aspect of flesh made to creep by the utterance of a Word, sentient to the horripilation of a Thought?"

For the Spirit of the Furnace made strange answer to him with whispering of fire: "*Vast thy faith, weird thy prayer! Has Thought feet, that man may perceive the trace of its passing? Canst thou measure me the blast of the Wind?*"

Nevertheless, with purpose unmoved, nine-and-forty times did Pu seek to fulfill the Emperor's command; nine-and-forty times he strove to obey the behest of the Son of Heaven. Vainly, alas! did he consume his substance; vainly did he expend his strength; vainly did he exhaust his knowledge: success smiled not upon him; and Evil visited his home, and Poverty sat in his dwelling, and Misery shivered at his hearth.

Sometimes, when the hour of trial came, it was found that the colors had become strangely transmuted in the firing, or had faded into ashen pallor, or had darkened into the fuliginous hue of forest-mould. And Pu, beholding these misfortunes, made wail to the Spirit of the

Furnace, praying: "O thou Spirit of Fire, how shall I render the likeness of lustrous flesh, the warm glow of living color, unless thou aid me?"

And the Spirit of the Furnace mysteriously answered him with murmuring of fire: "*Canst thou learn the art of that Infinite Enameller who hath made beautiful the Arch of Heaven—whose brush is Light; whose paints are the Colors of the Evening?*"

Sometimes, again, even when the tints had not changed, after the pricked and labored surface had seemed about to quicken in the heat, to assume the vibratility of living skin—even at the last hour all the labor of the workers proved to have been wasted; for the fickle substance rebelled against their efforts, producing only crinklings grotesque as those upon the rind of a withered fruit, or granulations like those upon the skin of a dead bird from which the feathers have been rudely plucked. And Pu wept, and cried out unto the Spirit of the Furnace: "O thou Spirit of Flame, how shall I be able to imitate the thrill of flesh touched by a Thought, unless thou wilt vouchsafe to lend me thine aid?"

And the Spirit of the Furnace mysteriously answered him with muttering of fire: "*Canst thou give ghost unto a stone? Canst thou thrill with a Thought the entrails of the granite hills?*"

Sometimes it was found that all the work indeed had not failed; for the color seemed good, and all faultless the matter of the vase appeared to be, having neither crack nor wrinkling nor crinkling; but the pliant softness of warm skin did not meet the eye; the flesh-tinted surface offered only the harsh aspect and hard glimmer of metal. All their exquisite toil to mock the pulpiness of sentient substance had left no trace; had been brought to naught by the breath of the furnace. And Pu, in his despair, shrieked to the Spirit of the Furnace: "O thou merciless divinity! O thou most pitiless god!—thou whom I have worshipped with ten thousand sacrifices!—for what fault hast thou abandoned me? for what error hast thou forsaken me? How may I, most wretched of men! ever render the aspect of flesh made to creep with the utterance of a Word, sentient to the titillation of a Thought, if thou wilt not aid me?"

And the Spirit of the Furnace made answer unto him with roaring of fire: "*Canst thou divide a Soul? Nay! . . . Thy life for the life of thy work!—thy soul for the soul of thy Vase!*"

And hearing these words Pu arose with a terrible resolve swelling at his heart, and made ready for the last and fiftieth time to fashion his work for the oven.

One hundred times did he sift the clay and the quartz, the *kao-ling* and the *tun*; one hundred times did he purify them in clearest water; one hundred times with tireless hands did he knead the creamy paste, mingling it at last with colors known only to himself. Then was the vase shapen and reshapen, and touched and retouched by the hands of Pu, until its blandness seemed to live, until it appeared to quiver and to palpitate, as with vitality from within, as with the quiver of rounded muscle undulating beneath the integument. For the hues of life were upon it and infiltrated throughout its innermost substance, imitating the carnation of blood-bright tissue, and the reticulated purple of the veins; and over all was laid the envelope of sun-colored *Pe-kia-ho*, the lucid and glossy enamel, half diaphanous, even like the substance that it counterfeited—the polished skin of a woman. Never since the making of the world had any work comparable to this been wrought by the skill of man.

Then Pu bade those who aided him that they should feed the furnace well with wood of *tcha*; but he told his resolve unto none. Yet after the oven began to glow, and he saw the work of his hands blossoming and blushing in the heat, he bowed himself before the Spirit of Flame, and murmured: "O thou Spirit and Master of Fire, I know the truth of thy words! I know that a Soul may never be divided! Therefore my life for the life of my work!—my soul for the soul of my Vase!"

And for nine days and for eight nights the furnaces were fed unceasingly with wood of *tcha*; for nine days and for eight nights men watched the wondrous vase crystallizing into being, rose-lighted by the breath of the flame. Now upon the coming of the ninth night, Pu bade all his weary comrades retire to, rest, for that the work was well-nigh done, and the success assured. "If you find me not here at sunrise," he said, "fear not to take forth the vase; for I know that the task will have been accomplished according to the command of the August." So they departed.

But in that same ninth night Pu entered the flame, and yielded up his ghost in the embrace of the Spirit of the Furnace, giving his life for the life of his work—his soul for the soul of his Vase.

And when the workmen came upon the tenth morning to take forth the porcelain marvel, even the bones of Pu had ceased to be; but lo! the Vase lived as they looked upon it: seeming to be flesh moved by the utterance of a Word, creeping to the titillation of a Thought. And whenever tapped by the finger it uttered a voice and a name—the voice of its maker, the name of its creator: PU.

And the son of Heaven, hearing of these things, and viewing the miracle of the vase, said unto those about him: "Verily, the Impossible hath been wrought by the strength of faith, by the force of obedience! Yet never was it our desire that so cruel a sacrifice should have been; we sought only to know whether the skill of the matchless artificer came from the Divinities or from the Demons—from heaven or from hell. Now, indeed, we discern that Pu hath taken his place among the gods." And the Emperor mourned exceedingly for his faithful servant. But he ordained that godlike honors should be paid unto the spirit of the marvelous artist, and that his memory should be revered forevermore, and that fair statues of him should be set up in all the cities of the Celestial Empire, and above all the toiling of the potteries, that the multitude of workers might unceasingly call upon his name and invoke his benediction upon their labors.

From GLIMPSES OF UNFAMILIAR JAPAN

Of Ghosts and Goblins

I

There was a Buddha, according to the Hokkekyō who "even assumed the shape of a goblin to preach to such as were to be converted by a goblin." And in the same Sûtra may be found this promise of the Teacher: "*While he is dwelling lonely in the wilderness, I will send thither goblins in great number to keep him company.*" The appalling character of this promise is indeed somewhat modified by the assurance that gods also are to be sent. But if ever I become a holy man, I shall take heed not to dwell in the wilderness, because I have seen Japanese goblins, and I do not like them.

Kinjurō showed them to me last night. They had come to town for the matsuri of our own ujigami, or parish-temple; and, as there were many curious things to be seen at the night festival, we started for the temple after dark, Kinjurō carrying a paper lantern painted with my crest.

It had snowed heavily in the morning; but now the sky and the sharp still air were clear as diamond; and the crisp snow made a pleasant crunching sound under our feet as we walked; and it occurred to me to say: "O Kinjurō, is there a God of Snow?"

"I cannot tell," replied Kinjurō. "There be many gods I do not know; and there is not any man who knows the names of all the gods. But there is the Yuki-Onna, the Woman of the Snow."

"And what is the Yuki-Onna?"

"She is the White One that makes the Faces in the snow. She does not any harm, only makes afraid. By day she lifts only her head, and frightens those who journey alone. But at night she rises up sometimes, taller than the trees, and looks about a little while, and then falls back in a shower of snow."[1]

"What is her face like?"

"It is all white, white. It is an enormous face. And it is a *lonesome* face."

---

[1] In other parts of Japan I have heard the Yuki-Onna described as a very beautiful phantom who lures young men to lonesome places for the purpose of sucking their blood.

[The word Kinjurō used was *samushii*. Its common meaning is "lonesome"; but he used it, I think, in the sense of "weird."]

"Did you ever see her, Kinjurō?"

"Master, I never saw her. But my father told me that once when he was a child, he wanted to go to a neighbor's house through the snow to play with another little boy; and that on the way he saw a great white Face rise up from the snow and look lonesomely about, so that he cried for fear and ran back. Then his people all went out and looked; but there was only snow; and then they knew that he had seen the Yuki-Onna."

"And in these days, Kinjurō, do people ever see her?"

"Yes. Those who make the pilgrimage to Yabumura, in the period called Dai-Kan, which is the Time of the Greatest Cold,[2] they sometimes see her."

"What is there at Yabumura, Kinjurō?"

"There is the Yabu-jinja, which is an ancient and famous temple of Yabu-no-Tenno-San—the God of Colds, Kaze-no-Kami. It is high upon a hill, nearly nine ri from Matsue. And the great matsuri of that temple is held upon the tenth and eleventh days of the Second Month. And on those days strange things may be seen. For one who gets a very bad cold prays to the deity of Yabu-jinja to cure it, and takes a vow to make a pilgrimage naked to the temple at the time of the matsuri."

"Naked?"

"Yes: the pilgrims wear only waraji, and a little cloth round their loins. And a great many men and women go naked through the snow to the temple, though the snow is deep at that time. And each man carries a bunch of gohei and a naked sword as gifts to the temple; and each woman carries a metal mirror. And at the temple, the priests receive them, performing curious rites. For the priests then, according to ancient custom, attire themselves like sick men, and lie down and groan, and drink, potions made of herbs, prepared after the Chinese manner."

"But do not some of the pilgrims die of cold, Kinjurō?"

"No: our Izumo peasants are hardy. Besides, they run swiftly, so that they reach the temple all warm. And before returning they put on thick warm robes. But sometimes, upon the way, they see the Yuki-Onna."

---

[2] In Izumo the Dai-Kan, or Period of Greatest Cold, falls in February.

II

Each side of the street leading to the miya was illuminated with a line of paper lanterns bearing holy symbols; and the immense court of the temple had been transformed into a town of booths, and shops, and temporary theatres. In spite of the cold, the crowd was prodigious. There seemed to be all the usual attractions of a matsuri, and a number of unusual ones. Among the familiar lures, I missed at this festival only the maiden wearing an obi of living snakes; probably it had become too cold for the snakes. There were several fortune-tellers and jugglers; there were acrobats and dancers; there was a man making pictures out of sand; and there was a menagerie containing an emu from Australia, and a couple of enormous bats from the Loo Choo Islands—bats trained to do several things. I did reverence to the gods, and bought some extraordinary toys; and then we went to look for the goblins. They were domiciled in a large permanent structure, rented to showmen on special occasions.

Gigantic characters signifying "IKI-NINGYŌ," painted upon the signboard at the entrance, partly hinted the nature of the exhibition. Iki-ningyō ("living images") somewhat correspond to our Occidental "wax figures"; but the equally realistic Japanese creations are made of much cheaper material. Having bought two wooden tickets for one sen each, we entered, and passed behind a curtain to find ourselves in a long corridor lined with booths, or rather matted compartments, about the size of small rooms. Each space, decorated with scenery appropriate to the subject, was occupied by a group of life-size figures. The group nearest the entrance, representing two men playing samisen and two geisha dancing, seemed to me without excuse for being, until Kinjurō had translated a little placard before it, announcing that one of the figures was a living person. We watched in vain for a wink or palpitation. Suddenly one of the musicians laughed aloud, shook his head, and began to play and sing. The deception was perfect.

The remaining groups, twenty-four in number, were powerfully impressive in their peculiar way, representing mostly famous popular traditions or sacred myths. Feudal heroisms, the memory of which stirs every Japanese heart; legends of filial piety; Buddhist miracles, and stories of emperors were among the subjects. Sometimes, however, the realism was brutal, as in one scene representing the body of a woman lying in a pool of blood, with brains scattered by a sword stroke. Nor was this unpleasantness altogether atoned for by her miraculous resuscitation in the adjoining compartment, where she reappeared returning thanks in a Nichiren temple, and converting her slaughterer, who happened, by some extraordinary accident, to go there at the same time.

At the termination of the corridor there hung a black curtain behind which screams could be heard. And above the black curtain was a placard inscribed with the promise of a gift to anybody able to traverse the mysteries beyond without being frightened.

"Master," said Kinjurō, "the goblins are inside."

We lifted the veil, and found ourselves in a sort of lane between hedges, and behind the hedges we saw tombs; we were in a graveyard. There were real weeds and trees, and sotoba and haka, and the effect was quite natural. Moreover, as the roof was very lofty, and kept invisible by a clever arrangement of lights, all seemed darkness only; and this gave one a sense of being out under the night, a feeling accentuated by the chill of the air. And here and there we could discern sinister shapes, mostly of superhuman stature, some seeming to wait in dim places, others floating above the graves. Quite near us, towering above the hedge on our right, was a Buddhist priest, with his back turned to us.

"A yamabushi, an exorciser?" I queried of Kinjurō.

"No," said Kinjurō; "see how tall he is. I think that must be a Tanuki-Bōzu."

The Tanuki-Bōzu is the priestly form assumed by the goblin-badger (*tanuki*) for the purpose of decoying belated travelers to destruction. We went on, and looked up into his face. It was a nightmare—his face.

"In truth a Tanuki-Bōzu," said Kinjurō. "What does the Master honorably think concerning it?"

Instead of replying, I jumped back; for the monstrous thing had suddenly reached over the hedge and clutched at me, with a moan. Then it fell back, swaying and creaking. It was moved by invisible strings.

"I think, Kinjurō, that it is a nasty, horrid thing. . . . But I shall not claim the present."

We laughed, and proceeded to consider a Three-Eyed Friar (*Mitsu-me-Nyūdō*). The Three-Eyed Friar also watches for the unwary at night. His face is soft and smiling as the face of a Buddha, but he has a hideous eye in the summit of his shaven pate, which can only be seen when seeing it does no good. The Mitsu-me-Nyūdō made a grab at Kinjurō, and startled him almost as much as the Tanuki-Bōzu had startled me.

Then we looked at the Yama-Uba—the "Mountain Nurse." She catches little children and nurses them for a while, and then devours them. In her face she has no mouth; but she has a mouth in the top of her head, under her hair. The Yama-Uba did not clutch at us, because her hands were occupied with a nice little boy, whom she was just going to eat. The child had been made wonderfully pretty to heighten the effect.

Then I saw the specter of a woman hovering in the air above a tomb at some distance, so that I felt safer in observing it. It had no eyes; its long hair hung loose; its white robe floated light as smoke. I thought of a statement in a composition by one of my pupils about ghosts: "*Their greatest Peculiarity is that They have no feet.*" Then I jumped again, for the thing, quite soundlessly but very swiftly, made through the air at me.

And the rest of our journey among the graves was little more than a succession of like experiences; but it was made amusing by the screams of women, and bursts of laughter from people who lingered only to watch the effect upon others of what had scared themselves.

III

Forsaking the goblins, we visited a little open-air theatre to see two girls dance. After they had danced awhile, one girl produced a sword and cut off the other girl's head, and put it upon a table, where it opened its mouth and began to sing. All this was very prettily done; but my mind was still haunted by the goblins. So I questioned Kinjurō:

"Kinjurō, those goblins of which we the ningyō have seen—do folk believe in the reality, thereof?"

"Not any more," answered Kinjurō—"not at least among the people of the city. Perhaps in the country it may not be so. We believe in the Lord Buddha; we believe in the ancient gods; and there be many who believe the dead sometimes return to avenge a cruelty or to compel an act of justice. But we do not now believe all that was believed in ancient time. . . .Master," he added, as we reached another queer exhibition, "it is only one sen to go to hell, if the Master would like to go"—

"Very good, Kinjurō," I made reply. "Pay two sen that we may both go to hell."

IV

And we passed behind a curtain into a big room full of curious clicking and squeaking noises. These noises were made by unseen wheels and pulleys moving a multitude of ningyō upon a broad shelf about breast- high, which surrounded the apartment upon three sides. These ningyō were not iki-ningyō, but very small images—puppets. They represented all things in the Under-World.

The first I saw was Sozu-Baba, the Old Woman of the River of Ghosts, who takes away the garments of Souls. The garments were hanging upon a tree behind her. She was tall; she rolled her green eyes and gnashed her long teeth, while the shivering of the little white souls before her was as a trembling of butterflies. Farther on appeared Emma

Dai-O, great King of Hell, nodding grimly. At his right hand, upon their tripod, the heads of Kaguhana and Mirume, the Witnesses, whirled as upon a wheel. At his left, a devil was busy sawing a Soul in two; and I noticed that he used his saw like a Japanese carpenter— pulling it towards him instead of pushing it. And then various exhibitions of the tortures of the damned. A liar bound to a post was having his tongue pulled out by a devil—slowly, with artistic jerks; it was already longer than the owner's body. Another devil was pounding another Soul in a mortar so vigorously that the sound of the braying could be heard above all the din of the machinery. A little farther on was a man being eaten alive by two serpents having women's faces; one serpent was white, the other blue. The white had been his wife, the blue his concubine. All the tortures known to medieval Japan were being elsewhere deftly practiced by swarms of devils. After reviewing them, we visited the Sai-no-Kawara, and saw Jizō with a child in his arms, and a circle of other children running swiftly around him, to escape from demons who brandished their clubs and ground their teeth.

Hell proved, however, to be extremely cold; and while meditating on the partial inappropriateness of the atmosphere, it occurred to me that in the common Buddhist picture-books of the Jigoku I had never noticed any illustrations of torment by cold. Indian Buddhism, indeed, teaches the existence of cold hells. There is one, for instance, where people's lips are frozen so that they can say only "Ah-ta-ta!"— wherefore that hell is called Atata. And there is the hell where tongues are frozen, and where people say only "Ah-baba!" for which reason it is called Ababa. And there is the Pundarika, or Great White-Lotus hell, where the spectacle of the bones laid bare by the cold is "like a blossoming of white lotus- flowers." Kinjurō thinks there are cold hells according to Japanese Buddhism; but he is not sure. And I am not sure that the idea of cold could be made very terrible to the Japanese. They confess a general liking for cold, and compose Chinese poems about the loveliness of ice and snow.

V

Out of hell, we found our way to a magic-lantern show being given in a larger and even much colder structure. A Japanese magic-lantern show is nearly always interesting in more particulars than one, but perhaps especially as evidencing the native genius for adapting Western inventions to Eastern tastes. A Japanese magic-lantern show is essentially dramatic. It is a play of which the dialogue is uttered by invisible personages, the actors and the scenery being only luminous shadows. "Wherefore it is peculiarly well suited to goblinries and weirdnesses of all kinds; and plays in which ghosts figure are the favorite subjects. As the hall was bitterly cold, I waited only long enough to see one performance—of which the following is an epitome:

SCENE 1.—A beautiful peasant girl and her aged mother, squatting together at home. Mother weeps violently, gesticulates agonizingly. From her frantic speech, broken by wild sobs, we learn that the girl must be sent as a victim to the Kami-Sama of some lonesome temple in the mountains. That god is a bad god. Once a year he shoots an arrow into the thatch of some farmer's house as a sign that he wants a girl—to eat! Unless the girl be sent to him at once, he destroys the crops and the cows. Exit mother, weeping and shrieking, and pulling out her grey hair. Exit girl, with downcast head, and air of sweet resignation.

SCENE II.—Before a wayside inn; cherry-trees in blossom. Enter coolies carrying, like a palanquin, a large box, in which the girl is supposed to be. Deposit box; enter to eat; tell story to loquacious landlord. Enter noble samurai, with two swords. Asks about box. Hears the story of the coolies repeated by loquacious landlord. Exhibits fierce indignation; vows that the Kami-Sama are good—do not eat girls. Declares that so-called Kami-Sama to be a devil. Observes that devils must be killed. Orders box opened. Sends girl home. Gets into box himself, and commands coolies under pain of death to bear him right quickly to that temple.

SCENE III.—Enter coolies, approaching temple through forest at night. Coolies afraid. Drop box and run. Exeunt coolies. Box alone in the dark. Enter veiled figure, all white. Figure moans unpleasantly; utters horrid cries. Box remains impassive. Figure removes veil, showing Its face—a skull with phosphoric eyes. [Audience unanimously utter the sound "Aaaaaa!"] Figure displays Its hands— monstrous and apish, with claws. [*Audience utter a second "Aaaaaa!"*] Figure approaches the box, touches the box, opens the box! Up leaps noble samurai. A wrestle; drums sound the roll of battle. Noble samurai practices successfully noble art of jiujutsu. Casts demon down, tramples upon him triumphantly, cuts off his head. Head suddenly enlarges, grows to the size of a house, tries to bite off head of samurai. Samurai slashes it with his sword. Head rolls backward, spitting fire, and vanishes. Finis. *Exeunt omnes.*

VI

The vision of the samurai and the goblin reminded Kinjurō of a queer tale, which he began to tell me as soon as the shadow-play was over. Ghastly stories are apt to fall flat after such an exhibition; but Kinjurō's stories are always peculiar enough to justify the telling under almost any circumstances. Wherefore I listened eagerly, in spite of the cold:

"A long time ago, in the days when Fox-women and goblins haunted this land, there came to the capital with her parents a samurai girl, so beautiful that all men who saw her fell enamored of her. And hundreds of young samurai desired and hoped to marry her, and made their desire known to her parents. For it has ever been the custom in Japan that marriages should be arranged by parents. But there are exceptions to all customs, and the case of this maiden was such an exception. Her parents declared that they intended to allow their daughter to choose her own husband, and that all who wished to win her would be free to woo her.

"Many men of high rank and of great wealth were admitted to the house as suitors; and each one courted her as he best knew how—with gifts, and with fair words, and with poems written in her honor, and with promises of eternal love. And to each one she spoke sweetly and hopefully; but she made strange conditions. For every suitor she obliged to bind himself by his word of honor as a samurai to submit to a test of his love for her, and never to divulge to living person what that test might be. And to this all agreed.

"But even the most confident suitors suddenly ceased their importunities after having been put to the test; and all of them appeared to have been greatly terrified by something. Indeed, not a few even fled away from the city, and could not be persuaded by their friends to return. But no one ever so much as hinted why. Therefore it was whispered by those who knew nothing of the mystery, that the beautiful girl must be either a Fox-woman or a goblin.

"Now, when all the wooers of high rank had abandoned their suit, there came a samurai who had no wealth but his sword. He was a good man and true, and of pleasing presence; and the girl seemed to like him. But she made him take the same pledge which the others had taken; and after he had taken it, she told him to return upon a certain evening.

"When that evening came, he was received at the house by none but the girl herself. With her own hands she set before him the repast of hospitality, and waited upon him, after which she told him that she wished him to go out with her at a late hour. To this he consented gladly, and inquired to what place she desired to go. But she replied nothing to his question, and all at once became very silent, and strange in her manner. And after a while she retired from the apartment, leaving him alone.

"Only long after midnight she returned, robed all in white—like a Soul—and, without uttering a word, signed to him to follow her. Out of the house they hastened while all the city slept. It was what is called an oborozuki-yo—'moon-clouded night.' Always upon such a night, 'tis said, do ghosts wander. She swiftly led the way; and the dogs howled as she flitted by; and she passed beyond the confines of the city to a place of knolls shadowed by enormous trees, where an ancient cemetery was. Into it she glided—a white shadow into blackness. He followed, wondering, his hand upon his sword. Then his eyes became accustomed to the gloom; and he saw.

"By a new-made grave she paused and signed to him to wait. The tools of the grave-maker were still lying there. Seizing one, she began to dig furiously, with strange haste and strength. At last her spade smote a coffin-lid and made it boom: another moment and the fresh white wood of the kwan was bare. She tore off the lid, revealing a corpse within—the corpse of a child. With goblin gestures she wrung an arm from the body, wrenched it in twain, and, squatting down, began to devour the upper half. Then, flinging to her lover the other half, she cried to him, 'Eat, if thou lovest me! this is what I eat!'

"Not even for a single instant did he hesitate. He squatted down upon the other side of the grave, and ate the half of the arm, and said, '*Kekkō degozarimasu! mo sukoshi chodai.*'[3] For that arm was made of the best kwashi[4] that Saikyō could produce.

"Then the girl sprang to her feet with a burst of laughter, and cried: 'You only, of all my brave suitors, did not run away! And I wanted a husband: who could not fear. I will marry you; I can love you: you are a *man!*'"

VII

"O Kinjurō," I said, as we took our way home, "I have heard and I have read many Japanese stories of the returning of the dead. Likewise you yourself have told me it is still believed the dead return, and why. But according both to that which I have read and that which you have told me, the coming back of the dead is never a thing to be desired. They return because of hate, or because of envy, or because they cannot rest for sorrow. But of any who return for that which is not evil—where is it written? Surely the common history of them is like that which we have this night seen: much that is horrible and much that is wicked and nothing of that which is beautiful or true."

Now this I said that I might tempt him. And he made even the answer I desired, by uttering the story which is hereafter set down:

"Long ago, in the days of a daimyo whose name has been forgotten, there lived in this old city a young man and a maid who loved each other very much. Their names are not remembered, but their story remains. From infancy they had been betrothed; and as children

---

[3] "It is excellent: I pray you give me a little more."
[4] Kwashi: Japanese confectionery.

they played together, for their parents were neighbors. And as they grew up, they became always fonder of each other.

"Before the youth had become a man, his parents died. But he was able to enter the service of a rich samurai, an officer of high rank, who had been a friend of his people. And his protector soon took him into great favor, seeing him to be courteous, intelligent, and apt at arms. So the young man hoped to find himself shortly in a position that would make it possible for him to marry his betrothed. But war broke out in the north and east; and he was summoned suddenly to follow his master to the field. Before departing, however, he was able to see the girl; and they exchanged pledges in the presence of her parents; and he promised, should he remain alive, to return within a year from that day to marry his betrothed.

"After his going much time passed without news of him, for there was no post in that time as now; and the girl grieved so much for thinking of the chances of war that she became all white and thin and weak. Then at last she heard of him through a messenger sent from the army to bear news to the daimyo and once again a letter was brought to her by another messenger. And thereafter there came no word. Long is a year to one who waits. And the year passed, and he did not return.

"Other seasons passed, and still he did not come; and she thought him dead; and she sickened and lay down, and died, and was buried. Then her old parents, who had no other child, grieved unspeakably, and came to hate their home for the lonesomeness of it. After a time they resolved to sell all they had, and to set out upon a sengaji—the great pilgrimage to the Thousand Temples of the Nichiren-Shū, which requires many years to perform. So they sold their small house with all that it contained, excepting the ancestral tablets, and the holy things which must never be sold, and the ihai of their buried daughter, which were placed, according to the custom of those about to leave their native place, in the family temple. Now the family was of the Nichiren-Shū; and their temple was Myōkōji.

"They had been gone only four days when the young man who had been betrothed to their daughter returned to the city. He had attempted, with the permission of his master, to fulfill his promise. But the provinces upon his way were full of war, and the roads and passes were guarded by troops, and he had been long delayed by many difficulties. And when he heard of his misfortune he sickened for grief, and many days remained without knowledge of anything, like one about to die.

"But when he began to recover his strength, all the pain of memory came back again; and he regretted that he had not died. Then he resolved to kill himself upon the grave of his betrothed; and, as soon as he was able to go out unobserved, he took his sword and went to the cemetery where the girl was buried: it is a lonesome place—the cemetery of Myōkōji. There he found her tomb, and knelt before it, and prayed and wept, and whispered to her that which he was about to do. And suddenly he heard her voice cry to him: '*Anata!*' and felt her hand upon his hand; and he turned, and saw her kneeling beside him, smiling, and beautiful as he remembered her, only a little pale. Then his heart leaped so that he could not speak for the wonder and the doubt and the joy of that moment. But she said: "Do not doubt: it is really I. I am not dead. It was all a mistake. I was buried, because my people thought me dead— buried too soon. And my own parents thought me dead, and went upon a pilgrimage. Yet you see, I am not dead—not a ghost. It is I: do not doubt it! And I have seen your heart, and that was worth all the waiting, and the pain . . . But now let us go away at once to another city, so that people may not know this thing and trouble us; for all still believe me dead."

"And they went away, no one observing them. And they went even to the village of Minobu, which is in the province of Kai. For there is a famous temple of the Nichiren-Shū in that place; and the girl had said: 'I know that in the course of their pilgrimage my parents will surely visit Minobu: so that if we dwell there, they will find us, and we shall be all again together.' And when they came to Minobu, she said: 'Let us open a little shop.' And they opened a little food-shop, on the wide way leading to the holy place; and there they sold cakes for children, and toys, and food for pilgrims. For two years they so lived and prospered; and there was a son born to them.

"Now when the child was a year and two months old, the parents of the wife came in the course of their pilgrimage to Minobu; and they stopped at the little shop to buy food. And seeing their daughter's betrothed, they cried out and wept and asked questions. Then he made them enter, and bowed down before them, and astonished them, saying: 'Truly as I speak it, your daughter is not dead; and she is my wife; and we have a son. And she is even now within the farther room, lying down with the child. I pray you go in at once and gladden her, for her heart longs for the moment of seeing you again.'

"So while he busied himself in making all things ready for their comfort, they entered the inner, room very softly—the mother first.

"They found the child asleep; but the mother they did not find. She seemed to have gone out for a little while only: her pillow was still warm. They waited long for her: then they began to seek her. But never was she seen again.

"And they understood only when they found beneath the coverings which had covered the mother and child, something which they remembered having left years before in the temple of Myōkōji—a little mortuary tablet, the ihai of their buried daughter."

I suppose I must have looked thoughtful after this tale; for the old man said:

"Perhaps the Master honorably thinks concerning the story that it is foolish?"

"Nay, Kinjurō, the story is in my heart."

From KOKORO

In Cholera-Time

I

China's chief ally in the late war, being deaf and blind, knew nothing, and still knows nothing, of treaties or of peace. It followed the returning armies of Japan, invaded the victorious empire, and killed about thirty thousand people during the hot season. It is still slaying; and the funeral pyres burn continually. Sometimes the smoke and the odor come wind-blown into my garden down from the hills behind the town, just to remind me that the cost of burning an adult of my own size is eighty sen—about half a dollar in American money at the present rate of exchange.

From the upper balcony of my house, the whole length of a Japanese street, with its rows of little shops, is visible down to the bay. Out of various houses in that street I have seen cholera-patients conveyed to the hospital—the last one (only this morning) my neighbor across the way, who kept a porcelain shop. He was removed by force, in spite of the tears and cries of his family. The sanitary law forbids the treatment of cholera in private houses; yet people try to hide their sick, in spite of fines and other penalties, because the public cholera-hospitals are overcrowded and roughly managed, and the patients are entirely separated from all who love them. But the police are not often deceived: they soon discover unreported cases, and come with litters and coolies. It seems cruel; but sanitary law must be cruel. My neighbor's wife followed the litter, crying, until the police obliged her to return to her desolate little shop. It is now closed up, and will probably never be opened again by the owners.

Such tragedies end as quickly as they begin. The bereaved, so soon as the law allows, remove their pathetic belongings, and disappear; and the ordinary life of the street goes on, by day and by night, exactly as if nothing particular had happened. Itinerant venders, with their bamboo poles and baskets or buckets or boxes, pass the empty houses, and utter their accustomed cries; religious processions go by, chanting fragments of sutras; the blind shampooer blows his melancholy whistle; the private watchman makes his heavy staff boom upon the gutter-flags; the boy who sells confectionery still taps his drum, and sings a love-song with a plaintive sweet voice, like a girl's:

You and I together. . . . I remained long; yet in the moment of going I thought I had only just come.

You and I together. . . . Still I think of the tea. Old or new tea of Uji it might have seemed to others; but to me it was Gyokorō tea, of the beautiful yellow of the yamabuki flower.

You and I together. . . . I am the telegraph-operator; you are the one who waits the message. I send my heart, and you receive it. What care we now if the posts should fall, if the wires be broken?

And the children sport as usual. They chase one another with screams and laughter; they dance in chorus; they catch dragon-flies and tie them to long strings; they sing burdens of the war, about cutting off Chinese heads:

> Chan-chan bozu no
> Kubi wo hané!

Sometimes a child vanishes; but the survivors continue their play. And this is wisdom.

It costs only forty-four sen to burn a child. The son of one of my neighbors was burned a few days ago. The little stones with which he used to play lie there in the sun just as he left them. . . . Curious, this child-love of stones! Stones are the toys not only of the children of the poor, but of all children at one period of existence: no matter how well supplied with other playthings, every Japanese child wants sometimes to play with stones. To the child-mind a stone is a marvelous thing, and ought so to be, since even to the understanding of the mathematician there can be nothing more wonderful than a common stone. The tiny urchin suspects the stone to be much more than it seems, which is an excellent suspicion; and if stupid grown-up folk did not untruthfully tell him that his plaything is not worth thinking about, he would never tire of it, and would always be finding something new and extraordinary in it. Only a very great mind could answer all a child's questions about stones.

According to popular faith, my neighbor's darling is now playing with small ghostly stones in the Dry Bed of the River of Souls, — wondering, perhaps, why they cast no shadows. The true poetry in the legend of the Sai-no-Kawara is the absolute naturalness of its principal idea—the phantom-continuation of that play which all little Japanese children play with stones.

II

The pipe-stem seller used to make his round with two large boxes suspended from a bamboo pole balanced upon his shoulder: one box containing stems of various diameters, lengths, and colors, together with tools for fitting them into metal pipes; and the other box containing a baby—his own baby. Sometimes I saw it peeping over the edge of the box, and smiling at the passers-by; sometimes I saw it lying, well wrapped up and fast asleep, in the bottom of the box; sometimes I saw it playing with toys. Many people, I was told, used to give it toys. One of the toys bore a curious resemblance to a mortuary tablet (ihai); and this I always observed in the box, whether the child were asleep or awake.

The other day I discovered that the pipe-stem seller had abandoned his bamboo pole and suspended boxes. He was coming up the street with a little hand-cart just big enough to hold his wares and his baby, and evidently built for that purpose in two compartments. Perhaps the baby had become too heavy for the more primitive method of conveyance. Above the cart fluttered a small white flag, bearing in cursive characters the legend Kiseru-rao kae (pipe-stems exchanged), and a brief petition for "honorable help," O-tasuké wo negaimasu. The child seemed well and happy; and I again saw the tablet-shaped object which had so often attracted my notice before. It was now fastened upright to a high box in the cart facing the infant's bed. As I watched the cart approaching, I suddenly felt convinced that the tablet was really an ihai: the sun shone full upon it, and there was no mistaking the conventional Buddhist text. This aroused my curiosity; and I asked Manyemon to tell the pipe-stem seller that we had a number of pipes needing fresh stems—which was true. Presently the cartlet drew up at our gate, and I went to look at it.

The child was not afraid, even of a foreign face—a pretty boy. He lisped and laughed and held out his arms, being evidently used to petting; and while playing with him I looked closely at the tablet. It was a Shinshū ihai, bearing a woman's kaimyō, or posthumous name; and Manyemon translated the Chinese characters for me:

Revered and of good rank in the Mansion of Excellence, the thirty-first day of the third month of the twenty-eighth year of Meiji.

Meantime a servant had fetched the pipes which needed new stems; and I glanced at the face of the artisan as he worked. It was the face of a man past middle age, with those worn, sympathetic lines about the mouth, dry beds of old smiles, which give to so many Japanese faces an indescribable expression of resigned gentleness.

Presently Manyemon began to ask questions; and when Manyemon asks questions, not to reply is possible for the wicked only. Sometimes behind that dear innocent old head I think I see the dawning of an aureole—the aureole of the Bosatsu.

The pipe-stem seller answered by telling his story. Two months after the birth of their little boy, his wife had died. In the last hour of her illness she had said: "From what time I die till three full years be past I pray you to leave the child always united with the Shadow of me: never let him be separated from my ihai, so that I may continue to care for him and to nurse him— since thou knowest that he should have the breast for three years. This, my last asking, I entreat thee, do not forget." But the mother being dead, the father could not labor as he had been wont to do, and also take care of so young a child, requiring continual attention both night and day; and he was too poor to hire a nurse. So he took to selling pipe-stems, as he could thus make a little money without leaving the child even for a minute alone. He could not afford to buy milk; but he had fed the boy for more than a year with rice gruel and cane syrup.

I said that the child looked very strong, and none the worse for lack of milk.

"That," declared Manyemon, in a tone of conviction bordering on reproof, "is because the dead mother nurses him. How should he want for milk?"

And the boy laughed softly, as if conscious of a ghostly caress.

From OUT OF THE EAST

The Dream of a Summer Day

I

The hotel seemed to me a paradise, and the maids thereof celestial beings. This was because I had just fled away from one of the Open Ports, where I had ventured to seek comfort in a European hotel, supplied with all "modern improvements." To find myself at ease once more in a yukata, seated upon cool, soft matting, waited upon by sweet-voiced girls, and surrounded by things of beauty, was therefore like a redemption from all the sorrows of the nineteenth century. Bamboo-shoots and lotus-bulbs were given me for breakfast, and a fan from heaven for a keepsake. The design upon that fan represented only the white rushing burst of one great wave on a beach, and sea-birds shooting in exultation through the blue overhead. But to behold it was worth all the trouble of the journey. It was a glory of light, a thunder of motion, a triumph of sea-wind—all in one. It made me want to shout when I looked at it.

Between the cedarn balcony pillars I could see the course of the pretty gray town following the shore-sweep—and yellow lazy junks asleep at anchor—and the opening of the bay between enormous green cliffs—and beyond it the blaze of summer to the horizon. In that horizon there were mountain shapes faint as old memories. And all things but the gray town, and the yellow junks, and the green cliffs, were blue.

Then a voice softly toned as a wind-bell began to tinkle words of courtesy into my reverie, and broke it; and I perceived that the mistress of the palace had come to thank me for the chadai,[5] and I prostrated myself before her. She was very young, and more than pleasant to look upon—like the moth-maidens, like the butterfly-women, of Kunisada. And I thought at once of death; for the beautiful is sometimes a sorrow of anticipation.

She asked whither I honorably intended to go, that she might order a kuruma for me. And I made answer:

"To Kumamoto. But the name of your house I much wish to know, that I may always remember it."

"My guest-rooms," she said, "are augustly insignificant, and my maidens honorably rude. But the house is called the House of Urashima. And now I go to order a kuruma."

The music of her voice passed; and I felt enchantment falling all about me—like the thrilling of a ghostly web. For the name was the name of the story of a song that bewitches men.

II

Once you hear the story, you will never be able to forget it. Every summer when I find myself on the coast—especially of very soft, still days—it haunts me most persistently. There are many native versions of it which have been the inspiration for countless works of art. But the most impressive and the most ancient is found in the "Manyefushifu," a collection of poems dating from the fifth to the ninth century. From this ancient version the great scholar Aston translated it into prose, and the great scholar Chamberlain into both prose and verse. But for English readers I think the most charming form of it is Chamberlain's version written for children, in the "Japanese Fairy-Tale Series,"—because of the delicious colored pictures by native artists. With that little book before me, I shall try to tell the legend over again in my own words.

Fourteen hundred and sixteen years ago, the fisher-boy Urashima Taro left the shore of Suminoyé in his boat.

Summer days were then as now—all drowsy and tender blue, with

---

[5] A little gift of money, always made to a hotel by the guest shortly after his arrival.

only some light, pure white clouds hanging over the mirror of the sea. Then, too, were the hills the same—far blue soft shapes melting into the blue sky. And the winds were lazy.

And presently the boy, also lazy, let his boat drift as he fished. It was a queer boat, unpainted and rudderless, of a shape you probably never saw. But still, after fourteen hundred years, there are such boats to be seen in front of the ancient fishing-hamlets of the coast of the Sea of Japan.

After long waiting, Urashima caught something, and drew it up to him. But he found it was only a tortoise.

Now a tortoise is sacred to the Dragon God of the Sea, and the period of its natural life is a thousand—some say ten thousand—years. So that to kill it is very wrong. The boy gently unfastened the creature from his line, and set it free, with a prayer to the gods.

But he caught nothing more. And the day was very warm; and sea and air and all things were very, very silent. And a great drowsiness grew upon him—and he slept in his drifting boat.

Then out of the dreaming of the sea rose up a beautiful girl—just as you can see her in the picture to Professor Chamberlain's "Urashima,"—robed in crimson and blue, with long black hair flowing down her back even to her feet, after the fashion of a prince's daughter fourteen hundred years ago.

Gliding over the waters she came, softly as air; and she stood above the sleeping boy in the boat, and woke him with a light touch, and said:

"Do not be surprised. My father, the Dragon King of the Sea, sent me to you, because of your kind heart. For tiday you set free a tortoise. And now we will go to my father's palace in the island where summer never dies; and I will be your flower-wife if you wish; and we shall live there happily forever."

And Urashima wondered more and more as he looked upon her; for she was more beautiful than any human being, and he could not but love her. Then he took one oar, and he took another, and they rowed away together—just as you may still see, off the far western coast, wife and husband rowing together, when the fishing-boats flit into the evening gold.

They rowed away softly and swiftly over the silent blue water down into the south—till they came to the island where summer never dies—and to the palace of the Dragon King of the Sea.

[Here the text of the little book suddenly shrinks away as you read, and faint blue ripplings flood the page; and beyond them in a fairy horizon you can see the long low soft shore of the island, and peaked roofs rising through evergreen foliage—the roofs of the Sea God's palace—like the palace of the Mikado Yuriaku, fourteen hundred and sixteen years ago.]

There strange servitors came to receive them in robes of ceremony—creatures of the Sea, who paid greeting to Urashima as the son-in-law of the Dragon King.

So the Sea God's daughter became the bride of Urashima; and it was a bridal of wondrous splendor; and in the Dragon Palace there was great rejoicing.

And each day for Urashima there were new wonders and new pleasures: wonders of the deepest deep brought up by the servants of the Ocean God; pleasures of that enchanted land where summer never dies. And so three years passed.

But in spite of all these things, the fisher-boy felt always a heaviness at his heart when he thought of his parents waiting alone. So that at last he prayed his bride to let him go home for a little while only, just to say one word to his father and mother—after which he would hasten hack to her.

At these words she began to weep; and for a long time she continued to weep silently. Then she said to him: "Since you wish to go, of course you must go. I fear your going very much; I fear we shall never see each other again. But I will give you a little box to take with you. It will help you to come hack to me if you will do what I tell you. Do not open it. Above all things, do not open it—no matter what may happen! Because, if you open it, you will never be able to come hack, and you will never see me again."

Then she gave him a little lacquered box tied about with a silken cord. [And that box can be seen unto this day in the temple of Kanagawa, by the seashore; and the priests there also keep Urashima Tarō's fishing line, and some strange jewels which he brought back with him from the realm of the Dragon King.]

But Urashima comforted his bride, and promised her never, never to open the box—never even to loosen the silken string. Then he passed away through the summer light over the ever-sleeping sea; and the shape of the island where summer never dies faded behind him like a dream; and he saw again before him the blue mountains of Japan, sharpening in the white glow of the northern horizon.

Again at last he glided into his native bay; again he stood upon its beach. But as he looked, there came upon him a great bewilderment—a weird doubt.

For the place was at once the same, and yet not the same. The cottage of his fathers had disappeared. There was a village; but the shapes of the houses were all strange, and the trees were strange, and the fields, and even the faces of the people. Nearly all remembered landmarks were gone; the Shintō temple appeared to have been rebuilt in a new place; the woods had vanished from the neighboring slopes. Only the voice of the little stream flowing through the settlement, and the forms of the mountains, were still the same. All else was unfamiliar and new. In vain he tried to find the dwelling of his parents; and the fisherfolk stared wonderingly at him; and he could not remember having ever seen any of those faces before.

There came along a very old man, leaning on a stick, and Urashima asked him the way to the house of the Urashima family. But the old man looked quite astonished, and made him repeat the question many times, and then cried out:

"Urashima Tarō! Where do you come from that you do not know the story? Urashima Tarō! Why, it is more than four hundred years since he was drowned, and a monument is erected to his memory in the graveyard. The graves of all his people are in that graveyard—the old graveyard which is not now used any more. Urashima Tarō! How can you he so foolish as to ask where his house is?" And the old man hobbled on, laughing at the simplicity of his questioner.

But Urashima went to the village graveyard—the old graveyard that was not used any more—and there he found his own tombstone, and the tombstones of his father and his mother and his kindred, and the tombstones of many others he had known. So old they were, so moss-eaten, that it was very hard to read the names upon them.

Then he knew himself the victim of some strange illusion, and he took his way hack to the beach—always carrying in his hand the box, the gift of the Sea God's daughter. But what was this illusion? And what could be in that box? Or might not that which was in the box be the cause of the illusion? Doubt mastered faith. Recklessly he broke the promise made to his beloved; he loosened the silken cord; he opened the box!

Instantly, without any sound, there burst from it a white cold spectral vapor that rose in air like a summer cloud, and began to drift away swiftly into the south, over the silent sea. There was nothing else in the box.

And Urashima then knew that he had destroyed his own happiness—that he could never again return to his beloved, the daughter of the Ocean King. So that he wept and cried out bitterly in his despair.

Yet for a moment only. In another, he himself was changed. An icy chill shot through all his blood; his teeth fell out; his face shriveled; his hair turned white as snow; his limbs withered; his strength ebbed; he sank down lifeless on the sand, crushed by the weight of four hundred winters.

Now in the official annals of the Emperors it is written that "in the twenty-first year of the Mikado Yuriaku, the boy Urashima of Midzunoyé, in the district of Yosa, in the province of Tango, a descendant of the divinity Shimanemi, went to Elysium [Hōraï] in a fishing-boat." After this there is no more news of Urashima during the reigns of thirty-one emperors and empresses—that is, from the fifth until the ninth century. And then the annals announce that "in the second year of Tenchiyō, in the reign of the Mikado Go-Junwa, the boy Urashima returned, and presently departed again, none knew whither."[6]

III

The fairy mistress came back to tell me that everything was ready, and tried to lift my valise in her slender hands—which I prevented her from doing, because it was heavy. Then she laughed, but would not suffer that I should carry it myself, and summoned a sea-creature with Chinese characters upon his back. I made obeisance to her; and she prayed me to remember the unworthy house despite the rudeness of the maidens. "And you will pay the kurumaya," she said, "only seventy-five sen."

Then I slipped into the vehicle; and in a few minutes the little gray town had vanished behind a curve. I was rolling along a white road overlooking the shore. To the right were pale brown cliffs; to the left only space and sea.

Mile after mile I rolled along that shore, looking into the infinite light. All was steeped in blue—a marvelous blue, like that which comes and goes in the heart of a great shell. Glowing blue sea met hollow blue sky in a brightness of electric fusion; and vast blue apparitions—the mountains of Higo—angled up through the blaze, like masses of amethyst. What a blue transparency! The universal color was broken only by the dazzling white of a few high summer clouds, motionlessly curled above one phantom peak in the offing. They threw down upon the water snowy tremulous lights. Midges of ships creeping far away seemed to pull long threads after them—the only sharp lines in all that hazy glory. But what divine clouds! White purified spirits of clouds, resting on their way to the beatitude of Nirvana? Or perhaps the mists escaped from Urashima's box a thousand years ago?

The gnat of the soul of me flitted out into that dream of blue, 'twixt sea and sun—hummed back to the shore of Suminoyé through the luminous ghosts of fourteen hundred summers. Vaguely I felt beneath me the drifting of a keel. It was the time of the Mikado Yuriaku. And the Daughter of the Dragon King said tinklingly, "Now we will go to my father's palace where it is always blue." "Why always blue?" I asked. "Because," she said, "I put all the clouds into the Box." "But I must go home," I answered resolutely. "Then," she said, "you will pay the kurumaya only seventy-five sen."

---

[6] See *The Classical Poetry of the Japanese*, by Professor Chamberlain, in Trübner's *Oriental Series*. According to Western chronology, Urashima went fishing in 477 A.D., and returned in 825.

Wherewith I woke into Doyō, or the Period of Greatest Heat, in the twenty-sixth year of Meiji—and saw proof of the era in a line of telegraph poles reaching out of sight on the land side of the way. The kuruma was still fleeing by the shore, before the same blue vision of sky, peak, and sea; but the white clouds were gone!—and there were no more cliffs close to the road, but fields of rice and of barley stretching to far-off hills. The telegraph lines absorbed my attention for a moment, because on the top wire, and only on the top wire, hosts of little birds were perched, all with their heads to the road, and nowise disturbed by our coming. They remained quite still, looking down upon us as mere passing phenomena. There were hundreds and hundreds in rank, for miles and miles. And I could not see one having its tail turned to the road. Why they sat thus, and what they were watching or waiting for, I could not guess. At intervals I waved my hat and shouted, to startle the ranks. Whereupon a few would rise up fluttering and chippering, and drop back again upon the wire in the same position as before. The vast majority refused to take me seriously.

The sharp rattle of the wheels was drowned by a deep booming; and as we whirled past a village I caught sight of an immense drum under an open shed, beaten by naked men.

"O kurumaya!" I shouted—"that—what is it?"

He, without stopping, shouted back: "Everywhere now the same thing is. Much time-in rain has not been: so the gods-to prayers are made, and drums are beaten." We flashed through other villages; and I saw and heard more drums of various sizes, and from hamlets invisible, over miles of parching rice-fields, yet other drums, like echoings, responded.

IV

Then I began to think about Urashima again. I thought of the pictures and poems and proverbs recording the influence of the legend upon the imagination of a race. I thought of an Izumo dancing-girl I saw at a banquet acting the part of Urashima, with a little lacquered box whence there issued at the tragical minute a mist of Kyōto incense. I thought about the antiquity of the beautiful dance—and therefore about vanished generations of dancing-girls—and therefore about dust in the abstract; which, again, led me to think of dust in the concrete, as bestirred by the sandals of the kurumaya to whom I was to pay only seventy-five sen. And I wondered how much of it might be old human dust, and whether in the eternal order of things the motion of hearts might be of more consequence than the motion of dust. Then my ancestral morality took alarm; and I tried to persuade myself that a story which had lived for a thousand years, gaining fresher charm with the passing of every century, could only have survived by virtue of some truth in it. But what truth? For the time being I could find no answer to this question.

The heat had become very great; and I cried:
"O kurumaya! the throat of Selfishness is dry; water desirable is."
He, still running, answered:
"The Village of the Long Beach inside of—not far—a great gush-water is. There pure august water will be given."
I cried again:
"O kurumaya!—those little birds as-for, why this way always facing?"
He, running still more swiftly, responded:
"All birds wind-to facing sit."
I laughed first at my own simplicity; then at my forgetfulness—remembering I had been told the same thing, somewhere or other, when a boy. Perhaps the mystery of Urashima might also have been created by forgetfulness.

I thought again about Urashima. I saw the Daughter of the Dragon King waiting vainly in the palace made beautiful for his welcome—and the pitiless return of the Cloud, announcing what had happened—and the loving uncouth sea-creatures, in their garments of great ceremony, trying to comfort her. But in the real story there was nothing of all this; and the pity of the people seemed to be all for Urashima. And I began to discourse with myself thus:

Is it right to pity Urashima at all? Of course he was bewildered by the gods. But who is not bewildered by the gods? What is Life itself but a bewilderment? And Urashima in his bewilderment doubted the purpose of the gods, and opened the box. Then he died without any trouble, and the people built a shrine to him as Urashima Miō-jin. Why, then, so much pity?

Things are quite differently managed in the West. After disobeying Western gods, we have still to remain alive and to learn the height and the breadth and the depth of superlative sorrow. We are not allowed to die quite comfortably just at the best possible time: much less are we suffered to become after death small gods in our own right. How can we pity the folly of Urashima after he had lived so long alone with visible gods.

Perhaps the fact that we do may answer the riddle. This pity must be self-pity; wherefore the legend may be the legend of a myriad souls. The thought of it comes just at a particular time of blue light and soft wind—and always like an old reproach. It has too intimate relation to a season and the feeling of a season not to be also related to something

real in one's life, or in the lives of one's ancestors. But what was that
real something? Who was the Daughter of the Dragon King? Where
was the island of unending summer? And what was the cloud in the
box?

I cannot answer all those questions. I know this only—which is not
at all new:

I have memory of a place and a magical time in which the Sun and
the Moon were larger and brighter than now. Whether it was of this life
or of some life before I cannot tell. But I know the sky was very much
more blue, and nearer to the world—almost as it seems to become
above the masts of a steamer steaming into equatorial summer. The sea
was alive, and used to talk—and the Wind made me cry out for joy
when it touched me. Once or twice during other years, in divine days
lived among the peaks, I have dreamed just for a moment that the same
wind was blowing—but it was only a remembrance.

Also in that place the clouds were wonderful, and of colors for
which there are no names at all—colors that used to make me hungry
and thirsty. I remember, too, that the days were ever so much longer
than these days—and that every day there were new wonders and new
pleasures for me. And all that country and time were softly ruled by
One who thought only of ways to make me happy. Sometimes I would
refuse to be made happy, and that always caused her pain, although she
was divine; and I remember that I tried very hard to be sorry. When day
was done, and there fell the great hush of the light before moonrise, she
would tell me stories that made me tingle from head to foot with
pleasure. I have never heard any other stories half so beautiful. And
when the pleasure became too great, she would sing a weird little song
which always brought sleep. At last there came a parting day; and she
wept, and told me of a charm she had given that I must never, never
lose, because it would keep me young, and give me power to return.
But I never returned. And the years went; and one day I knew that I had
lost the charm, and had become ridiculously old.

V

The Village of the Long Beach is at the foot of a green cliff near
the road, and consists of a dozen thatched cottages clustered about a
rocky pool, shaded by pines. The basin overflows with cold water,
supplied by a stream that leaps straight from the heart of the cliff—just
as folks imagine that a poem ought to spring straight from the heart of a
poet. It was evidently a favorite halting-place, judging by the number of
kuruma and of people resting. There were benches under the trees; and,
after having allayed thirst, I sat down to smoke and to look at the
women washing clothes and the travelers refreshing themselves at the

pool—while my kurumaya stripped, and proceeded to dash buckets of cold water over his body. Then tea was brought me by a young man with a baby on his back; and I tried to play with the baby, which said "Ah, bah!"

Such are the first sounds uttered by a Japanese babe. But they are purely Oriental; and in Romaji should be written *Aba*. And, as an utterance untaught, *Aba* is interesting. It is in Japanese child-speech the word for "good-by,"—precisely the last we would expect an infant to pronounce on entering into this world of illusion. To whom or to what is the little soul saying good-by?—to friends in a previous state of existence still freshly remembered?—to comrades of its shadowy journey from nobody—knows—where? Such theorizing is tolerably safe, from a pious point of view, since the child can never decide for us. What its thoughts were at that mysterious moment of first speech, it will have forgotten long before it has become able to answer questions.

Unexpectedly, a queer recollection came to me—resurrected, perhaps, by the sight of the young man with the baby—perhaps by the song of the water in the cliff: the recollection of a story:

Long, long ago there lived somewhere among the mountains a poor wood-cutter and his wife. They were very old, and had no children. Every day the husband went alone to the forest to cut wood, while the wife sat weaving at home.

One day the old man went farther into the forest than was his custom, to seek a certain kind of wood; and he suddenly found himself at the edge of a little spring he had never seen before. The water was strangely clear and cold, and he was thirsty; for the day was hot, and he had been working hard. So he doffed his great straw hat, knelt down, and took a long drink. That water seemed to refresh him in a most extraordinary way. Then he caught sight of his own face in the spring, and started back. It was certainly his own face, but not at all as he was accustomed to see it in the old mirror at home. It was the face of a very young man! He could not believe his eyes. He put up both hands to his head, which had been quite bald only a moment before. It was covered with thick black hair. And his face had become smooth as a boy's; every wrinkle was gone. At the same moment he discovered himself full of new strength. He stared in astonishment at the limbs that had been so long withered by age; they were now shapely and hard with dense young muscle. Unknowingly he had drunk at the Fountain of Youth; and that draught had transformed him.

First, he leaped high and shouted for joy; then he ran home faster than he had ever run before in his life. When he entered his house his wife was frightened—because she took him for a stranger; and when he told her the wonder, she could not at once believe him. But after a long time he was able to convince her that the young man she now saw before her was really her husband; and he told her where the spring was, and asked her to go there with him.

Then she said: "You have become so handsome and so young that you cannot continue to love an old woman; so I must drink some of that water immediately. But it will never do for both of us to be away from the house at the same time. Do you wait here while I go." And she ran to the woods all by herself.

She found the spring and knelt down, and began to drink. Oh! how cool and sweet that water was! She drank and drank and drank, and stopped for breath only to begin again.

Her husband waited for her impatiently; he expected to see her come back changed into a pretty slender girl. But she did not come back at all. He got anxious, shut up the house, and went to look for her.

When he reached the spring, he could not see her. He was just on the point of returning when he heard a little wail in the high grass near the spring. He searched there and discovered his wife's clothes and a baby—a very small baby, perhaps six months old!

For the old woman had drunk too deeply of the magical water; she had drunk herself far back beyond the time of youth into the period of speechless infancy.

He took up the child in his arms. It looked at him in a sad, wondering way. He carried it home—murmuring to it—thinking strange, melancholy thoughts.

In that hour, after my reverie about Urashima, the moral of this story seemed less satisfactory than in former time. Because by drinking too deeply of life we do not become young.

Naked and cool my kurumaya returned, and said that because of the heat he could not finish the promised run of twenty-five miles, but that he had found another runner to take me the rest of the way. For so much as he himself had done, he wanted fifty-five sen.

It was really very hot—more than 100° I afterwards learned; and far away there throbbed continually, like a pulsation of the beat itself, the sound of great drums beating for rain. And I thought of the Daughter of the Dragon King.

"Seventy-five sen, she told me," I observed; "and that promised to be done has not been done. Nevertheless, seventy-five sen to you shall be given—because I am afraid of the gods."

And behind a yet unwearied runner I fled away into the enormous blaze—in the direction of the great drums.

The Eternal Haunter

This year the Tōkyō color-prints—*Nishiki-è*—seem to me of unusual interest. They reproduce, or almost reproduce, the color-charm of the early broadsides; and they show a marked improvement in line-drawing. Certainly one could not wish for anything prettier than the best prints of the present season.

My latest purchase has been a set of weird studies—specters of all kinds known to the Far East, including many varieties not yet discovered in the West. Some are extremely unpleasant; but a few are really charming. Here, for example, is a delicious thing by "Chikanobu," just published, and for sale at the remarkable price of three sen!

Can you guess what it represents? . . . Yes, a girl—but what kind of a girl? Study it a little. . . . Very lovely, is she not, with that shy sweetness in her downcast gaze—that light and dainty grace, as of a resting butterfly? . . . No, she is not some Psyche of the most Eastern East, in the sense that you mean—but she is a soul. Observe that the cherry-flowers falling from the branch above, are passing *through* her form. See also the folds of her robe, below, melting into blue faint mist. How delicate and vapory the whole thing is! It gives you the feeling of spring; and all those fairy colors are the colors of a Japanese spring-morning. . . . No, she is not the personification of any season. Rather she is a dream—such a dream as might haunt the slumbers of Far-Eastern youth; but the artist did not intend her to represent a dream. . . . You cannot guess? Well, she is a tree-spirit—the Spirit of the Cherry-tree. Only in the twilight of morning or of evening she appears, gliding about her tree; and whoever sees her must love her. But, if approached, she vanishes back into the trunk, like a vapor absorbed. There is a legend of one tree-spirit who loved a man, and even gave him a son; but such conduct was quite at variance with the shy habits of her race. . .

You ask what is the use of drawing the Impossible? Your asking proves that you do not feel the charm of this vision of youth—this dream of spring. *I* hold that the Impossible bears a much closer relation to fact than does most of what we call the real and the commonplace. The Impossible may not be naked truth; but I think that it is usually truth—masked and veiled, perhaps, but eternal. Now to me this Japanese dream is true—true, at least, as human love is. Considered even as a ghost it is true. Whoever pretends not to believe in ghosts of any sort, lies to his own heart. Every man is haunted by ghosts. And this color-print reminds me of a ghost whom we all know—though most of us (poets excepted) are unwilling to confess the acquaintance.

Perhaps—for it happens to some of us—you may have seen this haunter, in dreams of the night, even during childhood. Then, of course, you could not know the beautiful shape bending above your rest: possibly you thought her to be an angel, or the soul of a dead sister. But in waking life we first become aware of her presence about the time when boyhood begins to ripen into youth.

This first of her apparitions is a shock of ecstasy, a breathless delight; but the wonder and the pleasure are quickly followed by a sense of sadness inexpressible—totally unlike any sadness ever felt before—though in her gaze there is only caress, and on her lips the most exquisite of smiles. And you cannot imagine the reason of that feeling until you have learned who she is—which is not an easy thing to learn.

Only a moment she remains; but during that luminous moment all the tides of your being set and surge to her with a longing for which there is not any word. And then—suddenly!—she is not; and you find that the sun has gloomed, the colors of the world turned grey.

Thereafter enchantment remains between you and all that you loved before—persons or things or places. None of them will ever seem again so near and dear as in other days.

Often she will return. Once that you have seen her she will never cease to visit you. And this haunting—ineffably sweet, inexplicably sad—may fill you with rash desire to wander over the world in search of somebody like her. But however long and far you wander, never will you find that somebody.

Later you may learn to fear her visits because of the pain they bring—the strange pain that you cannot understand. But the breadth of zones and seas cannot divide you from her; walls of iron cannot exclude her. Soundless and subtle as a shudder of ether is the motion of her.

Ancient her beauty as the heart of man—yet ever waxing fairer, forever remaining young. Mortals wither in Time as leaves in the frost of autumn; but Time only brightens the glow and the bloom of her endless youth.

All men have loved her; all must continue to love her. But none shall touch with his lips even the hem of her garment.

All men adore her; yet all she deceives, and many are the ways of her deception. Most often she lures her lover into the presence of some earthly maid, and blends herself incomprehensibly with the body of that maid, and works such sudden glamour that the human gaze becomes divine—that the human limbs shine through their raiment. But presently the luminous haunter detaches herself from the mortal, and leaves her dupe to wonder at the mockery of sense.

No man can describe her, though nearly all men have some time tried to do so. Pictured she cannot be—since her beauty itself is a ceaseless becoming, multiple to infinitude, and tremulous with perpetual quickening, as with flowing of light.

There is a story, indeed, that thousands of years ago some marvelous sculptor was able to fix in stone a single remembrance of her. But this doing became for many the cause of sorrow supreme; and the Gods decreed, out of compassion, that to no other mortal should ever be given power to work the like wonder. In these years we can worship only; we cannot portray.

But who is she?—what is she? . . . Ah! that is what I wanted you to ask. Well, she has never had a name; but I shall call her a tree-spirit.

The Japanese say that you can exorcise a tree-spirit—if you are cruel enough to do it—simply by cutting down her tree.

But you cannot exorcise the Spirit of whom I speak—nor ever cut down her tree.

For her tree is the measureless, timeless, billion-branching Tree of Life—even the World-Tree, Yggdrasil, whose roots are in Night and Death, whose head is above the Gods.

Seek to woo her—she is Echo. Seek to clasp her—she is Shadow. But her smile will haunt you into the hour of dissolution and beyond—through numberless lives to come.

And never will you return her smile—never, because of that which it awakens within you—the pain that you cannot understand.

And never, never shall you win to her—because she is the phantom light of long-expired suns—because she was shaped by the beating of infinite millions of hearts that are dust—because her witchery was made in the endless ebb and flow of the visions and hopes of youth, through countless forgotten cycles of your own incalculable past.

From GLEANINGS IN BUDDHA-FIELDS

Ningyō-No-Haka

Manyemon had coaxed the child indoors, and made her eat. She appeared to be about eleven years old, intelligent, and pathetically docile. Her name was Iné, which means "springing rice;" and her frail slimness made the name seem appropriate.

When she began, under Manyemon's gentle persuasion, to tell her story, I anticipated something queer from the accompanying change in her voice. She spoke in a high thin sweet tone, perfectly even—a tone changeless and unemotional as the chanting of the little kettle over its charcoal bed. Not infrequently in Japan one may hear a girl or a woman utter something touching or cruel or terrible in just such a steady, level, penetrating tone, but never anything indifferent. It always means that feeling is being kept under control.

"There were six of us at home," said Iné, "mother and father and father's mother, who was very old, and my brother and myself, and a little sister. Father was a hyōguya, a paper-hanger: he papered sliding-screens and also mounted kakemono. Mother was a hair-dresser. My brother was apprenticed to a seal-cutter.

"Father and mother did well: mother made even more money than father. We had good clothes and good food; and we never had any real sorrow until father fell sick.

"It was the middle of the hot season. Father had always been healthy: we did not think that his sickness was dangerous, and he did not think so himself. But the very next day he died. We were very much surprised. Mother tried to hide her heart, and to wait upon her customers as before. But she was not very strong, and the pain of father's death came too quickly. Eight days after father's funeral mother also died. It was so sudden that everybody wondered. Then the neighbors told us that we must make a *ningyō-no-haka* at once—or else there would be another death in our house. My brother said they were right; but he put off doing what they told him. Perhaps he did not have mercy enough, I do not know; but the haka was not made." . . .

"What is a ningyō-no-haka?" I interrupted.

"I think," Manyemon made answer, "that you have seen many *ningyō-no-haka* without knowing what they were; they look just like graves of children. It is believed that when two of a family die in the same year, a third also must soon die. There is a saying, *Always three graves.* So when two out of one family have been buried in the same year, a third grave is made next to the graves of those two, and in it is put a coffin containing only a little figure of straw—wara-ningyō; and over that grave a small tombstone is set up, bearing a kaimyō.[7] The priests of the temple to which the graveyard belongs write the kaimyō for these little gravestones. By making a *ningyō-no-haka* it is thought that a death may be prevented. . . . We listen for the rest, Iné."

The child resumed:

"There were still four of us—grandmother, brother, myself, and my little sister. My brother was nineteen years old. He had finished his apprenticeship just before father died: we thought that was like the pity of the gods for us. He had become the head of the house. He was very skillful in his business, and had many friends: therefore he could maintain us. He made thirteen yen the first month; that is very good for a seal-cutter. One evening he came home sick: he said that his head hurt him. Mother had then been dead forty-seven days. That evening he could not eat. Next morning he was not able to get up; he had a very

---

[7] The posthumous Buddhist name of the person buried is chiseled upon the tomb or haka.

hot fever: we nursed him as well as we could, and sat up at night to watch by him; but he did not get better. On the morning of the third day of his sickness we became frightened—because he began to talk to mother. It was the forty-ninth day after mother's death—the day the Soul leaves the house; and brother spoke as if mother was calling him: 'Yes, mother, yes!—in a little while I shall come!' Then he told us that mother was pulling him by the sleeve. He would point with his hand and call to us: 'There she is!—there!—do you not see her?' We would tell him that we could not see anything. Then he would say, 'Ah! you did not look quick enough: she is hiding now; she has gone down under the floor-mats.' All the morning he talked like that. At last grandmother stood up, and stamped her foot on the floor, and reproached mother— speaking very loud. 'Taka!' she said, 'Taka, what you do is very wrong. When you were alive we all loved you. None of us ever spoke unkind words to you. Why do you now want to take the boy? You know that he is the only pillar of our house. You know that if you take him there will not be any one to care for the ancestors. You know that if you take him, you will destroy the family name! O Taka, it is cruel! it is shameful! it is wicked!' Grandmother was so angry that all her body trembled. Then she sat down and cried; and I and my little sister cried. But our brother said that mother was still pulling him by the sleeve. When the sun went down, he died.

"Grandmother wept, and stroked us, and sang a little song that she made herself. I can remember it still:

> Oya no nai ko to
> Hamabé no chidori:
> Higuré-higuré ni
> Sodé shiboru.[8]

"So the third grave was made—but it was not a *ningyō-no-haka*; and that was the end of our house. We lived with kindred until winter, when grandmother died. She died in the night—when, nobody knew: in the morning she seemed to be sleeping, but she was dead. Then I and my little sister were separated. My sister was adopted by a tatamiya, a mat-maker—one of father's friends. She is kindly treated: she even goes to school!"

"Aa fushigi na koto da!—aa komatta ne?" murmured Manyemon.

---

[8] Children without parents, like the seagulls of the coast. Evening after evening the sleeves are wrung." The word *chidori*—indiscriminately applied to many kinds of birds— is here used for seagull. The cries of the seagull are thought to express melancholy and desolation: hence the comparison. The long sleeve of the Japanese robe is used to wipe the eyes as well as to hide the face in moments of grief. To "wring the sleeve"—that is, to wring the moisture from a tear-drenched sleeve—is a frequent expression in Japanese poetry.

Then there was a moment or two of sympathetic silence. Iné prostrated herself in thanks, and rose to depart. As she slipped her feet under the thongs of her sandals, I moved toward the spot where she had been sitting, to ask the old man a question. She perceived my intention, and immediately made an indescribable sign to Manyemon, who responded by checking me just as I was going to sit down beside him.

"She wishes," he said, "that the master will honorably strike the matting first."

"But why?" I asked in surprise—noticing only that under my unshod feet, the spot where the child had been kneeling felt comfortably warm.

Manyemon answered:

"She believes that to sit down upon the place made warm by the body of another is to take into one's own life all the sorrow of that other person—unless the place be stricken first."

Whereat I sat down without performing the rite; and we both laughed.

"Iné," said Manyemon, "the master takes your sorrows upon him. He wants"—I cannot venture to render Manyemon's honorifics—"to understand the pain of other people. You need not tear for him, Iné."

From In Ghostly Japan

Fragment

And it was at the hour of sunset that they came to the foot of the mountain. There was in that place no sign of life—neither token of water, nor trace of plant, nor shadow of flying bird—nothing but desolation rising to desolation. And the summit was lost in heaven.

Then the Bodhisattva said to his young companion: "What you have asked to see will be shown to you. But the place of the Vision is far; and the way is rude. Follow after me, and do not fear: strength will be given you."

Twilight gloomed about them as they climbed. There was no beaten path, nor any mark of former human visitation; and the way was over an endless heaping of tumbled fragments that rolled or turned beneath the foot. Sometimes a mass dislodged would clatter down with hollow echoings; sometimes the substance trodden would burst like an empty shell. . . . Stars pointed and thrilled; and the darkness deepened.

"Do not fear, my son," said the Bodhisattva, guiding: "danger there is none, though the way be grim."

Under the stars they climbed—fast, fast—mounting by help of power superhuman. High zones of mist they passed; and they saw below them, ever widening as they climbed, a soundless flood of cloud, like the tide of a milky sea.

Hour after hour they climbed; and forms invisible yielded to their tread with dull soft crashings; and faint cold fires lighted and died at every breaking.

And once the pilgrim-youth laid hand on a something smooth that was not stone—and lifted it—and dimly saw the cheekless gibe of death.

"Linger not thus, my son!" urged the voice of the teacher; "the summit that we must gain is very far away!"

On through the dark they climbed—and felt continually beneath them the soft strange breakings—and saw the icy fires worm and die— till the rim of the night turned grey, and the stars began to fail, and the east began to bloom.

Yet still they climbed—fast, fast—mounting by help of power superhuman. About them now was frigidness of death—and silence tremendous. . . . A gold flame kindled in the east.

Then first to the pilgrim's gaze the steeps revealed their nakedness; and a trembling seized him—and a ghastly fear. For there was not any ground—neither beneath him nor about him nor above him—but a heaping only, monstrous and measureless, of skulls and fragments of skulls and dust of bone—with a shimmer of shed teeth strown through the drift of it, like the shimmer of scrags of shell in the wrack of a tide.

"Do not fear, my son!" cried the voice of the Bodhisattva; "only the strong of heart can win to the place of the Vision!"

Behind them the world had vanished. Nothing remained but the clouds beneath, and the sky above, and the heaping of skulls between— up-slanting out of sight.

Then the sun climbed with the climbers; and there was no warmth in the light of him, but coldness sharp as a sword. And the horror of stupendous height, and the nightmare of stupendous depth, and the terror of silence, ever grew and grew, and weighed upon the pilgrim, and held his feet—so that suddenly all power departed from him, and he moaned like a sleeper in dreams.

"Hasten, hasten, my son!" cried the Bodhisattva: "the day is brief, and the summit is very far away."

But the pilgrim shrieked—"I fear! I fear unspeakably!—and the power has departed from me!"

"The power will return, my son," made answer the Bodhisattva. . . . "Look now below you and above you and about you, and tell me what you see."

"I cannot," cried the pilgrim, trembling and clinging; "I dare not look beneath! Before me and about me there is nothing but skulls of men."

"And yet, my son," said the Bodhisattva, laughing softly—"and yet you do not know of what this mountain is made."

The other, shuddering, repeated: "I fear!—unutterably I fear! . . . there is nothing but skulls of men!"

"A mountain of skulls it is," responded the Bodhisattva. "But know, my son, that all of them ARE YOUR OWN! Each has at some time been the nest of your dreams and delusions and desires. Not even one of them is the skull of any other being. All—all without exception—have been yours, in the billions of your former lives."

A Passional Karma

One of the never-failing attractions of the Tōkyō stage is the performance, by the famous Kikugorō and his company, of the *Botan-Dōrō*, or "Peony-Lantern." This weird play, of which the scenes are laid in the middle of the last century, is the dramatization of a romance by the novelist Enchō, written in colloquial Japanese, and purely Japanese in local color, though inspired by a Chinese tale. I went to see the play; and Kikugorō made me familiar with a new variety of the pleasure of fear. "Why not give English readers the ghostly part of the story?"—asked a friend who guides me betimes through the mazes of Eastern philosophy. "It would serve to explain some popular ideas of the supernatural which Western people know very little about. And I could help you with the translation."

I gladly accepted the suggestion; and we composed the following summary of the more extraordinary portion of Enchō's romance. Here and there we found it necessary to condense the original narrative; and we tried to keep close to the text only in the conversational passages— some of which happen to possess a particular quality of psychological interest.

—*This is the story of the Ghosts in the Romance of the Peony-Lantern*:

I

There once lived in the district of Ushigomé, in Yedo, a *hatamoto*[9] called Iijima Heizayémon, whose only daughter, Tsuyu, was beautiful as her name, which signifies "Morning Dew." Iijima took a second wife when his daughter was about sixteen; and, finding that O-Tsuyu could

---

[9] The *hatamoto* were samurai forming the special military force of the Shōgun. The name literally signifies "Banner-Supporters." These were the highest class of samurai— not only as the immediate vassals of the Shōgun, but as a military aristocracy.

not be happy with her mother-in-law, he had a pretty villa built for the girl at Yanagijima, as a separate residence, and gave her an excellent maidservant, called O-Yoné, to wait upon her.

O-Tsuyu lived happily enough in her new home until one day when the family physician, Yamamoto Shijō, paid her a visit in company with a young samurai named Hagiwara Shinzaburō, who resided in the Nedzu quarter. Shinzaburō was an unusually handsome lad, and very gentle; and the two young people fell in love with each other at sight. Even before the brief visit was over, they contrived— unheard by the old doctor—to pledge themselves to each other for life. And, at parting, O-Tsuyu whispered to the youth—"*Remember!* If you do not come to see me again, I shall certainly die!"

Shinzaburō never forgot those words; and he was only too eager to see more of O-Tsuyu. But etiquette forbade him to make the visit alone: he was obliged to wait for some other chance to accompany the doctor, who had promised to take him to the villa a second time. Unfortunately the old man did not keep this promise. He had perceived the sudden affection of O-Tsuyu; and he feared that her father would hold him responsible for any serious results. Iijima Heizayémon had a reputation for cutting off heads. And the more Shijō thought about the possible consequences of his introduction of Shinzaburō at the Iijima villa, the more he became afraid. Therefore he purposely abstained from calling upon his young friend.

Months passed; and O-Tsuyu, little imagining the true cause of Shinzaburō's neglect, believed that her love had been scorned. Then she pined away, and died. Soon afterwards, the faithful servant O-Yoné also died, through grief at the loss of her mistress; and the two were buried side by side in the cemetery of Shin-Banzui-In—a temple which still stands in the neighborhood of Dango-Zaka, where the famous chrysanthemum-shows are yearly held.

II

Shinzaburō knew nothing of what had happened; but his disappointment and his anxiety had resulted in a prolonged illness. He was slowly recovering, but still very weak, when he unexpectedly received another visit from Yamamoto Shijō. The old man made a number of plausible excuses for his apparent neglect. Shinzaburō said to him: "I have been sick ever since the beginning of spring; even now I cannot eat anything. . . . Was it not rather unkind of you never to call? I thought that we were to make another visit together to the house of the Lady Iijima; and I wanted to take to her some little present as a return for our kind reception. Of course I could not go by myself."

Shijō gravely responded—

"I am very sorry to tell you that the young lady is dead!"

"Dead!" repeated Shinzaburō, turning white—"did you say that she is dead?"

The doctor remained silent for a moment, as if collecting himself: then he resumed, in the quick light tone of a man resolved not to take trouble seriously:

"My great mistake was in having introduced you to her; for it seems that she fell in love with you at once. I am afraid that you must have said something to encourage this affection—when you were in that little room together. At all events, I saw how she felt towards you; and then I became uneasy—fearing that her father might come to hear of the matter, and lay the whole blame upon me. So—to be quite frank with you—I decided that it would be better not to call upon you; and I purposely stayed away for a long time. But, only a few days ago, happening to visit Iijima's house, I heard, to my great surprise, that his daughter had died, and that her servant O-Yoné had also died. Then, remembering all that had taken place, I knew that the young lady must have died of love for you. . . . [*Laughing*] Ah, you are really a sinful fellow! Yes, you are! [*Laughing*] Isn't it a sin to have been born so handsome that the girls die for love of you?[10] [*Seriously*] Well, we must leave the dead to the dead. It is no use to talk further about the matter; all that you now can do for her is to repeat the Nembutsu[11] . . . Goodbye."

And the old man retired hastily—anxious to avoid further converse about the painful event for which he felt himself to have been unwittingly responsible.

III

Shinzaburō long remained stupefied with grief by the news of O-Tsuyu's death. But as soon as he found himself again able to think clearly, he inscribed the dead girl's name upon a mortuary tablet, and placed the tablet in the Buddhist shrine of his house, and set offerings before it, and recited prayers. Every day thereafter he presented offerings, and repeated the *Nembutsu*; and the memory of O-Tsuyu was never absent from his thought.

Nothing occurred to change the monotony of his solitude before the time of the Bon—the great Festival of the Dead—which begins upon the thirteenth day of the seventh month. Then he decorated his house, and prepared everything for the festival; hanging out the lanterns that guide the returning spirits, and setting the food of ghosts on the

---

[10] Perhaps this conversation may seem strange to the Western reader; but it is true to life. The whole of the scene is characteristically Japanese.

[11] The invocation *Namu Amida Butsu!* ("Hail to the Buddha Amitâbha!")— repeated, as a prayer, for the sake of the dead.

shōryōdana, or Shelf of Souls. And on the first evening of the Bon, after sun-down, he kindled a small lamp before the tablet of O-Tsuyu, and lighted the lanterns.

The night was clear, with a great moon—and windless, and very warm. Shinzaburō sought the coolness of his veranda. Clad only in a light summer-robe, he sat there thinking, dreaming, sorrowing; sometimes fanning himself; sometimes making a little smoke to drive the mosquitoes away. Everything was quiet. It was a lonesome neighborhood, and there were few passers-by. He could hear only the soft rushing of a neighboring stream, and the shrilling of night-insects.

But all at once this stillness was broken by a sound of women's *geta*[12] approaching—*kara-kon, kara-kon*; and the sound drew nearer and nearer, quickly, till it reached the live-hedge surrounding the garden. Then Shinzaburō, feeling curious, stood on tiptoe, so as to look over the hedge; and he saw two women passing. One, who was carrying a beautiful lantern decorated with peony-flowers,[13] appeared to be a servant; the other was a slender girl of about seventeen, wearing a long-sleeved robe embroidered with designs of autumn-blossoms. Almost at the same instant both women turned their faces toward Shinzaburō; and to his utter astonishment, he recognized O-Tsuyu and her servant O-Yoné.

They stopped immediately; and the girl cried out—

"Oh, how strange! . . . Hagiwara Sama!"

Shinzaburō simultaneously called to the maid: "O-Yoné! Ah, you are O-Yoné!—I remember you very well."

"Hagiwara Sama!" exclaimed O-Yoné in a tone of supreme amazement. "Never could I have believed it possible! . . . Sir, we were told that you had died."

"How extraordinary!" cried Shinzaburō. "Why, I was told that both of you were dead!"

"Ah, what a hateful story!" returned O-Yoné. "Why repeat such unlucky words? . . . Who told you?"

"Please to come in," said Shinzaburō; "here we can talk better. The garden-gate is open."

So they entered, and exchanged greeting; and when Shinzaburō had made them comfortable, he said:

"I trust that you will pardon my discourtesy in not having called

---

[12] *Komageta* in the original. The geta is a wooden sandal, or clog, of which there are many varieties—some decidedly elegant. The *komageta,* or "pony-geta" is so-called because of the sonorous hoof-like echo which it makes on hard ground.

[13] The sort of lantern here referred to is no longer made; and its shape can best be understood by a glance at the picture accompanying this story. It was totally unlike the modern domestic band-lantern, painted with the owner's crest; but it was not altogether unlike some forms of lanterns still manufactured for the Festival of the Dead, and called *Bon-dōrō.* The flowers ornamenting it were not painted: they were artificial flowers of crêpe-silk, and were attached to the top of the lantern.

upon you for so long a time. But Shijō, the doctor, about a month ago, told me that you had both died."

"So it was he who told you?" exclaimed O-Yoné. "It was very wicked of him to say such a thing. Well, it was also Shijō who told us that *you* were dead. I think that he wanted to deceive you—which was not a difficult thing to do, because you are so confiding and trustful. Possibly my mistress betrayed her liking for you in some words which found their way to her father's ears; and, in that case, O-Kuni—the new wife—might have planned to make the doctor tell you that we were dead, so as to bring about a separation. Anyhow, when my mistress heard that you had died, she wanted to cut off her hair immediately, and to become a nun. But I was able to prevent her from cutting off her hair; and I persuaded her at last to become a nun only in her heart. Afterwards her father wished her to marry a certain young man; and she refused. Then there was a great deal of trouble—chiefly caused by O-Kuni; and we went away from the villa, and found a very small house in Yanaka-no-Sasaki. There we are now just barely able to live, by doing a little private work. . . . My mistress has been constantly repeating the *Nembutsu* for your sake. Tiday, being the first day of the Bon, we went to visit the temples; and we were on our way home—thus late—when this strange meeting happened."

"Oh, how extraordinary!" cried Shinzaburō. "Can it be true?-or is it only a dream? Here I, too, have been constantly reciting the *Nembutsu* before a tablet with her name upon it! Look!" And he showed them O-Tsuyu's tablet in its place upon the Shelf of Souls.

"We are more than grateful for your kind remembrance," returned O-Yoné, smiling. . . . "Now as for my mistress,"—she continued, turning towards O-Tsuyu, who had all the while remained demure and silent, half-hiding her face with her sleeve—"as for my mistress, she actually says that she would not mind being disowned by her father for the time of seven existences,[14] or even being killed by him, for your sake! Come! will you not allow her to stay here tonight?"

Shinzaburō turned pale for joy. He answered in a voice trembling with emotion:

"Please remain; but do not speak loud—because there is a troublesome fellow living close by—a *ninsomi*[15] called Hakuōdō Yusai, who tells peoples fortunes by looking at their faces. He is inclined to be curious; and it is better that he should not know."

---

[14] "For the time of seven existences,"—that is to say, for the time of seven successive lives. In Japanese drama and romance it is not uncommon to represent a father as disowning his child "for the time of seven lives." Such a disowning is called *shichi-shō madé no mandō*, a disinheritance for seven lives—signifying that in six future lives after the present the erring son or daughter will continue to feel the parental displeasure.

[15] The profession is not yet extinct. The *ninsomi* uses a kind of magnifying glass (or magnifying-mirror sometimes), called *tengankyō* or *ninsomégané*.

The two women remained that night in the house of the young samurai, and returned to their own home a little before daybreak. And after that night they came every night for seven nights—whether the weather were foul or fair—always at the same hour. And Shinzaburō became more and more attached to the girl; and the twain were fettered, each to each, by that bond of illusion which is stronger than bands of iron.

IV

Now there was a man called Tomozō, who lived in a small cottage adjoining Shinzaburō's residence, Tomozō and his wife O-Miné were both employed by Shinzaburō as servants. Both seemed to be devoted to their young master; and by his help they were able to live in comparative comfort.

One night, at a very late hour, Tomozō heard the voice of a woman in his master's apartment; and this made him uneasy. He feared that Shinzaburō, being very gentle and affectionate, might be made the dupe of some cunning wanton—in which event the domestics would be the first to suffer. He therefore resolved to watch; and on the following night he stole on tiptoe to Shinzaburō's dwelling, and looked through a chink in one of the sliding shutters. By the glow of a night-lantern within the sleeping-room, he was able to perceive that his master and a strange woman were talking together under the mosquito-net. At first he could not see the woman distinctly. Her back was turned to him; he only observed that she was very slim, and that she appeared to be very young—judging from the fashion of her dress and hair.[16] Putting his ear to the chink, he could hear the conversation plainly. The woman said:

"And if I should be disowned by my father, would you then let me come and live with you?"

Shinzaburō answered:

"Most assuredly I would—nay, I should be glad of the chance. But there is no reason to fear that you will ever be disowned by your father; for you are his only daughter, and he loves you very much. What I do fear is that some day we shall be cruelly separated."

She responded softly:

"Never, never could I even think of accepting any other man for my husband. Even if our secret were to become known, and my father were to kill me for what I have done, still—after death itself—I could never cease to think of you. And I am now quite sure that you yourself would not be able to live very long without me." . . . Then clinging closely to him, with her lips at his neck, she caressed him; and he

---

[16] The color and form of the dress, and the style of wearing the hair, are by Japanese custom regulated according to the age of the woman.

returned her caresses.

Tomozō wondered as he listened—because the language of the woman was not the language of a common woman, but the language of a lady of rank.[17] Then he determined at all hazards to get one glimpse of her face; and he crept round the house, backwards and forwards, peering through every crack and chink. And at last he was able to see; but therewith an icy trembling seized him; and the hair of his head stood up.

For the face was the face of a woman long dead—and the fingers caressing were fingers of naked bone—and of the body below the waist there was not anything: it melted off into thinnest trailing shadow. Where the eyes of the lover deluded saw youth and grace and beauty, there appeared to the eyes of the watcher horror only, and the emptiness of death. Simultaneously another woman's figure, and a weirder, rose up from within the chamber, and swiftly made toward the watcher, as if discerning his presence. Then, in uttermost terror, he fled to the dwelling of Hakuōdō Yusai, and, knocking frantically at the doors, succeeded in arousing him.

V

Hakuōdō Yusai, the *ninsomi*, was a very old man; but in his time he had travelled much, and he had heard and seen so many things that he could not be easily surprised. Yet the story of the terrified Tomozō both alarmed and amazed him. He had read in ancient Chinese books of love between the living and the dead; but he had never believed it possible. Now, however, he felt convinced that the statement of Tomozō was not a falsehood, and that something very strange was really going on in the house of Hagiwara. Should the truth prove to be what Tomozō imagined, then the young samurai was a doomed man.

"If the woman be a ghost,"—said Yusai to the frightened servant, "—if the woman be a ghost, your master must die very soon—unless something extraordinary can be done to save him. And if the woman be a ghost, the signs of death will appear upon his face. For the spirit of the living is *yōki*, and pure; the spirit of the dead is *inki*, and unclean: the one is Positive, the other Negative. He whose bride is a ghost cannot live. Even though in his blood there existed the force of a life of one hundred years, that force must quickly perish. . . . Still, I shall do all that I can to save Hagiwara Sama. And in the meantime, Tomozō, say nothing to any other person—not even to your wife—about this

---

[17] The forms of speech used by the samurai, and other superior classes, differed considerably from those of the popular idiom; but these differences could not be effectively rendered into English.

matter. At sunrise I shall call upon your master."

VI

When questioned next morning by Yusai, Shinzaburō at first attempted to deny that any women had been visiting the house; but finding this artless policy of no avail, and perceiving that the old man's purpose was altogether unselfish, he was finally persuaded to acknowledge what had really occurred, and to give his reasons for wishing to keep the matter a secret. As for the lady Iijima, he intended, he said, to make her his wife as soon as possible.

"Oh, madness!" cried Yusai—losing all patience in the intensity of his alarm. "Know, sir, that the people who have been coming here, night after night, are dead! Some frightful delusion is upon you! . . . Why, the simple fact that you long supposed O-Tsuyu to be dead, and repeated the *Nembutsu* for her, and made offerings before her tablet, is itself the proof! . . . The lips of the dead have touched you!—the hands of the dead have caressed you! . . . Even at this moment I see in your face the signs of death—and you will not believe! . . . Listen to me now, sir—I beg of you—if you wish to save yourself: otherwise you have less than twenty days to live. They told you—those people—that they were residing in the district of Shitaya, in Yanaka-no-Sasaki. Did you ever visit them at that place? No!—of course you did not! Then go tiday—as soon as you can—to Yanaka-no-Sasaki, and try to find their home! . . ."

And having uttered this counsel with the most vehement earnestness, Hakuōdō Yusai abruptly took his departure.

Shinzaburō, startled though not convinced, resolved after a moment's reflection to follow the advice of the *ninsomi*, and to go to Shitaya. It was yet early in the morning when he reached the quarter of Yanaka-no-Sasaki, and began his search for the dwelling of O-Tsuyu. He went through every street and side-street, read all the names inscribed at the various entrances, and made inquiries whenever an opportunity presented itself. But he could not find anything resembling the little house mentioned by O-Yoné; and none of the people whom he questioned knew of any house in the quarter inhabited by two single women. Feeling at last certain that further research would be useless, he turned homeward by the shortest way, which happened to lead through the grounds of the temple Shin-Banzui-In.

Suddenly his attention was attracted by two new tombs, placed side by side, at the rear of the temple. One was a common tomb, such as might have been erected for a person of humble rank: the other was a large and handsome monument; and hanging before it was a beautiful peony-lantern, which had probably been left there at the time of the

Festival of the Dead. Shinzaburō remembered that the peony-lantern carried by O-Yoné was exactly similar; and the coincidence impressed him as strange. He looked again at the tombs; but the tombs explained nothing. Neither bore any personal name—only the Buddhist *kaimyō,* or posthumous appellation. Then he determined to seek information at the temple. An acolyte stated, in reply to his questions, that the large tomb had been recently erected for the daughter of Iijima Heizayémon, the *hatamoto* of Ushigomé; and that the small tomb next to it was that of her servant O-Yoné, who had died of grief soon after the young lady's funeral.

Immediately to Shinzaburō's memory there recurred, with another and sinister meaning, the words of O-Yoné: "*We went away, and found a very small house in Yanaka-no-Sasaki. There we are now just barely able to live—by doing a little private work. . . .*" Here was indeed the very small house—and in Yanaka-no-Sasaki. But the little *private work* . . . ?

Terror-stricken, the samurai hastened with all speed to the house of Yusai, and begged for his counsel and assistance. But Yusai declared himself unable to be of any aid in such a case. All that he could do was to send Shinzaburō to the high-priest Ryōseki, of Shin-Banzui-In, with a letter praying for immediate religious help.

VII

The high-priest Ryōseki was a learned and a holy man. By spiritual vision he was able to know the secret of any sorrow, and the nature of the karma that had caused it. He heard unmoved the story of Shinzaburō, and said to him:

"A very great danger now threatens you, because of an error committed in one of your former states of existence. The karma that binds you to the dead is very strong; but if I tried to explain its character, you would not be able to understand. I shall therefore tell you only this—that the dead person has no desire to injure you out of hate, feels no enmity towards you: she is influenced, on the contrary, by the most passionate affection for you. Probably the girl has been in love with you from a time long preceding your present life—from a time of not less than three or four past existences; and it would seem that, although necessarily changing her form and condition at each succeeding birth, she has not been able to cease from following after you. Therefore it will not be an easy thing to escape from her influence. . . . But now I am going to lend you this powerful *mamori.*[18] It is a pure

---

[18] The Japanese word *mamori* has significations at least as numerous as those attaching to our own term "amulet." It would be impossible, in a mere footnote, even to suggest the variety of Japanese religious objects to which the name is given. In this instance, the *mamori* is a very small image, probably enclosed in a miniature shrine of

gold image of that Buddha called the Sea-Sounding Tathâgata—*Kai-On-Nyōrai*—because his preaching of the Law sounds through the world like the sound of the sea. And this little image is especially a *shiryō-yoké,*[19]—which protects the living from the dead. This you must wear, in its covering, next to your body—under the girdle. . . . Besides, I shall presently perform in the temple, a *segaki*-service[20] for the repose of the troubled spirit. . . . And here is a holy Sûtra, called *Ubō-Darani-Kyō*, or "Treasure-Raining Sûtra"[21] you must be careful to recite it every night in your house—without fail. . . . Furthermore I shall give you this package of *o-fuda;*[22] you must paste one of them over every opening of your house—no matter how small. If you do this, the power of the holy texts will prevent the dead from entering. But—whatever may happen—do not fail to recite the Sûtra."

Shinzaburō humbly thanked the high-priest; and then, taking with him the image, the Sûtra, and the bundle of sacred texts, he made all haste to reach his home before the hour of sunset.

VIII

With Yusai's advice and help, Shinzaburō was able before dark to fix the holy texts over all the apertures of his dwelling. Then the *ninsomi* returned to his own house—leaving the youth alone.

Night came, warm and clear. Shinzaburō made fast the doors, bound the precious amulet about his waist, entered his mosquito-net,

---

lacquer-work or metal, over which a silk cover is drawn. Such little images were often worn by *samurai* on the person. I was recently shown a miniature figure of Kwannon, in an iron case, which had been carried by an officer through the Satsuma war. He observed, with good reason, that it had probably saved his life; for it had stopped a bullet of which the dent was plainly visible.

[19] From *shiryō*, a ghost, and *yokeru*, to exclude. The Japanese have, two kinds of ghosts proper in their folk-lore: the spirits of the dead, *shiryō*; and the spirits of the living, *ikiryō*. A house or a person may be haunted by an *ikiryō* as well as by a *shiryō*.

[20] A special service—accompanying offerings of food, etc., to those dead having no living relatives or friends to care for them—is thus termed. In this case, however, the service would be of a particular and exceptional kind.

[21] The name would be more correctly written *Ubō-Darani-Kyō*. It is the Japanese pronunciation of the title of a very short Sûtra translated out of Sanskrit into Chinese by the Indian priest Amoghavajra, probably during the eighth century. The Chinese text contains transliterations of some mysterious Sanskrit words—apparently talismanic words—like those to be seen in Kern's translation of the Saddharma-Pundarika, ch. xxvi.

[22] *O-fuda* is the general name given to religious texts used as charms or talismans. They are sometimes stamped or burned upon wood, but more commonly written or printed upon narrow strips of paper. *O-fuda* are pasted above house-entrances, on the walls of rooms, upon tablets placed in household shrines, etc., etc. Some kinds are worn about the person; others are made into pellets, and swallowed as spiritual medicine. The text of the larger *o-fuda* is often accompanied by curious pictures or symbolic illustrations.

and by the glow of a night-lantern began to recite the *Ubō-Darani-Kyō*.
For a long time he chanted the words, comprehending little of their
meaning; then he tried to obtain some rest. But his mind was still too
much disturbed by the strange events of the day. Midnight passed; and
no sleep came to him. At last he heard the boom of the great temple-
bell of Dentsu-In announcing the eighth hour.[23]

It ceased; and Shinzaburō suddenly heard the sound of *geta*
approaching from the old direction—but this time more slowly: *karan-
koron, karan-koron*! At once a cold sweat broke over his forehead.
Opening the Sûtra hastily, with trembling hand, he began again to recite
it aloud. The steps came nearer and nearer—reached the live hedge—
stopped! Then, strange to say, Shinzaburō felt unable to remain under
his mosquito-net: something stronger even than his fear impelled him
to look; and, instead of continuing to recite the *Ubō-Darani-Kyō*, he
foolishly approached the shutters, and through a chink peered out into
the night. Before the house he saw O-Tsuyu standing, and O-Yoné with
the peony-lantern; and both of them were gazing at the Buddhist texts
pasted above the entrance. Never before—not even in what time she
lived—had O-Tsuyu appeared so beautiful; and Shinzaburō felt his
heart drawn towards her with a power almost resistless. But the terror
of death and the terror of the unknown restrained; and there went on
within him such a struggle between his love and his fear that he became
as one suffering in the body the pains of the Shō-netsu hell.[24]

Presently he heard the voice of the maid-servant, saying:

"My dear mistress, there is no way to enter. The heart of Hagiwara
Sama must have changed. For the promise that he made last night has
been broken; and the doors have been made fast to keep us out. . . . We
cannot go in tonight. . . . It will be wiser for you to make up your mind
not to think any more about him, because his feeling towards you has
certainly changed. It is evident that he does not want to see you. So it
will be better not to give yourself any more trouble for the sake of a
man whose heart is so unkind."

But the girl answered, weeping:

"Oh, to think that this could happen after the pledges which we
made to each other! . . . Often I was told that the heart of a man
changes as quickly as the sky of autumn; yet surely the heart of

---

[23] According to the old Japanese way of counting time, this *yatsudoki* or eighth hour
was the same as our two o'clock in the morning. Each Japanese hour was equal to two
European hours, so that there were only six hours instead of our twelve; and these six
hours were counted backwards in the order—9, 8, 7, 6, 5, 4. Thus the ninth hour
corresponded to our midday, or midnight; half-past nine to our one o'clock; eight to our
two o'clock. Two o'clock in the morning, also called "the Hour of the Ox," was the
Japanese hour of ghosts and goblins.

[24] *En-netsu* or *Shō-netsu* (Sanskrit "Tapana") is the sixth of the Eight Hot Hells of
Japanese Buddhism. One day of life in this hell is equal in duration to thousands (some
say millions) of human years.

Hagiwara Sama cannot be so cruel that he should really intend to exclude me in this way! . . . Dear Yoné, please find some means of taking me to him. . . . Unless you do, I will never, never go home again."

Thus she continued to plead, veiling her face with her long sleeves—and very beautiful she looked, and very touching; but the fear of death was strong upon her lover.

O-Yoné at last made answer—

"My dear young lady, why will you trouble your mind about a man who seems to be so cruel? . . . Well, let us see if there be no way to enter at the back of the house: come with me!"

And taking O-Tsuyu by the hand, she led her away toward the rear of the dwelling; and there the two disappeared as suddenly as the light disappears when the flame of a lamp is blown out.

IX

Night after night the shadows came at the Hour of the Ox; and nightly Shinzaburō heard the weeping of O-Tsuyu. Yet he believed himself saved—little imagining that his doom had already been decided by the character of his dependents.

Tomozō had promised Yusai never to speak to any other person— not even to O-Miné—of the strange events that were taking place. But Tomozō was not long suffered by the haunters to rest in peace. Night after night O-Yoné entered into his dwelling, and roused him from his sleep, and asked him to remove the *o-fuda* placed over one very small window at the back of his master's house. And Tomozō, out of fear, as often promised her to take away the *o-fuda* before the next sundown; but never by day could he make up his mind to remove it—believing that evil was intended to Shinzaburō. At last, in a night of storm, O-Yoné startled him from slumber with a cry of reproach, and stooped above his pillow, and said to him: "Have a care how you trifle with us! If, by to-morrow night, you do not take away that text, you shall learn how I can hate!" And she made her face so frightful as she spoke that Tomozō nearly died of terror.

O-Miné, the wife of Tomozō, had never till then known of these visits: even to her husband they had seemed like bad dreams. But on this particular night it chanced that, waking suddenly, she heard the voice of a woman talking to Tomozō. Almost in the same moment the talk-ing ceased; and when O-Miné looked about her, she saw, by the light of the night-lamp, only her husband—shuddering and white with fear. The stranger was gone; the doors were fast: it seemed impossible that anybody could have entered. Nevertheless the jealousy of the wife had been aroused; and she began to chide and to question Tomozō in such a manner that he thought himself obliged to betray the secret, and to explain the terrible dilemma in which he had been placed.

Then the passion of O-Miné yielded to wonder and alarm; but she was a subtle woman, and she devised immediately a plan to save her husband by the sacrifice of her master. And she gave Tomozō a cunning counsel—telling him to make conditions with the dead.

They came again on the following night at the Hour of the Ox; and O-Miné hid herself on hearing the sound of their coming—*karan-koron, karan-koron*! But Tomozō went out to meet them in the dark, and even found courage to say to them what his wife had told him to say:

"It is true that I deserve your blame; but I had no wish to cause you anger. The reason that the *o-fuda* has not been taken away is that my wife and I are able to live only by the help of Hagiwara Sama, and that we cannot expose him to any danger without bringing misfortune upon ourselves. But if we could obtain the sum of a hundred *ryō* in gold, we should be able to please you, because we should then need no help from anybody. Therefore if you will give us a hundred *ryō*, I can take the *o-fuda* away without being afraid of losing our only means of support."

When he had uttered these words, O-Yoné and O-Tsuyu looked at each other in silence for a moment. Then O-Yoné said:

"Mistress, I told you that it was not right to trouble this man, —as we have no just cause of ill will against him. But it is certainly useless to fret yourself about Hagiwara Sama, because his heart has changed towards you. Now once again, my dear young lady, let me beg you not to think any more about him!"

But O-Tsuyu, weeping, made answer:

"Dear Yoné, whatever may happen, I cannot possibly keep myself from thinking about him! You know that you can get a hundred *ryō* to have the *o-fuda* taken off. . . . Only once more, I pray, dear Yoné!— only once more bring me face to face with Hagiwara Sama—I beseech you!" And hiding her face with her sleeve, she thus continued to plead.

"Oh! why will you ask me to do these things?" responded O-Yoné. "You know very well that I have no money. But since you will persist in this whim of yours, in spite of all that I can say, I suppose that I must try to find the money somehow, and to bring it here to-morrow night. . . ." Then, turning to the faithless Tomozō, she said: "Tomozō, I must tell you that Hagiwara Sama now wears upon his body a *mamori* called by the name of *Kai-On-Nyōrai*, and that so long as he wears it we cannot approach him. So you will have to get that *mamori* away from him, by some means or other, as well as to remove the *o-fuda*."

Tomozō feebly made answer:

"That also I can do, if you will promise to bring me the hundred *ryō.*"

"Well, mistress," said O-Yoné, "you will wait—will you not—until to-morrow night?"

"Oh, dear Yoné!" sobbed the other—"have we to go back tonight again without seeing Hagiwara Sama? Ah! it is cruel!"

And the shadow of the mistress, weeping, was led away by the shadow of the maid.

X

Another day went, and another night came, and the dead came with it. But this time no lamentation was heard without the house of Hagiwara; for the faithless servant found his reward at the Hour of the Ox, and removed the *o-fuda.* Moreover he had been able, while his master was at the bath, to steal from its case the golden *mamori,* and to substitute for it an image of copper; and he had buried the *Kai-On-Nyōrai* in a desolate field. So the visitants found nothing to oppose their entering. Veiling their faces with their sleeves they rose and passed, like a streaming of vapor, into the little window from over which the holy text had been torn away. But what happened thereafter within the house Tomozō never knew.

The sun was high before he ventured again to approach his master's dwelling, and to knock upon the sliding-doors. For the first time in years he obtained no response; and the silence made him afraid. Repeatedly he called, and received no answer. Then, aided by O-Miné, he succeeded in effecting an entrance and making his way alone to the sleeping-room, where he called again in vain. He rolled back the rumbling shutters to admit the light; but still within the house there was no stir. At last he dared to lift a corner of the mosquito-net. But no sooner had he looked beneath than he fled from the house, with a cry of horror.

Shinzaburō was dead—hideously dead; and his face was the face of a man who had died in the uttermost agony of fear; and lying beside him in the bed were the bones of a woman! And the bones of the arms, and the bones of the hands, clung fast about his neck.

XI

Hakuōdō Yusai, the fortune-teller, went to view the corpse at the prayer of the faithless Tomozō. The old man was terrified and astonished at the spectacle, but looked about him with a keen eye. He soon perceived that the *o-fuda* had been taken from the little window at the back of the house; and on searching the body of Shinzaburō, he discovered that the golden *mamori* had been taken from its wrapping, and a copper image of Fudō put in place of it. He suspected Tomozō of the theft; but the whole occurrence was so very extraordinary that he thought it prudent to consult with the priest Ryōseki before taking further action. Therefore, after having made a careful examination of the premises, he betook himself to the temple Shin-Banzui-In, as quickly as his aged limbs could bear him.

Ryōseki, without waiting to hear the purpose of the old man's visit, at once invited him into a private apartment.

"You know that you are always welcome here," said Ryōseki. "Please seat yourself at ease. . . . Well, I am sorry to tell you that Hagiwara Sama is dead."

Yusai wonderingly exclaimed:

"Yes, he is dead; but how did you learn of it?"

The priest responded:

"Hagiwara Sama was suffering from the results of an evil karma; and his attendant was a bad man. What happened to Hagiwara Sama was unavoidable; his destiny had been determined from a time long before his last birth. It will be better for you not to let your mind be troubled by this event."

Yusai said:

"I have heard that a priest of pure life may gain power to see into the future for a hundred years; but truly this is the first time in my existence that I have had proof of such power. . . . Still, there is another matter about which I am very anxious. . . ."

"You mean," interrupted Ryōseki, "the stealing of the holy *mamori*, the *Kai-On-Nyōrai*. But you must not give yourself any concern about that. The image has been buried in a field; and it will be found there and returned to me during the eighth month of the coming year. So please do not be anxious about it."

More and more amazed, the old *ninsomi* ventured to observe:

"I have studied the *In-Yō*,[25] and the science of divination; and I make my living by telling peoples' fortunes; but I cannot possibly understand how you know these things."

Ryōseki answered gravely:

"Never mind how I happen to know them. . . . I now want to speak to you about Hagiwara's funeral. The House of Hagiwara has its own family-cemetery, of course; but to bury him there would not be proper. He must be buried beside O-Tsuyu, the Lady Iijima; for his karma-relation to her was a very deep one. And it is but right that you should erect a tomb for him at your own cost, because you have been indebted to him for many favors."

---

[25] The Male and Female principles of the universe, the Active and Passive forces of Nature. Yusai refers here to the old Chinese nature-philosophy—better known to Western readers by the name FENG-SHUI.

Thus it came to pass that Shinzaburō was buried beside O-Tsuyu, in the cemetery of Shin-Banzui-In, in Yanaka-no-Sasaki.

—Here ends the story of the Ghosts in the Romance of the Peony-Lantern.—

My friend asked me whether the story had interested me; and I answered by telling him that I wanted to go to the cemetery of Shin-Banzui-In—so as to realize more definitely the local color of the author's studies.

"I shall go with you at once," he said. "But what did you think of the personages?"

"To Western thinking," I made answer, "Shinzaburō is a despicable creature. I have been mentally comparing him with the true lovers of our old ballad-literature. They were only too glad to follow a dead sweetheart into the grave; and nevertheless, being Christians, they believed that they had only one human life to enjoy in this world. But Shinzaburō was a Buddhist—with a million lives behind him and a million lives before him; and he was too selfish to give up even one miserable existence for the sake of the girl that came back to him from the dead. Then he was even more cowardly than selfish. Although a samurai by birth and training, he had to beg a priest to save him from ghosts. In every way he proved himself contemptible; and O-Tsuyu did quite right in choking him to death."

"From the Japanese point of view, likewise," my friend responded, "Shinzaburō is rather contemptible. But the use of this weak character helped the author to develop incidents that could not otherwise, perhaps, have been so effectively managed. To my thinking, the only attractive character in the story is that of O-Yoné: type of the old-time loyal and loving servant—intelligent, shrewd, full of resource—faithful not only unto death, but beyond death. . . . Well, let us go to Shin-Banzui-In."

We found the temple uninteresting, and the cemetery an abomination of desolation. Spaces once occupied by graves had been turned into potato-patches. Between were tombs leaning at all angles out of the perpendicular, tablets made illegible by scurf, empty pedestals, shattered water-tanks, and statues of Buddhas without heads or hands. Recent rains had soaked the black soil—leaving here and there small pools of slime about which swarms of tiny frogs were hopping. Everything—excepting the potato-patches—seemed to have been neglected for years. In a shed just within the gate, we observed a woman cooking; and my companion presumed to ask her if she knew anything about the tombs described in the Romance of the Peony-Lantern.

"Ah! the tombs of O-Tsuyu and O-Yoné?" she responded, smiling; "you will find them near the end of the first row at the back of the temple—next to the statue of Jizō."

Surprises of this kind I had met with elsewhere in Japan.

We picked our way between the rain-pools and between the green ridges of young potatoes—whose roots were doubtless feeding on the sub-stance of many another O-Tsuyu and O-Yoné; and we reached at last two lichen-eaten tombs of which the inscriptions seemed almost obliterated. Beside the larger tomb was a statue of Jizō, with a broken nose.

"The characters are not easy to make out," said my friend—"but wait!". . . . He drew from his sleeve a sheet of soft white paper, laid it over the inscription, and began to rub the paper with a lump of clay. As he did so, the characters appeared in white on the blackened surface.

"*Eleventh day, third month—Rat, Elder Brother, Fire—Sixth year of Horéki* [A. D. 1756].' . . . This would seem to be the grave of some innkeeper of Nedzu, named Kichibei. Let us see what is on the other monument."

With a fresh sheet of paper he presently brought out the text of a kaimyō, and read—

"*En-myō-In,   Hō-yō-I-tei-ken-shi,   Hō-ni*': '*Nun-of-the-Law, Illustrious, Pure-of-heart-and-will, Famed-in-the-Law—inhabiting the Mansion-of-the-Preaching-of-Wonder.*'. . . . The grave of some Buddhist nun."

"What utter humbug!" I exclaimed. "That woman was only making fun of us."

"Now," my friend protested, "you are unjust to the, woman! You came here because you wanted a sensation; and she tried her very best to please you. You did not suppose that ghost-story was true, did you?"

Ingwa-banashi[26]

The daimyō's wife was dying, and knew that she was dying. She had not been able to leave her bed since the early autumn of the tenth Bunsei. It was now the fourth month of the twelfth Bunsei—the year 1829 by Western counting; and the cherry-trees were blossoming. She thought of the cherry-trees in her garden, and of the gladness of spring. She thought of her children. She thought of her husband's various concubines—especially the Lady Yukiko, nineteen years old.

---

[26] Lit., "a tale of *ingwa*." *Ingwa* is a Japanese Buddhist term for evil karma, or the evil consequence of faults committed in a former state of existence. Perhaps the curious title of the narrative is best explained by the Buddhist teaching that the dead have power to injure the living only in consequence of evil actions committed by their victims in some former life. Both title and narrative may be found in the collection of weird stories entitled *Hyaku-Monogatari*.

"My dear wife," said the daimyō, "you have suffered very much
for three long years. We have done all that we could to get you well—
watching beside you night and day, praying for you, and often fasting
for your sake, But in spite of our loving care, and in spite of the skill of
our best physicians, it would now seen that the end of your life is not
far off. Probably we shall sorrow more than you will sorrow because of
your having to leave what the Buddha so truly termed 'this burning-
house of the world.' I shall order to be performed—no matter what the
cost—every religious rite that can serve you in regard to your next
rebirth; and all of us will pray without ceasing for you, that you may
not have to wander in the Black Space, but may quickly enter Paradise,
and attain to Buddha-hood."

He spoke with the utmost tenderness, pressing her the while. Then,
with eyelids closed, she answered him in a voice thin as the voice of in
insect:

"I am grateful—most grateful—for your kind words. . . . Yes, it is
true, as you say, that I have been sick for three long years, and that I
have been treated with all possible care and affection. . . . Why, indeed,
should I turn away from the one true Path at the very moment of my
death? . . . Perhaps to think of worldly matters at such a time is not
right; but I have one last request to make—only one. . . . Call here to
me the Lady Yukiko; you know that I love her like a sister. I want to
speak to her about the affairs of this household."

Yukiko came at the summons of the lord, and, in obedience to a
sign from him, knelt down beside the couch. The daimyō's wife opened
her eyes, and looked at Yukiko, and spoke:

"Ah, here is Yukiko! . . . I am so pleased to see you, Yukiko! . . .
Come a little closer—so that you can hear me well: I am not able to
speak loud. . . . Yukiko, I am going to die. I hope that you will be
faithful in all things to our dear lord; for I want you to take my place
when I am gone. . . . I hope that you will always be loved by him—yes,
even a hundred times more than I have been—and that you will very
soon be promoted to a higher rank, and become his honored wife. . . .
And I beg of you always to cherish our dear lord: never allow another
woman to rob you of his affection. . . . This is what I wanted to say to
you, dear Yukiko. . . . Have you been able to understand?"

"Oh, my dear Lady," protested Yukiko, "do not, I entreat you, say
such strange things to me! You well know that I am of poor and mean
condition: how could I ever dare to aspire to become the wife of our
lord!"

"Nay, nay!" returned the wife, huskily—"this is not a time for
words of ceremony: let us speak only the truth to each other. After my
death, you will certainly be promoted to a higher place; and I now
assure you again that I wish you to become the wife of our lord—yes, I

wish this, Yukiko, even more than I wish to become a Buddha! . . . Ah, I had almost forgotten!—I want you to do something for me, Yukiko. You know that in the garden there is a *yaē-zakura*,[27] which was brought here, the year before last, from Mount Yoshino in Yamato. I have been told that it is now in full bloom; and I wanted so much to see it in flower! In a little while I shall be dead; I must see that tree before I die. Now I wish you to carry me into the garden—at once, Yukiko—so that I can see it. . . . Yes, upon your back, Yukiko; take me upon your back. . . ."

While thus asking, her voice had gradually become clear and strong—as if the intensity of the wish had given her new force: then she suddenly burst into tears. Yukiko knelt motionless, not knowing what to do; but the lord nodded assent.

"It is her last wish in this world," he said. "She always loved cherry-flowers; and I know that she wanted very much to see that Yamato-tree in blossom. Come, my dear Yukiko, let her have her will."

As a nurse turns her back to a child, that the child may cling to it, Yukiko offered her shoulders to the wife, and said:

"Lady, I am ready: please tell me how I best can help you."

"Why, this way!"—responded the dying woman, lifting herself with an almost superhuman effort by clinging to Yukiko's shoulders. But as she stood erect, she quickly slipped her thin hands down over the shoulders, under the robe, and clutched the breasts of the girl,, and burst into a wicked laugh.

"I have my wish!" she cried—"I have my wish for the cherry-bloom,[28]—but not the cherry-bloom of the garden! . . . I could not die before I got my wish. Now I have it!—oh, what a delight!"

And with these words she fell forward upon the crouching girl, and died.

The attendants at once attempted to lift the body from Yukiko's shoulders, and to lay it upon the bed. But—strange to say!—this seemingly easy thing could not be done. The cold hands had attached themselves in some unaccountable way to the breasts of the girl— appeared to have grown into the quick flesh. Yukiko became senseless with fear and pain.

Physicians were called. They could not understand what had taken place. By no ordinary methods could the hands of the dead woman be unfastened from the body of her victim; they so clung that any effort to

---

[27] *Yaē-zakura, yaē-no-sakura*, a variety of Japanese cherry-tree that bears double-blossoms.

[28] In Japanese poetry and proverbial phraseology, the physical beauty of a woman is compared to the cherry-flower; while feminine moral beauty is compared to the plum-flower.

remove them brought blood. This was not because the fingers held: it was because the flesh of the palms had united itself in some inexplicable manner to the flesh of the breasts!

At that time the most skilful physician in Yedo was a foreigner—a Dutch surgeon. It was decided to summon him. After a careful examination he said that he could not understand the case, and that for the immediate relief of Yukiko there was nothing to be done except to cut the hands from the corpse. He declared that it would be dangerous to attempt to detach them from the breasts. His advice was accepted; and the hands' were amputated at the wrists. But they remained clinging to the breasts; and there they soon darkened and dried up—like the hands of a person long dead.

Yet this was only the beginning of the horror.

Withered and bloodless though they seemed, those hands were not dead. At intervals they would stir—stealthily, like great grey spiders. And nightly thereafter—beginning always at the Hour of the Ox,[29]— they would clutch and compress and torture. Only at the Hour of the Tiger the pain would cease.

Yukiko cut off her hair, and became a mendicant-nun—taking the religious name of Dassetsu. She had an *ihai* (mortuary tablet) made, bearing the *kaimyō* of her dead mistress—*"Myō-Kō-In-Den Chizan-Ryō-Fu Daishī"*; and this she carried about with her in all her wanderings; and every day before it she humbly besought the dead for pardon, and performed a Buddhist service in order that the jealous spirit might find rest. But the evil karma that had rendered such an affliction possible could not soon be exhausted. Every night at the Hour of the Ox, the hands never failed to torture her, during more than seventeen years—according to the testimony of those persons to whom she last told her story, when she stopped for one evening at the house of Noguchi Dengozayémon, in the village of Tanaka in the district of Kawachi in the province of Shimotsuké. This was in the third year of Kōkwa (1846). Thereafter nothing more was ever heard of her.

---

[29] In ancient Japanese time, the Hour of the Ox was the special hour of ghosts. It began at 2 A.M., and lasted until 4 A.M.—for the old Japanese hour was double the length of the modern hour. The Hour of the Tiger began at 4 A.M.

Story of a Tengu[30]

In the days of the Emperor Go-Reizei, there was a holy priest living in the temple of Saito, on the mountain called Hiyei-Zan, near Kyōto. One summer day this good priest, after a visit to the city, was returning to his temple by way of Kita-no-Ōji, when he saw some boys ill-treating a kite. They had caught the bird in a snare, and were beating it with sticks. "Oh, the, poor creature!" compassionately exclaimed the priest; "why do you torment it so, children?" One of the boys made answer: "We want to kill it to get the feathers." Moved by pity, the priest persuaded the boys to let him have the kite in exchange for a fan that he was carrying; and he set the bird free. It had not been seriously hurt, and was able to fly away.

Happy at having performed this Buddhist act of merit, the priest then resumed his walk. He had not proceeded very far when he saw a strange monk come out of a bamboo-grove by the road-side, and hasten towards him. The monk respectfully saluted him, and said: "Sir, through your compassionate kindness my life has been saved; and I now desire to express my gratitude in a fitting manner." Astonished at hearing himself thus addressed, the priest replied: "Really, I cannot remember to have ever seen you before: please tell me who you are." "It is not wonderful that you cannot recognize me in this form," returned the monk: "I am the kite that those cruel boys were tormenting at Kita-no-Ōji. You saved my life; and there is nothing in this world more precious than life. So I now wish to return your kindness in some way or other. If there be anything that you would like to have, or to know, or to see—anything that I can do for you, in short—please to tell me; for as I happen to possess, in a small degree, the Six Supernatural Powers, I am able to gratify almost any wish that you can express." On hearing these words, the priest knew that he was speaking with a Tengu; and he frankly made answer: "My friend, I have long ceased to care for the things of this world: I am now seventy years of age; neither fame nor pleasure has any attraction for me. I feel anxious only about my future birth; but as that is a matter in which no one can help me, it were useless to ask about it. Really, I can think of but one thing worth

---

[30] This story may be found in the curious old Japanese book called *Jikkun-Shō*. The same legend has furnished the subject of an interesting *Nō*-play, called *Dai-É* ("The Great Assembly").

In Japanese popular art, the Tengu are commonly represented either as winged men with beak-shaped noses, or as birds of prey. There are different kinds of Tengu; but all are supposed to be mountain-haunting spirits, capable of assuming many forms, and occasionally appearing as crows, vultures, or eagles. Buddhism appears to class the Tengu among the Mârakâyikas.

wishing for. It has been my life-long regret that I was not in India in the time of the Lord Buddha, and could not attend the great assembly on the holy mountain Gridhrakûta. Never a day passes in which this regret does not come to me, in the hour of morning or of evening prayer. Ah, my friend! if it were possible to conquer Time and Space, like the Bodhisattvas, so that I could look upon that marvelous assembly, how happy should I be!"—"Why," the Tengu exclaimed, "that pious wish of yours can easily be satisfied. I perfectly well remember the assembly on the Vulture Peak; and I can cause everything that happened there to reappear before you, exactly as it occurred. It is our greatest delight to represent such holy matters. . . . Come this way with me!"

And the priest suffered himself to be led to a place among pines, on the slope of a hill. "Now," said the Tengu, "you have only to wait here for awhile, with your eyes shut. Do not open them until you hear the voice of the Buddha preaching the Law. Then you can look. But when you see the appearance of the Buddha, you must not allow your devout feelings to influence you in any way; you must not bow down, nor pray, nor utter any such exclamation as, '*Even so, Lord*!' or '*O thou Blessed One*!' You must not speak at all. Should you make even the least sign of reverence, something very unfortunate might happen to me." The priest gladly promised to follow these injunctions; and the Tengu hurried away as if to prepare the spectacle.

The day waned and passed, and the darkness came; but the old priest waited patiently beneath a tree, keeping his eyes closed. At last a voice suddenly resounded above him—a wonderful voice, deep and clear like the pealing of a mighty bell—the voice of the Buddha Sâkyamuni proclaiming the Perfect Way. Then the priest, opening his eyes in a great radiance, perceived that all things had been changed: the place was indeed the Vulture Peak—the holy Indian mountain Gridhrakûta; and the time was the time of the Sûtra of the Lotos of the Good Law. Now there were no pines about him, but strange shining trees made of the Seven Precious Substances, with foliage and fruit of gems; and the ground was covered with Mandârava and Manjûshaka flowers showered from heaven; and the night was filled with fragrance and splendor and the sweetness of the great Voice. And in mid-air, shining as a moon above the world, the priest beheld the Blessed One seated upon the Lion-throne, with Samantabhadra at his right hand, and Mañjusrî at his left—and before them assembled—immeasurably spreading into Space, like a flood Of stars—the hosts of the Mahâsattvas and the Bodhisattvas with their countless following: "gods, demons, Nâgas, goblins, men, and beings not human." Sâriputra he saw, and Kâsyapa, and Ânanda, with all the disciples of the Tathâgata—and the Kings of the Devas—and the Kings of the Four Directions, like pillars of fire—and the great Dragon-Kings—and the

Gandharvas and Garudas—and the Gods of the Sun and the Moon and the Wind—and the shining myriads of Brahma's heaven. And incomparably further than even the measureless circling of the glory of these, he saw—made visible by a single ray of light that shot from the forehead of the Blessed One to pierce beyond uttermost Time—the eighteen hundred thousand Buddha-fields of the Eastern Quarter with all their habitants—and the beings in each of the Six States of Existence—and even the shapes of the Buddhas extinct, that had entered into Nirvâna. These, and all the gods, and all the demons, he saw bow down before the Lion-throne; and he heard that multitude incalculable of beings praising the Sûtra of the Lotos of the Good Law—like the roar of a sea before the Lord. Then forgetting utterly his pledge—foolishly dreaming that he stood in the very presence of the very Buddha—he cast himself down in worship with tears of love and thanksgiving; crying out with a loud voice, "*O thou Blessed One!*" . . .

Instantly with a shock as of earthquake the stupendous spectacle disappeared; and the priest found himself alone in the dark, kneeling upon the grass of the mountain-side. Then a sadness unspeakable fell upon him, because of the loss of the vision, and because of the thoughtlessness that had caused him to break his word. As he sorrowfully turned his steps homeward, the goblin-monk once more appeared before him, and said to him in tones of reproach and pain: "Because you did not keep the promise which you made to me, and heedlessly allowed your feelings to overcome you, the Gohotendó, who is the Guardian of the Doctrine, swooped down suddenly from heaven upon us, and smote us in great anger, crying out, '*How do ye dare thus to deceive a pious person?*' Then the other monks, whom I had assembled, all fled in fear. As for myself, one of my wings has been broken—so that now I cannot fly." And with these words the Tengu vanished forever.

From Shadowings

The Reconciliation[31]

There was a young Samurai of Kyōto who had been reduced to poverty by the ruin of his lord, and found himself obliged to leave his home, and to take service with the Governor of a distant province. Before quitting the capital, this Samurai divorced his wife—a good and beautiful woman—under the belief that he could better obtain promotion by another alliance. He then married the daughter of a family of some distinction, and took her with him to the district whither

---

[31] The original story is to be found in the curious volume entitled *Konséki-Monogatari.*

he had been called.

But it was in the time of the thoughtlessness of youth, and the sharp experience of want, that the Samurai could not understand the worth of the affection so lightly cast away. His second marriage did not prove a happy one; the character of his new wife was hard and selfish; and he soon found every cause to think with regret of Kyōto days. Then he discovered that he still loved his first wife—loved her more than he could ever love the second; and he began to feel how unjust and how thankless he had been. Gradually his repentance deepened into a remorse that left him no peace of mind. Memories of the woman he had wronged—her gentle speech, her smiles, her dainty, pretty ways, her faultless patience—continually haunted him. Sometimes in dreams he saw her at her loom, weaving as when she toiled night and day to help him during the years of their distress: more often he saw her kneeling alone in the desolate little room where he had left her, veiling her tears with her poor worn sleeve. Even in the hours of official duty, his thoughts would wander back to her: then he would ask himself how she was living, what she was doing. Something in his heart assured him that she could not accept another husband, and that she never would refuse to pardon him. And he secretly resolved to seek her out as soon as he could return to Kyōto—then to beg her forgiveness, to take her back, to do everything that a man could do to make atonement. But the years went by.

At last the Governor's official term expired, and the Samurai was free. "Now I will go back to my dear one," he vowed to himself. "Ah, what a cruelty—what a folly to have divorced her!" He sent his second wife to her own people (she had given him no children); and hurrying to Kyōto, he went at once to seek his former companion—not allowing himself even the time to change his travelling-garb.

When he reached the street where she used to live, it was late in the night—the night of the tenth day of the ninth month; and the city was silent as a cemetery. But a bright moon made everything visible; and he found the house without difficulty. It had a deserted look: tall weeds were growing on the roof. He knocked at the sliding-doors, and no one answered. Then, finding that the doors had not been fastened from within, he pushed them open, and entered. The front room was matless and empty: a chilly wind was blowing through crevices in the planking; and the moon shone through a ragged break in the wall of the alcove. Other rooms presented a like forlorn condition. The house, to all seeming, was unoccupied. Nevertheless, the Samurai determined to visit one other apartment at the further end of the dwelling—a very small room that had been his wife's favorite resting-place. Approaching the sliding-screen that closed it, he was startled to perceive a glow within. He pushed the screen aside, and uttered a cry of joy; for he saw her there—sewing by the light of a paper-lamp. Her eyes at the same instant met his own; and with a happy smile she greeted him—asking only: "When did you come back to Kyōto? How did you find your way here to me, through all those black rooms?" The years had not changed her. Still she seemed as fair and young as in his fondest memory of her; but sweeter than any memory there came to him the music of her voice, with its trembling of pleased wonder.

Then joyfully he took his place beside her, and told her all: how deeply he repented his selfishness—how wretched he had been without her—how constantly he had regretted her—how long he had hoped and planned to make amends; caressing her the while, and asking her forgiveness over and over again. She answered him, with loving gentleness, according to his heart's desire—entreating him to cease all self-reproach. It was wrong, she said, that he should have allowed himself to suffer on her account: she had always felt that she was not worthy to be his wife. She knew that he had separated from her, notwithstanding, only because of poverty; and while he lived with her, he had always been kind; and she had never ceased to pray for his happiness. But even if there had been a reason for speaking of amends, this honorable visit would be ample amends; what greater happiness than thus to see him again, though it were only for a moment? "Only for a moment!" he answered, with a glad laugh—"say, rather, for the time of seven existences! My loved one, unless you forbid, I am coming back to live with you always—always—always! Nothing shall ever separate us again. Now I have means and friends: we need not fear poverty. To-morrow my goods will be brought here; and my servants will come to wait upon you; and we shall make this house beautiful. . . . Tonight," he added, apologetically, "I came thus late—without even changing my dress—only because of the longing I had to see you, and to tell you this." She seemed greatly pleased by these words; and in her turn she told him about all that had happened in Kyōto since the time of his departure—excepting her own sorrows, of which she sweetly refused to speak. They chatted far into the night: then she conducted him to a warmer room, facing south—a room that had been their bridal chamber in former time. "Have you no one in the house to help you?" he asked, as she began to prepare the couch for him. "No," she answered, laughing cheerfully: "I could not afford a servant; so I have been living all alone." "You will have plenty of servants to-morrow," he said—"good servants—and everything else that you need." They lay down to rest—not to sleep: they had too much to tell each other; and they talked of the past and the present and the future, until the dawn was grey. Then, involuntarily, the Samurai closed his eyes, and slept.

When he awoke, the daylight was streaming through the chinks of the sliding-shutters; and he found himself, to his utter amazement, lying upon the naked boards of a moldering floor. . . . Had he only dreamed a dream? No: she was there; she slept. . . . He bent above her—and looked—and shrieked; for the sleeper had no face! . . . Before him, wrapped in its grave-sheet only, lay the corpse of a woman—a corpse so wasted that little remained save the bones, and the long black tangled hair.

Slowly—as he stood shuddering and sickening in the sun—the icy horror yielded to a despair so intolerable, a pain so atrocious, that he clutched at the mocking shadow of a doubt. Feigning ignorance of the neighborhood, he ventured to ask his way to the house in which his wife had lived.

"There is no one in that house," said the person questioned. "It used to belong to the wife of a Samurai who left the city several years ago. He divorced her in order to marry another woman before he went away; and she fretted a great deal, and so became sick. She had no relatives in Kyōto, and nobody to care for her; and she died in the autumn of the same year—on the tenth day of the ninth month. . . ."

A Legend of Fugen-Bosatsu[32]

There was once a very pious and learned priest, called Shōku Shōnin, who lived in the province of Harima. For many years he meditated daily upon the chapter of Fugen-Bosatsu [the Bodhisattva Samantabhadra] in the Sûtra of the Lotos of the Good Law; and he used to pray, every morning and evening, that he might at some time be permitted to behold Fugen-Bosatsu as a living presence, and in the form described in the holy text.[33]

One evening, while he was reciting the Sûtra, drowsiness overcame him; and he fell asleep leaning upon his *kyōsoku*.[34] Then he dreamed; and in his dream a voice told him that, in order to see Fugen-

---

[32] From the old story-book, *Jikkun-shō*.

[33] The priest's desire was probably inspired by the promises recorded in the chapter entitled "The Encouragement of Samantabhadra" (see Kern's translation of the Saddharma Pundarîka in the *Sacred Books of the East*—pp. 433-434): "Then the Bodhisattva Mahâsattva Samantabhadra said to the Lord: . . . 'When a preacher who applies himself to this Dharmaparyâya shall take a walk, then, O Lord, will I mount a white elephant with six tusks, and betake myself to the place where that preacher is walking, in order to protect this Dharmaparyâya. And when that preacher, applying himself to this Dharmaparyâya, forgets, be it but a single word or syllable, then will I mount the white elephant with six tusks, and show my face to that preacher, and repeat this entire Dharmaparyâya.'"—But these promises refer to "the end of time."

[34] The *Kyōsoku* is a kind of padded arm-rest, or arm-stool, upon which the priest leans one arm while reading. The use of such an arm-rest is not confined, however, to the Buddhist clergy.

Bosatsu, he must go to the house of a certain courtesan, known as the "Yujō-no-Chōja,"[35] who lived in the town of Kanzaki. Immediately upon awakening he resolved to go to Kanzaki; and, making all possible haste, he reached the town by the evening of the next day.

When he entered the house of the *yujō*, he found many persons already there assembled—mostly young men of the capital, who had been attracted to Kanzaki by the fame of the woman's beauty. They were feasting and drinking; and the *yujō* was playing a small hand-drum (*tsuzumi*), which she used very skillfully, and singing a song. The song which she sang was an old Japanese song about a famous shrine in the town of Murozumi; and the words were these:

Within the sacred water-tank[36] of Murozumi in Suwō,
Even though no wind be blowing,
The surface of the water is always rippling.

The sweetness of the voice filled everybody with surprise and delight. As the priest, who had taken a place apart, listened and wondered, the girl suddenly fixed her eyes upon him; and in the same instant he saw her form change into the form of Fugen-Bosatsu, emitting from her brow a beam of light that seemed to pierce beyond the limits of the universe, and riding a snow-white elephant with six tusks. And still she sang—but the song also was now transformed; and the words came thus to the ears of the priest:

On the Vast Sea of Cessation,
Though the Winds of the Six Desires and of the Five Corruptions
    never blow,
Yet the surface of that deep is always covered
With the billowings of Attainment to the Reality-in-Itself.

Dazzled by the divine ray, the priest closed his eyes: but through their lids he still distinctly saw the vision. When he opened them again, it was gone: he saw only the girl with her hand-drum, and heard only the song about the water of Murozumi. But he found that as often as he shut his eyes he could see Fugen-Bosatsu on the six-tusked elephant, and could hear the mystic Song of the Sea of Cessation. The other persons present saw only the *yujō*: they had not beheld the manifestation.

---

[35] A *yujō*, in old days, was a singing-girl as well as a courtesan. The term "Yujō-no-Chōja," in this case, would mean simply "the first (or best) of yujō."

[36] *Mitarai*. *Mitarai* (or *mitarashi*) is the name especially given to the water-tanks, or water-fonts—of stone or bronze—placed before Shintō shrines in order that the worshipper may purify his lips and hands before making prayer. Buddhist tanks are not so named.

Then the singer suddenly disappeared from the banquet-room—
none could say when or how. From that moment the revelry ceased;
and gloom took the place of joy. After having waited and sought for the
girl to no purpose, the company dispersed in great sorrow. Last of all,
the priest departed, bewildered by the emotions of the evening. But
scarcely had he passed beyond the gate, when the *yujō* appeared before
him, and said: "Friend, do not speak yet to any one of what you have
seen this night." And with these words she vanished away—leaving the
air filled with a delicious fragrance.

The monk by whom the foregoing legend was recorded, comments
upon it thus: The condition of a *yujō* is low and miserable, since she is
condemned to serve the lusts of men. Who therefore could imagine that
such a woman might be the *nirmanakaya*, or incarnation, of a
Bodhisattva. But we must remember that the Buddhas and the
Bodhisattvas may appear in this world in countless different forms;
choosing, for the purpose of their divine compassion, even the most
humble or contemptible shapes when such shapes can serve them to
lead men into the true path, and to save them from the perils of illusion.

The Corpse-Rider[37]

The body was cold as ice; the heart had long ceased to beat: yet
there were no other signs of death. Nobody even spoke of burying the
woman. She had died of grief and anger at having been divorced. It
would have been useless to bury her—because the last undying wish of
a dying person for vengeance can burst asunder any tomb and rift the
heaviest graveyard stone. People who lived near the house in which she
was lying fled from their homes. They knew that she was only *waiting
for the return of the man who had divorced her.*

At the time of her death he was on a journey. When he came back
and was told what had happened, terror seized him. "If I can find no
help before dark," he thought to himself, "she will tear me to pieces." It
was yet only the Hour of the Dragon;[38] but he knew that he had no time
to lose.

He went at once to an *inyōshi*[39] and begged for succor. The *inyōshi*
knew the story of the dead woman; and he had seen the body. He said
to the supplicant: "A very great danger threatens you. I will try to save
you. But you must promise to do whatever I shall tell you to do. There

---

[37] From the *Konséki-Monogatari.*

[38] *Tatsu no Koku*, or the Hour of the Dragon, by old Japanese time, began at about
eight o'clock in the morning.

[39] *Inyōshi*, a professor or master of the science of *in-yō*—the old Chinese nature-
philosophy, based upon the theory of a male and a female principle pervading the
universe.

is only one way by which you can be saved. It is a fearful way. But
unless you find the courage to attempt it, she will tear you limb from
limb. If you can be brave, come to me again in the evening before
sunset." The man shuddered; but he promised to do whatever should be
required of him.

At sunset the *inyōshi* went with him to the house where the body
was lying. The *inyōshi* pushed open the sliding-doors, and told his
client to enter. It was rapidly growing dark. "I dare not!" gasped the
man, quaking from head to foot; "I dare not even look at her!" "You
will have to do much more than look at her," declared the *inyōshi*; "and
you promised to obey. Go in!" He forced the trembler into the house
and led him to the side of the corpse.

The dead woman was lying on her face. "Now you must get astride
upon her," said the *inyōshi*, "and sit firmly on her back, as if you were
riding a horse. . . . Come!—you must do it!" The man shivered so that
the *inyōshi* had to support him—shivered horribly; but he obeyed.
"Now take her hair in your hands," commanded the *inyōshi*—"half in
the right hand, half in the left. . . . So! . . . You must grip it like a bridle.
Twist your hands in it—both hands—tightly. That is the way! . . .
Listen to me! You must stay like that till morning. You will have
reason to be afraid in the night—plenty of reason. But whatever may
happen, never let go of her hair. If you let go—even for one second—
she will tear you into gobbets!"
The *inyōshi* then whispered some mysterious words into the ear of
the body, and said to its rider: "Now, for my own sake, I must leave
you alone with her. . . . Remain as you are! . . . Above all things,
remember that you must not let go of her hair." And he went away—
closing the doors behind him.

Hour after hour the man sat upon the corpse in black fear; and the
hush of the night deepened and deepened about him till he screamed to
break it. Instantly the body sprang beneath him, as to cast him off; and
the dead woman cried out loudly, "Oh, how heavy it is! Yet I shall
bring that fellow here now!"
Then tall she rose, and leaped to the doors, and flung them open,
and rushed into the night—always bearing the weight of the man. But
he, shutting his eyes, kept his hands twisted in her long hair—tightly,
tightly—though fearing with such a fear that he could not even moan.
How far she went, he never knew. He saw nothing: he heard only the
sound of her naked feet in the dark—*picha-picha, picha-picha*—and
the hiss of her breathing as she ran.
At last she turned, and ran back into the house, and lay down upon
the floor exactly as at first. Under the man she panted and moaned till

the cocks began to crow. Thereafter she lay still.

But the man, with chattering teeth, sat upon her until the *inyōshi* came at sunrise. "So you did not let go of her hair!"—observed the *inyōshi*, greatly pleased. "That is well . . . Now you can stand up." He whispered again into the ear of the corpse, and then said to the man: "You must have passed a fearful night; but nothing else could have saved you. Hereafter you may feel secure from her vengeance."

The conclusion of this story I do not think to be morally satisfying. It is not recorded that the corpse-rider became insane, or that his hair turned white: we are told only that "he worshipped the *inyōshi* with tears of gratitude." A note appended to the recital is equally disappointing. "It is reported," the Japanese author says, "that a grandchild of the man [*who rode the corpse*] still survives, and that a grandson of the *inyōshi* is at this very time living in a village called Otokunoi-mura [*probably pronounced Otonoi-mura*]."

This village-name does not appear in any Japanese directory of tiday. But the names of many towns and villages have been changed since the foregoing story was written.

The Sympathy of Benten[40]

In Kyōto there is a famous temple called Amadera. Sadazumi Shinnō, the fifth son of the Emperor Seiwa, passed the greater part of his life there as a priest; and the graves of many celebrated persons are to be seen in the temple-grounds.

But the present edifice is not the ancient Amadera. The original temple, after the lapse of ten centuries, fell into such decay that it had to be entirely rebuilt in the fourteenth year of Genroku (1701 A. D.).

A great festival was held to celebrate the rebuilding of the Amadera; and among the thousands of persons who attended that festival there was a young scholar and poet named Hanagaki Baishū. He wandered about the newly-laid-out grounds and gardens, delighted by all that he saw, until he reached the place of a spring at which he had often drunk in former times. He was then surprised to find that the soil about the spring had been dug away, so as to form a square pond, and that at one corner of this pond there had been set up a wooden tablet bearing the words *Tanjō-Sui* ("Birth-Water").[41] He also saw that a small, but very handsome temple of the Goddess Benten had been erected beside the pond. While he was looking at this new temple, a

---

[40] The original story is in the *Otogi-Hyaku-Monogatari*

[41] The word *tanjō* (birth) should here be understood in its mystical Buddhist meaning of new life or rebirth, rather than in the western signification of birth.

sudden gust of wind blew to his feet a *tanzaku*,[42] on which the
following poem had been written:

Shirushi aréto
Iwai zo somuru
Tama hōki,
Toruté bakari no
Chigiri narétomo.

This poem—a poem on first love (*hatsu koi*), composed by the
famous Shunrei Kyō—was not unfamiliar to him; but it had been
written upon the *tanzaku* by a female hand, and so exquisitely that he
could scarcely believe his eyes. Something in the form of the
characters—an indefinite grace—suggested that period of youth
between childhood and womanhood; and the pure rich color of the ink
seemed to bespeak the purity and goodness of the writer's heart.[43]

Baishū carefully folded up the *tanzaku*, and took it home with him.
When he looked at it again the writing appeared to him even more
wonderful than at first. His knowledge in calligraphy assured him only
that the poem had been written by some girl who was very young, very
intelligent, and probably very gentle-hearted. But this assurance
sufficed to shape within his mind the image of a very charming person;
and he soon found himself in love with the unknown. Then his first
resolve was to seek out the writer of the verses, and, if possible, make
her his wife. . . . Yet how was he to find her? Who was she? Where did
she live? Certainly he could hope to find her only through the favor of
the Gods.

But presently it occurred to him that the Gods might be very
willing to lend their aid. The *tanzaku* had come to him while he was
standing in front of the temple of Benten-Sama; and it was to this
divinity in particular that lovers were wont to pray for happy union.
This reflection impelled him to beseech the Goddess for assistance. He
went at once to the temple of Benten-of-the-Birth-Water (*Tanjō-sui-no-
Benten*) in the grounds of the Amadera; and there, with all the fervor of

---

[42] *Tanzaku* is the name given to the long strips or ribbons of paper, usually colored,
upon which poems are written perpendicularly. Poems written upon *tanzaku* are
suspended to trees in flower, to wind-bells, to any beautiful object in which the poet has
found an inspiration.

[43] It is difficult for the inexperienced European eye to distinguish in Chinese or
Japanese writing those characteristics implied by our term "hand"—in the sense of
individual style. But the Japanese scholar never forgets the peculiarities of a handwriting
once seen; and he can even guess at the approximate age of the writer. Chinese and
Japanese authors claim that the color (quality) of the ink used tells something of the
character of the writer. As every person grounds or prepares his or her own ink, the
deeper and clearer black would at least indicate something of personal carefulness and of
the sense of beauty.

his heart, he made his petition: "O Goddess, pity me!—help me to find where the young person lives who wrote the *tanzaku*!—vouchsafe me but one chance to meet her—even if only for a moment!" And after having made this prayer, he began to perform a seven days' religious service (*nanuka-mairi*)[44] in honor of the Goddess; vowing at the same time to pass the seventh night in ceaseless worship before her shrine.

Now on the seventh night—the night of his vigil—during the hour when the silence is most deep, he heard at the main gateway of the temple-grounds a voice calling for admittance. Another voice from within answered; the gate was opened; and Baishū saw an old man of majestic appearance approaching with slow steps. This venerable person was clad in robes of ceremony; and he wore upon his snow-white head a black cap (*eboshi*) of the form indicating high rank. Reaching the little temple of Benten, he knelt down in front of it, as if respectfully awaiting some order. Then the outer door of the temple was opened; the hanging curtain of bamboo behind it, concealing the inner sanctuary, was rolled half-way up; and a *chigo*[45] came forward—a beautiful boy, with long hair tied back in the ancient manner. He stood at the threshold, and said to the old man in a clear loud voice:

"There is a person here who has been praying for a love-union not suitable to his present condition, and otherwise difficult to bring about. But as the young man is worthy of Our pity, you have been called to see whether something can be done for him. If there should prove to be any relation between the parties from the period of a former birth, you will introduce them to each other."

On receiving this command, the old man bowed respectfully to the *chigo*: then, rising, he drew from the pocket of his long left sleeve a crimson cord. One end of this cord he passed round Baishū's body, as if to bind him with it. The other end he put into the flame of one of the temple-lamps; and while the cord was there burning, he waved his hand three times, as if to summon somebody out of the dark.

Immediately, in the direction of the Amadera, a sound of coming steps was heard; and in another moment a girl appeared—a charming girl, fifteen or sixteen years old. She approached gracefully, but very shyly—hiding the lower part of her face with a fan; and she knelt down beside Baishū. The *chigo* then said to Baishū:

"Recently you have been suffering much heart-pain; and this desperate love of yours has even impaired your health. We could not

---

[44] There are many kinds of religious exercises called *mairi*. The performer of a *nanuka-mairi* pledges himself to pray at a certain temple every day for seven days in succession.

[45] The term *chigo* usually means the page of a noble household, especially an Imperial page. The *chigo* who appears in this story is of course a supernatural being—the court-messenger of the Goddess, and her mouthpiece.

allow you to remain in so unhappy a condition; and We therefore summoned the Old-Man-under-the-Moon[46] to make you acquainted with the writer of that *tanzaku*. She is now beside you."

With these words, the *chigo* retired behind the bamboo curtain. Then the old man went away as he had come; and the young girl followed him. Simultaneously Baishū heard the great bell of the Amadera sounding the hour of dawn. He prostrated himself in thanksgiving before the shrine of Benten-of-the-Birth-Water, and proceeded homeward—feeling as if awakened from some delightful dream—happy at having seen the charming person whom he had so fervently prayed to meet—unhappy also because of the fear that he might never meet her again.

But scarcely had he passed from the gateway into the street, when he saw a young girl walking alone in the same direction that he was going; and, even in the dusk of the dawn, he recognized her at once as the person to whom he had been introduced before the temple of Benten. As he quickened his pace to overtake her, she turned and saluted him with a graceful bow. Then for the first time he ventured to speak to her; and she answered him in a voice of which the sweetness filled his heart with joy. Through the yet silent streets they walked on, chatting happily, till they found themselves before the house where Baishū lived. There he paused—spoke to the girl of his hopes and fears. Smiling, she asked: "Do you not know that I was sent for to become your wife?" And she entered with him.

Becoming his wife, she delighted him beyond expectation by the charm of her mind and heart. Moreover, he found her to be much more accomplished than he had supposed. Besides being able to write so wonderfully, she could paint beautiful pictures; she knew the art of arranging flowers, the art of embroidery, the art of music; she could weave and sew; and she knew everything in regard to the management of a house.

It was in the early autumn that the young people had met; and they lived together in perfect accord until the winter season began. Nothing, during those months, occurred to disturb their peace. Baishū's love for his gentle wife only strengthened with the passing of time. Yet, strangely enough, he remained ignorant of her history—knew nothing about her family. Of such matters she had never spoken; and, as the Gods had given her to him, he imagined that it would not be proper to question her. But neither the Old-Man-under-the-Moon nor any one

---

[46] *Gekkawō.* This is a poetical appellation for the God of Marriage, more usually known as *Musubi-no-kami.* Throughout this story there is an interesting mingling of Shintō and Buddhist ideas.

else came—as he had feared—to take her away. Nobody even made any inquiries about her. And the neighbors, for some undiscoverable reason, acted as if totally unaware of her presence.

Baishū wondered at all this. But stranger experiences were awaiting him.

One winter morning he happened to be passing through a somewhat remote quarter of the city, when he heard himself loudly called by name, and saw a man-servant making signs to him from the gateway of a private residence. As Baishū did not know the man's face, and did not have a single acquaintance in that part of Kyōto, he was more than startled by so abrupt a summons. But the servant, coming forward, saluted him with the utmost respect, and said, "My master greatly desires the honor of speaking with you: deign to enter for a moment." After an instant of hesitation, Baishū allowed himself to be conducted to the house. A dignified and richly dressed person, who seemed to be the master, welcomed him at the entrance, and led him to the guest-room. When the courtesies due upon a first meeting had been fully exchanged, the host apologized for the informal manner of his invitation, and said:

"It must have seemed to you very rude of us to call you in such a way. But perhaps you will pardon our impoliteness when I tell you that we acted thus upon what I firmly believe to have been an inspiration from the Goddess Benten. Now permit me to explain.

"I have a daughter, about sixteen years old, who can write rather well,[47] and do other things in the common way: she has the ordinary nature of woman. As we were anxious to make her happy by finding a good husband for her, we prayed the Goddess Benten to help us; and we sent to every temple of Benten in the city a *tanzaku* written by the girl. Some nights later, the Goddess appeared to me in a dream, and said: 'We have heard your prayer, and have already introduced your daughter to the person who is to become her husband. During the coming winter he will visit you.' As I did not understand this assurance that a presentation had been made, I felt some doubt; I thought that the dream might have been only a common dream, signifying nothing. But last night again I saw Benten-Sama in a dream; and she said to me: 'To-morrow the young man, of whom I once spoke to you, will come to this street: then you can call him into your house, and ask him to become the husband of your daughter. He is a good young man; and later in life he will obtain a much higher rank than he now holds.' Then Benten-Sama told me your name, your age, your birthplace, and

---

[47] As it is the old Japanese rule that parents should speak depreciatingly of their children's accomplishments the phrase "rather well" in this connection would mean, for the visitor, "wonderfully well." For the same reason the expressions "common way" and "ordinary nature," as subsequently used, would imply almost the reverse of the literal meaning.

described your features and dress so exactly that my servant found no difficulty in recognizing you by the indications which I was able to give him."

This explanation bewildered Baishū instead of reassuring him; and his only reply was a formal return of thanks for the honor which the master of the house had spoken of doing him. But when the host invited him to another room, for the purpose of presenting him to the young lady, his embarrassment became extreme. Yet he could not reasonably decline the introduction. He could not bring himself, under such extraordinary circumstances, to announce that he already had a wife—a wife given to him by the Goddess Benten herself; a wife from whom he could not even think of separating. So, in silence and trepidation, he followed his host to the apartment indicated.

Then what was his amazement to discover, when presented to the daughter of the house, that she was the very same person whom he had already taken to wife!

The same—yet not the same.

She to whom he had been introduced by the Old-Man-under-the-Moon, was only the soul of the beloved.

She to whom he was now to be wedded, in her father's house, was the body.

Benten had wrought this miracle for the sake of her worshippers.

The original story breaks off suddenly at this point, leaving several matters unexplained. The ending is rather unsatisfactory. One would like to know something about the mental experiences of the real maiden during the married life of her phantom. One would also like to know what became of the phantom—whether it continued to lead an independent existence; whether it waited patiently for the return of its husband; whether it paid a visit to the real bride. And the book says nothing about these things. But a Japanese friend explains the miracle thus:

"The spirit-bride was really formed out of the *tanzaku*. So it is possible that the real girl did not know anything about the meeting at the temple of Benten. When she wrote those beautiful characters upon the *tanzaku*, something of her spirit passed into them. Therefore it was possible to evoke from the writing the double of the writer."

The Gratitude of the Samébito[48]

There was a man named Tawaraya Tōtarō, who lived in the Province of Ōmi. His house was situated on the shore of Lake Biwa, not far from the famous temple called Ishiyamadera. He had some property, and lived in comfort; but at the age of twenty-nine he was still unmarried. His greatest ambition was to marry a very beautiful woman; and he had not been able to find a girl to his liking.

One day, as he was passing over the Long Bridge of Séta,[49] he saw a strange being crouching close to the parapet. The body of this being resembled the body of a man, but was black as ink; its face was like the face of a demon; its eyes were green as emeralds; and its beard was like the beard of a dragon. Tōtarō was at first very much startled. But the green eyes looked at him so gently that after a moment's hesitation he ventured to question the creature. Then it answered him, saying: "I am a *Samébito*,[50]—a Shark-Man of the sea; and until a short time ago I was in the service of the Eight Great Dragon-Kings [*Hachi-Dai-Ryū-Ō*] as a subordinate officer in the Dragon-Palace [*Ryūgū*].[51] But because of a small fault which I committed, I was dismissed from the Dragon-Palace, and also banished from the Sea. Since then I have been wandering about here—unable to get any food, or even a place to lie down. If you can feel any pity for me, do, I beseech you, help me to find a shelter, and let me have something to eat!"

This petition was uttered in so plaintive a tone, and in so humble a manner, that Tōtarō's heart was touched. "Come with me," he said. "There is in my garden a large and deep pond where you may live as long as you wish; and I will give you plenty to eat."

The *Samébito* followed Tōtarō home, and appeared to be much pleased with the pond.

Thereafter, for nearly half a year, this strange guest dwelt in the pond, and was every day supplied by Tōtarō with such food as sea-creatures like.

---

[48] The original of this story may be found in the book called *Kibun-Anbaiyoshi*.

[49] The Long Bridge of Séta (*Séta-no-Naga-Hashi*), famous in Japanese legend, is nearly eight hundred feet in length, and commands a beautiful view. This bridge crosses the waters of the Setagawa near the junction of the stream with Lake Biwa. Ishiyamadera, one of the most picturesque Buddhist temples in Japan, is situated within a short distance from the bridge.

[50] Literally, "a Shark-Person," but in this story the *Samébito* is a male. The characters for *Samébito* can also be read *Kōjin*—which is the usual reading. In dictionaries the word is loosely rendered by "merman" or "mermaid;" but as the above description shows, the *Samébito* or *Kōjin* of the Far East is a conception having little in common with the Western idea of a merman or mermaid.

[51] *Ryūgū* is also the name given to the whole of that fairy-realm beneath the sea which figures in so many Japanese legends.

[From this point of the original narrative the Shark-Man is referred to, not as a monster, but as a sympathetic Person of the male sex.]

Now, in the seventh month of the same year, there was a female pilgrimage (*nyonin-mōdé*) to the great Buddhist temple called Miidera, in the neighboring town of Ōtsu; and Tōtarō went to Ōtsu to attend the festival. Among the multitude of women and young girls there assembled, he observed a person of extraordinary beauty. She seemed about sixteen years old; her face was fair and pure as snow; and the loveliness of her lips assured the beholder that their every utterance would sound "as sweet as the voice of a nightingale singing upon a plum-tree." Tōtarō fell in love with her at sight. When she left the temple he followed her at a respectful distance, and discovered that she and her mother were staying for a few days at a certain house in the neighboring village of Séta. By questioning some of the village folk, he was able also to learn that her name was Tamana; that she was unmarried; and that her family appeared to be unwilling that she should marry a man of ordinary rank—for they demanded as a betrothal-gift a casket containing ten thousand jewels.[52]

Tōtarō returned home very much dismayed by this information. The more that he thought about the strange betrothal-gift demanded by the girl's parents, the more he felt that he could never expect to obtain her for his wife. Even supposing that there were as many as ten thousand jewels in the whole country, only a great prince could hope to procure them.

But not even for a single hour could Tōtarō banish from his mind the memory of that beautiful being. It haunted him so that he could neither eat nor sleep; and it seemed to become more and more vivid as the days went by. And at last he became ill—so ill that he could not lift his head from the pillow. Then he sent for a doctor.

The doctor, after having made a careful examination, uttered an exclamation of surprise. "Almost any kind of sickness," he said, "can be cured by proper medical treatment, except the sickness of love. Your ailment is evidently love-sickness. There is no cure for it. In ancient times Rōya-Ō Hakuyo died of that sickness; and you must prepare yourself to die as he died." So saying, the doctor went away, without even giving any medicine to Tōtarō.

---

[52] *Tama* in the original. This word *tama* has a multitude of meanings; and as here used it is quite as indefinite as our own terms "jewel," "gem," or "precious stone." Indeed, it is more indefinite, for it signifies also a bead of coral, a ball of crystal, a polished stone attached to a hairpin, etc., etc. Later on, however, I venture to render it by "ruby,"—for reasons which need no explanation.

About this time the Shark-Man that was living in the garden-pond heard of his master's sickness, and came into the house to wait upon Tōtarō. And he tended him with the utmost affection both by day and by night. But he did not know either the cause or the serious nature of the sickness until nearly a week later, when Tōtarō, thinking himself about to die, uttered these words of farewell:

"I suppose that I have had the pleasure of caring for you thus long, because of some relation that grew up between us in a former state of existence. But now I am very sick indeed, and every day my sickness becomes worse; and my life is like the morning dew which passes away before the setting of the sun. For your sake, therefore, I am troubled in mind. Your existence has depended upon my care; and I fear that there will be no one to care for you and to feed you when I am dead. . . . My poor friend! . . . Alas! our hopes and our wishes are always disappointed in this unhappy world!"

No sooner had Tōtarō spoken these words than the Samébito uttered a strange wild cry of pain, and began to weep bitterly. And as he wept, great tears of blood streamed from his green eyes and rolled down his black cheeks and dripped upon the floor. And, falling, they were blood; but, having fallen, they became hard and bright and beautiful—became jewels of inestimable price, rubies splendid as crimson fire. For when men of the sea weep, their tears become precious stones.

Then Tōtarō, beholding this marvel, was so amazed and overjoyed that his strength returned to him. He sprang from his bed, and began to pick up and to count the tears of the Shark-Man, crying out the while: "My sickness is cured! I shall live! I shall live!"

Therewith, the Shark-Man, greatly astonished, ceased to weep, and asked Tōtarō to explain this wonderful cure; and Tōtarō told him about the young person seen at Miidera, and about the extraordinary marriage-gift demanded by her family. "As I felt sure," added Tōtarō, "that I should never be able to get ten thousand jewels, I supposed that my suit would be hopeless. Then I became very unhappy, and at last fell sick. But now, because of your generous weeping, I have many precious stones; and I think that I shall be able to marry that girl. Only—there are not yet quite enough stones; and I beg that you will be good enough to weep a little more, so as to make up the full number required."

But at this request the Samébito shook his head, and answered in a tone of surprise and of reproach:

"Do you think that I am like a harlot—able to weep whenever I wish? Oh, no! Harlots shed tears in order to deceive men; but creatures of the sea cannot weep without feeling real sorrow. I wept for you because of the true grief that I felt in my heart at the thought that you were going to die. But now I cannot weep for you, because you have told me that your sickness is cured."

"Then what am I to do?" plaintively asked Tōtarō. "Unless I can get ten thousand jewels, I cannot marry the girl!"

The Samébito remained for a little while silent, as if thinking. Then he said:

"Listen! Tiday I cannot possibly weep any more. But to-morrow let us go together to the Long Bridge of Séta, taking with us some wine and some fish. We can rest for a time on the bridge; and while we are drinking the wine and eating the fish, I shall gaze in the direction of the Dragon-Palace, and try, by thinking of the happy days that I spent there, to make myself feel homesick—so that I can weep."

Tōtarō joyfully assented.

Next morning the two, taking plenty of wine and fish with them, went to the Séta bridge, and rested there, and feasted. After having drunk a great deal of wine, the Samébito began to gaze in the direction of the Dragon-Kingdom, and to think about the past. And gradually, under the softening influence of the wine, the memory of happier days filled his heart with sorrow, and the pain of homesickness came upon him, so that he could weep profusely. And the great red tears that he shed fell upon the bridge in a shower of rubies; and Tōtarō gathered them as they fell, and put them into a casket, and counted them until he had counted the full number of ten thousand. Then he uttered a shout of joy.

Almost in the same moment, from far away over the lake, a delightful sound of music was heard; and there appeared in the offing, slowly rising from the waters, like some fabric of cloud, a palace of the color of the setting sun.

At once the Samébito sprang upon the parapet of the bridge, and looked, and laughed for joy. Then, turning to Tōtarō, he said:

"There must have been a general amnesty proclaimed in the Dragon-Realm; the Kings are calling me. So now I must bid you farewell. I am happy to have had one chance of befriending you in return for your goodness to me."

With these words he leaped from the bridge; and no man ever saw him again. But Tōtarō presented the casket of red jewels to the parents of Tamana, and so obtained her in marriage.

From A JAPANESE MISCELLANY

Of a Promise Kept[53]

"I shall return in the early autumn," said Akana Soyëmon several hundred years ago—when bidding good-bye to his brother by adoption, young Hasébé Samon. The time was spring; and the place was the village of Kato in the province of Harima. Akana was an Izumo samurai; and he wanted to visit his birthplace.

Hasébé said:

"Your Izumo—the Country of the Eight-Cloud Rising—is very distant. Perhaps it will therefore be difficult for you to promise to return here upon any particular day. But, if we were to know the exact day, we should feel happier. We could then prepare a feast of welcome; and we could watch at the gateway for your coming."

"Why, as for that," responded Akana, "I have been so much accustomed to travel that I can usually tell beforehand how long it will take me to reach a place; and I can safely promise you to be here upon a particular day. Suppose we say the day of the festival Chōyō?"

"That is the ninth day of the ninth month," said Hasébé; "then the chrysanthemums will be in bloom, and we can go together to look at them. How pleasant! . . . So you promise to come back on the ninth day of the ninth month?"

"On the ninth day of the ninth month," repeated Akana, smiling farewell. Then he strode away from the village of Kato in the province of Harima; and Hasébé Samon and the mother of Hasébé looked after him with tears in their eyes.

"Neither the Sun nor the Moon," says an old Japanese proverb, "ever halt upon their journey." Swiftly the months went by; and the autumn came—the season of chrysanthemums. And early upon the morning of the ninth day of the ninth month Hasébé prepared to welcome his adopted brother. He made ready a feast of good things, bought wine, decorated the guest-room, and filled the vases of the alcove with chrysanthemums of two colors. Then his mother, watching him, said: "The province of Izumo, my son, is more than one hundred ri[54] from this place; and the journey thence over the mountains is difficult and weary; and you cannot be sure that Akana will be able to come tiday. Would it not be better, before you take all this trouble, to wait for his coming?" "Nay, mother!" Hasébé made answer—"Akana promised to be here tiday: he could not break a promise! And if he

---

[53] Related in the *Ugétsu Monogatari.*
[54] A ri is about equal to two and a half English miles.

were to see us beginning to make preparation after his arrival, he would know that we had doubted his word; and we should be put to shame."

The day was beautiful, the sky without a cloud, and the air so pure that the world seemed to be a thousand miles wider than usual. In the morning many travelers passed through the village—some of them samurai; and Hasébé, watching each as he came, more than once imagined that he saw Akana approaching. But the temple-bells sounded the hour of midday; and Akana did not appear. Through the afternoon also Hasébé watched and waited in vain. The sun set; and still there was no sign of Akana. Nevertheless Hasébé remained at the gate, gazing down the road. Later his mother went to him, and said: "The mind of a man, my son—as our proverb declares—may change as quickly as the sky of autumn. But your chrysanthemum-flowers will still be fresh to-morrow. Better now to sleep; and in the morning you can watch again for Akana, if you wish." "Rest well, mother," returned Hasébé; "but I still believe that he will come." Then the mother went to her own room; and Hasébé lingered at the gate.

The night was pure as the day had been: all the sky throbbed with stars; and the white River of Heaven shimmered with unusual splendor. The village slept; the silence was broken only by the noise of a little brook, and by the faraway barking of peasants' dogs. Hasébé still waited—waited until he saw the thin moon sink behind the neighboring hills. Then at last he began to doubt and to fear. Just as he was about to re-enter the house, he perceived in the distance a tall man approaching—very lightly and quickly; and in the next moment he recognized Akana.

"Oh!" cried Hasébé, springing to meet him—"I have been waiting for you from the morning until now! . . . So you really did keep your promise after all. . . . But you must be tired, poor brother!—come in; everything is ready for you." He guided Akana to the place of honor in the guest-room, and hastened to trim the lights, which were burning low. "Mother," continued Hasébé, "felt a little tired this evening, and she has already gone to bed; but I shall awaken her presently." Akana shook his head, and made a little gesture of disapproval. "As you will, brother," said Hasébé; and he set warm food and wine before the traveler. Akana did not touch the food or the wine, but remained motionless and silent for a short time. Then, speaking in whisper—as if fearful of awakening the mother, he said:

"Now I must tell you how it happened that I came thus late. When I returned to Izumo I found that the people had almost forgotten the kindness of our former ruler, the good Lord Enya, and were seeking the favor of the usurper Tsunéhisa, who had possessed himself of the Tonda Castle. But I had to visit my cousin, Akana Tanji, though he had accepted service under Tsunéhisa, and was living, as a retainer, within the castle grounds. He persuaded me to present myself before Tsunéhisa: I yielded chiefly in order to observe the character of the new ruler, whose face I had never seen. He is a skilled soldier, and of great courage; but he is cunning and cruel. I found it necessary to let him know that I could never enter into his service. After I left his presence he ordered my cousin to detain me—to keep me confined within the house. I protested that I had promised to return to Harima upon the ninth day of the ninth month; but I was refused permission to go. I then hoped to escape from the castle at night; but I was constantly watched; and until tiday I could find no way to fulfill my promise . . ."

"Until tiday!" exclaimed Hasébé in bewilderment; "the castle is more than a hundred ri from here!"

"Yes," returned Akana; "and no living man can travel on foot a hundred ri in one day. But I felt that, if I did not keep my promise, you could not think well of me; and I remembered the ancient proverb, 'Tama yoku ichi nichi ni sen ri wo yuku' ['The soul of a man can journey a thousand ri in a day']. Fortunately I had been allowed to keep my sword; thus only was I able to come to you. . . . Be good to our mother."

With these words he stood up, and in the same instant disappeared.

Then Hasébé knew that Akana had killed himself in order to fulfill the promise.

At earliest dawn Hasébé Samon set out for the Castle Tonda, in the province of Izumo. Reaching Matsué, he there learned that, on the night of the ninth day of the ninth month, Akana Soyémon had performed harakiri in the house of Akana Tanji, in the grounds of the castle. Then Hasébé went to the house of Akana Tanji, and reproached Akana Tanji for the treachery done, and slew him in the midst of his family, and escaped without hurt. And when the Lord Tsunéhisa had heard the story, he gave commands that Hasébé should not be pursued. For, although an unscrupulous and cruel man himself, the Lord Tsunéhisa could respect the love of truth in others, and could admire the friendship and the courage of Hasébé Samon.

Of a Promise Broken[55]

I

"I am not afraid to die," said the dying wife; "there is only one thing that troubles me now. I wish that I could know who will take my place in this house."

"My dear one," answered the sorrowing husband, "nobody shall

---

[55] Izumo legend.

ever take your place in my home. I will never, never marry again."

At the time that he said this he was speaking out of his heart; for he loved the woman whom he was about to lose.

"On the faith of a samurai?" she questioned, with a feeble smile.

"On the faith of a samurai," he responded—stroking the pale thin face.

"Then, my dear one," she said, "you will let me be buried in the garden—will you not?—near those plum-trees that we planted at the further end? I wanted long ago to ask this; but I thought, that if you were to marry again, you would not like to have my grave so near you. Now you have promised that no other woman shall take my place; so I need not hesitate to speak of my wish. . . . I want so much to be buried in the garden! I think that in the garden I should sometimes hear your voice, and that I should still be able to see the flowers in the spring."

"It shall be as you wish," he answered. "But do not now speak of burial: you are not so ill that we have lost all hope."

"*I* have," she returned; "I shall die this morning. . . . But you will bury me in the garden?"

"Yes," he said—"under the shade of the plum-trees that we planted; and you shall have a beautiful tomb there."

"And will you give me a little bell?"

"Bell—?"

"Yes: I want you to put a little bell in the coffin—such a little bell as the Buddhist pilgrims carry. Shall I have it?"

"You shall have the little bell—and anything else that you wish."

"I do not wish for anything else," she said. . . . "My dear one, you have been very good to me always. Now I can die happy."

Then she closed her eyes and died—as easily as a tired child falls asleep. She looked beautiful when she was dead; and there was a smile upon her face.

She was buried in the garden, under the shade of the trees that she loved; and a small bell was buried with her. Above the grave was erected a handsome monument, decorated with the family crest, and bearing the kaimyô:

"Great   Elder   Sister,   Luminous-Shadow-of-the-Plum-Flower-Chamber, dwelling in the Mansion of the Great Sea of Compassion."

But, within a twelve-month after the death of his wife, the relatives and friends of the samurai began to insist that he should marry again. "You are still a young man," they said, "and an only son; and you have no children. It is the duty of a samurai to marry. If you die childless, who will there be to make the offerings and to remember the ancestors?"

By many such representations he was at last persuaded to marry again. The bride was only seventeen years old; and he found that he could love her dearly, notwithstanding the dumb reproach of the tomb in the garden.

II

Nothing took place to disturb the happiness of the young wife until the seventh day after the wedding—when her husband was ordered to undertake certain duties requiring his presence at the castle by night. On the first evening that he was obliged to leave her alone, she felt uneasy in a way that she could not explain—vaguely afraid without knowing why. When she went to bed she could not sleep. There was a strange oppression in the air—an indefinable heaviness like that which sometimes precedes the coming of a storm.

About the Hour of the Ox she heard, outside in the night, the clanging of a bell—a Buddhist pilgrim's bell; and she wondered what pilgrim could be passing through the samurai quarter at such a time. Presently, after a pause, the bell sounded much nearer. Evidently the pilgrim was approaching the house; but why approaching from the rear, where no road was? . . . Suddenly the dogs began to whine and howl in an unusual and horrible way; and a fear came upon her like the fear of dreams. . . . That ringing was certainly in the garden. . . . She tried to get up to waken a servant. But she found that she could not rise—could not move—could not call. . . . And nearer, and still more near, came the clang of the bell; and oh! how the dogs howled! . . . Then, lightly as a shadow steals, there glided into the room a Woman—though every door stood fast, and every screen unmoved—a Woman robed in a grave-robe, and carrying a pilgrim's bell. Eyeless she came—because she had long been dead; and her loosened hair streamed down about her face; and she looked without eyes through the tangle of it, and spoke without a tongue:

"Not in this house—not in this house shall you stay! Here I am mistress still. You shall go; and you shall tell to none the reason of your going. If you tell HIM, I will tear you into pieces!"

So speaking, the haunter vanished. The bride became senseless with fear. Until the dawn she so remained.

Nevertheless, in the cheery light of day, she doubted the reality of what she had seen and heard. The memory of the warning still weighed upon her so heavily that she did not dare to speak of the vision, either to her husband or to any one else; but she was almost able to persuade herself that she had only dreamed an ugly dream, which had made her ill.

On the following night, however, she could not doubt. Again, at the Hour of the Ox, the dogs began to howl and whine; again the bell resounded—approaching slowly from the garden; again the listener vainly strove to rise and call; again the dead came into the room, and hissed:

"You shall go; and you shall tell to no one why you must go! If you even whisper it to HIM, I will tear you in pieces!" . . .

This time the haunter came close to the couch—and bent and muttered and mowed above it. . . .

Next morning, when the samurai returned from the castle, his young wife prostrated herself before him in supplication:

"I beseech you," she said, "to pardon my ingratitude and my great rudeness in thus addressing you: but I want to go home; I want to go away at once."

"Are you not happy here?" he asked, in sincere surprise. "Has any one dared to be unkind to you during my absence?"

"It is not that—" she answered, sobbing. "Everybody here has been only too good to me. . . . But I cannot continue to be your wife; I must go away. . . ."

"My dear," he exclaimed, in great astonishment, "it is very painful to know that you have had any cause for unhappiness in this house. But I cannot even imagine why you should want to go away—unless somebody has been very unkind to you. . . . Surely you do not mean that you wish for a divorce?"

She responded, trembling and weeping, —

"If you do not give me a divorce, I shall die!"

He remained for a little while silent—vainly trying to think of some cause for this amazing declaration. Then, without betraying any emotion, he made answer:

"To send you back now to your people, without any fault on your part, would seem a shameful act. If you will tell me a good reason for your wish—any reason that will enable me to explain matters honorably—I can write you a divorce. But unless you give me a reason, a good reason, I will not divorce you—for the honor of our house must be kept above reproach."

And then she felt obliged to speak; and she told him everything— adding, in an agony of terror:

"Now that I have let you know, she will kill me!—she will kill me! . . ."

Although a brave man, and little inclined to believe in phantoms, the samurai was more than startled for the moment. But a simple and natural explanation of the matter soon presented itself to his mind.

"My dear," he said, "you are now very nervous; and I fear that some one has been telling you foolish stories. I cannot give you a divorce merely because you have had a bad dream in this house. But I am very sorry indeed that you should have been suffering in such a way during my absence. Tonight, also, I must be at the castle; but you shall not be alone. I will order two of the retainers to keep watch in your room; and you will be able to sleep in peace. They are good men; and they will take all possible care of you."

Then he spoke to her so considerately and so affectionately that she became almost ashamed of her terrors, and resolved to remain in the house.

III

The two retainers left in charge of the young wife were big, brave, simple-hearted men—experienced guardians of women and children. They told the bride pleasant stories to keep her cheerful. She talked with them a long time, laughed at their good-humored fun, and almost forgot her fears. When at last she lay down to sleep, the men-at-arms took their places in a corner of the room, behind a screen, and began a game of go[56]—speaking only in whispers, that she might not be disturbed. She slept like an infant.

But again at the Hour of the Ox she awoke with a moan of terror—for she heard the bell! . . . It was already near, and was coming nearer. She started up; she screamed; but in the room there was no stir—only a silence as of death—a silence growing—a silence thickening. She rushed to the men-at-arms: they sat before their checker-table—motionless—each staring at the other with fixed eyes. She shrieked to them: she shook them: they remained as if frozen. . . .

Afterwards they said that they had heard the bell—heard also the cry of the bride—even felt her try to shake them into wakefulness; and that, nevertheless, they had not been able to move or speak. From the same moment they had ceased to hear or to see: a black sleep had seized upon them.

Entering his bridal-chamber at dawn, the samurai beheld, by the light of a dying lamp, the headless body of his young wife, lying in a pool of blood. Still squatting before their unfinished game, the two retainers slept. At their master's cry they sprang up, and stupidly stared at the horror on the floor. . . .

The head was nowhere to be seen; and the hideous wound showed that it had not been cut off, but *torn off*. A trail of blood led from the chamber to an angle of the outer gallery, where the storm-doors

---

[56] A game resembling draughts, but much more complicated.

appeared to have been riven apart. The three men followed that trail into the garden—over reaches of grass—over spaces of sand—along the bank of an iris-bordered pond—under heavy shadowings of cedar and bamboo. And suddenly, at a turn, they found themselves face to face with a nightmare-thing that chippered like a bat: the figure of the long-buried woman, erect before her tomb—in one hand clutching a bell, in the other the dripping head. . . . For a moment the three stood numbed. Then one of the men-at-arms, uttering a Buddhist invocation, drew, and struck at the shape. Instantly it crumbled down upon the soil—an empty scattering of grave-rags, bones, and hair; and the bell rolled clanking out of the ruin. But the fleshless right hand, though parted from the wrist, still writhed; and its fingers still gripped at the bleeding head—and tore, and mangled—as the claws of the yellow crab cling fast to a fallen fruit. . . .

"That is a wicked story," I said to the friend who had related it. "The vengeance of the dead—if taken at all—should have been taken upon the man."

"Men think so," he made answer. "But that is not the way that a woman feels. . . ."

He was right.

Before the Supreme Court

The great Buddhist priest, Mongaku Shōnin, says in his book Kyō-gyō Shin-shō:

"Many of those gods whom the people worship are unjust gods [*jajin*]: therefore such gods are not worshipped by persons who revere the Three Precious Things. And even persons who obtain favors from those gods, in answer to prayer, usually find at a later day that such favors cause misfortune."

This truth is well exemplified by a story recorded in the book Nihon-Rei-Iki.

During the time of the Emperor Shōmu there lived in the district called Yamadagori, in the province of Sanuki, a man named Fushiki no Shin. He had but one child, a daughter called Kinumé. Kinumé was a fine-looking girl, and very strong; but, shortly after she had reached her eighteenth year, a dangerous sickness began to prevail in that part of the country, and she was attacked by it. Her parents and friends then made offerings on her behalf to a certain Pest-God, and performed great austerities in honor of the Pest-God—beseeching him to save her.

After having lain in a stupor for several days, the sick girl one evening came to herself, and told her parents a dream that she had dreamed. She had dreamed that the Pest-God appeared to her, and said: "Your people have been praying to me so earnestly for you, and have been worshipping me so devoutly, that I really wish to save you. But I cannot do so except by giving you the life of some other person. Do you happen to know of any other girl who has the same name as yours?" "I remember," answered Kinumé, "that in Utarigori there is a girl whose name is the same as mine." "Point her out to me," the God said, touching the sleeper; and at the touch she rose into the air with him; and, in less than a second, the two were in front of the house of the other Kinumé, in Utarigori. It was night; but the family had not yet gone to bed, and the daughter was washing something in the kitchen. "That is the girl," said Kinumé of Yamadagori. The Pest-God took out of a scarlet bag at his girdle a long sharp instrument shaped like a chisel; and, entering the house, he drove the sharp instrument into the forehead of Kinumé of Utarigori. Then Kinumé of Utarigori sank to the floor in great agony; and Kinumé of Yamadagori awoke, and related the dream.

Immediately after having related it, however, she again fell into a stupor. For three days she remained without knowledge of the world; and her parents began to despair of her recovery. Then once more she opened her eyes, and spoke. But almost in the same moment she rose from her bed, looked wildly about the room, and rushed out of the house, exclaiming: "This is not my home!—you are not my parents!" . . .

Something strange had happened.

Kinumé of Utarigori had died after having been stricken by the Pest-God. Her parents sorrowed greatly; and the priests of their parish-temple performed a Buddhist service for her; and her body was burned in a field outside the village. Then her spirit descended to the Meido, the world of the dead, and was summoned to the tribunal of Emma-Dai-Ō—the King and Judge of Souls. But no sooner had the Judge cast eyes upon her than he exclaimed: "This girl is the Utarigori-Kinumé: she ought not to have been brought here so soon! Send her back at once to the Shaba-world, and fetch me the other Kinumé—the Yamadagori girl!" Then the spirit of Kinumé of Utarigori made moan before King Emma, and complained, saying: "Great Lord, it is more than three days since I died; and by this time my body must have been burned; and, if you now send me back to the Shaba-world, what shall I do? My body has been changed into ashes and smoke; I shall have no body!" "Do not be anxious," the terrible King answered; "I am going to give you the body of Kinumé of Yamadagori—for her spirit must be brought here to me at once. You need not fret about the burning of your body: you will find the body of the other Kinumé very much better." And scarcely had he finished speaking when the spirit of Kinumé of Utarigori revived in the body of Kinumé of Yamadagori.

Now when the parents of Kinumé of Yamadagori saw their sick girl spring up and run away, exclaiming, "This is not my home!"-they imagined her to be out of her mind, and they ran after her, calling out: "Kinumé, where are you going?-wait for a moment, child! you are much too ill to run like that!" But she escaped from them, and ran on without stopping, until she came to Utarigori, and to the house of the family of the dead Kinumé. There she entered, and found the old people; and she saluted them, crying: "Oh, how pleasant to be again at home! . . . Is it well with you, dear parents?" They did not recognize her, and thought her mad; but the mother spoke to her kindly, asking: "Where have you come from, child?" "From the Meido I have come," Knume made answer. "I am your own child, Kinumé, returned to you from the dead. But I have now another body, mother." And she related all that had happened; and the old people wondered exceedingly, yet did not know what to believe. Presently the parents of Kinumé of Yamadagori also came to the house, looking for their daughter; and then the two fathers and the two mothers consulted together, and made the girl repeat her story, and questioned her over and over again. But she replied to every question in such a way that the truth of her statements could not be doubted. At last the mother of the Yamadagori Kinumé, after having related the strange dream which her sick daughter had dreamed, said to the parents of the Utarigori Kinumé: "We are satisfied that the spirit of this girl is the spirit of your child. But you know that her body is the body of our child; and we think that both families ought to have a share in her. So we would ask you to agree that she be considered hence-forward the daughter of both families." To this proposal the Utarigori parents joyfully consented; and it is recorded that in after-time Kinumé inherited the property of both households.

"This story," says the Japanese author of the Bukkyō Hyakkwa Zenshō, "may be found on the left side of the twelfth sheet of the first volume of the Nihon-Rei-Iki."

The Story of Kwashin Koji

During the period of Tenshō there lived, in one of the northern districts of Kyoto, an old man whom the people called Kwashin Koji. He wore a long white beard, and was always dressed like a Shinto priest; but he made his living by exhibiting Buddhist pictures and by preaching Buddhist doctrine. Every fine day he used to go to the grounds of the temple Gion, and there suspend to some tree a large kakemono on which were depicted the punishments of the various hells. This kakemono was so wonderfully painted that all things represented in it seemed to be real; and the old man would discourse to the people crowding to see it, and explain to them the Law of Cause and Effect—pointing out with a Buddhist staff [nyoi], which he always carried, each detail of the different torments, and exhorting everybody to follow the teachings of the Buddha. Multitudes assembled to look at the picture and to hear the old man preach about it; and sometimes the mat which he spread before him, to receive contributions, was covered out of sight by the heaping of coins thrown upon it.

Oda Nobunaga was at that time ruler of Kyōto and of the surrounding provinces. One of his retainers, named Arakawa, during a visit to the temple of Gion, happened to see the picture being displayed there; and he afterwards talked about it at the palace. Nobunaga was interested by Arakawa's description, and sent orders to Kwashin Koji to come at once to the palace, and to bring the picture with him.

When Nobunaga saw the kakemono he was not able to conceal his surprise at the vividness of the work: the demons and the tortured spirits actually appeared to move before his eyes; and he heard voices crying out of the picture; and the blood there represented seemed to be really flowing—so that he could not help putting out his finger to feel if the painting was wet. But the finger was not stained, -for the paper proved to be perfectly dry. More and more astonished, Nobunaga asked who had made the wonderful picture. Kwashin Koji answered that it had been painted by the famous Oguri Sōtan—after he had performed the rite of self-purification every day for a hundred days, and practiced great austerities, and made earnest prayer for inspiration to the divine Kwannon of Kiyomidzu Temple.

Observing Nobunaga's evident desire to possess the kakemono, Arakawa then asked Kwashin Koji whether he would "offer it up," as a gift to the great lord. But the old man boldly answered: "This painting is the only object of value that I possess; and I am able to make a little money by showing it to the people. Were I now to present this picture to the lord, I should deprive myself of the only means which I have to make my living. However, if the lord be greatly desirous to possess it, let him pay me for it the sum of one hundred ryō of gold. With that amount of money I should be able to engage in some profitable business. Otherwise, I must refuse to give up the picture."

Nobunaga did not seem to be pleased at this reply; and he remained silent. Arakawa presently whispered something in the ear of the lord, who nodded assent; and Kwashin Koji was then dismissed, with a small present of money.

But when the old man left the palace, Arakawa secretly followed him—hoping for a chance to get the picture by foul means. The chance came; for Kwashin Koji happened to take a road leading directly to the heights beyond the town. When he reached a certain lonesome spot at the foot of the hills, where the road made a sudden turn, he was seized by Arakawa, who said to him: "Why were you so greedy as to ask a hundred ryō of gold for that picture? Instead of a hundred ryō of gold, I am now going to give you one piece of iron three feet long." Then Arakawa drew his sword, and killed the old man, and took the picture.

The next day Arakawa presented the kakemono—still wrapped up as Kwashin Koji had wrapped before leaving the palace—to Oda Nobunaga, who ordered it to be hung up forthwith. But, when it was unrolled, both Nobunaga and his retainer were astounded to find that there was no picture at all—nothing but a blank surface. Arakawa could not explain how the original painting had disappeared; and as he had been guilty—whether willingly or unwillingly—of deceiving his master, it was decided that he should be punished. Accordingly he was sentenced to remain in confinement for a considerable time.

Scarcely had Arakawa completed his term of imprisonment, when news was brought to him that Kwashin Koji was exhibiting the famous picture in the grounds of Kitano Temple. Arakawa could hardly believe his ears; but the information inspired him with a vague hope that he might be able, in some way or other, to secure the kakemono, and thereby redeem his recent fault. So he quickly assembled some of his followers, and hurried to the temple; but when he reached it he was told that Kwashin Koji had gone away.

Several days later, word was brought to Arakawa that Kwashin Koji was exhibiting the picture at Kiyomidzu Temple, and preaching about it to an immense crowd. Arakawa made all haste to Kiyomidzu; but he arrived there only in time to see the crowd disperse, -for Kwashin Koji had again disappeared.

At last one day Arakawa unexpectedly caught sight of Kwashin Koji in a wine-shop, and there captured him. The old man only laughed good-humoredly on finding himself seized, and said: -I will go with you; but please wait until I drink a little wine." To this request Arakawa made no objection; and Kwashin Koji thereupon drank, to the amazement of the bystanders, twelve bowls of wine. After drinking the twelfth he declared himself satisfied; and Arakawa ordered him to be bound with a rope, and taken to Nobunaga's residence.

In the court of the palace Kwashin Koji was examined at once by the Chief Officer, and sternly reprimanded. Finally the Chief Officer said to him: "It is evident that you have been deluding people by magical practices; and for this offence alone you deserve to be heavily punished. However, if you will now respectfully offer up that picture to the Lord Nobunaga, we shall this time overlook your fault. Otherwise we shall certainly inflict upon you a very severe punishment."

At this menace Kwashin Koji laughed in a bewildered way, and exclaimed: "It is not I who have been guilty of deluding people." Then, turning to Arakawa, he cried out: "You are the deceiver! You wanted to flatter the lord by giving him that picture; and you tried to kill me in order to steal it. Surely, if there be any such thing as crime, that was a crime! As luck would have it, you did not succeed in killing me; but if you had succeeded, as you wished, what would you have been able to plead in excuse for such an act? You stole the picture, at all events. The picture that I now have is only a copy. And after you stole the picture, you changed your mind about giving it to Lord Nobunaga; and you devised a plan to keep it for yourself. So you gave a blank kakemono to Lord Nobunaga; and, in order to conceal your secret act and purpose, you pretended that I had deceived you by substituting a blank kakemono for the real one. Where the real picture now is, I do not know. You probably do."

At these words Arakawa became so angry that he rushed towards the prisoner, and would have struck him but for the interference of the guards. And this sudden outburst of anger caused the Chief Officer to suspect that Arakawa was not altogether innocent. He ordered Kwashin Koji to be taken to prison for the time being; and he then proceeded to question Arakawa closely. Now Arakawa was naturally slow of speech; and on this occasion, being greatly excited, he could scarcely speak at all; and he stammered, and contradicted himself, and betrayed every sign of guilt. Then the Chief Officer ordered that Arakawa should be beaten with a stick until he told the truth. But it was not possible for him even to seem to tell the truth. So he was beaten with a bamboo until his senses departed from him, and he lay as if dead.

Kwashin Koji was told in the prison about what had happened to Arakawa; and he laughed. But after a little while he said to the jailer: "Listen! That fellow Arakawa really behaved like a rascal; and I purposely brought this punishment upon him, in order to correct his evil inclinations. But now please say to the Chief Officer that Arakawa must have been ignorant of the truth, and that I shall explain the whole matter satisfactorily."

Then Kwashin Koji was again taken before the Chief Officer, to whom he made the following declaration: "In any picture of real excellence there must be a ghost; and such a picture, having a will of its own, may refuse to be separated from the person who gave it life, even from its rightful owner. There are many stories to prove that really great pictures have souls. It is well known that some sparrows, painted upon a sliding-screen [fusuma] by Hōgen Yenshin, once flew away, leaving blank the spaces which they had occupied upon the surface. Also it is well known that a horse, painted upon a certain kakemono, used to go out at night to eat grass. Now, in this present case, I believe the truth to be that, inasmuch as the Lord Nobunaga never became the rightful owner of my kakemono, the picture voluntarily vanished from the paper when it was unrolled in his presence. But if you will give me the price that I first asked, -one hundred ryō of gold, -I think that the painting will then reappear, of its own accord, upon the now blank paper. At all events, let us try! There is nothing to risk—since, if the picture does not reappear, I shall at once return the money."

On hearing of these strange assertions, Nobunaga ordered the hundred ryō to be paid, and came in person to observe the result. The kakemono was then unrolled before him; and, to the amazement of all present, the painting reappeared, with all its detail. But the colors seemed to have faded a little; and the figures of the souls and the demons did not look really alive, as before. Perceiving this difference, the lord asked Kwashin Koji to explain the reason of it; and Kwashin Koji replied: "The value of the painting, as you first saw it, was the value of a painting beyond all price. But the value of the painting, as you now see it, represents exactly what you paid for it—one hundred ryō of gold. . . . How could it be otherwise?" On hearing this answer, all present felt that it would be worse than useless to oppose the old man any further. He was immediately set at liberty; and Arakawa was also liberated, as he had more than expiated his fault by the punishment which he had undergone.

Now Arakawa had a younger brother named Buichi—also a retainer in the service of Nobunaga. Buichi was furiously angry because Arakawa had been beaten and imprisoned; and he resolved to kill Kwashin Koji. Kwashin Koji no sooner found himself again at liberty than he went straight to a wine-shop, and called for wine. Buichi rushed after him into the shop, struck him down, and cut off his head. Then, taking the hundred ryō that had been paid to the old man, Buichi wrapped up the head and the gold together in a cloth, and hurried home to show them to Arakawa. But when he unfastened the cloth he found, instead of the head, only an empty wine-gourd, and only a lump of filth instead of the gold. . . . And the bewilderment of the brothers was presently increased by the information that the headless body had disappeared from the wine-shop—none could say how or when.

Nothing more was heard of Kwashin Koji until about a month later, when a drunken man was found one evening asleep in the gateway of Lord Nobunaga's palace, and snoring so loud that every snore sounded like the rumbling of distant thunder. A retainer discovered that the drunkard was Kwashin Koji. For this insolent offence, the old fellow was at once seized and thrown into the prison.

But he did not awake; and in the prison he continued to sleep without interruption for ten days and ten nights—all the while snoring so that the sound could be heard to a great distance.

About this time, the Lord Nobunaga came to his death through the treachery of one of his captains, Akéchi Mitsuhidé, who thereupon usurped rule. But Mitsuhidé's power endured only for a period of twelve days.

Now when Mitsuhidé became master of Kyoto, he was told of the case of Kwashin Koji; and he ordered that the prisoner should be brought before him. Accordingly Kwashin Koji was summoned into the presence of the new lord; but Mitsuhidé spoke to him kindly, treated him as a guest, and commanded that a good dinner should be served to him. When the old man had eaten, Mitsuhidé said to him: "I have heard that you are very fond of wine; -how much wine can you drink at a single sitting?" Kwashin Koji answered: "I do not really know how much; I stop drinking only when I feel intoxication coming on." Then the lord set a great wine-cup[57] before Kwashin Koji, and told a servant to fill the cup as often as the old man wished. And Kwashin Koji emptied the great cup ten times in succession, and asked for more; but the servant made answer that the wine-vessel was exhausted. All present were astounded by this drinking-feat; and the lord asked Kwashin Koji, "Are you not yet satisfied, Sir?" "Well, yes," replied Kwashin Koji, "I am somewhat satisfied; and now, in return for your august kindness, I shall display a little of my art. Be therefore so good as to observe that screen." He pointed to a large eight-folding screen upon which were painted the Eight Beautiful Views of the Lake of Omi (Omi-Hakkei); and everybody looked at the screen. In one of the views the artist had represented, far away on the lake, a man rowing a boat— the boat occupying, upon the surface of the screen, a space of less than an inch in length. Kwashin Koji then waved his hand in the direction of the boat; and all saw the boat suddenly turn, and begin to move toward the foreground of the picture. It grew rapidly larger and larger as it approached; and presently the features of the boatman became clearly distinguishable. Still the boat drew nearer—always becoming larger— until it appeared to be only a short distance away. And, all of a sudden, the water of the lake seemed to overflow—out of the picture into the room; -and the room was flooded; and the spectators girded up their robes in haste, as the water rose above their knees. In the same moment the boat appeared to glide out of the screen, -a real fishing-boat; -and the creaking of the single oar could be heard. Still the flood in the room

---

[57] The term "bowl" would better indicate the kind of vessel to which the storyteller refers. Some of the so-called cups, used on festival occasions, were very large—shallow lacquered basins capable of holding considerably more than a quart. To empty one of the largest size, at a draught, was considered no small feat.

continued to rise until the spectators were standing up to their girdles in water. Then the boat came close up to Kwashin Koji; and Kwashin Koji climbed into it; and the boatman turned about, and began to row away very swiftly. And, as the boat receded, the water in the room began to lower rapidly, -seeming to ebb back into the screen. No sooner had the boat passed the apparent foreground of the picture than the room was dry again! But still the painted vessel appeared to glide over the painted water, -retreating further into the distance, and ever growing smaller, till at last it dwindled to a dot in the offing. And then it disappeared altogether; and Kwashin Koji disappeared with it. He was never again seen in Japan.

The Story of Umétsu Chūbei[58]

Umétsu Chūbei was a young samurai of great strength and courage. He was in the service of the Lord Tomura Jūdayū, whose castle stood upon a lofty hill in the neighborhood of Yokoté, in the province of Dewa. The houses of the lord's retainers formed a small town at the base of the hill.

Umétsu was one of those selected for night-duty at the castle-gates. There were two night-watches; the first beginning at sunset and ending at midnight; the second beginning at midnight and ending at sunrise.

Once, when Umétsu happened to be on the second watch, he met with a strange adventure. While ascending the hill at midnight, to take his place on guard, he perceived a woman standing at the last upper turn of the winding road leading to the castle. She appeared to have a child in her arms, and to be waiting for somebody. Only the most extraordinary circumstances could account for the presence of a woman in that lonesome place at so late an hour; and Umétsu remembered that goblins were wont to assume feminine shapes after dark, in order to deceive and destroy men. He therefore doubted whether the seeming woman before him was really a human being; and when he saw her hasten towards him, as if to speak, he intended to pass her by without a word. But he was too much surprised to do so when the woman called him by name, and said, in a very sweet voice: "Good Sir Umétsu, tonight I am in great trouble, and I have a most painful duty to perform: will you not kindly help me by holding this baby for one little moment?" And she held out the child to him.

Umétsu did not recognize the woman, who appeared to be very young: he suspected the charm of the strange voice, suspected a supernatural snare, suspected everything; but he was naturally kind; and he felt that it would be unmanly to repress a kindly impulse through fear of goblins. Without replaying, he took the child. "Please

---

[58] Related in the Bukkyō-Hyakkwa-Zenshō.

hold it till I come back," said the woman: "I shall return in a very little while." "I will hold it," he answered; and immediately the woman turned from him, and, leaving the road, sprang soundlessly down the hill so lightly and so quickly that he could scarcely believe his eyes. She was out of sight in a few seconds.

Umétsu the first looked at the child. It was very small, and appeared to have been just born. It was very still in his hands; and it did not cry at all.

Suddenly it seemed to be growing larger. He looked at it again. . . . No: it was the same small creature; and it had not even moved. Why had he imagined that it was growing larger?

In another moment he knew why; and he felt a chill strike through him. The child was not growing larger; *but it was growing heavier.* . . . At first it had seemed to weight only seven or eight pounds: then its weight had gradually doubled—tripled—quadrupled. Now it could not weigh less than fifty pounds; and still it was getting heavier and heavier. . . . A hundred pounds!—a hundred and fifty!—two hundred! . . . Umétsu knew that he had been deluded—that he had not been speaking with any mortal woman—that the child was not human. But he had made a promise; and a samurai was bound by his promise. So he kept the infant in his arms; and it continued to grow heavier and heavier. . . two hundred and fifty!—three hundred!—four hundred pounds! . . . What was going to happen he could not imagine; but he resolved not to be afraid, and not to let the child go while his strength lasted. . . . Five hundred!—five hundred and fifty!—six hundred pounds! All his muscles began to quiver with the strain; and still the weight increased. . . . "Namu Amida Butsu!" he groaned—"Namu Amida Butsu!—Namu Amida Butsu!" Even as he uttered the holy invocation for the third time, the weight passed away from him with a shock; and he stood stupefied, with empty hands—for the child had unaccountably disappeared. But almost in the same instant he saw the mysterious woman returning as quickly as she had gone. Still panting she came to him; and he then first saw that she was very fair; but her brow dripped with sweat; and her sleeves were bound back with tasuki-cords, as if she had been working hard.

"Kind Sir Umétsu," she said, "you do not know how great a service you have done me. I am the Ujigami[59] of this place; and tonight one of my Ujiko found herself in the pains of childbirth, and prayed to me for aid. But the labor proved to be very difficult; and I soon saw that, by my own power alone, I might not be able to save her: therefore I sought for the help of your strength and courage. And the child that I

---

[59] Ujigami is the title given to the tutelary Shintō divinity of a parish or district. All persons living in that parish of district, and assisting in the maintenance of the temple (miya) of the deity, are call "Ujiko."

laid in your hands was the child that had not yet been born; and in the time that you first felt the child becoming heavier and heavier, the danger was very great—for the Gates of Birth were closed. And when you felt the child become so heavy that you despaired of being able to bear the weight much longer—in that same moment the mother seemed to be dead, and the family wept for her. Then you three times repeated the prayer, Namu Amida Butsu!—and the third time that you uttered it the power of the Lord Buddha came to our aid, and the Gates of Birth were opened. . . . And for that which you have done you shall be fitly rewarded. To a brave samurai no gift can be more serviceable than strength: therefore, not only to you, but likewise to your children and to your children's children, great strength shall be given."

And, with this promise, the divinity disappeared.

Umétsu Chūbei, wondering greatly, resumed his way to the castle. At sunrise, on being relieved from duty, he proceeded as usual to wash his face and hands before making his morning prayer. But when he began to wring the towel which had served him, he was surprised to feel the tough material snap asunder in his hands. He attempted to twist together the separated portions; and again the stuff parted—like so much wet paper. He tried to wring the four thicknesses; and the result was the same. Presently, after handling various objects of bronze and of iron which yielded to his touch like clay, he understood that he had come into full possession of the great strength promised, and that he would have to be careful thenceforward when touching things, lest they should crumble in his fingers.

On returning home, he made inquiry as to whether any child had been born in the settlement during the night. Then he learned that a birth had actually taken place at the very hour of his adventure, and that the circumstances had been exactly as related to him by the Ujigami.

The children of Umétsu Chūbei inherited their father's strength. Several of his descendants—all remarkably powerful men—were still living in the province of Dewa at the time when this story was written.

From KOTTO

The Legend of Yurei-Daki

Near the village of Kurosaka, in the province of Hōki, there is a waterfall called Yurei-Daki, or The Cascade of Ghosts. Why it is so called I do not know. Near the foot of the fall there is a small Shintō shrine of the god of the locality, whom the people name Taki-Daimyōjin; and in front of the shrine is a little wooden money-box—*saisen-bako*—to receive the offerings of believers. And there is a story about that money-box.

One icy winter's evening, thirty-five years ago, the women and girls employed at a certain asa-toriba, or hemp-factory, in Kurosaka, gathered around the big brazier in the spinning-room after their day's work had been done. Then they amused themselves by telling ghost-stories. By the time that a dozen stories had been told, most of the gathering felt uncomfortable; and a girl cried out, just to heighten the pleasure of fear, "Only think of going this night, all by one's self, to the Yurei-Daki!" The suggestion provoked a general scream, followed by nervous bursts of laughter. . . . "I'll give all the hemp I spun today," mockingly said one of the party, "to the person who goes!" "So will I," exclaimed another. "And I," said a third. "All of us," affirmed a fourth. . . . Then from among the spinners stood up one Yasumoto O-Katsu, the wife of a carpenter; she had her only son, a boy of two years old, snugly wrapped up and asleep upon her back. "Listen," said O-Katsu; "if you will all really agree to make over to me all the hemp spun today, I will go to the Yurei-Daki." Her proposal was received with cries of astonishment and of defiance. But after having been several times repeated, it was seriously taken. Each of the spinners in turn agreed to give up her share of the day's work to O-Katsu, providing that O-Katsu should go to the Yurei-Daki. "But how are we to know if she really goes there?" a sharp voice asked. "Why, let her bring back the money-box of the god," answered an old woman whom the spinners called Obaa-San, the Grandmother; "that will be proof enough." "I'll bring it," cried O-Katsu. And out she darted into the street, with her sleeping boy upon her back.

The night, was frosty, but clear. Down the empty street O-Katsu hurried; and she saw that all the house fronts were tightly closed, because of the piercing cold. Out of the village, and along the high road she ran—pichà-pichà—with the great silence of frozen rice-fields on either hand, and only the stars to light her. Half an hour she followed the open road; then she turned down a narrower way, winding under cliffs. Darker and rougher the path became as she proceeded; but she knew it well, and she soon heard the dull roar of the water. A few minutes more, and the way widened into a glen—and the dull roar suddenly became a loud clamor—and before her she saw, looming against a mass of blackness, the long glimmering of the fall. Dimly she perceived the shrine—the money-box. She rushed forward—put out her hand. . . .

"Oi! O-Katsu-San!"[60] suddenly called a warning voice above the

---

[60] The exclamation Oi! is used to call the attention of a person: it is the Japanese equivalent for such English exclamations as "Halloa!" "Ho, there!" etc.

crash of the water.

O-Katsu stood motionless—stupefied by terror.

"Oi! O-Katsu-San!" again pealed the voice—this time with more of menace in its tone.

But O-Katsu was really a bold woman. At once recovering from her stupefaction, she snatched up the money-box and ran. She neither heard nor saw anything more to alarm her until she reached the highroad, where she stopped a moment to take breath. Then she ran on steadily—pichà-pichà—till she got to Kurosaka, and thumped at the door of the asa-toriba.

How the women and the girls cried out as she entered, panting, with the money-box of the god in her hand! Breathlessly they heard her story; sympathetically they screeched when she told them of the Voice that had called her name, twice, out of the haunted water. . . . What a woman! Brave O-Katsu!—well had she earned the hemp! . . . "But your boy must be cold, O-Katsu!" cried the Obaa-San, "let us have him here by the fire!"

"He ought to be hungry," exclaimed the mother; "I must give him his milk presently." . . . "Poor O-Katsu!" said the Obaa-San, helping to remove the wraps in which the boy had been carried—"why, you are all wet behind!" Then, with a husky scream, the helper vociferated, "*Arà! it is blood!*"

And out of the wrappings unfastened there fell to the floor a blood-soaked bundle of baby clothes that left exposed two very small brown feet, and two very small brown hands—nothing more. The child's head had been torn off! . . .

In a Cup of Tea

Have you ever attempted to mount some old tower stairway, spiring up through darkness, and in the heart of that darkness found yourself at the cobwebbed edge of nothing? Or have you followed some coast path, cut along the face of a cliff, only to discover yourself, at a turn, on the jagged verge of a break? The emotional worth of such experience—from a literary point of view—is proved by the force of the sensations aroused, and by the vividness with which they are remembered.

Now there have been curiously preserved, in old Japanese story-books, certain fragments of fiction that produce an almost similar emotional experience. . . . Perhaps the writer was lazy; perhaps he had a quarrel with the publisher; perhaps he was suddenly called away from his little table, and never came back; perhaps death stopped the writing-brush in the very middle of a sentence. But no mortal man can ever tell us exactly why these things were left unfinished. . . . I select a typical example.

On the fourth day of the first month of the third Tenwa—that is to say, about two hundred and twenty years ago—the lord Nakagawa Sado, while on his way to make a New Year's visit, halted with his train at a tea-house in Hakusan, in the Hongō district of Yedo. While the party were resting there, one of the lord's attendants—a wakatō[61] named Sekinai—feeling very thirsty, filled for himself a large water-cup with tea. He was raising the cup to his lips when he suddenly perceived, in the transparent yellow infusion, the image or reflection of a face that was not his own. Startled, he looked around, but could see no one near him. The face in the tea appeared, from the coiffure, to be the face of a young samurai: it was strangely distinct, and very handsome—delicate as the face of a girl. And it seemed the reflection of a *living* face; for the eyes and the lips were moving. Bewildered by this mysterious apparition, Sekinai threw away the tea, and carefully examined the cup. It proved to be a very cheap water-cup, with no artistic devices of any sort. He found and filled another cup; and again the face appeared in the tea. He then ordered fresh tea, and refilled the cup; and once more the strange face appeared—this time with a mocking smile. But Sekinai did not allow himself to be frightened. "Whoever you are," he muttered, "you shall delude me no further!"— then he swallowed the tea, face and all, and went his way, wondering whether he had swallowed a ghost.

Late in the evening of the same day, while on watch in the palace of the lord Nakagawa, Sekinai was surprised by the soundless coming of a stranger into the apartment. This stranger, a richly dressed young samurai, seated himself directly in front of Sekinai, and, saluting the wakatō with a slight bow, observed:

"I am Shikibu Heinai—met you today for the first time. . . . You do not seem to recognize me."

He spoke in a very low, but penetrating voice. And Sekinai was astonished to find before him the same sinister, handsome face of which he had seen, and swallowed, the apparition in a cup of tea. It was smiling now, as the phantom had smiled; but the steady gaze of the eyes, above the smiling lips, was at once a challenge and an insult.

"No, I do not recognize you," returned Sekinai, angry but cool; "and perhaps you will now be good enough to inform me how you obtained admission to this house?"

[In feudal times the residence of a lord was strictly guarded at all hours; and no one could enter unannounced, except through some unpardonable negligence on the part of the armed watch.]

---

[61] The armed attendant of a *samurai* was thus called. The relation of the wakatō to the *samurai* was that of squire to knight.

"Ah, you do not recognize me!" exclaimed the visitor, in a tone of irony, drawing a little nearer as he spoke. "No, you do not recognize me! Yet you took upon yourself this morning to do me a deadly injury! . . ."

Sekinai instantly seized the tantō[62] at his girdle, and made a fierce thrust at the throat of the man. But the blade seemed to touch no substance. Simultaneously and soundlessly the intruder leaped sideward to the chamber-wall, *and through it*! . . . The wall showed no trace of his exit. He had traversed it only as the light of a candle passes through lantern-paper.

When Sekinai made report of the incident, his recital astonished and puzzled the retainers. No stranger had been seen either to enter or to leave the palace at the hour of the occurrence; and no one in the service of the lord Nakagawa had ever heard of the name "Shikibu Heinai."

On the following night Sekinai was off duty, and remained at home with his parents. At a rather late hour he was informed that some strangers had called at the house, and desired to speak with him for a moment. Taking his sword, he went to the entrance, and there found three armed men—apparently retainers—waiting in front of the doorstep. The three bowed respectfully to Sekinai; and one of them said:

"Our names are Matsuoka Bungō, Tsuchibashi Bungō, and Okamura Heiroku. We are retainers of the noble Shikibu Heinai. When our master last night deigned to pay you a visit, you struck him with a sword. He was much will hurt, and has been obliged to go to the hot springs, where his wound is now being treated. But on the sixteenth day of the coming month he will return; and he will then fitly repay you for the injury done him. . . ."

Without waiting to hear more, Sekinai leaped out, sword in hand, and slashed right and left, at the strangers. But the three men sprang to the wall of the adjoining building, and flitted up the wall like shadows, and. . . .

Here the old narrative breaks off; the rest of the story existed only in some brain that has been dust for a century.

I am able to imagine several possible endings; but none of them would satisfy an Occidental imagination. I prefer to let the reader attempt to decide for himself the probable consequence of swallowing a Soul.

---

[62] The shorter of the two swords carried by samurai. The longer sword was called *katana*.

Ikiryō[63]

Formerly, in the quarter of Reiganjima, in Yedo, there was a great porcelain shop called the Setomonodana, kept by a rich man named Kihei. Kihei had in his employ, for many years, a head clerk named Rokubei. Under Rokubei's care the business prospered; and at last it grew so large that Rokubei found himself unable to manage it without help. He therefore asked and obtained permission to hire an experienced assistant; and he then engaged one of his own nephews—a young man about twenty-two years old, who had learned the porcelain trade in Ōsaka.

The nephew proved a very capable assistant—shrewder in business than his experienced uncle. His enterprise extended the trade of the house, and Kihei was greatly pleased. But about seven months after his engagement, the young man became very ill, and seemed likely to die. The best physicians in Yedo were summoned to attend him; but none of them could understand the nature of his sickness. They prescribed no medicine, and expressed the opinion that such a sickness could only have been caused by some secret grief.

Rokubei imagined that it might be a case of lovesickness. He therefore said to his nephew:

"I have been thinking that, as you are still very young, you might have formed some secret attachment which is making you unhappy— perhaps even making you ill. If this be the truth, you certainly ought to tell me all about your troubles. Here I stand to you in the place of a father, as you are far away from your parents; and if you have any anxiety or sorrow, I am ready to do for you whatever a father should do. If money can help you, do not be ashamed to tell me, even though the amount be large. I think that I could assist you; and I am sure that Kihei would be glad to do anything to make you happy and well."

The sick youth appeared to be embarrassed by these kindly assurances; and for some little time he remained silent. At last he answered:

"Never in this world can I forget those generous words. But I have no secret attachment—no longing for any woman. This sickness of mine is not a sickness that doctors can cure; and money could not help me in the least. The truth is, that I have been so persecuted in this house that I scarcely care to live. Everywhere—by day and by night, whether in the shop or in my room, whether alone or in company—I have been unceasingly followed and tormented by the Shadow of a woman. And it

---

[63] Literally, "living spirit,"—that is to say, the ghost of a person still alive. An *ikiryō* may detach itself from the body under the influence of anger, and proceed to haunt and torment the individual by whom the anger was caused.

is long, long since I have been able to get even one night's rest. For so soon as I close my eyes, the Shadow of the woman takes me by the throat and strives to strangle me. So I cannot sleep. . . ."

"And why did you not tell me this before?" asked Rokubei.

"Because I thought," the nephew answered, "that it would be of no use to tell you. The Shadow is not the ghost of a dead person. It is made by the hatred of a living person—a person whom you very well know."

"What person?" questioned Rokubei, in great astonishment.[64]

"The mistress of this house," whispered the youth—"the wife of Kihei Sama. . . . She wishes to kill me."

Rokubei was bewildered by this confession. He doubted nothing of what his nephew had said; but he could not imagine a reason for the haunting. An ikiryō might be caused by disappointed love, or by violent hate—without the knowledge of the person from whom it had emanated. To suppose any love in this case was impossible; the wife of Kihei was considerably more than fifty years of age. But, on the other hand, what could the young clerk have done to provoke hatred—a hatred capable of producing an ikiryō? He had been irreproachably well conducted, unfailingly courteous, and earnestly devoted to his duties. The mystery troubled Rokubei; but, after careful reflection, he decided to tell everything to Kihei, and to request an investigation.

Kihei was astounded; but in the time of forty years he had never had the least reason to doubt the word of Rokubei. He therefore summoned his wife at once, and carefully questioned her, telling her, at the same time, what the sick clerk had said. At first she turned pale, and wept; but, after some hesitation, she answered frankly:

"I suppose that what the new clerk has said about the ikiryō is true—though I really tried never to betray, by word or look, the dislike which I could not help feeling for him. You know that he is very skilful in commerce—very shrewd in everything that he does. And you have given him much authority in this house—power over the apprentices and the servants. But our only son, who should inherit this business, is very simple-hearted and easily deceived; and I have long been thinking that your clever new clerk might so delude our boy as to get possession of all this property. Indeed, I am certain that your clerk could at any time, without the least difficulty, and without the least risk to himself, ruin our business and ruin our son. And with this certainty in my mind, I cannot help fearing and hating the man. I have often and often wished that he were dead; I have even wished that it were in my own power to kill him. . . . Yes, I know that it is wrong to hate any one in such a way; but I could not check the feeling. Night and day I have been wishing

---

[64] An ikiryō is seen only by the person haunted.—For another illustration of this curious belief, see the paper entitled "The Stone Buddha" in my *Out of the East*, p. 171.

evil to that clerk. So I cannot doubt that he has really seen the thing of which he spoke to Rokubei."

"How absurd of you," exclaimed Kihei, "to torment yourself thus! Up to the present time that clerk has done no single thing for which he could be blamed; and you have caused him to suffer cruelly. . . . Now if I should send him away, with his uncle, to another town, to establish a branch business, could you not endeavor to think more kindly of him?"

"If I do not see his face or hear his voice," the wife answered—"if you will only send him away from this house—then I think that I shall be able to conquer my hatred of him."

"Try to do so," said Kihei; "for, if you continue to hate him as you have been hating him, he will certainly die, and you will then be guilty of having caused the death of a man who has done us nothing but good. He has been, in every way, a most excellent servant."

Then Kihei quickly made arrangements for the establishment of a branch house in another city; and he sent Rokubei there with the clerk, to take charge. And thereafter the ikiryō ceased to torment the young man, who soon recovered his health.

The Story of O-Kamé

O-Kamé, daughter of the rich Gonyémon of Nagoshi, in the province of Tosa, was very fond of her husband, Hachiyémon. She was twenty-two, and Hachiyémon twenty-five. She was so fond of him that people imagined her to be jealous. But he never gave her the least cause for jealousy; and it is certain that no single unkind word was ever spoken between them.

Unfortunately the health of O-Kamé was feeble. Within less than two years after her marriage she was attacked by a disease, then prevalent in Tosa, and the best doctors were not able to cure her. Persons seized by this malady could not eat or drink; they remained constantly drowsy and languid, and troubled by strange fancies. And, in spite of constant care, O-Kamé grew weaker and weaker, day by day, until it became evident, even to herself, that she was going to die.

Then she called her husband, and said to him:

"I cannot tell you how good you have been to me during this miserable sickness of mine. Surely no one could have been more kind. But that only makes it all the harder for me to leave you now. . . . Think! I am not yet even twenty-five—and I have the best husband in all this world—and yet I must die! . . . Oh, no, no! it is useless to talk to me about hope; the best Chinese doctors could do nothing for me. I did think to live a few months longer; but when I saw my face this morning in the mirror, I knew that I must die today—yes, this very day. And there is something that I want to beg you to do for me—if you wish me to die quite happy."

"Only tell me what it is," Hachiyémon answered; "and if it be in my power to do, I shall be more than glad to do it."

"No, no—you will not be glad to do it," she returned: "you are still so young! It is difficult—very, very difficult—even to ask you to do such a thing; yet the wish for it is like a fire burning in my breast. I must speak it before I die. . . . My dear, you know that sooner or later, after I am dead, they will want you to take another wife. Will you promise me—can you promise me—not to marry again? . . ."

"Only that!" Hachiyémon exclaimed. "Why, if that be all that you wanted to ask for, your wish is very easily granted. With all my heart I promise you that no one shall ever take your place."

"Aa! uréshiya!" cried O-Kamé, half-rising from her couch; "oh, how happy you have made me!"

And she fell back dead.

Now the health of Hachiyémon appeared to fail after the death of O-Kamé. At first the change in his aspect was attributed to natural grief, and the villagers only said, "How fond of her he must have been!" But, as the months went by, he grew paler and weaker, until at last he became so thin and wan that he looked more like a ghost than a man. Then people began to suspect that sorrow alone could not explain this sudden decline of a man so young. The doctors said that Hachiyémon was not suffering from any known form of disease: they could not account for his condition; but they suggested that it might have been caused by some very unusual trouble of mind. Hachiyémon's parents questioned him in vain; he had no cause for sorrow, he said, other than what they already knew. They counseled him to remarry; but he protested that nothing could ever induce him to break his promise to the dead.

Thereafter Hachiyémon continued to grow visibly weaker, day by day; and his family despaired of his life. But one day his mother, who felt sure that he had been concealing something from her, adjured him so earnestly to tell her the real cause of his decline, and wept so bitterly before him, that he was not able to resist her entreaties.

"Mother," he said, "it is very difficult to speak about this matter, either to you or to any one; and, perhaps, when I have told you everything, you will not be able to believe me. But the truth is that O-Kamé can find no rest in the other world, and that the Buddhist services repeated for her have been said in vain. Perhaps she will never be able to rest unless I go with her on the long black journey. For every night she returns, and lies down by my side. Every night, since the day of her funeral, she has come back. And sometimes I doubt if she be really dead; for she looks and acts just as when she lived—except that she talks to me only in whispers. And she always bids me tell no one that she comes. It may be that she wants me to die; and I should not care to live for my own sake only. But it is true, as you have said, that my body really belongs to my parents, and that I owe to them the first duty. So now, mother, I tell you the whole truth. . . . Yes: every night she comes, just as I am about to sleep; and she remains until dawn. As soon as she hears the temple-bell, she goes away."

When the mother of Hachiyémon had heard these things, she was greatly alarmed; and, hastening at once to the parish-temple, she told the priest all that her son had confessed, and begged for ghostly help. The priest, who was a man of great age and experience, listened without surprise to the recital, and then said to her:

"It is not the first time that I have known such a thing to happen; and I think that I shall be able to save your son. But he is really in great danger. I have seen the shadow of death upon his face; and, if O-Kamé return but once again, he will never behold another sunrise. Whatever can be done for him must be done quickly. Say nothing of the matter to your son; but assemble the members of both families as soon as possible, and tell them to come to the temple without delay. For your son's sake it will be necessary to open the grave of O-Kamé."

So the relatives assembled at the temple; and when the priest had obtained their consent to the opening of the sepulchre, he led the way to the cemetery. Then, under his direction, the tombstone of O-Kamé was shifted, the grave opened, and the coffin raised. And when the coffin-lid had been removed, all present were startled; for O-Kamé sat before them with a smile upon her face, seeming as comely as before the time of her sickness; and there was not any sign of death upon her. But when the priest told his assistants to lift the dead woman out of the coffin, the astonishment changed to fear; for the corpse was blood-warm to the touch, and still flexible as in life, notwithstanding the squatting posture in which it had remained so long.[65]

It was borne to the mortuary chapel; and there the priest, with a writing-brush, traced upon the brow and breast and limbs of the body the Sanskrit characters (Bonji) of certain holy talismanic words. And he performed a Ségaki-service for the spirit of O-Kamé, before suffering her corpse to be restored to the ground.

She never again visited her husband; and Hachiyémon gradually recovered his health and strength. But whether he always kept his promise, the Japanese story-teller does not say.

---

[65] The Japanese dead are placed in a sitting posture in the coffin—which is almost square in form.

The Story of Chūgorō

Along time ago there lived, in the Koishikawa quarter of Yedo, a hatamoto named Suzuki, whose yashiki was situated on the bank of the Yedogawa, not far from the bridge called Naka-no-hashi. And among the retainers of this Suzuki there was an ashigaru[66] named Chūgorō. Chūgorō was a handsome lad, very amiable and clever, and much liked by his comrades.

For several years Chūgorō remained in the service of Suzuki, conducting himself so well that no fault was found with him. But at last the other ashigaru discovered that Chūgorō was in the habit of leaving the yashiki every night, by way of the garden, and staying out until a little before dawn. At first they said nothing to him about this strange behavior; for his absences did not interfere with any regular duty, and were supposed to be caused by some love-affair. But after a time he began to look pale and weak; and his comrades, suspecting some serious folly, decided to interfere. Therefore, one evening, just as he was about to steal away from the house, an elderly retainer called him aside, and said:

"Chūgorō, my lad, we know that you go out every night and stay away until early morning; and we have observed that you are looking unwell. We fear that you are keeping bad company, and injuring your health. And unless you can give a good reason for your conduct, we shall think that it is our duty to report this matter to the Chief Officer. In any case, since we are your comrades and friends, it is but right that we should know why you go out at night, contrary to the custom of this house."

Chūgorō appeared to be very much embarrassed and alarmed by these words. But after a short silence he passed into the garden, followed by his comrade. When the two found themselves well out of hearing of the rest, Chūgorō stopped, and said:

"I will now tell you everything; but I must entreat you to keep my secret. If you repeat what I tell you, some great misfortune may befall me.

"It was in the early part of last spring—about five months ago— that I first began to go out at night, on account of a love-affair. One evening, when I was returning to the yashiki after a visit to my parents, I saw a woman standing by the riverside, not far from the main gateway. She was dressed like a person of high rank; and I thought it strange that a woman so finely dressed should be standing there alone at such an hour. But I did not think that I had any right to question her; and I was about to pass her by, without speaking, when she stepped

---

[66] The ashigaru were the lowest class of retainers in military service.

forward and pulled me by the sleeve. Then I saw that she was very young and handsome.

"'Will you not walk with me as far as the bridge?' she said; 'I have something to tell you.'

"Her voice was very soft and pleasant; and she smiled as she spoke; and her smile was hard to resist. So I walked with her toward the bridge; and on the way she told me that she had often seen me going in and out of the yashiki, and had taken a fancy to me. 'I wish to have you for my husband,' she said; 'if you can like me, we shall be able to make each other very happy.' I did not know how to answer her; but I thought her very charming.

"As we neared the bridge, she pulled my sleeve again, and led me down the bank to the very edge of the river. 'Come in with me,' she whispered, and pulled me toward the water. It is deep there, as you know; and I became all at once afraid of her, and tried to turn back. She smiled, and caught me by the wrist, and said, 'Oh, you must never be afraid with me!' And, somehow, at the touch of her hand, I became more helpless than a child. I felt like a person in a dream who tries to run, and cannot move hand or foot.

"Into the deep water she stepped, and drew me with her; and I neither saw nor heard nor felt anything more until I found myself walking beside her through what seemed to be a great palace, full of light. I was neither wet nor cold: everything around me was dry and warm and beautiful. I could not understand where I was, nor how I had come there. The woman led me by the hand: we passed through room after room—through ever so many rooms, all empty, but very fine— until we entered into a guest-room of a thousand mats. Before a great alcove, at the farther end, lights were burning, and cushions laid as for a feast; but I saw no guests. She led me to the place of honor, by the alcove, and seated herself in front of me, and said: 'This is my home: do you think that you could be happy with me here?' As she asked the question she smiled; and I thought that her smile was more beautiful than anything else in the world; and out of my heart I answered, 'Yes. . . .'

"In the same moment I remembered the story of Urashima; and I imagined that she might be the daughter of a god; but I feared to ask her any questions. . . . Presently maid-servants came in, bearing rice-wine and many dishes, which they set before us. Then she who sat before me said: 'Tonight shall be our bridal night, because you like me; and this is our wedding-feast.' We pledged ourselves to each other for the time of seven existences; and after the banquet we were conducted to a bridal chamber, which had been prepared for us.

"It was yet early in the morning when she awoke me, and said: 'My dear one, you are now indeed my husband. But for reasons which I cannot tell you, and which you must not ask, it is necessary that our marriage remain secret. To keep you here until daybreak would cost both of us our lives. Therefore do not, I beg of you, feel displeased because I must now send you back to the house of your lord. You can come to me tonight again, and every night hereafter, at the same hour that we first met. Wait always for me by the bridge; and you will not have to wait long. But remember, above all things, that our marriage must be a secret, and that, if you talk about it, we shall probably be separated forever.'

"I promised to obey her in all things—remembering the fate of Urashima—and she conducted me through many rooms, all empty and beautiful, to the entrance. There she again took me by the wrist, and everything suddenly became dark, and I knew nothing more until I found myself standing alone on the river bank, close to the Naka-no-hashi. When I got back to the yashiki, the temple bells had not yet begun to ring.

"In the evening I went again to the bridge, at the hour she had named, and I found her waiting for me. She took me with her, as before, into the deep water, and into the wonderful place where we had passed our bridal night. And every night, since then, I have met and parted from her in the same way. Tonight she will certainly be waiting for me, and I would rather die than disappoint her: therefore I must go. . . . But let me again entreat you, my friend, never to speak to any one about what I have told you."

The elder ashigaru was surprised and alarmed by this story. He felt that Chūgorō had told him the truth; and the truth suggested unpleasant possibilities. Probably the whole experience was an illusion, and an illusion produced by some evil power for a malevolent end. Nevertheless, if really bewitched, the lad was rather to be pitied than blamed; and any forcible interference would be likely to result in mischief. So the ashigaru answered kindly:

"I shall never speak of what you have told me—never, at least, while you remain alive and well. Go and meet the woman; but— beware of her! I fear that you are being deceived by some wicked spirit."

Chūgorō only smiled at the old man's warning, and hastened away. Several hours later he reentered the yashiki, with a strangely dejected look. "Did you meet her?" whispered his comrade. "No," replied Chūgorō; "she was not there. For the first time, she was not there. I think that she will never meet me again. I did wrong to tell you; I was very foolish to break my promise. . . ." The other vainly tried to console him. Chūgorō lay down, and spoke no word more. He was trembling from head to foot, as if he had caught a chill.

When the temple bells announced the hour of dawn, Chūgorō tried to get up, and fell back senseless. He was evidently sick—deathly sick. A Chinese physician was summoned.

"Why, the man has no blood!" exclaimed the doctor, after a careful examination; "there is nothing but water in his veins! It will be very difficult to save him. . . . What malfeasance is this?"

Everything was done that could be done to save Chūgorō's life— but in vain. He died as the sun went down. Then his comrade related the whole story.

"Ah! I might have suspected as much!" exclaimed the doctor. . . . "No power could have saved him. He was not the first whom she destroyed."

"Who is she?—or what is she?" the ashigaru asked—"a Fox-Woman?"

"No; she has been haunting this river from ancient time. She loves the blood of the young. . . ."

"A Serpent-Woman?—A Dragon-Woman?"

"No, no! If you were to see her under that bridge by daylight, she would appear to you a very loathsome creature."

"But what kind of a creature?"

"Simply a Frog—a great and ugly Frog!"

From KWAIDAN

The Story of Mimi-Nashi-Hōïchi

More than seven hundred years ago, at Dan-no-ura, in the Straits of Shimonoséki, was fought the last battle of the long contest between the Heiké, or Taira clan, and the Genji, or Minamoto clan. There the Heiké perished utterly, with their women and children, and their infant emperor likewise—now remembered as Antoku Tennō. And that sea and shore have been haunted for seven hundred years . . . Elsewhere I told you about the strange crabs found there, called Heiké crabs, which have human faces on their backs, and are said to be the spirits of the Heiké warriors.[67] But there are many strange things to be seen and heard along that coast. On dark nights thousands of ghostly fires hover about the beach, or flit above the waves—pale lights which the fishermen call *Oni-bi*, or demon-fires; and, whenever the winds are up, a sound of great shouting comes from that sea, like a clamor of battle.

In former years the Heiké were much more restless than they now are. They would rise about ships passing in the night, and try to sink them; and at all times they would watch for swimmers, to pull them

---

[67] See my *Kottō*, for a description of these curious crabs.

down. It was in order to appease those dead that the Buddhist temple, Amidaji, was built at Akamagaséki.[68] A cemetery also was made close by, near the beach; and within it were set up monuments inscribed with the names of the drowned emperor and of his great vassals; and Buddhist services were regularly performed there, on behalf of the spirits of them. After the temple had been built, and the tombs erected, the Heiké gave less trouble than before; but they continued to do queer things at intervals—proving that they had not found the perfect peace.

Some centuries ago there lived at Akamagaséki a blind man named Hōïchi, who was famed for his skill in recitation and in playing upon the *biwa*.[69] From childhood he had been trained to recite and to play; and while yet a lad he had surpassed his teachers. As a professional biwa-hōshi he became famous chiefly by his recitations of the history of the Heiké and the Genji; and it is said that when he sang the song of the battle of Dan-no-ura "even the goblins [*kijin*] could not refrain from tears."

At the outset of his career, Hōïchi was very poor; but he found a good friend to help him. The priest of the Amidaji was fond of poetry and music; and he often invited Hōïchi to the temple, to play and recite. Afterwards, being much impressed by the wonderful skill of the lad, the priest proposed that Hōïchi should make the temple his home; and this offer was gratefully accepted. Hōïchi was given a room in the temple-building; and, in return for food and lodging, he was required only to gratify the priest with a musical performance on certain evenings, when otherwise disengaged.

One summer night the priest was called away, to perform a Buddhist service at the house of a dead parishioner; and he went there with his acolyte, leaving Hōïchi alone in the temple. It was a hot night; and the blind man sought to cool himself on the verandah before his sleeping-room. The verandah overlooked a small garden in the rear of the Amidaji. There Hōïchi waited for the priest's return, and tried to relieve his solitude by practicing upon his biwa. Midnight passed; and the priest did not appear. But the atmosphere was still too warm for comfort within doors; and Hōïchi remained outside. At last he heard steps approaching from the back gate. Somebody crossed the garden,

---

[68] Or, Shimonoséki. The town is also known by the name of Bakkan.

[69] The *biwa*, a kind of four-stringed lute, is chiefly used in musical recitative. Formerly the professional minstrels who recited the *Heiké-Monogatari*, and other tragical histories, were called *biwa-hōshi*, or "lute-priests." The origin of this appellation is not clear; but it is possible that it may have been suggested by the fact that "lute-priests" as well as blind shampooers, had their heads shaven, like Buddhist priests. The *biwa* is played with a kind of plectrum, called *bachi*, usually made of horn.

advanced to the verandah, and halted directly in front of him—but it was not the priest. A deep voice called the blind man's name—abruptly and unceremoniously, in the manner of a samurai summoning an inferior:—

"Hōïchi!"

Hōïchi was too much startled, for the moment, to respond; and the voice called again, in a tone of harsh command—

"Hōïchi!"

"*Hai!*"[70] answered the blind man, frightened by the menace in the voice—"I am blind!—I cannot know who calls!"

"There is nothing to fear," the stranger exclaimed, speaking more gently. "I am stopping near this temple, and have been sent to you with a message. My present lord, a person of exceedingly high rank, is now staying in Akamagaséki, with many noble attendants. He wished to view the scene of the battle of Dan-no-ura; and today he visited that place. Having heard of your skill in reciting the story of the battle, he now desires to hear your performance: so you will take your biwa and come with me at once to the house where the august assembly is waiting."

In those times, the order of a samurai was not to be lightly disobeyed. Hōïchi donned his sandals, took his biwa, and went away with the stranger, who guided him deftly, but obliged him to walk very fast. The hand that guided was iron; and the clank of the warrior's stride proved him fully armed—probably some palace-guard on duty. Hōïchi's first alarm was over: he began to imagine himself in good luck; for, remembering the retainer's assurance about a "person of exceedingly high rank," he thought that the lord who wished to hear the recitation could not be less than a daimyō of the first class. Presently the samurai halted; and Hōïchi became aware that they had arrived at a large gateway; and he wondered, for he could not remember any large gate in that part of the town, except the main gate of the Amidaji. "*Kaimon!*"[71] the samurai called—and there was a sound of unbarring; and the twain passed on. They traversed a space of garden, and halted again before some entrance; and the retainer cried in a loud voice, "Within there! I have brought Hōïchi." Then came sounds of feet hurrying, and screens sliding, and rain-doors opening, and voices of women in converse. By the language of the women Hōïchi knew them to be domestics in some noble household; but he could not imagine to what place he had been conducted. Little time was allowed him for conjecture. After he had been helped to mount several stone steps, upon the last of which he was told to leave his sandals, a woman's hand

---

[70] A response to show that one has heard and is listening attentively.
[71] A respectful term, signifying the opening of a gate. It was used by samurai when calling to the guards on duty at a lord's gate for admission.

guided him along interminable reaches of polished planking, and round pillared angles too many to remember, and over widths amazing of matted floor—into the middle of some vast apartment. There he thought that many great people were assembled: the sound of the rustling of silk was like the sound of leaves in a forest. He heard also a great humming of voices—talking in undertones; and the speech was the speech of courts.

Hōïchi was told to put himself at ease, and he found a kneeling-cushion ready for him. After having taken his place upon it, and tuned his instrument, the voice of a woman—whom he divined to be the *Rōjo*, or matron in charge of the female service—addressed him, saying—

"It is now required that the history of the Heiké be recited, to the accompaniment of the biwa."

Now the entire recital would have required a time of many nights: therefore Hōïchi ventured a question:—

"As the whole of the story is not soon told, what portion is it augustly desired that I now recite?"

The woman's voice made answer:—

"Recite the story of the battle at Dan-no-ura—for the pity of it is the most deep."[72]

Then Hōïchi lifted up his voice, and chanted the chant of the fight on the bitter sea—wonderfully making his biwa to sound like the straining of oars and the rushing of ships, the whirr and the hissing of arrows, the shouting and trampling of men, the crashing of steel upon helmets, the plunging of slain in the flood. And to left and right of him, in the pauses of his playing, he could hear voices murmuring praise: "How marvelous an artist!"—"Never in our own province was playing heard like this!"—"Not in all the empire is there another singer like Hōïchi!" Then fresh courage came to him, and he played and sang yet better than before; and a hush of wonder deepened about him. But when at last he came to tell the fate of the fair and helpless—the piteous perishing of the women and children—and the death-leap of Nii-no-Ama, with the imperial infant in her arms—then all the listeners uttered together one long, long shuddering cry of anguish; and thereafter they wept and wailed so loudly and so wildly that the blind man was frightened by the violence and grief that he had made. For much time the sobbing and the wailing continued. But gradually the sounds of lamentation died away; and again, in the great stillness that followed, Hōïchi heard the voice of the woman whom he supposed to be the Rōjo.

She said:—

---

[72] Or the phrase might be rendered, "for the pity of that part is the deepest." The Japanese word for pity in the original text is "*awaré.*"

"Although we had been assured that you were a very skillful player upon the biwa, and without an equal in recitative, we did not know that any one could be so skillful as you have proved yourself tonight. Our lord has been pleased to say that he intends to bestow upon you a fitting reward. But he desires that you shall perform before him once every night for the next six nights—after which time he will probably make his august return-journey. To-morrow night, therefore, you are to come here at the same hour. The retainer who tonight conducted you will be sent for you . . . There is another matter about which I have been ordered to inform you. It is required that you shall speak to no one of your visits here, during the time of our lord's august sojourn at Akamagaséki. As he is traveling incognito,[73] he commands that no mention of these things be made . . . You are now free to go back to your temple."

After Hōïchi had duly expressed his thanks, a woman's hand conducted him to the entrance of the house, where the same retainer, who had before guided him, was waiting to take him home. The retainer led him to the verandah at the rear of the temple, and there bade him farewell.

It was almost dawn when Hōïchi returned; but his absence from the temple had not been observed—as the priest, coming back at a very late hour, had supposed him asleep. During the day Hōïchi was able to take some rest; and he said nothing about his strange adventure. In the middle of the following night the samurai again came for him, and led him to the august assembly, where he gave another recitation with the same success that had attended his previous performance. But during this second visit his absence from the temple was accidentally discovered; and after his return in the morning he was summoned to the presence of the priest, who said to him, in a tone of kindly reproach:—

"We have been very anxious about you, friend Hōïchi. To go out, blind and alone, at so late an hour, is dangerous. Why did you go without telling us? I could have ordered a servant to accompany you. And where have you been?"

Hōïchi answered, evasively—

"Pardon me kind friend! I had to attend to some private business; and I could not arrange the matter at any other hour."

The priest was surprised, rather than pained, by Hōïchi's reticence: he felt it to be unnatural, and suspected something wrong. He feared that the blind lad had been bewitched or deluded by some evil spirits. He did not ask any more questions; but he privately instructed the men-

---

[73] "Traveling incognito" is at least the meaning of the original phrase—"making a disguised august-journey" (*shinobi no go-ryokō*).

servants of the temple to keep watch upon Hōïchi's movements, and to follow him in case that he should again leave the temple after dark.

On the very next night, Hōïchi was seen to leave the temple; and the servants immediately lighted their lanterns, and followed after him. But it was a rainy night, and very dark; and before the temple-folks could get to the roadway, Hōïchi had disappeared. Evidently he had walked very fast—a strange thing, considering his blindness; for the road was in a bad condition. The men hurried through the streets, making inquiries at every house which Hōïchi was accustomed to visit; but nobody could give them any news of him. At last, as they were returning to the temple by way of the shore, they were startled by the sound of a biwa, furiously played, in the cemetery of the Amidaji. Except for some ghostly fires—such as usually flitted there on dark nights—all was blackness in that direction. But the men at once hastened to the cemetery; and there, by the help of their lanterns, they discovered Hōïchi—sitting alone in the rain before the memorial tomb of Antoku Tennō, making his biwa resound, and loudly chanting the chant of the battle of Dan-no-ura. And behind him, and about him, and everywhere above the tombs, the fires of the dead were burning, like candles. Never before had so great a host of *Oni-bi* appeared in the sight of mortal man . . .

"Hōïchi San!—Hōïchi San!" the servants cried—"you are bewitched! . . . Hōïchi San!"

But the blind man did not seem to hear. Strenuously he made his biwa to rattle and ring and clang; more and more wildly he chanted the chant of the battle of Dan-no-ura. They caught hold of him; they shouted into his ear—

"Hōïchi San!—Hōïchi San!—come home with us at once!"

Reprovingly he spoke to them:—

"To interrupt me in such a manner, before this august assembly, will not be tolerated."

Whereat, in spite of the weirdness of the thing, the servants could not help laughing. Sure that he had been bewitched, they now seized him, and pulled him up on his feet, and by main force hurried him back to the temple—where he was immediately relieved of his wet clothes, by order of the priest. Then the priest insisted upon a full explanation of his friend's astonishing behavior.

Hōïchi long hesitated to speak. But at last, finding that his conduct had really alarmed and angered the good priest, he decided to abandon his reserve; and he related everything that had happened from the time of first visit of the samurai.

The priest said:—

"Hōïchi, my poor friend, you are now in great danger! How unfortunate that you did not tell me all this before! Your wonderful skill in music has indeed brought you into strange trouble. By this time you must be aware that you have not been visiting any house whatever, but have been passing your nights in the cemetery, among the tombs of the Heiké; and it was before the memorial-tomb of Antoku Tennō that our people tonight found you, sitting in the rain. All that you have been imagining was illusion—except the calling of the dead. By once obeying them, you have put yourself in their power. If you obey them again, after what has already occurred, they will tear you in pieces. But they would have destroyed you, sooner or later, in any event . . . Now I shall not be able to remain with you tonight: I am called away to perform another service. But, before I go, it will be necessary to protect your body by writing holy texts upon it."

Before sundown the priest and his acolyte stripped Hōïchi: then, with their writing-brushes, they traced upon his breast and back, head and face and neck, limbs and hands and feet—even upon the soles of his feet, and upon all parts of his body—the text of the holy sûtra called *Hannya-Shin-Kyō.*[74] When this had been done, the priest instructed Hōïchi, saying:—

"Tonight, as soon as I go away, you must seat yourself on the verandah, and wait. You will be called. But, whatever may happen, do not answer, and do not move. Say nothing and sit still—as if meditating. If you stir, or make any noise, you will be torn asunder. Do not get frightened; and do not think of calling for help—because no help could save you. If you do exactly as I tell you, the danger will pass, and you will have nothing more to fear."

After dark the priest and the acolyte went away; and Hōïchi seated himself on the verandah, according to the instructions given him. He laid his biwa on the planking beside him, and, assuming the attitude of meditation, remained quite still—taking care not to cough, or to breathe audibly. For hours he stayed thus.

Then, from the roadway, he heard the steps coming. They passed the gate, crossed the garden, approached the verandah, stopped—

---

[74] The Smaller Pragña-Pâramitâ-Hridaya-Sûtra is thus called in Japanese. Both the smaller and larger sûtras called Pragña-Pâramitâ ("Transcendent Wisdom") have been translated by the late Professor Max Müller, and can be found in volume xlix. of the *Sacred Books of the East* ("Buddhist Mahâyâna Sûtras").—Apropos of the magical use of the text, as described in this story, it is worth remarking that the subject of the sûtra is the Doctrine of the Emptiness of Forms—that is to say, of the unreal character of all phenomena or noumena . . . "Form is emptiness; and emptiness is form. Emptiness is not different from form; form is not different from emptiness. What is form—that is emptiness. What is emptiness—that is form . . . Perception, name, concept, and knowledge, are also emptiness . . . There is no eye, ear, nose, tongue, body, and mind . . . But when the envelopment of consciousness has been annihilated, then he [*the seeker*] becomes free from all fear, and beyond the reach of change, enjoying final Nirvâna."

directly in front of him.

"Hōïchi!" the deep voice called. But the blind man held his breath, and sat motionless.

"Hōïchi!" grimly called the voice a second time. Then a third time—savagely:—

"Hōïchi!"

Hōïchi remained as still as a stone—and the voice grumbled:—

"No answer!—that won't do! . . . Must see where the fellow is." . . .

There was a noise of heavy feet mounting upon the verandah. The feet approached deliberately—halted beside him. Then, for long minutes—during which Hōïchi felt his whole body shake to the beating of his heart—there was dead silence.

At last the gruff voice muttered close to him:—

"Here is the biwa; but of the biwa-player I see—only two ears! . . . So that explains why he did not answer: he had no mouth to answer with—there is nothing left of him but his ears . . . Now to my lord those ears I will take—in proof that the august commands have been obeyed, so far as was possible" . . .

At that instant Hōïchi felt his ears gripped by fingers of iron, and torn off! Great as the pain was, he gave no cry. The heavy footfalls receded along the verandah—descended into the garden—passed out to the roadway—ceased. From either side of his head, the blind man felt a thick warm trickling; but he dared not lift his hands . . .

Before sunrise the priest came back. He hastened at once to the verandah in the rear, stepped and slipped upon something clammy, and uttered a cry of horror; for he say, by the light of his lantern, that the clamminess was blood. But he perceived Hōïchi sitting there, in the attitude of meditation—with the blood still oozing from his wounds.

"My poor Hōïchi!" cried the startled priest—"what is this? . . . You have been hurt?

At the sound of his friend's voice, the blind man felt safe. He burst out sobbing, and tearfully told his adventure of the night.

"Poor, poor Hōïchi!" the priest exclaimed—"all my fault!—my very grievous fault! . . . Everywhere upon your body the holy texts had been written—except upon your ears! I trusted my acolyte to do that part of the work; and it was very, very wrong of me not to have made sure that he had done it! . . . Well, the matter cannot now be helped; we can only try to heal your hurts as soon as possible . . . Cheer up, friend!—the danger is now well over. You will never again be troubled by those visitors."

With the aid of a good doctor, Hōïchi soon recovered from his injuries. The story of his strange adventure spread far and wide, and soon made him famous. Many noble persons went to Akamagaséki to hear him recite; and large presents of money were given to him—so that he became a wealthy man . . . But from the time of his adventure, he was known only by the appellation of *Mimi-nashi-Hōïchi*: "Hōïchi-the-Earless."

Jikininki

Once, when Musō Kokushi, a priest of the Zen sect, was journeying alone through the province of Mino,[75] he lost his way in a mountain-district where there was nobody to direct him. For a long time he wandered about helplessly; and he was beginning to despair of finding shelter for the night, when he perceived, on the top of a hill lighted by the last rays of the sun, one of those little hermitages, called *anjitsu*, which are built for solitary priests. It seemed to be in ruinous condition; but he hastened to it eagerly, and found that it was inhabited by an aged priest, from whom he begged the favor of a night's lodging. This the old man harshly refused; but he directed Musō to a certain hamlet, in the valley adjoining where lodging and food could be obtained.

Musō found his way to the hamlet, which consisted of less than a dozen farm-cottages; and he was kindly received at the dwelling of the headman. Forty or fifty persons were assembled in the principal apartment, at the moment of Musō's arrival; but he was shown into a small separate room, where he was promptly supplied with food and bedding. Being very tired, he lay down to rest at an early hour; but a little before midnight he was roused from sleep by a sound of loud weeping in the next apartment. Presently the sliding-screens were gently pushed apart; and a young man, carrying a lighted lantern, entered the room, respectfully saluted him, and said:—

"Reverend Sir, it is my painful duty to tell you that I am now the responsible head of this house. Yesterday I was only the eldest son. But when you came here, tired as you were, we did not wish that you should feel embarrassed in any way: therefore we did not tell you that father had died only a few hours before. The people whom you saw in the next room are the inhabitants of this village: they all assembled here to pay their last respects to the dead; and now they are going to another village, about three miles off—for by our custom, no one of us may remain in this village during the night after a death has taken place. We make the proper offerings and prayers; then we go away, leaving the corpse alone. Strange things always happen in the house where a corpse

---

[75] The southern part of present-day Gifu Prefecture.

has thus been left: so we think that it will be better for you to come away with us. We can find you good lodging in the other village. But perhaps, as you are a priest, you have no fear of demons or evil spirits; and, if you are not afraid of being left alone with the body, you will be very welcome to the use of this poor house. However, I must tell you that nobody, except a priest, would dare to remain here tonight."

Musō made answer:—

"For your kind intention and your generous hospitality and am deeply grateful. But I am sorry that you did not tell me of your father's death when I came; for, though I was a little tired, I certainly was not so tired that I should have found difficulty in doing my duty as a priest. Had you told me, I could have performed the service before your departure. As it is, I shall perform the service after you have gone away; and I shall stay by the body until morning. I do not know what you mean by your words about the danger of staying here alone; but I am not afraid of ghosts or demons: therefore please to feel no anxiety on my account."

The young man appeared to be rejoiced by these assurances, and expressed his gratitude in fitting words. Then the other members of the family, and the folk assembled in the adjoining room, having been told of the priest's kind promises, came to thank him—after which the master of the house said:—

"Now, reverend Sir, much as we regret to leave you alone, we must bid you farewell. By the rule of our village, none of us can stay here after midnight. We beg, kind Sir, that you will take every care of your honorable body, while we are unable to attend upon you. And if you happen to hear or see anything strange during our absence, please tell us of the matter when we return in the morning."

All then left the house, except the priest, who went to the room where the dead body was lying. The usual offerings had been set before the corpse; and a small Buddhist lamp—*tōmyō*—was burning. The priest recited the service, and performed the funeral ceremonies—after which he entered into meditation. So meditating he remained through several silent hours; and there was no sound in the deserted village. But, when the hush of the night was at its deepest, there noiselessly entered a Shape, vague and vast; and in the same moment Musō found himself without power to move or speak. He saw that Shape lift the corpse, as with hands, devour it, more quickly than a cat devours a rat—beginning at the head, and eating everything: the hair and the bones and even the shroud. And the monstrous Thing, having thus consumed the body, turned to the offerings, and ate them also. Then it went away, as mysteriously as it had come.

When the villagers returned next morning, they found the priest awaiting them at the door of the headman's dwelling. All in turn saluted him; and when they had entered, and looked about the room, no one expressed any surprise at the disappearance of the dead body and the offerings. But the master of the house said to Musō:—

"Reverent Sir, you have probably seen unpleasant things during the night: all of us were anxious about you. But now we are very happy to find you alive and unharmed. Gladly we would have stayed with you, if it had been possible. But the law of our village, as I told you last evening, obliges us to quit our houses after a death has taken place, and to leave the corpse alone. Whenever this law has been broken, heretofore, some great misfortune has followed. Whenever it is obeyed, we find that the corpse and the offerings disappear during our absence. Perhaps you have seen the cause."

Then Musō told of the dim and awful Shape that had entered the death-chamber to devour the body and the offerings. No person seemed to be surprised by his narration; and the master of the house observed:—

"What you have told us, reverend Sir, agrees with what has been said about this matter from ancient time."

Musō then inquired:—

"Does not the priest on the hill sometimes perform the funeral service for your dead?"

"What priest?" the young man asked.

"The priest who yesterday evening directed me to this village," answered Musō. "I called at his *anjitsu* on the hill yonder. He refused me lodging, but told me the way here."

The listeners looked at each other, as in astonishment; and, after a moment of silence, the master of the house said:—

"Reverend Sir, there is no priest and there is no *anjitsu* on the hill. For the time of many generations there has not been any resident-priest in this neighborhood."

Musō said nothing more on the subject; for it was evident that his kind hosts supposed him to have been deluded by some goblin. But after having bidden them farewell, and obtained all necessary information as to his road, he determined to look again for the hermitage on the hill, and so to ascertain whether he had really been deceived. He found the *anjitsu* without any difficulty; and, this time, its aged occupant invited him to enter. When he had done so, the hermit humbly bowed down before him, exclaiming:—"Ah! I am ashamed!—I am very much ashamed!—I am exceedingly ashamed!"

"You need not be ashamed for having refused me shelter," said Musō. "you directed me to the village yonder, where I was very kindly treated; and I thank you for that favor.

"I can give no man shelter," the recluse made answer; and it is not for the refusal that I am ashamed. I am ashamed only that you should have seen me in my real shape—for it was I who devoured the corpse and the offerings last night before your eyes . . . Know, reverend Sir, that I am a *jikininki*,[76]—an eater of human flesh. Have pity upon me, and suffer me to confess the secret fault by which I became reduced to this condition.

"A long, long time ago, I was a priest in this desolate region. There was no other priest for many leagues around. So, in that time, the bodies of the mountain-folk who died used to be brought here—sometimes from great distances—in order that I might repeat over them the holy service. But I repeated the service and performed the rites only as a matter of business; I thought only of the food and the clothes that my sacred profession enabled me to gain. And because of this selfish impiety I was reborn, immediately after my death, into the state of a *jikininki*. Since then I have been obliged to feed upon the corpses of the people who die in this district: every one of them I must devour in the way that you saw last night . . . Now, reverend Sir, let me beseech you to perform a Ségaki-service[77] for me: help me by your prayers, I entreat you, so that I may be soon able to escape from this horrible state of existence" . . .

No sooner had the hermit uttered this petition than he disappeared; and the hermitage also disappeared at the same instant. And Musō Kokushi found himself kneeling alone in the high grass, beside an ancient and moss-grown tomb of the form called *go-rin-ishi*,[78] which seemed to be the tomb of a priest.

Mujina

On the Akasaka Road, in Tōkyō, there is a slope called Kii-no-kuni-zaka—which means the Slope of the Province of Kii. I do not know why it is called the Slope of the Province of Kii. On one side of this slope you see an ancient moat, deep and very wide, with high green banks rising up to some place of gardens; and on the other side of the

---

[76] Literally, a man-eating goblin. The Japanese narrator gives also the Sanscrit term, "Râkshasa;" but this word is quite as vague as *jikininki*, since there are many kinds of Râkshasas. Apparently the word *jikininki* signifies here one of the *Baramon-Rasetsu-Gaki*—forming the twenty-sixth class of pretas enumerated in the old Buddhist books.

[77] A Ségaki-service is a special Buddhist service performed on behalf of beings supposed to have entered into the condition of *gaki* (pretas), or hungry spirits. For a brief account of such a service, see my *Japanese Miscellany*.

[78] Literally, "five-circle [or five-zone] stone." A funeral monument consisting of five parts superimposed—each of a different form—symbolizing the five mystic elements: Ether, Air, Fire, Water, Earth.

road extend the long and lofty walls of an imperial palace. Before the era of street-lamps and jinrikishas, this neighborhood was very lonesome after dark; and belated pedestrians would go miles out of their way rather than mount the Kii-no-kuni-zaka, alone, after sunset.

All because of a Mujina that used to walk there.[79]

The last man who saw the Mujina was an old merchant of the Kyōbashi quarter, who died about thirty years ago. This is the story, as he told it:—

One night, at a late hour, he was hurrying up the Kii-no-kuni-zaka, when he perceived a woman crouching by the moat, all alone, and weeping bitterly. Fearing that she intended to drown herself, he stopped to offer her any assistance or consolation in his power. She appeared to be a slight and graceful person, handsomely dressed; and her hair was arranged like that of a young girl of good family. "O-jochū,"[80] he exclaimed, approaching her—"O-jochū, do not cry like that! . . . Tell me what the trouble is; and if there be any way to help you, I shall be glad to help you." (He really meant what he said; for he was a very kind man.) But she continued to weep—hiding her face from him with one of her long sleeves. "O-jochū," he said again, as gently as he could—"please, please listen to me! . . . This is no place for a young lady at night! Do not cry, I implore you!—only tell me how I may be of some help to you!" Slowly she rose up, but turned her back to him, and continued to moan and sob behind her sleeve. He laid his hand lightly upon her shoulder, and pleaded:—"O-jochū!—O-jochū!—O-jochū! . . . Listen to me, just for one little moment! . . . O-jochū!—O-jochū!" . . . Then that O-jochū turned around, and dropped her sleeve, and stroked her face with her hand; and the man saw that she had no eyes or nose or mouth—and he screamed and ran away.[81]

Up Kii-no-kuni-zaka he ran and ran; and all was black and empty before him. On and on he ran, never daring to look back; and at last he saw a lantern, so far away that it looked like the gleam of a firefly; and he made for it. It proved to be only the lantern of an itinerant *soba*-seller,[82] who had set down his stand by the road-side; but any light and any human companionship was good after that experience; and he flung himself down at the feet of the *soba*-seller, crying out, "Ah!—aa!!—aa!!!" . . .

---

[79] A kind of badger. Certain animals were thought to be able to transform themselves and cause mischief for humans.

[80] O-jochū ("honorable damsel"), a polite form of address used in speaking to a young lady whom one does not know.

[81] An apparition with a smooth, totally featureless face, called a *"nopperabo,"* is a stock part of the Japanese pantheon of ghosts and demons.

[82] *Soba* is a preparation of buckwheat, somewhat resembling vermicelli.

"*Koré! koré!*"[83] roughly exclaimed the soba-man. "Here! what is the matter with you? Anybody hurt you?"

"No—nobody hurt me," panted the other—"only . . . *Aa!—aa!*"

"—Only scared you?" queried the peddler, unsympathetically. "Robbers?"

"Not robbers—not robbers," gasped the terrified man . . . "I saw . . . I saw a woman—by the moat; and she showed me . . . *Aa!* I cannot tell you what she showed me!" . . .

"*Hé!*[84] Was it anything like THIS that she showed you?" cried the soba-man, stroking his own face—which therewith became like unto an Egg . . . And, simultaneously, the light went out.

Rokuro-Kubi

Nearly five hundred years ago there was a samurai, named Isogai Héïdazaëmon Takétsura, in the service of the Lord Kikuji, of Kyūshū. This Isogai had inherited, from many warlike ancestors, a natural aptitude for military exercises, and extraordinary strength. While yet a boy he had surpassed his teachers in the art of swordsmanship, in archery, and in the use of the spear, and had displayed all the capacities of a daring and skillful soldier. Afterwards, in the time of the Eikyō[85] war, he so distinguished himself that high honors were bestowed upon him. But when the house of Kikuji came to ruin, Isogai found himself without a master. He might then easily have obtained service under another daimyo; but as he had never sought distinction for his own sake alone, and as his heart remained true to his former lord, he preferred to give up the world. so he cut off his hair, and became a traveling priest—taking the Buddhist name of Kwairyō.

But always, under the *koromo*[86] of the priest, Kwairyō kept warm within him the heart of the samurai. As in other years he had laughed at peril, so now also he scorned danger; and in all weathers and all seasons he journeyed to preach the good Law in places where no other priest would have dared to go. For that age was an age of violence and disorder; and upon the highways there was no security for the solitary traveler, even if he happened to be a priest.

In the course of his first long journey, Kwairyō had occasion to visit the province of Kai.[87] One evening, as he was traveling through the mountains of that province, darkness overcame him in a very lonesome district, leagues away from any village. So he resigned

---

[83] An exclamation of annoyed alarm.
[84] Well!
[85] The period of Eikyō lasted from 1429 to 1441.
[86] The upper robe of a Buddhist priest is thus called.
[87] Present-day Yamanashi Prefecture.

himself to pass the night under the stars; and having found a suitable grassy spot, by the roadside, he lay down there, and prepared to sleep. He had always welcomed discomfort; and even a bare rock was for him a good bed, when nothing better could be found, and the root of a pine-tree an excellent pillow. His body was iron; and he never troubled himself about dews or rain or frost or snow.

Scarcely had he lain down when a man came along the road, carrying an axe and a great bundle of chopped wood. This woodcutter halted on seeing Kwairyō lying down, and, after a moment of silent observation, said to him in a tone of great surprise:—

"What kind of a man can you be, good Sir, that you dare to lie down alone in such a place as this? . . . There are haunters about here— many of them. are you not afraid of Hairy Things?"

"My friend," cheerfully answered Kwairyō, "I am only a wandering priest—a 'Cloud-and-Water-Guest,' as folks call it: *Unsui-no-ryokaku.*[88] And I am not in the least afraid of Hairy Things—if you mean goblin-foxes, or goblin-badgers, or any creatures of that kind. As for lonesome places, I like them: they are suitable for meditation. I am accustomed to sleeping in the open air: and I have learned never to be anxious about my life."

"You must be indeed a brave man, Sir Priest," the peasant responded, "to lie down here! This place has a bad name—a very bad name. But, as the proverb has it, *Kunshi ayayuki ni chikayorazu* ['The superior man does not needlessly expose himself to peril']; and I must assure you, Sir, that it is very dangerous to sleep here. Therefore, although my house is only a wretched thatched hut, let me beg of you to come home with me at once. In the way of food, I have nothing to offer you; but there is a roof at least, and you can sleep under it without risk."

He spoke earnestly; and Kwairyō, liking the kindly tone of the man, accepted this modest offer. The woodcutter guided him along a narrow path, leading up from the main road through mountain-forest. It was a rough and dangerous path—sometimes skirting precipices— sometimes offering nothing but a network of slippery roots for the foot to rest upon—sometimes winding over or between masses of jagged rock. But at last Kwairyō found himself upon a cleared space at the top of a hill, with a full moon shining overhead; and he saw before him a small thatched cottage, cheerfully lighted from within. The woodcutter led him to a shed at the back of the house, whither water had been conducted, through bamboo-pipes, from some neighboring stream; and the two men washed their feet. Beyond the shed was a vegetable garden, and a grove of cedars and bamboos; and beyond the trees appeared the glimmer of a cascade, pouring from some loftier height,

---

[88] A term for itinerant priests.

and swaying in the moonshine like a long white robe.

As Kwairyō entered the cottage with his guide, he perceived four persons—men and women—warming their hands at a little fire kindled in the *ro*[89] of the principle apartment. They bowed low to the priest, and greeted him in the most respectful manner. Kwairyō wondered that persons so poor, and dwelling in such a solitude, should be aware of the polite forms of greeting. "These are good people," he thought to himself; "and they must have been taught by some one well acquainted with the rules of propriety." Then turning to his host—the *aruji*, or house-master, as the others called him—Kwairyō said:—

"From the kindness of your speech, and from the very polite welcome given me by your household, I imagine that you have not always been a woodcutter. Perhaps you formerly belonged to one of the upper classes?"

Smiling, the woodcutter answered:—

"Sir, you are not mistaken. Though now living as you find me, I was once a person of some distinction. My story is the story of a ruined life—ruined by my own fault. I used to be in the service of a daimyo; and my rank in that service was not inconsiderable. But I loved women and wine too well; and under the influence of passion I acted wickedly. My selfishness brought about the ruin of our house, and caused the death of many persons. Retribution followed me; and I long remained a fugitive in the land. Now I often pray that I may be able to make some atonement for the evil which I did, and to reestablish the ancestral home. But I fear that I shall never find any way of so doing. Nevertheless, I try to overcome the karma of my errors by sincere repentance, and by helping as afar as I can, those who are unfortunate."

Kwairyō was pleased by this announcement of good resolve; and he said to the *aruji*:—

"My friend, I have had occasion to observe that man, prone to folly in their youth, may in after years become very earnest in right living. In the holy sûtras it is written that those strongest in wrong-doing can become, by power of good resolve, the strongest in right-doing. I do not doubt that you have a good heart; and I hope that better fortune will come to you. Tonight I shall recite the sûtras for your sake, and pray that you may obtain the force to overcome the karma of any past errors."

With these assurances, Kwairyō bade the *aruji* good-night; and his host showed him to a very small side-room, where a bed had been made ready. Then all went to sleep except the priest, who began to read

---

[89] A sort of little fireplace, contrived in the floor of a room, is thus described. The *ro* is usually a square shallow cavity, lined with metal and half-filled with ashes, in which charcoal is lighted.

the sutras by the light of a paper lantern. Until a late hour he continued to read and pray: then he opened a little window in his little sleeping-room, to take a last look at the landscape before lying down. The night was beautiful: there was no cloud in the sky: there was no wind; and the strong moonlight threw down sharp black shadows of foliage, and glittered on the dews of the garden. Shrillings of crickets and bell-insects[90] made a musical tumult; and the sound of the neighboring cascade deepened with the night. Kwairyō felt thirsty as he listened to the noise of the water; and, remembering the bamboo aqueduct at the rear of the house, he thought that he could go there and get a drink without disturbing the sleeping household. Very gently he pushed apart the sliding-screens that separated his room from the main apartment; and he saw, by the light of the lantern, five recumbent bodies—without heads!

For one instant he stood bewildered—imagining a crime. But in another moment he perceived that there was no blood, and that the headless necks did not look as if they had been cut. Then he thought to himself:—"Either this is an illusion made by goblins, or I have been lured into the dwelling of a Rokuro-Kubi . . .[91] In the book Sōshinki[92] it is written that if one find the body of a Rokuro-Kubi without its head, and remove the body to another place, the head will never be able to join itself again to the neck. And the book further says that when the head comes back and finds that its body has been moved, it will strike itself upon the floor three times—bounding like a ball—and will pant as in great fear, and presently die. Now, if these be Rokuro-Kubi, they mean me no good; so I shall be justified in following the instructions of the book." . . .

He seized the body of the aruji by the feet, pulled it to the window, and pushed it out. Then he went to the back-door, which he found barred; and he surmised that the heads had made their exit through the smoke-hole in the roof, which had been left open. Gently unbarring the door, he made his way to the garden, and proceeded with all possible caution to the grove beyond it. He heard voices talking in the grove; and he went in the direction of the voices—stealing from shadow to shadow, until he reached a good hiding-place. Then, from behind a trunk, he caught sight of the heads—all five of them—flitting about, and chatting as they flitted. They were eating worms and insects which they found on the ground or among the trees. Presently the head of the aruji stopped eating and said:—

"Ah, that traveling priest who came tonight!—how fat all his body

---

[90] Direct translation of "*suzumushi*," a kind of cricket with a distinctive chirp like a tiny bell, whence the name.

[91] Now a *rokuro-kubi* is ordinarily conceived as a goblin whose neck stretches out to great lengths, but which nevertheless always remains attached to its body.

[92] A Chinese collection of stories on the supernatural.

is! When we shall have eaten him, our bellies will be well filled . . . I
was foolish to talk to him as I did; it only set him to reciting the sûtras
on behalf of my soul! To go near him while he is reciting would be
difficult; and we cannot touch him so long as he is praying. But as it is
now nearly morning, perhaps he has gone to sleep . . . Some one of you
go to the house and see what the fellow is doing."

Another head—the head of a young woman—immediately rose up
and flitted to the house, lightly as a bat. After a few minutes it came
back, and cried out huskily, in a tone of great alarm:—

"That traveling priest is not in the house; he is gone! But that is not
the worst of the matter. He has taken the body of our aruji; and I do not
know where he has put it."

At this announcement the head of the aruji—distinctly visible in
the moonlight—assumed a frightful aspect: its eyes opened
monstrously; its hair stood up bristling; and its teeth gnashed. Then a
cry burst from its lips; and—weeping tears of rage—it exclaimed:—

"Since my body has been moved, to rejoin it is not possible! Then I
must die! . . . And all through the work of that priest! Before I die I will
get at that priest!—I will tear him!—I will devour him! . . . *And there
he is*—behind that tree!—hiding behind that tree! See him!—the fat
coward!" . . .

In the same moment the head of the *aruji*, followed by the other
four heads, sprang at Kwairyō. But the strong priest had already armed
himself by plucking up a young tree; and with that tree he struck the
heads as they came—knocking them from him with tremendous blows.
Four of them fled away. But the head of the aruji, though battered again
and again, desperately continued to bound at the priest, and at last
caught him by the left sleeve of his robe. Kwairyō, however, as quickly
gripped the head by its topknot, and repeatedly struck it. It did not
release its hold; but it uttered a long moan, and thereafter ceased to
struggle. It was dead. But its teeth still held the sleeve; and, for all his
great strength, Kwairyō could not force open the jaws.

With the head still hanging to his sleeve he went back to the house,
and there caught sight of the other four Rokuro-Kubi squatting
together, with their bruised and bleeding heads reunited to their bodies.
But when they perceived him at the back-door all screamed, "The
priest! the priest!"—and fled, through the other doorway, out into the
woods.

Eastward the sky was brightening; day was about to dawn; and
Kwairyō knew that the power of the goblins was limited to the hours of
darkness. He looked at the head clinging to his sleeve—its face all
fouled with blood and foam and clay; and he laughed aloud as he

thought to himself: "What a *miyagé!*[93]—the head of a goblin!" After which he gathered together his few belongings, and leisurely descended the mountain to continue his journey.

Right on he journeyed, until he came to Suwa in Shinano;[94] and into the main street of Suwa he solemnly strode, with the head dangling at his elbow. Then woman fainted, and children screamed and ran away; and there was a great crowding and clamoring until the *torité* (as the police in those days were called) seized the priest, and took him to jail. For they supposed the head to be the head of a murdered man who, in the moment of being killed, had caught the murderer's sleeve in his teeth. As the Kwairyō, he only smiled and said nothing when they questioned him. So, after having passed a night in prison, he was brought before the magistrates of the district. Then he was ordered to explain how he, a priest, had been found with the head of a man fastened to his sleeve, and why he had dared thus shamelessly to parade his crime in the sight of people.

Kwairyō laughed long and loudly at these questions; and then he said:—

"Sirs, I did not fasten the head to my sleeve: it fastened itself there—much against my will. And I have not committed any crime. For this is not the head of a man; it is the head of a goblin; and, if I caused the death of the goblin, I did not do so by any shedding of blood, but simply by taking the precautions necessary to assure my own safety." . . . And he proceeded to relate the whole of the adventure—bursting into another hearty laugh as he told of his encounter with the five heads.

But the magistrates did not laugh. They judged him to be a hardened criminal, and his story an insult to their intelligence. Therefore, without further questioning, they decided to order his immediate execution—all of them except one, a very old man. This aged officer had made no remark during the trial; but, after having heard the opinion of his colleagues, he rose up, and said:—

"Let us first examine the head carefully; for this, I think, has not yet been done. If the priest has spoken truth, the head itself should bear witness for him . . . Bring the head here!"

So the head, still holding in its teeth the *koromo* that had been stripped from Kwairyō's shoulders, was put before the judges. The old man turned it round and round, carefully examined it, and discovered, on the nape of its neck, several strange red characters. He called the attention of his colleagues to these, and also bad them observe that the edges of the neck nowhere presented the appearance of having been cut

---

[93] A present made to friends or to the household on returning from a journey is thus called. Ordinarily, of course, the *miyagé* consists of something produced in the locality to which the journey has been made: this is the point of Kwairyō's jest.

[94] Present-day Nagano Prefecture.

by any weapon. On the contrary, the line of severance was smooth as the line at which a falling leaf detaches itself from the stem . . . Then said the elder:—

"I am quite sure that the priest told us nothing but the truth. This is the head of a Rokuro-Kubi. In the book Nan-hō-ï-butsu-shi it is written that certain red characters can always be found upon the nape of the neck of a real Rokuro-Kubi. There are the characters: you can see for yourselves that they have not been painted. Moreover, it is well known that such goblins have been dwelling in the mountains of the province of Kai from very ancient time . . . But you, Sir," he exclaimed, turning to Kwairyō—"what sort of sturdy priest may you be? Certainly you have given proof of a courage that few priests possess; and you have the air of a soldier rather than a priest. Perhaps you once belonged to the samurai-class?"

"You have guessed rightly, Sir," Kwairyō responded. "Before becoming a priest, I long followed the profession of arms; and in those days I never feared man or devil. My name then was Isogai Héïdazaëmon Takétsura of Kyūshū: there may be some among you who remember it."

At the mention of that name, a murmur of admiration filled the court-room.; for there were many present who remembered it. And Kwairyō immediately found himself among friends instead of judges— friends anxious to prove their admiration by fraternal kindness. With honor they escorted him to the residence of the daimyō, who welcomed him, and feasted him, and made him a handsome present before allowing him to depart. When Kwairyō left Suwa, he was as happy as any priest is permitted to be in this transitory world. As for the head, he took it with him—jocosely insisting that he intended it for a *miyagé*.

And now it only remains to tell what became of the head.

A day or two after leaving Suwa, Kwairyō met with a robber, who stopped him in a lonesome place, and bade him strip. Kwairyō at once removed his *koromo*, and offered it to the robber, who then first perceived what was hanging to the sleeve. Though brave, the highwayman was startled: he dropped the garment, and sprang back. Then he cried out:—"You!—what kind of a priest are you? Why, you are a worse man than I am! It is true that I have killed people; but I never walked about with anybody's head fastened to my sleeve . . . Well, Sir priest, I suppose we are of the same calling; and I must say that I admire you! . . . Now that head would be of use to me: I could frighten people with it. Will you sell it? You can have my robe in exchange for your *koromo*; and I will give you five ryō for the head."

Kwairyō answered:—

"I shall let you have the head and the robe if you insist; but I must tell you that this is not the head of a man. It is a goblin's head. So, if you buy it, and have any trouble in consequence, please to remember that you were not deceived by me."

"What a nice priest you are!" exclaimed the robber. "You kill men, and jest about it! . . . But I am really in earnest. Here is my robe; and here is the money; and let me have the head . . . What is the use of joking?"

"Take the thing," said Kwairyō. "I was not joking. The only joke—if there be any joke at all—is that you are fool enough to pay good money for a goblin's head." And Kwairyō, loudly laughing, went upon his way.

Thus the robber got the head and the *koromo*; and for some time he played goblin-priest upon the highways. But, reaching the neighborhood of Suwa, he there leaned the true story of the head; and he then became afraid that the spirit of the Rokuro-Kubi might give him trouble. So he made up his mind to take back the head to the place from which it had come, and to bury it with its body. He found his way to the lonely cottage in the mountains of Kai; but nobody was there, and he could not discover the body. Therefore he buried the head by itself, in the grove behind the cottage; and he had a tombstone set up over the grave; and he caused a Ségaki-service to be performed on behalf of the spirit of the Rokuro-Kubi. And that tombstone—known as the Tombstone of the Rokuro-Kubi—may be seen (at least so the Japanese story-teller declares) even unto this day.

Yuki-Onna

In a village of Musashi Province,[95] there lived two woodcutters: Mosaku and Minokichi. At the time of which I am speaking, Mosaku was an old man; and Minokichi, his apprentice, was a lad of eighteen years. Every day they went together to a forest situated about five miles from their village. On the way to that forest there is a wide river to cross; and there is a ferry-boat. Several times a bridge was built where the ferry is; but the bridge was each time carried away by a flood. No common bridge can resist the current there when the river rises.

Mosaku and Minokichi were on their way home, one very cold evening, when a great snowstorm overtook them. They reached the ferry; and they found that the boatman had gone away, leaving his boat on the other side of the river. It was no day for swimming; and the woodcutters took shelter in the ferryman's hut—thinking themselves

---

[95] An ancient province whose boundaries took in most of present-day Tokyo, and parts of Saitama and Kanagawa prefectures.

lucky to find any shelter at all. There was no brazier in the hut, nor any place in which to make a fire: it was only a two-mat[96] hut, with a single door, but no window. Mosaku and Minokichi fastened the door, and lay down to rest, with their straw rain-coats over them. At first they did not feel very cold; and they thought that the storm would soon be over.

The old man almost immediately fell asleep; but the boy, Minokichi, lay awake a long time, listening to the awful wind, and the continual slashing of the snow against the door. The river was roaring; and the hut swayed and creaked like a junk at sea. It was a terrible storm; and the air was every moment becoming colder; and Minokichi shivered under his rain-coat. But at last, in spite of the cold, he too fell asleep.

He was awakened by a showering of snow in his face. The door of the hut had been forced open; and, by the snow-light (*yuki-akari*), he saw a woman in the room—a woman all in white. She was bending above Mosaku, and blowing her breath upon him; and her breath was like a bright white smoke. Almost in the same moment she turned to Minokichi, and stooped over him. He tried to cry out, but found that he could not utter any sound. The white woman bent down over him, lower and lower, until her face almost touched him; and he saw that she was very beautiful—though her eyes made him afraid. For a little time she continued to look at him; then she smiled, and she whispered:—"I intended to treat you like the other man. But I cannot help feeling some pity for you—because you are so young . . . You are a pretty boy, Minokichi; and I will not hurt you now. But, if you ever tell anybody— even your own mother—about what you have seen this night, I shall know it; and then I will kill you . . . Remember what I say!"

With these words, she turned from him, and passed through the doorway. Then he found himself able to move; and he sprang up, and looked out. But the woman was nowhere to be seen; and the snow was driving furiously into the hut. Minokichi closed the door, and secured it by fixing several billets of wood against it. He wondered if the wind had blown it open; he thought that he might have been only dreaming, and might have mistaken the gleam of the snow-light in the doorway for the figure of a white woman: but he could not be sure. He called to Mosaku, and was frightened because the old man did not answer. He put out his hand in the dark, and touched Mosaku's face, and found that it was ice! Mosaku was stark and dead . . .

By dawn the storm was over; and when the ferryman returned to his station, a little after sunrise, he found Minokichi lying senseless beside the frozen body of Mosaku. Minokichi was promptly cared for, and soon came to himself; but he remained a long time ill from the

---

[96] That is to say, with a floor-surface of about six feet square.

effects of the cold of that terrible night. He had been greatly frightened also by the old man's death; but he said nothing about the vision of the woman in white. As soon as he got well again, he returned to his calling—going alone every morning to the forest, and coming back at nightfall with his bundles of wood, which his mother helped him to sell.

One evening, in the winter of the following year, as he was on his way home, he overtook a girl who happened to be traveling by the same road. She was a tall, slim girl, very good-looking; and she answered Minokichi's greeting in a voice as pleasant to the ear as the voice of a song-bird. Then he walked beside her; and they began to talk. The girl said that her name was O-Yuki;[97] that she had lately lost both of her parents; and that she was going to Yedo,[98] where she happened to have some poor relations, who might help her to find a situation as a servant. Minokichi soon felt charmed by this strange girl; and the more that he looked at her, the handsomer she appeared to be. He asked her whether she was yet betrothed; and she answered, laughingly, that she was free. Then, in her turn, she asked Minokichi whether he was married, or pledge to marry; and he told her that, although he had only a widowed mother to support, the question of an "honorable daughter-in-law" had not yet been considered, as he was very young . . . After these confidences, they walked on for a long while without speaking; but, as the proverb declares, *Ki ga aréba, mé mo kuchi hodo ni mono wo iu*: "When the wish is there, the eyes can say as much as the mouth." By the time they reached the village, they had become very much pleased with each other; and then Minokichi asked O-Yuki to rest awhile at his house. After some shy hesitation, she went there with him; and his mother made her welcome, and prepared a warm meal for her. O-Yuki behaved so nicely that Minokichi's mother took a sudden fancy to her, and persuaded her to delay her journey to Yedo. And the natural end of the matter was that Yuki never went to Yedo at all. She remained in the house, as an "honorable daughter-in-law."

O-Yuki proved a very good daughter-in-law. When Minokichi's mother came to die—some five years later—her last words were words of affection and praise for the wife of her son. And O-Yuki bore Minokichi ten children, boys and girls—handsome children all of them, and very fair of skin.

The country-folk thought O-Yuki a wonderful person, by nature

---

[97] This name, signifying "Snow," is not uncommon. On the subject of Japanese female names, see my paper in the volume entitled *Shadowings*.

[98] Also spelled *Edo*, the former name of Tokyo.

different from themselves. Most of the peasant-women age early; but O-Yuki, even after having become the mother of ten children, looked as young and fresh as on the day when she had first come to the village.

One night, after the children had gone to sleep, O-Yuki was sewing by the light of a paper lamp; and Minokichi, watching her, said:—

"To see you sewing there, with the light on your face, makes me think of a strange thing that happened when I was a lad of eighteen. I then saw somebody as beautiful and white as you are now—indeed, she was very like you." . . .

Without lifting her eyes from her work, O-Yuki responded:—

"Tell me about her . . . Where did you see her?

Then Minokichi told her about the terrible night in the ferryman's hut—and about the White Woman that had stooped above him, smiling and whispering—and about the silent death of old Mosaku. And he said:—

"Asleep or awake, that was the only time that I saw a being as beautiful as you. Of course, she was not a human being; and I was afraid of her—very much afraid—but she was so white! . . . Indeed, I have never been sure whether it was a dream that I saw, or the Woman of the Snow." . . .

O-Yuki flung down her sewing, and arose, and bowed above Minokichi where he sat, and shrieked into his face:—

"It was I—I—I! Yuki it was! And I told you then that I would kill you if you ever said one work about it! . . . But for those children asleep there, I would kill you this moment! And now you had better take very, very good care of them; for if ever they have reason to complain of you, I will treat you as you deserve!" . . .

Even as she screamed, her voice became thin, like a crying of wind; then she melted into a bright white mist that spired to the roof-beams, and shuddered away through the smoke-hole . . . Never again was she seen.

The Story of Aoyagi

In the era of Bummei [1469-1486] there was a young samurai called Tomotada in the service of Hatakéyama Yoshimuné, the Lord of Noto.[99] Tomotada was a native of Echizen;[100] but at an early age he had been taken, as page, into the palace of the daimyo of Noto, and had been educated, under the supervision of that prince, for the profession of arms. As he grew up, he proved himself both a good scholar and a

---

[99] An ancient province corresponding to the northern part of present-day Ishikawa Prefecture.

[100] An ancient province corresponding to the eastern part of present-day Fukui Prefecture.

good soldier, and continued to enjoy the favor of his prince. Being gifted with an amiable character, a winning address, and a very handsome person, he was admired and much liked by his samurai-comrades.

When Tomotada was about twenty years old, he was sent upon a private mission to Hosokawa Masamoto, the great daimyō of Kyōto, a kinsman of Hatakéyama Yoshimuné. Having been ordered to journey through Echizen, the youth requested and obtained permission to pay a visit, on the way, to his widowed mother.

It was the coldest period of the year when he started; and, though mounted upon a powerful horse, he found himself obliged to proceed slowly. The road which he followed passed through a mountain-district where the settlements were few and far between; and on the second day of his journey, after a weary ride of hours, he was dismayed to find that he could not reached his intended halting-place until late in the night. He had reason to be anxious; for a heavy snowstorm came on, with an intensely cold wind; and the horse showed signs of exhaustion. But in that trying moment, Tomotada unexpectedly perceived the thatched room of a cottage on the summit of a near hill, where willow-trees were growing. With difficulty he urged his tired animal to the dwelling; and he loudly knocked upon the storm-doors, which had been closed against the wind. An old woman opened them, and cried out compassionately at the sight of the handsome stranger: "Ah, how pitiful!—a young gentleman traveling alone in such weather! . . . Deign, young master, to enter."

Tomotada dismounted, and after leading his horse to a shed in the rear, entered the cottage, where he saw an old man and a girl warming themselves by a fire of bamboo splints. They respectfully invited him to approach the fire; and the old folks then proceeded to warm some rice-wine, and to prepare food for the traveler, whom they ventured to question in regard to his journey. Meanwhile the young girl disappeared behind a screen. Tomotada had observed, with astonishment, that she was extremely beautiful—though her attire was of the most wretched kind, and her long, loose hair in disorder. He wondered that so handsome a girl should be living in such a miserable and lonesome place.

The old man said to him:—

"Honored Sir, the next village is far; and the snow is falling thickly. The wind is piercing; and the road is very bad. Therefore, to proceed further this night would probably be dangerous. Although this hovel is unworthy of your presence, and although we have not any comfort to offer, perhaps it were safer to remain tonight under this miserable roof . . . We would take good care of your horse."

Tomotada accepted this humble proposal—secretly glad of the chance thus afforded him to see more of the young girl. Presently a coarse but ample meal was set before him; and the girl came from behind the screen, to serve the wine. She was now reclad, in a rough but cleanly robe of homespun; and her long, loose hair had been neatly combed and smoothed. As she bent forward to fill his cup, Tomotada was amazed to perceive that she was incomparably more beautiful than any woman whom he had ever before seen; and there was a grace about her every motion that astonished him. But the elders began to apologize for her, saying: "Sir, our daughter, Aoyagi,[101] has been brought up here in the mountains, almost alone; and she knows nothing of gentle service. We pray that you will pardon her stupidity and her ignorance." Tomotada protested that he deemed himself lucky to be waited upon by so comely a maiden. He could not turn his eyes away from her—though he saw that his admiring gaze made her blush; and he left the wine and food untasted before him. The mother said: "Kind Sir, we very much hope that you will try to eat and to drink a little—though our peasant-fare is of the worst—as you must have been chilled by that piercing wind." Then, to please the old folks, Tomotada ate and drank as he could; but the charm of the blushing girl still grew upon him. He talked with her, and found that her speech was sweet as her face. Brought up in the mountains as she might have been; but, in that case, her parents must at some time been persons of high degree; for she spoke and moved like a damsel of rank. Suddenly he addressed her with a poem— which was also a question—inspired by the delight in his heart:—

"Tadzunétsuru,
Hana ka toté koso,
Hi wo kurasé,
Akénu ni otoru
Akané sasuran?"

["*Being on my way to pay a visit, I found that which I took to be a flower: therefore here I spend the day . . . Why, in the time before dawn, the dawn-blush tint should glow—that, indeed, I know not.*"][102]

---

[101] The name signifies "Green Willow;"—though rarely met with, it is still in use.

[102] The poem may be read in two ways; several of the phrases having a double meaning. But the art of its construction would need considerable space to explain, and could scarcely interest the Western reader. The meaning which Tomotada desired to convey might be thus expressed:—"While journeying to visit my mother, I met with a being lovely as a flower; and for the sake of that lovely person, I am passing the day here . . . Fair one, wherefore that dawn-like blush before the hour of dawn?—can it mean that you love me?"

Without a moment's hesitation, she answered him in these verses:—

> "Izuru hi no
> Honoméku iro wo
> Waga sodé ni
> Tsutsumaba asu mo
> Kimiya tomaran."

["*If with my sleeve I hid the faint fair color of the dawning sun—then, perhaps, in the morning my lord will remain.*"][103]

Then Tomotada knew that she accepted his admiration; and he was scarcely less surprised by the art with which she had uttered her feelings in verse, than delighted by the assurance which the verses conveyed. He was now certain that in all this world he could not hope to meet, much less to win, a girl more beautiful and witty than this rustic maid before him; and a voice in his heart seemed to cry out urgently, "Take the luck that the gods have put in your way!" In short he was bewitched—bewitched to such a degree that, without further preliminary, he asked the old people to give him their daughter in marriage—telling them, at the same time, his name and lineage, and his rank in the train of the Lord of Noto.

They bowed down before him, with many exclamations of grateful astonishment. But, after some moments of apparent hesitation, the father replied:—

"Honored master, you are a person of high position, and likely to rise to still higher things. Too great is the favor that you deign to offer us; indeed, the depth of our gratitude therefore is not to be spoken or measured. But this girl of ours, being a stupid country-girl of vulgar birth, with no training or teaching of any sort, it would be improper to let her become the wife of a noble samurai. Even to speak of such a matter is not right . . . But, since you find the girl to your liking, and have condescended to pardon her peasant-manners and to overlook her great rudeness, we do gladly present her to you, for an humble handmaid. Deign, therefore, to act hereafter in her regard according to your august pleasure."

Ere morning the storm had passed; and day broke through a cloudless east. Even if the sleeve of Aoyagi hid from her lover's eyes the rose-blush of that dawn, he could no longer tarry. But neither could he resign himself to part with the girl; and, when everything had been prepared for his journey, he thus addressed her parents:—

---

[103] Another reading is possible; but this one gives the signification of the *answer* intended.

"Though it may seem thankless to ask for more than I have already received, I must again beg you to give me your daughter for wife. It would be difficult for me to separate from her now; and as she is willing to accompany me, if you permit, I can take her with me as she is. If you will give her to me, I shall ever cherish you as parents . . . And, in the meantime, please to accept this poor acknowledgment of your kindest hospitality."

So saying, he placed before his humble host a purse of gold *ryō*. But the old man, after many prostrations, gently pushed back the gift, and said:—

"Kind master, the gold would be of no use to us; and you will probably have need of it during your long, cold journey. Here we buy nothing; and we could not spend so much money upon ourselves, even if we wished . . . As for the girl, we have already bestowed her as a free gift; she belongs to you: therefore it is not necessary to ask our leave to take her away. Already she has told us that she hopes to accompany you, and to remain your servant for as long as you may be willing to endure her presence. We are only too happy to know that you deign to accept her; and we pray that you will not trouble yourself on our account. In this place we could not provide her with proper clothing— much less with a dowry. Moreover, being old, we should in any event have to separate from her before long. Therefore it is very fortunate that you should be willing to take her with you now."

It was in vain that Tomotada tried to persuade the old people to accept a present: he found that they cared nothing for money. But he saw that they were really anxious to trust their daughter's fate to his hands; and he therefore decided to take her with him. So he placed her upon his horse, and bade the old folks farewell for the time being, with many sincere expressions of gratitude.

"Honored Sir," the father made answer, "it is we, and not you, who have reason for gratitude. We are sure that you will be kind to our girl; and we have no fears for her sake." . . .

[*Here, in the Japanese original, there is a queer break in the natural course of the narration, which therefrom remains curiously inconsistent. Nothing further is said about the mother of Tomotada, or about the parents of Aoyagi, or about the daimyō of Noto. Evidently the writer wearied of his work at this point, and hurried the story, very carelessly, to its startling end. I am not able to supply his omissions, or to repair his faults of construction; but I must venture to put in a few explanatory details, without which the rest of the tale would not hold together . . . It appears that Tomotada rashly took Aoyagi with him to Kyōto, and so got into trouble; but we are not informed as to where the couple lived afterwards.*]

... Now a samurai was not allowed to marry without the consent of his lord; and Tomotada could not expect to obtain this sanction before his mission had been accomplished. He had reason, under such circumstances, to fear that the beauty of Aoyagi might attract dangerous attention, and that means might be devised of taking her away from him. In Kyōto he therefore tried to keep her hidden from curious eyes. But a retainer of Lord Hosokawa one day caught sight of Aoyagi, discovered her relation to Tomotada, and reported the matter to the daimyō. Thereupon the daimyō—a young prince, and fond of pretty faces—gave orders that the girl should be brought to the place; and she was taken thither at once, without ceremony.

Tomotada sorrowed unspeakably; but he knew himself powerless. He was only an humble messenger in the service of a far-off daimyō; and for the time being he was at the mercy of a much more powerful daimyō, whose wishes were not to be questioned. Moreover Tomotada knew that he had acted foolishly—that he had brought about his own misfortune, by entering into a clandestine relation which the code of the military class condemned. There was now but one hope for him—a desperate hope: that Aoyagi might be able and willing to escape and to flee with him. After long reflection, he resolved to try to send her a letter. The attempt would be dangerous, of course: any writing sent to her might find its way to the hands of the daimyō; and to send a love-letter to any inmate of the place was an unpardonable offense. But he resolved to dare the risk; and, in the form of a Chinese poem, he composed a letter which he endeavored to have conveyed to her. The poem was written with only twenty-eight characters. But with those twenty-eight characters he was about to express all the depth of his passion, and to suggest all the pain of his loss:—[104]

> Kōshi ō-son gojin wo ou;
> Ryokuju namida wo tarété rakin wo hitataru;
> Komon hitotabi irité fukaki koto umi no gotoshi;
> Koré yori shorō koré rojin

[Closely, *closely the youthful prince now follows after the gem-bright maid*;
The tears of the fair one, falling, have moistened all her robes.
But the august lord, having one become enamored of her—the depth of his longing is like the depth of the sea.

---

[104] So the Japanese story-teller would have us believe—although the verses seem commonplace in translation. I have tried to give only their general meaning: an effective literal translation would require some scholarship.

*Therefore it is only I that am left forlorn—only I that am left to
wander alone.*]

On the evening of the day after this poem had been sent, Tomotada
was summoned to appear before the Lord Hosokawa. The youth at once
suspected that his confidence had been betrayed; and he could not
hope, if his letter had been seen by the daimyō, to escape the severest
penalty. "Now he will order my death," thought Tomotada; "but I do
not care to live unless Aoyagi be restored to me. Besides, if the death-
sentence be passed, I can at least try to kill Hosokawa." He slipped his
swords into his girdle, and hastened to the palace.

On entering the presence-room he saw the Lord Hosokawa seated
upon the dais, surrounded by samurai of high rank, in caps and robes of
ceremony. All were silent as statues; and while Tomotada advanced to
make obeisance, the hush seemed to his sinister and heavy, like the
stillness before a storm. But Hosokawa suddenly descended from the
dais, and, while taking the youth by the arm, began to repeat the words
of the poem:—"*Kōshi ō-son gojin wo ou.*" . . . And Tomotada, looking
up, saw kindly tears in the prince's eyes.
Then said Hosokawa:—
"Because you love each other so much, I have taken it upon myself
to authorize your marriage, in lieu of my kinsman, the Lord of Noto;
and your wedding shall now be celebrated before me. The guests are
assembled; the gifts are ready."
At a signal from the lord, the sliding-screens concealing a further
apartment were pushed open; and Tomotada saw there many dignitaries
of the court, assembled for the ceremony, and Aoyagi awaiting him in
bride's apparel . . . Thus was she given back to him; and the wedding
was joyous and splendid; and precious gifts were made to the young
couple by the prince, and by the members of his household.

For five happy years, after that wedding, Tomotada and Aoyagi
dwelt together. But one morning Aoyagi, while talking with her
husband about some household matter, suddenly uttered a great cry of
pain, and then became very white and still. After a few moments she
said, in a feeble voice: "Pardon me for thus rudely crying out—but the
paid was so sudden! . . . My dear husband, our union must have been
brought about through some Karma-relation in a former state of
existence; and that happy relation, I think, will bring us again together
in more than one life to come. But for this present existence of ours, the
relation is now ended; we are about to be separated. Repeat for me, I
beseech you, the *Nembutsu*-prayer—because I am dying."
"Oh! what strange wild fancies!" cried the startled husband—"you
are only a little unwell, my dear one! . . . lie down for a while, and rest;

and the sickness will pass." . . .

"No, no!" she responded—"I am dying!—I do not imagine it; I know! . . . And it were needless now, my dear husband, to hide the truth from you any longer:—I am not a human being. The soul of a tree is my soul; the heart of a tree is my heart; the sap of the willow is my life. And some one, at this cruel moment, is cutting down my tree; that is why I must die! . . . Even to weep were now beyond my strength!— quickly, quickly repeat the *Nembutsu* for me . . . quickly! . . . Ah! . . .

With another cry of pain she turned aside her beautiful head, and tried to hide her face behind her sleeve. But almost in the same moment her whole form appeared to collapse in the strangest way, and to sank down, down, down—level with the floor. Tomotada had spring to support her; but there was nothing to support! There lay on the matting only the empty robes of the fair creature and the ornaments that she had worn in her hair: the body had ceased to exist . . .

Tomotada shaved his head, took the Buddhist vows, and became an itinerant priest. He traveled through all the provinces of the empire; and, at holy places which he visited, he offered up prayers for the soul of Aoyagi. Reaching Echizen, in the course of his pilgrimage, he sought the home of the parents of his beloved. But when he arrived at the lonely place among the hills, where their dwelling had been, he found that the cottage had disappeared. There was nothing to mark even the spot where it had stood, except the stumps of three willows— two old trees and one young tree—that had been cut down long before his arrival.

Beside the stumps of those willow-trees he erected a memorial tomb, inscribed with divers holy texts; and he there performed many Buddhist services on behalf of the spirits of Aoyagi and of her parents.

The Dream of Akinosuké

In the district called Toïchi of Yamato Province,[105] there used to live a gōshi named Miyata Akinosuké . . . [Here I must tell you that in Japanese feudal times there was a privileged class of soldier-farmers— free-holders—corresponding to the class of yeomen in England; and these were called gōshi.]

In Akinosuké's garden there was a great and ancient cedar-tree, under which he was wont to rest on sultry days. One very warm afternoon he was sitting under this tree with two of his friends, fellow-gōshi, chatting and drinking wine, when he felt all of a sudden very drowsy—so drowsy that he begged his friends to excuse him for taking

---

[105] Present-day Nara Prefecture.

a nap in their presence. Then he lay down at the foot of the tree, and dreamed this dream:—

He thought that as he was lying there in his garden, he saw a procession, like the train of some great daimyō descending a hill near by, and that he got up to look at it. A very grand procession it proved to be—more imposing than anything of the kind which he had ever seen before; and it was advancing toward his dwelling. He observed in the van of it a number of young men richly appareled, who were drawing a great lacquered palace-carriage, or *gosho-guruma*, hung with bright blue silk. When the procession arrived within a short distance of the house it halted; and a richly dressed man—evidently a person of rank—advanced from it, approached Akinosuké, bowed to him profoundly, and then said:—

"Honored Sir, you see before you a *kérai* [vassal] of the Kokuō of Tokoyo.[106] My master, the King, commands me to greet you in his august name, and to place myself wholly at your disposal. He also bids me inform you that he augustly desires your presence at the palace. Be therefore pleased immediately to enter this honorable carriage, which he has sent for your conveyance."

Upon hearing these words Akinosuké wanted to make some fitting reply; but he was too much astonished and embarrassed for speech; and in the same moment his will seemed to melt away from him, so that he could only do as the *kérai* bade him. He entered the carriage; the *kérai* took a place beside him, and made a signal; the drawers, seizing the silken ropes, turned the great vehicle southward; and the journey began.

In a very short time, to Akinosuké's amazement, the carriage stopped in front of a huge two-storied gateway (*rōmon*), of a Chinese style, which he had never before seen. Here the *kérai* dismounted, saying, "I go to announce the honorable arrival,"—and he disappeared. After some little waiting, Akinosuké saw two noble-looking men, wearing robes of purple silk and high caps of the form indicating lofty rank, come from the gateway. These, after having respectfully saluted him, helped him to descend from the carriage, and led him through the great gate and across a vast garden, to the entrance of a palace whose front appeared to extend, west and east, to a distance of miles. Akinosuké was then shown into a reception-room of wonderful size and splendor. His guides conducted him to the place of honor, and respectfully seated themselves apart; while serving-maids, in costume of ceremony, brought refreshments. When Akinosuké had partaken of the refreshments, the two purple-robed attendants bowed low before

---

[106] This name "Tokoyo" is indefinite. According to circumstances it may signify any unknown country—or that undiscovered country from whose bourn no traveler returns—or that Fairyland of far-eastern fable, the Realm of Hōrai. The term "Kokuō" means the ruler of a country—therefore a king. The original phrase, *Tokoyo no Kokuō*, might be rendered here as "the Ruler of Hōrai," or "the King of Fairyland."

him, and addressed him in the following words—each speaking alternately, according to the etiquette of courts:—

"It is now our honorable duty to inform you . . . as to the reason of your having been summoned hither . . . Our master, the King, augustly desires that you become his son-in-law; . . . and it is his wish and command that you shall wed this very day . . . the August Princess, his maiden-daughter . . . We shall soon conduct you to the presence-chamber . . . where His Augustness even now is waiting to receive you . . . But it will be necessary that we first invest you . . . with the appropriate garments of ceremony."[107]

Having thus spoken, the attendants rose together, and proceeded to an alcove containing a great chest of gold lacquer. They opened the chest, and took from it various roes and girdles of rich material, and a *kamuri*, or regal headdress. With these they attired Akinosuké as befitted a princely bridegroom; and he was then conducted to the presence-room, where he saw the Kokuō of Tokoyo seated upon the *daiza*,[108] wearing a high black cap of state, and robed in robes of yellow silk. Before the *daiza*, to left and right, a multitude of dignitaries sat in rank, motionless and splendid as images in a temple; and Akinosuké, advancing into their midst, saluted the king with the triple prostration of usage. The king greeted him with gracious words, and then said:—

"You have already been informed as to the reason of your having been summoned to Our presence. We have decided that you shall become the adopted husband of Our only daughter; and the wedding ceremony shall now be performed."

As the king finished speaking, a sound of joyful music was heard; and a long train of beautiful court ladies advanced from behind a curtain to conduct Akinosuké to the room in which he bride awaited him.

The room was immense; but it could scarcely contain the multitude of guests assembled to witness the wedding ceremony. All bowed down before Akinosuké as he took his place, facing the King's daughter, on the kneeling-cushion prepared for him. As a maiden of heaven the bride appeared to be; and her robes were beautiful as a summer sky. And the marriage was performed amid great rejoicing.

Afterwards the pair were conducted to a suite of apartments that had been prepared for them in another portion of the palace; and there they received the congratulations of many noble persons, and wedding gifts beyond counting.

---

[107] The last phrase, according to old custom, had to be uttered by both attendants at the same time. All these ceremonial observances can still be studied on the Japanese stage.

[108] This was the name given to the estrade, or dais, upon which a feudal prince or ruler sat in state. The term literally signifies "great seat."

Some days later Akinosuké was again summoned to the throne-room. On this occasion he was received even more graciously than before; and the King said to him:—

In the southwestern part of Our dominion there is an island called Raishū. We have now appointed you Governor of that island. You will find the people loyal and docile; but their laws have not yet been brought into proper accord with the laws of Tokoyo; and their customs have not been properly regulated. We entrust you with the duty of improving their social condition as far as may be possible; and We desire that you shall rule them with kindness and wisdom. All preparations necessary for your journey to Raishū have already been made."

So Akinosuké and his bride departed from the palace of Tokoyo, accompanied to the shore by a great escort of nobles and officials; and they embarked upon a ship of state provided by the king. And with favoring winds they safety sailed to Raishū, and found the good people of that island assembled upon the beach to welcome them.

Akinosuké entered at once upon his new duties; and they did not prove to be hard. During the first three years of his governorship he was occupied chiefly with the framing and the enactment of laws; but he had wise counselors to help him, and he never found the work unpleasant. When it was all finished, he had no active duties to perform, beyond attending the rites and ceremonies ordained by ancient custom. The country was so healthy and so fertile that sickness and want were unknown; and the people were so good that no laws were ever broken. And Akinosuké dwelt and ruled in Raishū for twenty years more—making in all twenty-three years of sojourn, during which no shadow of sorrow traversed his life.

But in the twenty-fourth year of his governorship, a great misfortune came upon him; for his wife, who had borne him seven children—five boys and two girls—fell sick and died. She was buried, with high pomp, on the summit of a beautiful hill in the district of Hanryōkō; and a monument, exceedingly splendid, was placed upon her grave. But Akinosuké felt such grief at her death that he no longer cared to live.

Now when the legal period of mourning was over, there came to Raishū, from the Tokoyo palace, a *shisha*, or royal messenger. The *shisha* delivered to Akinosuké a message of condolence, and then said to him:—

"These are the words which our august master, the King of Tokoyo, commands that I repeat to you: 'We will now send you back to your own people and country. As for the seven children, they are the grandsons and granddaughters of the King, and shall be fitly cared for. Do not, therefore, allow you mind to be troubled concerning them.'"

On receiving this mandate, Akinosuké submissively prepared for his departure. When all his affairs had been settled, and the ceremony of bidding farewell to his counselors and trusted officials had been concluded, he was escorted with much honor to the port. There he embarked upon the ship sent for him; and the ship sailed out into the blue sea, under the blue sky; and the shape of the island of Raishū itself turned blue, and then turned grey, and then vanished forever . . . And Akinosuké suddenly awoke—under the cedar-tree in his own garden!

For a moment he was stupefied and dazed. But he perceived his two friends still seated near him—drinking and chatting merrily. He stared at them in a bewildered way, and cried aloud—

"How strange!"

"Akinosuké must have been dreaming," one of them exclaimed, with a laugh. "What did you see, Akinosuké, that was strange?"

Then Akinosuké told his dream—that dream of three-and-twenty years' sojourn in the realm of Tokoyo, in the island of Raishū; and they were astonished, because he had really slept for no more than a few minutes.

One gōshi said:—

"Indeed, you saw strange things. We also saw something strange while you were napping. A little yellow butterfly was fluttering over your face for a moment or two; and we watched it. Then it alighted on the ground beside you, close to the tree; and almost as soon as it alighted there, a big, big ant came out of a hole and seized it and pulling it down into the hole. Just before you woke up, we saw that very butterfly come out of the hole again, and flutter over your face as before. And then it suddenly disappeared: we do not know where it went."

"Perhaps it was Akinosuké's soul," the other gōshi said; "certainly I thought I saw it fly into his mouth . . . But, even if that butterfly *was* Akinosuké's soul, the fact would not explain his dream."

"The ants might explain it," returned the first speaker. "Ants are queer beings—possibly goblins . . . Anyhow, there is a big ant's nest under that cedar-tree." . . .

"Let us look!" cried Akinosuké, greatly moved by this suggestion. And he went for a spade.

The ground about and beneath the cedar-tree proved to have been excavated, in a most surprising way, by a prodigious colony of ants. The ants had furthermore built inside their excavations; and their tiny constructions of straw, clay, and stems bore an odd resemblance to miniature towns. In the middle of a structure considerably larger than the rest there was a marvelous swarming of small ants around the body of one very big ant, which had yellowish wings and a long black head.

"Why, there is the King of my dream!" cried Akinosuké; "and there is the palace of Tokoyo! . . . How extraordinary! . . . Raishū ought to lie somewhere southwest of it—to the left of that big root . . . Yes!— here it is! . . . How very strange! Now I am sure that I can find the mountain of Hanryōkō, and the grave of the princess." . . .

In the wreck of the nest he searched and searched, and at last discovered a tiny mound, on the top of which was fixed a water-worn pebble, in shape resembling a Buddhist monument. Underneath it he found—embedded in clay—the dead body of a female ant.

Riki-Baka

His name was Riki, signifying Strength; but the people called him Riki-the-Simple, or Riki-the-Fool—"Riki-Baka,"—because he had been born into perpetual childhood. For the same reason they were kind to him—even when he set a house on fire by putting a lighted match to a mosquito-curtain, and clapped his hands for joy to see the blaze. At sixteen years he was a tall, strong lad; but in mind he remained always at the happy age of two, and therefore continued to play with very small children. The bigger children of the neighborhood, from four to seven years old, did not care to play with him, because he could not learn their songs and games. His favorite toy was a broomstick, which he used as a hobby-horse; and for hours at a time he would ride on that broomstick, up and down the slope in front of my house, with amazing peals of laughter. But at last he became troublesome by reason of his noise; and I had to tell him that he must find another playground. He bowed submissively, and then went off—sorrowfully trailing his broomstick behind him. Gentle at all times, and perfectly harmless if allowed no chance to play with fire, he seldom gave anybody cause for complaint. His relation to the life of our street was scarcely more than that of a dog or a chicken; and when he finally disappeared, I did not miss him. Months and months passed by before anything happened to remind me of Riki.

"What has become of Riki?" I then asked the old woodcutter who supplies our neighborhood with fuel. I remembered that Riki had often helped him to carry his bundles.

"Riki-Baka?" answered the old man. "Ah, Riki is dead—poor fellow! . . . Yes, he died nearly a year ago, very suddenly; the doctors said that he had some disease of the brain. And there is a strange story now about that poor Riki

"When Riki died, his mother wrote his name, 'Riki-Baka,' in the palm of his left hand—putting 'Riki' in the Chinese character, and

'Baka' in *kana*.[109] And she repeated many prayers for him—prayers that he might be reborn into some more happy condition.

"Now, about three months ago, in the honorable residence of Nanigashi-Sama,[110] in Kōjimachi,[111] a boy was born with characters on the palm of his left hand; and the characters were quite plain to read—'RIKI-BAKA'!

"So the people of that house knew that the birth must have happened in answer to somebody's prayer; and they caused inquiry to be made everywhere. At least a vegetable-seller brought word to them that there used to be a simple lad, called Riki-Baka, living in the Ushigomé quarter, and that he had died during the last autumn; and they sent two men-servants to look for the mother of Riki.

"Those servants found the mother of Riki, and told her what had happened; and she was glad exceedingly—for that Nanigashi house is a very rich and famous house. But the servants said that the family of Nanigashi-Sama were very angry about the word 'Baka' on the child's hand. 'And where is your Riki buried?' the servants asked. 'He is buried in the cemetery of Zendōji,' she told them. 'Please to give us some of the clay of his grave,' they requested.

"So she went with them to the temple Zendōji, and showed them Riki's grave; and they took some of the grave-clay away with them, wrapped up in a *furoshiki*. . . .[112] They gave Riki's mother some money—ten yen." . . .[113]

"But what did they want with that clay?" I inquired.

"Well," the old man answered, "you know that it would not do to let the child grow up with that name on his hand. And there is no other means of removing characters that come in that way upon the body of a child: *you must rub the skin with clay taken from the grave of the body of the former birth.*" . . .

---

[109] Kana: the Japanese phonetic alphabet.
[110] "So-and-so": appellation used by Hearn in place of the real name.
[111] A section of Tokyo.
[112] A square piece of cotton-goods, or other woven material, used as a wrapper in which to carry small packages.
[113] Ten yen is nothing now, but was a formidable sum then.

From THE ROMANCE OF THE MILKY WAY,
AND OTHER STUDIES & STORIES

The Mirror Maiden

In the period of the Ashikaga Shōgunate the shrine of Ogawachi-Myōjin, at Minami-Isé, fell into decay; and the daimyō of the district, the Lord Kitahataké, found himself unable, by reason of war and other circumstances, to provide for the reparation of the building. Then the Shintō priest in charge, Matsumura Hyōgo, sought help at Kyōto from the great daimyō Hosokawa, who was known to have influence with the Shōgun. The Lord Hosokawa received the priest kindly, and promised to speak to the Shōgun about the condition of Ogawachi-Myōjin. But he said that, in any event, a grant for the restoration of the temple could not be made without due investigation and considerable delay; and he advised Matsumura to remain in the capital while the matter was being arranged. Matsumura therefore brought his family to Kyōto, and rented a house in the old Kyōgoku quarter.

This house, although handsome and spacious, had been long unoccupied. It was said to be an unlucky house. On the northeast side of it there was a well; and several former tenants had drowned themselves in that well, without any known cause. But Matsumura, being a Shintō priest, had no fear of evil spirits; and he soon made himself very comfortable in his new home.

In the summer of that year there was a great drought. For months no rain had fallen in the Five Home-Provinces; the river-beds dried up, the wells failed; and even in the capital there was a dearth of water. But the well in Matsumura's garden remained nearly full; and the water—which was very cold and clear, with a faint bluish tinge—seemed to be supplied by a spring. During the hot season many people came from all parts of the city to beg for water; and Matsumura allowed them to draw as much as they pleased. Nevertheless the supply did not appear to be diminished.

But one morning the dead body of a young servant, who had been sent from a neighboring residence to fetch water, was found floating in the well. No cause for a suicide could be imagined; and Matsumura, remembering many unpleasant stories about the well, began to suspect some invisible malevolence. He went to examine the well, with the intention of having a fence built around it; and while standing there alone he was startled by a sudden motion in the water, as of something alive. The motion soon ceased; and then he perceived, clearly reflected in the still surface, the figure of a young woman, apparently about nineteen or twenty years of age. She seemed to be occupied with her toilet: he distinctly saw her touching her lips with béni[114] At first her face was visible in profile only; but presently she turned towards him and smiled. Immediately he felt a strange shock at his heart, and a dizziness came upon him like the dizziness of wine, and everything became dark, except that smiling face—white and beautiful as moonlight, and always seeming to grow more beautiful, and to be drawing him down—down—down into the darkness. But with a desperate effort he recovered his will and closed his eyes. When he opened them again, the face was gone, and the light had returned; and he found himself leaning down over the curb of the well. A moment more of that dizziness—a moment more of that dazzling lure—and he would never again have looked upon the sun . . .

Returning to the house, he gave orders to his people not to approach the well under any circumstances, or allow any person to draw water from it. And the next day he had a strong fence built round the well.

About a week after the fence had been built, the long drought was broken by a great rain-storm, accompanied by wind and lightning and thunder—thunder so tremendous that the whole city shook to the rolling of it, as if shaken by an earthquake. For three days and three nights the downpour and the lightnings and the thunder continued; and the Kamogawa rose as it had never risen before, carrying away many bridges. During the third night of the storm, at the Hour of the Ox, there was heard a knocking at the door of the priest's dwelling, and the voice of a woman pleading for admittance. But Matsumura, warned by his experience at the well, forbade his servants to answer the appeal. He went himself to the entrance, and asked:

"Who calls?"

A feminine voice responded:

"Pardon! it is I—Yayoi![115] . . . I have something to say to Matsumura Sama—something of great moment. Please open!" . . .

Matsumura half opened the door, very cautiously; and he saw the same beautiful face that had smiled upon him from the well. But it was not smiling now: it had a very sad look.

"Into my house you shall not come," the priest exclaimed. "You are not a human being, but a Well-Person. . . . Why do you thus wickedly try to delude and destroy people?"

The Well-Person made answer in a voice musical as a tinkling of jewels (tama-wo-korogasu-koē.):

"It is of that very matter that I want to speak. . . . I have never wished to injure human beings. But from ancient time a Poison-Dragon

---

[114] A kind of rouge, now used only to color the lips.
[115] This name, though uncommon, is still in use.

dwelt in that well. He was the Master of the Well; and because of him the well was always full. Long ago I fell into the water there, and so became subject to him; and he had power to make me lure people to death, in order that he might drink their blood. But now the Heavenly Ruler has commanded the Dragon to dwell hereafter in the lake called Torii-no-Iké, in the Province of Shinshū; and the gods have decided that he shall never be allowed to return to this city. So tonight, after he had gone away, I was able to come out, to beg for your kindly help. There is now very little water in the well, because of the Dragon's departure; and if you will order search to be made, my body will be found there. I pray you to save my body from the well without delay; and I shall certainly return your benevolence." . . .

So saying, she vanished into the night.

Before dawn the tempest had passed; and when the sun arose there was no trace of cloud in the pure blue sky. Matsumura sent at an early hour for well-cleaners to search the well. Then, to everybody's surprise, the well proved to be almost dry. It was easily cleaned; and at the bottom of it were found some hair-ornaments of a very ancient fashion, and a metal mirror of curious form—but no trace of any body, animal or human.

Matusmura imagined, however, that the mirror might yield some explanation of the mystery; for every such mirror is a weird thing, having a soul of its own—and the soul of a mirror is feminine. This mirror, which seemed to be very old, was deeply crusted with scurf. But when it had been carefully cleaned, by the priest's order, it proved to be of rare and costly workmanship; and there were wonderful designs upon the back of it—also several characters. Some of the characters had become indistinguishable; but there could still be discerned part of a date, and ideographs signifying, "third month, the third day." Now the third month used to be termed *Yayoi* (meaning, the Month of Increase); and the third day of the third month, which is a festival day, is still called Yayoi-no-sekku. Remembering that the Well-Person called herself "Yayoi," Matsumura felt almost sure that his ghostly visitant had been none other than the Soul of the Mirror.

He therefore resolved to treat the mirror with all the consideration due to a Spirit. After having caused it to be carefully repolished and resilvered, he had a case of precious wood made for it, and a particular room in the house prepared to receive it. On the evening of the same day that it had been respectfully deposited in that room, Yayoi herself unexpectedly appeared before the priest as he sat alone in his study. She looked even more lovely than before; but the light of her beauty was now soft as the light of a summer moon shining through pure white clouds. After having humbly saluted Matsumura, she said in her sweetly tinkling voice:

"Now that you have saved me from solitude and sorrow, I have come to thank you. . . . I am indeed, as you supposed, the Spirit of the Mirror. It was in the time of the Emperor Saimei that I was first brought here from Kudara; and I dwelt in the august residence until the time of the Emperor Saga, when I was augustly bestowed upon the Lady Kamo, Naishinnō of the Imperial Court.[116] Thereafter I became an heirloom in the House of Fujiwara, and so remained until the period of Hōgen, when I was dropped into the well. There I was left and forgotten during the years of the great war.[117] The Master of the Well[118] was a venomous Dragon, who used to live in a lake that once covered a great part of this district. After the lake had been filled in, by government order, in order that houses might be built upon the place of it, the Dragon took possession of the well; and when I fell into the well I became subject to him; and he compelled me to lure many people to their deaths. But the gods have banished him forever. . . . Now I have one more favor to beseech: I entreat that you will cause me to be offered up to the Shōgun, the Lord Yoshimasa, who by descent is related to my former possessors. Do me but this last great kindness, and it will bring you good-fortune. . . . But I have also to warn you of a danger. In this house, after to-morrow, you must not stay, because it will be destroyed." . . . And with these words of warning Yayoi disappeared.

Matsumura was able to profit by this premonition. He removed his people and his belongings to another district the next day; and almost immediately afterwards another storm arose, even more violent than the first, causing a flood which swept away the house in which he had been residing.

Some time later, by favor of the Lord Hosokawa, Matsumura was enabled to obtain an audience of the Shōgun Yoshimasa, to whom he presented the mirror, together with a written account of its wonderful history. Then the prediction of the Spirit of the Mirror was fulfilled; for the Shōgun, greatly pleased with this strange gift, not only bestowed

---

[116] The Emperor Saimei reigned from 655 to 662 (A.D.); the Emperor Saga from 810 to 842.—Kudara was an ancient kingdom in southwestern Korea, frequently mentioned in early Japanese history.—A Naishinnō was of Imperial blood. In the ancient court-hierarchy there were twenty-five ranks or grades of noble ladies;—that of Naishinnō was seventh in order of precedence.

[117] For centuries the wives of the emperors and the ladies of the Imperial Court were chosen from the Fujiwara clan—The period called Hōgen lasted from 1156 to 1159: the war referred to is the famous war between the Taira and Minamoto clans.

[118] In old-time belief every lake or spring had its invisible guardian, supposed to sometimes take the form of a serpent or dragon. The spirit of a lake or pond was commonly spoken of as Iké-no-Mushi, the Master of the Lake. Here we find the title "Master" given to a dragon living in a well; but the guardian of wells is really the god Suijin.

costly presents upon Matsumura, but also made an ample grant of money for the rebuilding of the Temple of Ogawachi-Myōjin.

The Story of Itō Norisuké

In the town of Uji, in the province of Yamashiro, there lived, about six hundred years ago, a young samurai named Itō Tatéwaki Norisuké, whose ancestors were of the Héïké clan. Itō was of handsome person and amiable character, a good scholar and apt at arms. But his family were poor; and he had no patron among the military nobility—so that his prospects were small. He lived in a very quiet way, devoting himself to the study of literature, and having (says the Japanese story-teller) "only the Moon and the Wind for friends."

One autumn evening, as he was taking a solitary walk in the neighborhood of the hill called Kotobikiyama, he happened to overtake a young girl who was following the same path. She was richly dressed, and seemed to be about eleven or twelve years old. Itō greeted her, and said, "The sun will soon be setting, damsel, and this is rather a lonesome place. May I ask if you have lost your way?" She looked up at him with a bright smile, and answered deprecatingly: "Nay! I am a miya-dzukai,[119] serving in this neighborhood; and I have only a little way to go."

By her use of the term miya-dzukai, Itō knew that the girl must be in the service of persons of rank; and her statement surprised him, because he had never heard of any family of distinction residing in that vicinity. But he only said: "I am returning to Uji, where my home is. Perhaps you will allow me to accompany you on the way, as this is a very lonesome place."

She thanked him gracefully, seeming pleased by his offer; and they walked on together, chatting as they went. She talked about the weather, the flowers, the butterflies, and the birds; about a visit that she had once made to Uji, about the famous sights of the capital, where she had been born; and the moments passed pleasantly for Itō, as he listened to her fresh prattle. Presently, at a turn in the road, they entered a hamlet, densely shadowed by a grove of young trees.

[Here I must interrupt the story to tell you that, without having actually seen them, you cannot imagine how dark some Japanese country villages remain even in the brightest and hottest weather. In the neighborhood of Tōkyō itself there are many villages of this kind. At a short distance from such a settlement you see no houses: nothing is visible but a dense grove of evergreen trees. The grove, which is usually composed of young cedars and bamboos, serves to shelter the

---

[119] August-residence servant.

village from storms, and also to supply timber for various purposes. So closely are the trees planted that there is no room to pass between the trunks of them: they stand straight as masts, and mingle their crests so as to form a roof that excludes the sun. Each thatched cottage occupies a clear space in the plantation, the trees forming a fence about it, double the height of the building. Under the trees it is always twilight, even at high noon; and the houses, morning or evening, are half in shadow. What makes the first impression of such a village almost disquieting is, not the transparent gloom, which has a certain weird charm of its own, but the stillness. There may be fifty or a hundred dwellings; but you see nobody; and you hear no sound but the twitter of invisible birds, the occasional crowing of cocks, and the shrilling of cicada. Even the cicada, however, find these groves too dim, and sing faintly; being sun-lovers, they prefer the trees outside the village. I forgot to say that you may sometimes hear a viewless shuttle—chaka-ton, chaka-ton; but that familiar sound, in the great green silence, seems an elfish happening. The reason of the hush is simply that the people are not at home. All the adults, excepting some feeble elders, have gone to the neighboring fields, the women carrying their babies on their backs; and most of the children have gone to the nearest school, perhaps not less than a mile away. Verily, in these dim hushed villages, one seems to behold the mysterious perpetuation of conditions recorded in the texts of Kwang-Tze:

"The ancients who had the nourishment of the world wished for nothing, and the world had enough:—they did nothing, and all things were transformed:—their stillness was abysmal, and the people were all composed."]

. . . The village was very dark when Itō reached it; for the sun had set, and the after-glow made no twilight in the shadowing of the trees. "Now, kind sir," the child said, pointing to a narrow lane opening upon the main road, "I have to go this way." "Permit me, then, to see you home," Itō responded; and he turned into the lane with her, feeling rather than seeing his way. But the girl soon stopped before a small gate, dimly visible in the gloom—a gate of trelliswork, beyond which the lights of a dwelling could be seen. "Here," she said, "is the honorable residence in which I serve. As you have come thus far out of your way, kind sir, will you not deign to enter and to rest a while?" Itō assented. He was pleased by the informal invitation; and he wished to learn what persons of superior condition had chosen to reside in so lonesome a village. He knew that sometimes a family of rank would retire in this manner from public life, by reason of government displeasure or political trouble; and he imagined that such might be the history of the occupants of the dwelling before him. Passing the gate, which his young guide opened for him, he found himself in a large quaint garden. A miniature landscape, traversed by a winding stream, was faintly distinguishable. "Deign for one little moment to wait," the child said; "I go to announce the honorable coming;" and hurried toward the house. It was a spacious house, but seemed very old, and built in the fashion of another time. The sliding doors were not closed; but the lighted interior was concealed by a beautiful bamboo curtain extending along the gallery front. Behind it shadows were moving— shadows of women; and suddenly the music of a koto rippled into the night. So light and sweet was the playing that Itō could scarcely believe the evidence of his senses. A slumberous feeling of delight stole over him as he listened—a delight strangely mingled with sadness. He wondered how any woman could have learned to play thus—wondered whether the player could be a woman—wondered even whether he was hearing earthly music; for enchantment seemed to have entered into his blood with the sound of it.

The soft music ceased; and almost at the same moment Itō found the little miya-dzukai beside him. "Sir," she said, "it is requested that you will honorably enter." She conducted him to the entrance, where he removed his sandals; and an aged woman, whom he thought to be the Rōjo, or matron of the household, came to welcome him at the threshold. The old woman then led him through many apartments to a large and well-lighted room in the rear of the house, and with many respectful salutations requested him to take the place of honor accorded to guests of distinction. He was surprised by the stateliness of the chamber, and the curious beauty of its decorations. Presently some maid-servants brought refreshments; and he noticed that the cups and other vessels set before him were of rare and costly workmanship, and ornamented with a design indicating the high rank of the possessor. More and more he wondered what noble person had chosen this lonely retreat, and what happening could have inspired the wish for such solitude. But the aged attendant suddenly interrupted his reflections with the question:

"Am I wrong in supposing that you are Itō Sama, of Uji—Itō Tatéwaki Norisuké?"

Itō bowed in assent. He had not told his name to the little miya-dzukai, and the manner of the inquiry startled him.

"Please do not think my question rude," continued the attendant. "An old woman like myself may ask questions without improper curiosity. When you came to the house, I thought that I knew your face; and I asked your name only to clear away all doubt, before speaking of other matters. I have some thing of moment to tell you. You often pass through this village, and our young Himégimi-Sama[120] happened one morning to see you going by; and ever since that moment she has been thinking about you, day and night. Indeed, she thought so much that she became ill; and we have been very uneasy about her. For that reason I took means to find out your name and residence; and I was on the point of sending you a letter when—so unexpectedly!—you came to our gate with the little attendant. Now, to say how happy I am to see you is not possible; it seems almost too fortunate a happening to be true! Really I think that this meeting must have been brought about by the favor of Enmusubi-no-Kami—that great God of Izumo who ties the knots of fortunate union. And now that so lucky a destiny has led you hither, perhaps you will not refuse—if there be no obstacle in the way of such a union—to make happy the heart of our Himégimi-Sama?"

For the moment Itō did not know how to reply. If the old woman had spoken the truth, an extraordinary chance was being offered to him. Only a great passion could impel the daughter of a noble house to seek, of her own will, the affection of an obscure and masterless samurai, possessing neither wealth nor any sort of prospects. On the other hand, it was not in the honorable nature of the man to further his own interests by taking advantage of a feminine weakness. Moreover, the circumstances were disquietingly mysterious. Yet how to decline the proposal, so unexpectedly made, troubled him not a little. After a short silence, he replied:

"There would be no obstacle, as I have no wife, and no betrothed, and no relation with any woman. Until now I have lived with my parents; and the matter of my marriage was never discussed by them. You must know that I am a poor samurai, without any patron among persons of rank; and I did not wish to marry until I could find some chance to improve my condition. As to the proposal which you have done me the very great honor to make, I can only say that I know myself yet unworthy of the notice of any noble maiden."

The old woman smiled as if pleased by these words, and responded:

"Until you have seen our Himégimi-Sama, it were better that you make no decision. Perhaps you will feel no hesitation after you have seen her. Deign now to come with me, that I may present you to her."

She conducted him to another larger guest-room, where preparations for a feast had been made, and having shown him the place of honor, left him for a moment alone. She returned accompanied by the Himégimi-Sama; and, at the first sight of the young mistress, Itō felt again the strange thrill of wonder and delight that had come to him in the garden, as he listened to the music of the *koto*. Never had he

---

[120] A scarcely translatable honorific title compounded of the word himé (princess) and kimi (sovereign, master or mistress, lord or lady, etc.).

dreamed of so beautiful a being. Light seemed to radiate from her presence, and to shine through her garments, as the light of the moon through flossy clouds; her loosely flowing hair swayed about her as she moved, like the boughs of the drooping willow bestirred by the breezes of spring; her lips were like flowers of the peach besprinkled with morning dew. Itō was bewildered by the vision. He asked himself whether he was not looking upon the person of Amano-kawara-no-Ori-Himé herself—the Weaving-Maiden who dwells by the shining River of Heaven.

Smiling, the aged woman turned to the fair one, who remained speechless, with downcast eyes and flushing cheeks, and said to her:

"See, my child!—at the moment when we could least have hoped for such a thing, the very person whom you wished to meet has come of his own accord. So fortunate a happening could have been brought about only by the will of the high gods. To think of it makes me weep for joy." And she sobbed aloud. "But now," she continued, wiping away her tears with her sleeve, "it only remains for you both—unless either prove unwilling, which I doubt—to pledge yourselves to each other, and to partake of your wedding feast."

Itō answered by no word: the incomparable vision before him had numbed his will and tied his tongue. Maid-servants entered, bearing dishes and wine: the wedding feast was spread before the pair; and the pledges were given. Itō nevertheless remained as in a trance: the marvel of the adventure, and the wonder of the beauty of the bride, still bewildered him. A gladness, beyond aught that he had ever known before, filled his heart—like a great silence. But gradually he recovered his wonted calm; and thereafter he found himself able to converse without embarrassment. Of the wine he partook freely; and he ventured to speak, in a self-depreciating but merry way, about the doubts and fears that had oppressed him. Meanwhile the bride remained still as moonlight, never lifting her eyes, and replying only by a blush or a smile when he addressed her.

Itō said to the aged attendant:

"Many times, in my solitary walks, I have passed through this village without knowing of the existence of this honorable dwelling. And ever since entering here, I have been wondering why this noble household should have chosen so lonesome a place of sojourn. . . . Now that your Himégimi-Sama and I have become pledged to each other, it seems to me a strange thing that I do not yet know the name of her august family."

At this utterance, a shadow passed over the kindly face of the old woman; and the bride, who had yet hardly spoken, turned pale, and appeared to become painfully anxious. After some moments of silence, the aged woman responded:

"To keep our secret from you much longer would be difficult; and I think that, under any circumstances, you should be made aware of the facts, now that you are one of us. Know then, Sir Itō, that your bride is the daughter of Shigéhira-Kyō, the great and unfortunate San-mi Chūjō."

At those words—"Shigéhira-Kyō, San-mi Chūjō"—the young samurai felt a chill, as of ice, strike through all his veins. Shigéhira-Kyō, the great Héïké general and statesman, had been dust for centuries. And Itō suddenly understood that everything around him— the chamber and the lights and the banquet—was a dream of the past; that the forms before him were not people, but shadows of people dead.

But in another instant the icy chill had passed; and the charm returned, and seemed to deepen about him; and he felt no fear. Though his bride had come to him out of Yomi—out of the place of the Yellow Springs of death—his heart had been wholly won. Who weds a ghost must become a ghost; yet he knew himself ready to die, not once, but many times, rather than betray by word or look one thought that might bring a shadow of pain to the brow of the beautiful illusion before him. Of the affection proffered he had no misgiving: the truth had been told him when any unloving purpose might better have been served by deception. But these thoughts and emotions passed in a flash, leaving him resolved to accept the strange situation as it had presented itself, and to act just as he would have done if chosen, in the years of Jü-ei, by Shigéhira's daughter.

"Ah, the pity of it!" he exclaimed; "I have heard of the cruel fate of the august Lord Shigéhira."

"Aye," responded the aged woman, sobbing as she spoke; "it was indeed a cruel fate. His horse, you know, was killed by an arrow, and fell upon him; and when he called for help, those who had lived upon his bounty deserted him in his need. Then he was taken prisoner, and sent to Kamakura, where they treated him shamefully, and at last put him to death.[121] His wife and child—this dear maid here—were then in hiding; for everywhere the Héïké were being sought out and killed. When the news of the Lord Shigéhira's death reached us, the pain proved too great for the mother to bear, so the child was left with no one to care for her but me—since her kindred had all perished or

---

[121] Shigéhira, after a brave fight in defense of the capital,—then held by the Taïra (or Héïké) party,—was surprised and routed by Yoshitsuné, leader of the Minamoto forces. A soldier named Iyénaga, who was a skilled archer, shot down Shigéhira's horse; and Shigéhira fell under the struggling animal. He cried to an attendant to bring another horse; but the man fled. Shigéhira was then captured by Iyénaga, and eventually given up to Yoritomo, head of the Minamoto clan, who caused him to be sent in a cage to Kamakura. There, after sundry humiliations, he was treated for a time with consideration,—having been able, by a Chinese poem, to touch even the cruel heart of Yoritomo. But in the following year he was executed by request of the Buddhist priests of Nanto, against whom he had formerly waged war by order of Kiyomori.

disappeared. She was only five years old. I had been her milk-nurse, and I did what I could for her. Year after year we wandered from place to place, traveling in pilgrim-garb. . . . But these tales of grief are ill-timed," exclaimed the nurse, wiping away her tears; "pardon the foolish heart of an old woman who cannot forget the past. See! the little maid whom I fostered has now become a Himégimi-Sama indeed!—were we living in the good days of the Emperor Takakura, what a destiny might be reserved for her! However, she has obtained the husband whom she desired; that is the greatest happiness. . . . But the hour is late. The bridal-chamber has been prepared; and I must now leave you to care for each other until morning."

She rose, and sliding back the screens parting the guest-room from the adjoining chamber, ushered them to their sleeping apartment. Then, with many words of joy and congratulation, she withdrew; and Itō was left alone with his bride.

As they reposed together, Itō said:

"Tell me, my loved one, when was it that you first wished to have me for your husband."

(For everything appeared so real that he had almost ceased to think of the illusion woven around him.)

She answered, in a voice like a dove's voice:

"My august lord and husband, it was at the temple of Ishiyama, where I went with my foster-mother, that I saw you for the first time. And because of seeing you, the world became changed to me from that hour and moment. But you do not remember, because our meeting was not in this, your present life: it was very, very long ago. Since that time you have passed through many deaths and births, and have had many comely bodies. But I have remained always that which you see me now: I could not obtain another body, nor enter into another state of existence, because of my great wish for you. My dear lord and husband, I have waited for you through many ages of men."

And the bridegroom felt nowise afraid at hearing these strange words, but desired nothing more in life, or in all his lives to come, than to feel her arms about him, and to hear the caress of her voice.

But the pealing of a temple-bell proclaimed the coming of dawn. Birds began to twitter; a morning breeze set all the trees a-whispering. Suddenly the old nurse pushed apart the sliding screens of the bridal-chamber, and exclaimed:

"My children, it is time to separate! By daylight you must not be together, even for an instant: that were fatal! You must bid each other good-bye."

Without a word, Itō made ready to depart. He vaguely understood the warning uttered, and resigned himself wholly to destiny. His will belonged to him no more; he desired only to please his shadowy bride.

She placed in his hands a little suzuri, or ink-stone, curiously carved, and said:

"My young lord and husband is a scholar; therefore this small gift will probably not be despised by him. It is of strange fashion because it is old, having been augustly bestowed upon my father by the favor of the Emperor Takakura. For that reason only, I thought it to be a precious thing."

Itō, in return, besought her to accept for a remembrance the kōgai[122] of his sword, which were decorated with inlaid work of silver and gold, representing plum-flowers and nightingales.

Then the little miya-dzukai came to guide him through the garden, and his bride with her foster-mother accompanied him to the threshold.

As he turned at the foot of the steps to make his parting salute, the old woman said:

"We shall meet again the next Year of the Boar, at the same hour of the same day of the same month that you came here. This being the Year of the Tiger, you will have to wait ten years. But, for reasons which I must not say, we shall not be able to meet again in this place; we are going to the neighborhood of Kyōto, where the good Emperor Takakura and our fathers and many of our people are dwelling. All the Héïké will be rejoiced by your coming. We shall send a kago[123] for you on the appointed day."

Above the village the stars were burning as Itō passed the gate; but on reaching the open road he saw the dawn brightening beyond leagues of silent fields. In his bosom he carried the gift of his bride. The charm of her voice lingered in his ears—and nevertheless, had it not been for the memento which he touched with questioning fingers, he could have persuaded himself that the memories of the night were memories of sleep, and that his life still belonged to him.

But the certainty that he had doomed himself evoked no least regret: he was troubled only by the pain of separation, and the thought of the seasons that would have to pass before the illusion could be renewed for him. Ten years!—and every day of those years would seem how long! The mystery of the delay he could not hope to solve; the secret ways of the dead are known to the gods alone.

Often and often, in his solitary walks, Itō revisited the village at Kotobikiyama, vaguely hoping to obtain another glimpse of the past. But never again, by night or by day, was he able to find the rustic gate in the shadowed lane; never again could he perceive the figure of the

---

[122] This was the name given to a pair of metal rods attached to a sword-sheath, and used like chop-sticks. They were sometimes exquisitely ornamented.

[123] A kind of palanquin.

little miya-dzukai, walking alone in the sunset-glow.

The village people, whom he questioned carefully, thought him bewitched. No person of rank, they said, had ever dwelt in the settlement; and there had never been, in the neighborhood, any such garden as he described. But there had once been a great Buddhist temple near the place of which he spoke; and some gravestones of the temple-cemetery were still to be seen. Itō discovered the monuments in the middle of a dense thicket. They were of an ancient Chinese form, and were covered with moss and lichens. The characters that had been cut upon them could no longer be deciphered.

Of his adventure Itō spoke to no one. But friends and kindred soon perceived a great change in his appearance and manner. Day by day he seemed to become more pale and thin, though physicians declared that he had no bodily ailment; he looked like a ghost, and moved like a shadow. Thoughtful and solitary he had always been, but now he appeared indifferent to everything which had formerly given him pleasure—even to those literary studies by means of which he might have hoped to win distinction. To his mother—who thought that marriage might quicken his former ambition, and revive his interest in life—he said that he had made a vow to marry no living woman. And the months dragged by.

At last came the Year of the Boar, and the season of autumn; but I to could no longer take the solitary walks that he loved. He could not even rise from his bed. His life was ebbing, though none could divine the cause; and he slept so deeply and so long that his sleep was often mistaken for death.

Out of such a sleep he was startled, one bright evening, by the voice of a child; and he saw at his bedside the little miya-dsukai who had guided him, ten years before, to the gate of the vanished garden. She saluted him, and smiled, and said: "I am bidden to tell you that you will be received tonight at Ōhara, near Kyōto, where the new home is, and that a kago has been sent for you." Then she disappeared.

Itō knew that he was being summoned away from the light of the sun; but the message so rejoiced him that he found strength to sit up and call his mother. To her he then for the first time related the story of his bridal, and he showed her the ink-stone which had been given him. He asked that it should be placed in his coffin—and then he died.

The ink-stone was buried with him. But before the funeral ceremonies it was examined by experts, who said that it had been made in the period of Jō-an (1169 A.D.), and that it bore the seal-mark of an artist who had lived in the time of the Emperor Takakura.

THE END